Shadowspell Academy

The Culling Trials

SHADOWSPELL ACADEMY

THE
CULLING TRIALS

K.F. BREENE
SHANNON MAYER

SKY PONY PRESS
NEW YORK

First Sky Pony Press omnibus edition 2019

Sky Pony Press books may be purchased in bulk at special discounts for sales promotion, corporate gifts, fund-raising, or educational purposes. Special editions can also be created to specifications. For details, contact the Special Sales Department, Sky Pony Press, 307 West 36th Street, 11th Floor, New York, NY 10018 or info@skyhorsepublishing.com.

Sky Pony® is a registered trademark of Skyhorse Publishing, Inc.®, a Delaware corporation.

Visit our website at www.skyponypress.com.

10 9 8 7 6 5 4 3 2 1

Library of Congress Cataloging-in-Publication Data is available on file.

Cover design and artwork by Ravven

Hardcover ISBN: 978-1-5107-5510-9

Printed in the United States of America

BOOK ONE

CHAPTER 1

D amn it, Wild, hold her tight or she's going to gore me!"

"Easier said . . . than done . . . old man . . ." I labored to hold on as Bluebell, our fifteen-hundred-pound longhorn, tried to swing her great head around and get a look at my dad, who was sewing up a gaping hole in her side. She'd had a run in with Whiskers, our massive bull, unfortunately named by my sister when she was younger. Whiskers wasn't known for being easy on the ladies. He was probably still pissed about the name. "She's in a really . . . *really* . . ." I flexed my hands around the smooth horn, cursing under my breath as my fingers slid closer to the tip. "Bad mood!"

I barely heard him huff out a laugh.

I gritted my teeth and dug my heels into the loose soil, pushing against the metal of our makeshift chute for leverage. The ramshackle affair groaned and crackled. Bluebell stomped her foot in impatience or maybe pain, and a splatter of mud flew up and slapped my face. The glop of rank-smelling muck slid over the corner of my mouth and infiltrated my lips before I could close them. I fought not to gag, settled for spitting to the side and tried not to taste what had just landed on my tongue.

Much as I loved being a farm girl, moments like these made me wish for a house in the city. Houston. Dallas. Anywhere in Texas but the great nowhere I called home, a quarter mile from the nearest neighbor and a tiny town five miles beyond that. The moment was fleeting, and I spat again, clearing the last of the sludge from my mouth.

That had better *be mud . . .*

I craned my neck to get a view of my dad.

"Johnson, you good?" I hollered.

His failing body had a harder and harder time keeping up each year, an open secret in our family. A cripple before his time, he couldn't dance out of the way of a pissed off cow like he once had. Dad was in his mid-forties, but moved as if he were a hundred plus. His hands were still steadier than anyone's, though, when it came to stitching up the animals . . . assuming I could keep the cow's big butts in our crappy cow chute, of course, something I wasn't excelling at in that moment.

"Good," he called out, strain in his voice. "Just slow going. Thick hide on our ol' Bluebell, you know."

Bluebell jerked to the side, dragging my feet through the mud. With a growl and a heave, I yanked her back to nearly straight and held on. The chute groaned and the weld closest to me began to open. If it broke free, we'd be wrestling with Bluebell in a whole new arena.

"Come on, you fat cow, stop fighting!" I growled, as frustrated as a woodpecker on an iron post.

She let out a bellow and jerked her head toward him again. My knee bashed into the metal panel and I yelped, barely keeping my grip on her horn. Bluebell shifted gears fast, slamming her shoulder into the panel and using it as leverage. Damn it, smart cows were going to be the end of me. The other end of the panel swung out and smacked my dad, sending him flying.

He yelled, and there was the distinct sound of a body hitting the mud.

I'm sure he hoped it was mud, at any rate.

"Tell me you didn't break your neck!" I called out, breathing hard and pushing aside a sudden spike of anxiety. My knee throbbed, but I barely felt it over the worry. "Dad?"

There was a good five seconds that felt like a heck of a lot longer where he didn't answer.

"I'm fine," he grunt-laughed, and I let out a breath I didn't know I'd been holding. His dark hair and ballcap slowly appeared above the cow's shoulder again. "I didn't see that one coming. One day, we'll get a proper chute. One of those big head gates maybe."

"We sure will. Just gotta start playing that lotto."

"I keep telling you to get a ticket. With your luck, all our problems would be over."

I laughed and pulled on Bluebell's horn again, adjusting my grip. If only that were true, I'd scrounge up a few bucks and make the long trek into town tomorrow for a stack of tickets. Sadly, it was my older brother, Tommy, who'd always been the lucky one. Whole lot of good it had done him in the end.

A black cloud settled over me at that wayward thought, and grief, old but still raw, churned in my gut like soured milk. I shook my head to dislodge the heavy pallor and forced myself to focus on the task at hand. What had happened to Tommy was in the past. Too late to change it.

I bent my head and wiped the sweat from my face onto my upper arm. The end of summer in Texas was as hot as the devil's thong and about as humid. The rain the night before hadn't been any help to us.

"Stop daydreaming, Johnson," I said, a little too seriously. My hands slid farther, sweat making them slick. "I can't hold her much longer."

You'd think that after losing his wife and oldest son long before their times, my dad's outlook on life in general would have dimmed. No, that pessimism was left to me. I no longer even had my best childhood friend to help carry the load. At least Rory, the kid I'd grown up with, had found a better life. He still had a future, unlike Mom and Tommy.

I just wished he hadn't forgotten me so completely.

"Almost got it done, Wild, just two more stitches," Dad said.

I breathed slowly, my muscles spazzing after holding Bluebell's horn for so long. "Fat head," I grumbled at her. "You're lucky one of us likes you."

She let out a long, low moo, rolled her eye closest to me, and I relaxed my hand, thinking she was calming down.

Big mistake.

As soon as I let off the pressure, Bluebell jerked her head to the side, and my fingers slid to the tip of the horn. "Dad, I can't hold her!"

He couldn't move fast enough; I knew it. I clutched with my fingernails, my upper body shaking with effort, nails digging in as I snarled with the effort.

"Hurry!"

Dad limped away from Bluebell, hunched over, but two steps were enough to put him out of her range. I let go of her and she whipped her head to the side, her horns ripping through the space where he'd been standing only a moment before.

I backed up and bent at the waist, hands on my knees as I blew out a few deep breaths. My body trembled from my shoulders down to my calves. I was going to be sore in the morning.

Who needed the gym when you had to wrestle with cows on a regular basis?

"Good job, Wild. I finished up that last stitch. Keep her and that calf of hers separate from the others for a few days before letting them back in with the rest of the herd." Dad spoke over his shoulder, his instructions given in a pain-filled voice as he limped toward the house.

I understood why. If he stopped to talk, he might not get going again. The last time, I'd had to carry him into the house. It had been more than humiliating for him. What father wanted his teenage daughter to care for him like that? Certainly not a Texan, a rough neck, born and bred.

"Got it." I stood upright and stretched my hands over my head, my back cracking with a long series of pops that sent a shiver down my spine. I patted Bluebell on the forehead and scratched her behind one ear. "You're a turd, you know that? The man was just trying to help you."

She mooed at me and licked my jeans like nothing more than an oversized dog, her horns carefully kept away from me now that she wasn't being restrained.

"Total turd," I muttered as I checked to make sure my dad was out of the small corral before I let her loose. She'd go for him, even now that he wasn't bothering her. He was basically the vet around here, and she didn't like going to the doctor.

I watched as he slipped through the main gate and latched it behind him. He didn't talk about what ailed him, just called it *The Sickness*, as if that meant something. And honestly, it must've. At least to my mother when she was alive. But to the kids, no explanation was given, and if we asked, we were punished, or he'd just shrug and walk away. We didn't think he'd outlive our mother. But life has a way of randomly kicking you in the gut. My family got kicked more often than most.

I chewed my lip as I looked out over our sprawling ranch. Dad's optimism couldn't change the fact that our bills kept mounting while our revenue slowly decreased—only money would do that. Maybe I *should* start playing the lotto. Couldn't hurt at this point and it wasn't like the few dollars a week I'd spend would save us in the end any other way.

I sighed and unlatched our makeshift chute, letting Bluebell into the small corral.

"There you go, turd," I muttered, patting her hip as she went by.

She mooed softly at her six-month-old calf, who'd hid in the corner of the corral while we worked, and he ran over to her, rubbing against her head as she licked him all over.

I worked to get two of the panels unlatched and lifted them, balancing them on my shoulder, and then carefully made my way to the side of the corral to stack them with the others.

"What a waste of a life."

I startled at the unfamiliar voice, and turned slowly, seeing a solid man with a crew cut and aviators leaning against the fence. I hadn't heard the crunch of tires on gravel.

A glance behind him, then a sweep with my gaze, told me why—he didn't have a car. Or at least not one within sight.

I frowned. Strangers out this way were rare, but walking strangers rarer still, especially if they didn't have one holy book or another clutched between their palms.

Stalling for time, I headed to grab another panel, assessing him while I did so. He was five foot eight or nine, a few inches shorter than me, with a lean body poised in such a way that there was no mistaking the loosely contained power coiled within him. He reminded me of the mountain lions that occasionally came through the farm. Even when they were still, you could see the potential in them to launch at you with the blink of an eye. Sideburns crawled down his square face, otherwise clean of stubble.

Although his clothing was dark and non-descript, he wore a patch on his right shoulder, the symbol done up with red lines in a series of angles. At this distance, I couldn't make out the details, but even still, a memory floated up out of the darkness. A patch on one of my mom's old jackets.

Web of Wyrd.

"Girl," the man said, clearly short on patience.

"I'm eighteen, mister," I said before I dropped the panel. Metal clanged, giving me a moment to turn. "Call me *woman*. Or lady, if you're interested in a fat lip."

He stared at me across the space, and the push of his focus nearly made me step back. Cold shivers worked up my spine, everything in my body screaming *danger!*

"Derelict, then," he said. Our versions of compromise didn't line up too well, but he didn't give me time to say so. "Where is the boy?"

"Didn't take to the vocabulary lessons in school, huh?" I took two slow steps, outwardly loose and relaxed, and leaned an elbow against the nearest fence. I didn't trust the raging energy I felt pulsing from him, even from the distance. It spoke of a predator, and if I spooked, that would make me the prey. I didn't know much about people, but I knew a great deal about animals—he was not someone to turn your back on and live.

"The boy has been summoned," the man said. "I must speak with him."

"Can't. He's not home from school." I checked my watch. "He'll be getting loaded up on the bus. I wouldn't mess with the bus driver, Ms. Everdeen, though. She isn't allowed to smoke during her school run, and it makes her so cranky, she grows horns to hold up her halo."

The stranger's lips pulled to the side in a smirk, and he minutely shook his head. "It's a pity you elected not to go to school. You're a natural."

He took a step back and I couldn't help a confused frown. I didn't have the money for college, but why should he care? Is that what he'd meant about a waste of a life? Because when you were flat broke, and your family depended on you to survive, staying on the farm was a matter of necessity.

"See that the boy gets the envelope," the stranger said, walking toward the long driveway. "I'll be around later to discuss the particulars."

"What you really need is to discuss those sideburns with a barber," I mumbled, watching him silently make his way along the fence.

I blinked and swept my gaze out over the farm. A pang of regret hit me thinking about college. All kids dreamed about what they wanted to be when they grew up, and I hadn't been the exception. I'd never thought mediocre grades and a penchant to talk back would keep me from setting my footprints on the moon, or becoming a vet, or once, when I'd been in a really down moment, becoming a mortician. And I'd been right—the grades hadn't held me back. My sense of duty had.

Well, that, and a serious lack of funds.

I probably should've tried harder in school. Kept my mouth shut a little more. Then maybe I could've gotten a scholarship like Tommy had. Then again, look how his big break had turned out.

His chance at a better life had turned into a death certificate. No, I was better off with the farm. At least I knew the dangers here.

Replaying what the stranger had said, something about the envelope he'd mentioned but neglected to give me twanged my memory banks. A cold sweat popped along my skin and I turned back to the stranger to ask him a question, only to see . . . nothing.

He was gone.

"No way," I said softly, taking a few steps toward the driveway and road far beyond. The land was flat and cleared—I should've still seen him. Even if he'd started running, he couldn't have disappeared that quickly and I would have heard him on the gravel if he'd sprinted. Yet . . . there was no sign of him.

A strange tremor worked through my body, the warning of danger taking root. Something wasn't right with that man. He was trouble. I could feel it all the way to the marrow of my bones.

CHAPTER 2

An hour later, after I'd finished the last of the chores outside, I stood in the kitchen of our rundown, termite-ridden, hundred-year-old farmhouse, heart and mind racing, as I stared down at the pockmarked and cracked kitchen table. The clutter that usually choked the surface had been cleared away to Lord knew where. The kitchen counter had been set to rights, everything tucked into cabinets, or maybe the garbage can. The mostly empty canisters of sugar and flour were lined up, nice and tidy.

There was no way my father had done this, not with the knocks he'd taken in the pasture. The twins wouldn't have bothered even if they were home.

A hefty manila envelope lay in the exact center of the table, and when I saw it, one of the last memories I had of my older brother rushed over me.

"You guys will never believe what I got!" Tommy set the fat manila envelope on the clean kitchen table like it contained a bar of gold. He stepped back and fist pumped the air. "Guy came up to me and said it was special delivery. It's not mine yet, but, Dad . . ." he grinned like a maniac, "all our prayers have been answered. This is what we've been waiting for."

"Why?" I inched forward, Tommy's smile infectious. "What is it?"

"It's . . ." He shook his head and reached forward to gingerly touch the envelope, clearly caught up in the moment and unable to get the words out.

"What?" I chuckled and stood beside him, anticipation filling me.

"An invitation to the trials," my father said softly. "To school, if you pass."

A strange heaviness dragged at my father's words, threads of fear and hope mingled tightly together.

"School?" I asked. "But . . . I thought we couldn't afford it?"

"That's the thing, Wild." My brother beamed. "The envelope has—"

"No." My father stood and pulled the envelope with him. He pinched the flap closed. "No, Thomas. You are not to discuss the contents of the envelope with anyone but me. Your mother . . ." My father's jaw set in that stubborn way I knew from when my mother was alive. He hadn't said no to her often, but occasionally, when she tried to enforce something he didn't agree with, he'd dig in his heels as hard as any of the thick-headed longhorns in the pasture. I wondered what in that envelope had set him off.

"We'll talk about it, Thomas, just you and me," he said, turning away. "We'll see what they have to say. I'd hate to pass up an opportunity because of old superstitions."

Tommy shrugged at me, as confused as I was, apparently, his eyes glittering with excitement before he followed Dad from the room.

Three years later, I stared down at an identical manila envelope, curiosity eating away at me. Just like before, there was nothing written on the envelope, no name, no *do not open*, but I knew. This envelope was for my little brother, Billy. The stranger had asked for him by gender if not by name. And even if he hadn't, I would have known anyway, as certainly as I'd known my father would let Tommy run off to that prestigious college.

Whoever had sent both envelopes was trying to poach the boys of this family, one by one.

This time, though, I had the power to stop it.

"Dad?" I called, still staring at that envelope like I might a hornet trapped in an outhouse with me.

"In here, Wild," he called from the living room, easy to hear in our small house. "I'm just taking a break for a minute."

"Did you hear anyone in here earlier?" I asked, my hands shaking.

"Do you mean the twins?" He paused. "Isn't it early for them to be home?"

I shook my head, frustration eating at me. First, the stranger had shown up without my noticing, then he'd vanished on the way to the driveway, and now this? Why had he cleaned my kitchen, and how had he done it quietly enough not to bother Dad?

"Dad, you need anything?" I yelled louder than needed.

"No, Wild, I'm good. I'll just take another minute, if you don't need me."

That minute would last the next few days if he held to the usual pattern of recuperation. My old man was too proud to call it like it was.

"It's fine, Dad."

I snatched up that envelope and reached for the knife hanging at my belt. What I knew of the school was very little. My brother had passed the trials, whatever those were, and been admitted into the academy. My father had been ecstatic in one beat and strangely guilt-ridden the next.

Tommy had thrived in his first year, jumping to top in his class (like always). He'd had whatever my dad lacked—according to my dad's mumbling one night after a few glasses of celebratory Scotch. All was going great . . . until, without warning, our lives were turned upside down.

A notice was left on our doorstep that Tommy had died in a freak accident. The details were classified, they'd said, although no one cared to explain why. When my father pressed, he was stonewalled. Ignored like a stranger. They didn't even send Tommy's body home. Sure, they'd sent a pine box, but it had been empty. For some reason, my father didn't raise a fuss about that. When I pleaded with him, he cut me off in much the same way he would when asked about *The Sickness*. The topic was closed for discussion. End of story.

No one from the school had attended the funeral. We'd received no condolences. Hell, even Rory, our lifelong family friend—nearly a brother, we were so close—hadn't bothered to come home. Hell, maybe he didn't know. The only address I had for him was from a postcard he'd sent. We were alone in our grief, in the dark about the cause and completely powerless to do anything about any of it.

After the funeral, my father never mentioned the school again. He'd kept on hoping for a better life, acting as though someone would ride in and rescue us. As though something might come of all his dreaming. Which had left me to carry the weight of Tommy's loss these last two years.

And here we were again. This accursed envelope. This death threat tolling Billy's name.

The heavily worn handle of my knife, made from a longhorn, was comfortable against my palm. My parents had made it for me ages ago, back when I was starting to help out on the land. Back when the family had been whole and happy.

Back before freak accidents like the one that had taken my mother, and phantom schools that didn't allow an investigation or offer an explanation when one of their students died mysteriously. Back when life had been good.

I slipped the gleaming edge into the opening. I slid it through the top of the envelope, the paper cutting clean with a sharp tearing sound.

A deep breath and my knife firmly in my hand in case something nasty fell out, I grabbed a corner and dumped the contents of the envelope onto the worn wood. Metal trinkets clattered across the table, followed by a silver envelope and gleaming new smart watch. Finally, a wad of cash bound with a thick rubber band. The bill on top made my eyes widen. A quick flip through the stack and I could barely breathe.

Hundred dollar bills. All of them.

No wonder my brother had nearly peed himself with excitement when he'd gotten his envelope.

My lip curled in distaste.

They intended to bribe my younger brother in the same way. To entice him to his death, just like Tommy.

Fat freaking chance.

Memories filtered through my mind, unbidden. The Costco run that had filled our pantry, cabinets, and storehouse with staples that would last for the year. The clothes my brother had claimed Rory had helped him steal from a big store in Dallas. I remembered Dad muttering about a gift horse and the full-ride scholarship, cloaked in guilt while simultaneously beaming in pride.

I hadn't really understood the conflicting emotions rolling off our father in waves. At fifteen, I hadn't had the wind knocked out of me yet. The twins had been old enough to enjoy the windfall of good fortune but too young to make sense of it.

Finally, one last memory filtered through as I stood in front of more money than I'd seen in my entire life.

Tommy, Rory, and I had been sitting underneath the weeping willow at the far end of the acreage on a sweltering late summer day, not unlike today. Tommy was supposed to leave for the academy the following morning, and this was our last goodbye. Rory had leaned forward to look Tommy square in the eyes and said, "Never trust someone that throws money at you, Tank. People like that have more money than sense, and more sense than morals. Think fast, and make friends slow, or not at all."

It had been good advice. Advice Rory was probably following, wherever he was.

A familiar sadness washed over me. A year after Tommy left, Rory had headed out west without even a proper goodbye. He'd stuck a note to the outside of my window, the way he'd done for years, only this one wasn't "meet me in the apple orchard" or "I found a stack of fireworks." This one had crushed me.

"Off to the West Coast. Chasing dreams. Be safe, Wild." That was all it had said, signed as always with the slash of an R. Aside from an occasional postcard, I hadn't heard from him since. Clearly, he'd moved on from this nowhere town and his hard life.

I heaved a sigh. At least he was alive. He'd better have been, at any rate, though his dad would never let us know if something had happened.

I lowered myself onto the chair in our kitchen, the contents of the envelope spread around me, and leaned my elbows heavily on the table. Then, unable to help myself, I set my hand up beside the stack of money for a quick measurement. Just over four inches or so.

I thought back to Tommy's first year at the academy. To the windfall that had given us a year's worth of supplies, clothes, and improvements. Given what I knew of finances from my few years of handling the farm without much help, I could only guess how much money sat in that stack. All told, it had to be nearly forty grand. Maybe more, but I'd have to count it and I didn't have time for that before the twins got home.

As if my thoughts had summoned it, the clock above the kitchen door chimed three times and I jumped. I let my breath out slowly, trying to calm my nerves. Three already? I was way behind.

With shaking hands I tried to ignore, I grabbed the watch and a shiver rolled over me, cold air whispering up my arm to my shoulder. I shoved it into the envelope, followed by the money that threatened to cling to my hand. Everything inside, I rushed the whole package upstairs to my room on the third floor, the only room up there. I needed to talk to my dad about all this, alone, and with the twins due home any minute, now wasn't the time. It would have to wait until tonight.

A loose floorboard under my bed used to be my favorite stashing spot, but the twins and my dad knew it and they regularly snooped to see if I'd put aside any good chocolate. I did a slow turn. My room wasn't big and I didn't have a lot of choices.

"Closet," I said and shoved the package into an old backpack. That would have to do for now.

Ten seconds later, the thundering of feet on the floorboards downstairs, followed by a stampede up the stairs, announced the twins' arrival.

"Slow down before you bust a plank!" I yelled from my room.

"Hey!" Sam stuck her head into my room, wild red curls spilling in every direction as if they were a living creature on her head. "What's for dinner?"

I shook my own head, a few dark strands loosening from my ponytail, and hurried toward the door, brushing past her. "I don't know. It's been a busy day."

Billy met me on the stairs as I headed down, his hands lifted in the air, shock written all over his face. "What do you mean, *you don't know*?"

"I'm leaving it up to my first and finest cooking pupils." I put my hand on the wall to scoot around him, jumping over the last step that was dodgy on the best of days. It needed to be replaced—I just hadn't gotten around to it.

"You're teaching people to cook?" Billy ran down after me, stopping in the kitchen doorway. "But you're not any good at it. How can you teach anything other than how not to burn stuff?"

"Then I look forward to the students outperforming the master. Step right up, you heathens, and let's learn some stuff!"

Billy's eyes widened as understanding dawned. "I have home-work," he shouted, backing away. "Lots of homework. Summer school is really all about the homework."

"I do too," Sam said, crashing into Billy's back before she could stop herself. "And chores."

"And chores!" Billy chorused.

I grinned as I grabbed a pan out of the cabinet.

"Are you sure you don't want to help me? You can plan the whole menu if you do." I turned my back so I could school my features. If they knew I was upset, they'd start asking questions. As it was, they were always on high alert for the next bad thing to happen. I couldn't blame them really. At nearly sixteen, they'd experienced more heartache and loss than most middle-aged people. "Just think, you could plan out the entire week ahead of time, so you'd always know what would be for dinner. What a relief that would be, huh?"

Billy scratched his head, his unruly hair as dark as Sam's was red. They might have been twins but they couldn't have been more opposite. "I think I'd rather a surprise every night."

"I'd much rather a surprise," Sam agreed with him, ganging up on me yet again. "Wild, listen to this. Remember that boy—"

"Jaaaaysus, not this again," Billy drawled, and I promptly forced out a laugh. Another day, I would have laughed for real.

Sam frowned and then her hand shot out, a mere blur as she smacked him upside the head. "At least I can talk to my crush face-to-face. All you've seen of Miss Gothic lady what's-her-face is a few pics and words on a screen! How's that chat group, anyway, grandpa?"

Billy's face turned red. "You're just jealous that I have more Facebook friends than you do."

"Facebook is for old people."

"I wish I had a phone instead of that crappy ol' library computer so I could do Snapchat," Billy muttered.

I twisted my lips to the side in unease, wishing I could buy them flashy new devices—or even an old used one. We didn't have any cellphones or computers to our name—we couldn't afford it. Anything online needed to be done at the library or the high school, including their social media presences, something I didn't even have. Not that it mattered. I had no friends anymore to hook up with.

"I'm going to marry that boy one day," Sam said. "He's going to be your brother-in-law." She lifted her nose and stared down it at her twin. A dare for him to speak if I ever saw it.

"Marry him tomorrow so I can have your room too." Billy grinned as he swiped an apple off the counter.

"She'd probably ask to move him in here, then you'd be out of a room altogether," I said, badgering him.

Sam's scowl deepened until I wasn't even sure her eyes were open. They paused for a moment, like two cats eyeing each other up, and then they tore out of the house, Billy leading, Sam close behind, screaming at him not to be a jackass.

"Language!" I yelled after them, not that it did any good, or that I ever expected it to. But Mom had attempted to raise us as well-behaved, softly spoken, non-swearing children, and she'd want me to take up her mantle.

I was doing a terrible job. But then, she'd done a terrible job, too, if I was any proof.

Reality seeped back in and my grin slid from my face. I leaned against the counter. I had to focus on one thing at a time. Dinner. I had to get dinner ready. We didn't have much, but we had livestock and a few green thumbs between us. We'd put one of the older cows—Annabelle—in the freezer the month before, which meant we ate better than most this far below the poverty line.

I cooked on autopilot as my mind worked over just what I was going to do.

"Dad?" I called as I flipped the steaks in the frying pan with the dip in the middle. With the twins out of the house doing their afternoon chores, this would be a good time to talk to him alone.

Maybe the only time before he turned in early as was his nightly schedule.

"Yeah, Wild?" he called back in a thick voice. I knew full well he was napping, another routine part of our days, but this couldn't wait.

I moved the steaks off the heat and washed my hands quickly before snagging a tea towel to dry them. I wound the towel around my hands, worrying the material as I walked to the TV room at the front of the house.

Dad was leaned back in his recliner, legs propped by a cushion, his head supported by a pillow. "I was just going to get up," he murmured, his eyes at half mast, but he didn't make a move. The lie was one he told often enough that we all just acted like it was truth.

I swallowed and nodded. Crap, this was harder than I'd thought it would be.

"You going to strangle me with that?" He lifted a trembling finger and pointed at the tea towel I'd stretched between my hands.

"I'll wait until your back is turned. It's easier that way." I grinned to complement the joke but knew it didn't reach my eyes. I took a breath and dove in. "Listen, I was thinking 'bout Tommy. Thinking about that scholarship—"

"No, we don't talk about that," he said.

"We have to," I said softly. He wasn't the only one hurt by the loss of Tommy, so I tread lightly. "I know you don't want to, Dad, but we have to. I'm not a child any longer." The urge to take his hand swept over me and I pushed it away. Not because I didn't care, but because of the tension in his frame. He did not want to tell me what had happened.

"Why now?" He frowned. "Why do you say we have to?"

"Can you trust me? Just tell me what happened to Tommy, about how the scholarship worked."

I thought his face paled, but he shook it off. "I'm not supposed to talk about it, Wild. Not just because I don't want to relive it." He rubbed a hand over his face and a good minute went by before he spoke again.

"All right, I'll tell you what I can." Dad swallowed hard and the tension in him went from caged fear to pain in a split second. "I should never have let him go," my dad whispered, the grief in his voice like an arrow straight through me. He closed his eyes. "Your mother was right all along, God rest her soul. I was blinded by pride and hope. That was the worst decision I've ever made. Believing he would be safe. That he'd be the one to defeat the system."

My heart beat faster. My father had known Tommy would be in danger?

"Did . . . did he get money for going?" I asked, wanting to be sure. "And a watch, and a few . . . trinkets?"

"Money wasn't worth his life. Money wasn't worth losing him. But it wasn't just the money. It was vanity, Wild. My boy was offered something I'd only ever dreamed of . . . I wanted to live through him." His dark eyes pleaded with me in the dim light of the room. "I wanted him to be more than his old, broken man. More than this crippled sack of bones. I wondered if he'd be like his mother. If he'd wield that kind of power. She was so damn majestic. I hated that she had to give it up because of a rumor about that curse. Because of the bleating of an—"

His lips thinned and he shook his head again, deflating. "But she was right all along. If I'd only listened to her. If I'd only acted on what she'd made me promise, Thomas would be safe. We'd still have him here, safe with us."

I stared with my mouth open, feeling the depth underlying his words, like standing on an iceberg and wondering how much of it existed below the surface. Even though he was saying more than he'd ever said about the situation with Tommy, so much of his speech didn't make sense.

"What if another envelope came?" I asked softly, knowing what he'd say.

Or so I thought. My father surprised me.

"I expected it before now," he said, his tone resolute. "Your mother felt the power in you from day one, Wild. From your first cry. Your strength only ever blossomed. It didn't have peaks and valleys, like the others. It only ever grew. She wanted to hide you, most of all. And she tried. Her friend used her blood to cast this place into the shadows. But the blood magic faded after her accident. As soon as they came for Tommy, I knew you'd be next. It was only a matter of time."

Blood magic. Spells. Power. His words sent shivers through me, fear and . . . excitement. Then his meaning finally sunk in.

I surely looked like a big-mouthed bass standing there, jaw hanging open wide.

"Me? There's power in me?" I asked, dumbfounded. Mom had told us bedtime stories about magic, but that's all they were—stories. Had Dad's sickness addled his brain?

He ignored my question. "Did he come?"

I worked to catch up to him while my brain struggled to make sense of his words. "Who, sideburns guy?"

"Did someone come with an envelope?"

"Yes, but—"

Dad shook his head, slowly. "No, Wild. No buts. We will not speak with him. You saw what happened to Tommy. It's too dangerous. Tommy was a target, and you will be, too, even more so than your brother. Your mother left that place to stay safe. You'll stay away for the same reason."

I couldn't wrap my head around what he was saying. They were the kinds of words that threatened to change the shape of all you knew. Questions lined up in my head like little toy soldiers. What place did Mom leave? The same school as Tommy? Why was it dangerous?

"But . . ." I started.

"No, Wild, and that's final." He cranked up the volume on the TV, his way of ending the conversation. "Give the money back. Give it all back. They won't have another of my children. *They will not!*"

He shifted his gaze to the TV, and I stared at him a moment before I turned and trudged back to the kitchen in a fog, my mind whirling. What did my father mean, "my power continued to grow"? Did he mean physical strength? I was surely much stronger than the average girl, but I'd always attributed that to a hard life dealing with large animals. A girl needed a certain amount of strength to work the farm and keep up with the men.

But what did any of that have to do with a college scholarship that included stacks of cash, fancy watches, and trinkets? And why were Tommy and me targets? Targets of what?

None of this made any sense, starting with sideburns dude somehow sneaking onto the property. Not to mention that the envelope wasn't even for me. Whatever my father thought he knew, clearly he was mistaken. Except for the fact that he should've said no when Tommy had wanted to go, of course.

Suddenly the guilt I'd seen in Dad all those years made a lot more sense. My mother had somehow known Tommy would get asked to this college, whatever it was, and she'd made my Dad promise not to commit. Only, my father had bent to the excitement, and his own desire to live vicariously through Tommy.

One thought kept niggling at me—why hadn't I gotten an envelope if my father was so sure they'd want me? They'd skipped right over me.

"It's a pity you elected not to go to school. You're a natural."

Sideburns had said that, as though it had been my choice to be passed up. As though I'd rejected the invitation already. Yet . . . my father would've said if one had already come. Right?

I pushed that from my mind. The past didn't matter. What did matter was the envelope coming for too-young Billy.

It struck me that Sam hadn't gotten one either. Whatever my dad thought, my initial assessment held firm—this college, school, whatever it was, was going after the younger males of this family. They were trying to pick them off.

First things first, I needed to find out the nature of this college.

CHAPTER 3

A couple hours later, after I served up dinner and all but force-fed the twins their greens, I slipped into the quiet hush of my room and closed the door. The yellow package was still in my closet, right where I'd stashed it. I grabbed it and unceremoniously dumped the contents onto the bed. Five trinkets spilled out first. They reminded me of something, I couldn't quite put my finger on. Each one was tiny, barely bigger than a quarter, but three dimensional. A knife, a gravestone, a pawprint, a tiny stick, and a blank coin. I rolled them through my fingers, then dropped them back to the bed. No clues there.

I zeroed in on the letter in the shiny silver envelope. If anything held answers, that did; I was sure of it.

A quick slit of the paper with my knife, and I pulled out a piece of thick cardstock with feathered edges. Soft vibrations ran up through my fingers as I touched the card. As I watched in utter confusion, embossed letters etched themselves into the cream-colored paper, dancing and swirling across the expensive paper as they formed words.

"What the hell?"

I angled the card away from the light and leaned in to see better, but upon closer inspection, the words were stationary. My dad's babbling about magic must have set off my imagination. My eyes slid over the message and immediately sweat beaded along my brow and slid down my face, one droplet landing on the paper, next to the words I couldn't un-see. Words that could not have been any worse.

> Billy Johnson,
>
> Your presence is requested at the Culling Trials.
> You don't choose an Academy. An Academy chooses you.
> Report to the address below within forty-eight hours or your family will die.
> Time is ticking.

I stared at the words for a long time, longer than I should have considering the last line, then shook the paper, wondering if the letters would rearrange themselves into a more favorable message. Nothing happened, of course. My eyes had been playing tricks on me earlier. I turned the paper over and searched the back for a customer service number or an April Fool's note. It was late July, but maybe someone was getting a head start on their tomfoolery. Blankness greeted me, a solid white of nothing.

I squinted at the address listed below the message. Upstate New York somewhere.

Crystal Lake Wild Forest, Roscoe, New York.

The ink glittered, as if the threat to my family were a young girl's art project.

The message seemed preposterous. What college threatened people to show up and learn or else? On what planet was that rational?

The same college that covers up students' deaths.

I gritted my teeth as the message in front of me finally sank in. It almost seemed like I could feel the intent behind the embossed words: You will show up regardless, but if we have to make you, your family will die.

I eyed the watch on the bed, its screen a solid black. They'd even sent their own timekeeper. How thoughtful.

If Tommy had been given a watch, I would've seen it. He would've been too proud not to wear it. He also couldn't have gotten a card with a message like this—there was no way he would've been beaming about his acceptance to a school that would threaten his family.

Right?

Given all the skeletons that had gone dancing around the living room earlier, I wasn't sure of anything anymore. Time to hold Dad's feet to the fire and get the rest of the story.

I took the stairs quickly but with light steps, not wanting to bring the twins out of their rooms. In the living room, I gently shook my dad awake. It appeared he hadn't bothered to head to bed. Another part of our routine. "Dad."

"Hmm?" His eyes fluttered opened and it took a moment for him to focus on the card held three feet from his face. "What is it?"

"Dad, did Tommy get an invitation with that manila envelope he got from that school?" I asked.

"Did . . . what?" My dad rubbed his eyes and struggled to sit up.

I shook the card a little, drawing his eyes to the glittering message.

"Did Tommy get something like this?" I repeated.

His brows lowered, and the sleep fled from his eyes as they traced the words. "What . . . ? No. Thomas didn't get anything like that. He only got a message about the Culling Trials, not the threat. Is that how they're running things now? The older families must be pushing back. The Helix family wouldn't stand for this. Wait a minute . . . is that?" He took the card and held it away from his face so he could see better. "That says Billy's name. It can't be." His hand shook as he stared at me over the top of it, the fear heavy in his eyes.

"Yeah." I took the, now bent, card. "The envelope didn't come for me. It came for Billy."

"But . . ." My father struggled to get his feet down in the recliner so he could properly sit up. "Billy is still in high school. He isn't ready for college yet."

I fought not to crumple the card in my hand. "I know. And he's not going. What is this place, Dad? How is this even legal? You have to give me some answers. We have to figure out how to stop this."

He sighed and rubbed his temple with a gnarled finger. "Sweet Jesus, this can't be happening. Not again." He held up an empty glass to me. "Bring me another glass of elixir, Wild," he said softly.

Without money to spend on Scotch these days, he had to settle for moonshine, what he liked to call elixir. We had a couple of bottles—a present one of the neighbors had given me for hunting down a lone wolf that had terrorized both of our livestock. Dad rarely drank it, saving it for Christmas and special occasions—or for when life and his pain got too heavy to bear.

"Sure, Dad," I said, then gritted my teeth, refusing to give in to despair. I'd been taking care of things around here for the last few years. So far, I'd kept us above water . . . or at least we weren't drowning yet. Whatever it took, we'd find a way around this. Billy would not end up like Tommy.

A flash of yellow snagged my attention when I stepped into the kitchen, and I found myself staring at a second manila folder on the kitchen table.

"Buckets of crud . . ." My voice drifted away as cold trickled down my spine.

He'd been in here again—the dude with the bad sideburns. Him, or someone like him. We'd all been home, going about our lives, and none of us had noticed a stranger in our midst. He was like a ghost!

"Billy! Sam!" I yelled. The chances were slim to none, but I entertained the faint hope that I was wrong. That they'd brought the envelope home from summer school.

Before they could answer, or even emerge from their room, I rushed to the back door and yanked it open. He should still be out there, although I didn't actually expect to see him.

Early evening blanketed the sweeping fields to the side of our house and settled firmly on the barn off to my left. A deep *moo* drifted through the dense evening and the sound of crickets throbbed in the dying light. I usually loved this time of the day, but now it all seemed tainted by the intruder. As though the serenity was washed through with his danger.

I flicked on the porch light and jogged to the edge of the cracked concrete walkway. I squinted into the deep twilight, just bright enough to reveal one clear boot tread in the still damp dirt. Just one, as though he'd stepped down with the intention that I'd notice his presence . . . before vanishing again.

"What?" Sam stepped out of the house and into the evening light. I turned back to look at her, hands on her hips and an eyebrow arched. "What's the matter?"

Billy jogged out behind her, his brows pinched. "What's up?"

I spun on my heel and marched toward them. "Did you hear anyone come in?"

They both looked around in confusion, the sass in Sam fading.

"Where?" she asked as I brushed by her. "You mean in the house?"

Well, that was a no.

"Close the door," I barked, worry making me sharper than usual. "Lock it. All the locks."

"What's going on?" Billy asked, hurrying in behind Sam. He didn't wait for an answer before he threw the deadbolt and locked the knob.

"It's happening again." My dad staggered as he neared the door to the kitchen and put a large-knuckled hand on the door frame to stabilize himself. Sam ran forward to help him, slipping under his free arm. Dad's eyes locked on mine. "Wild, we can't let him go. They'll kill him. Thomas was the top of his class—if he couldn't make it through, Billy surely won't."

"Me?" Billy pointed at his chest. "What did I do? I swear it wasn't me!"

"Guilty conscience," Sam muttered. He scowled at her.

"Stop." I held up my hand. "Just hold on. They're not taking Billy anywhere. Sam, Billy, get to bed."

Billy shook his head. "If this is about me, I have a right—"

I silenced him with a look. "It's *not* about you. It's about *me*. Get on with ya. Both of you. Go to bed. We'll talk about this in the morning."

They hesitated, they knew as well as I did that we didn't talk about things in this house—and I pointed at the staircase.

"Go on, now. Let me talk to Dad for a while. We'll figure this out."

They muttered complaints, but after a stern word from my father, they stomped up the stairs. I waited until their bedroom door slammed before I snatched up the second manila envelope and ripped it open, finding a packet of paper. The five symbols emblazoned across the top in impossibly vivid colors matched the trinkets I had received in the first envelope. I scanned the text even as my dad gave me some of the same information.

"It's a school for exceptional people," he said, his words slightly slurring. He reached, grasping for a chair. I grabbed his hand, feeling the strength that was still there, little as it was. Our palms pressed together as I helped him down into it, one-handed. My eyes slid to the additional items as he kept talking. "Only the very privileged go there, Wild, and not privileged in the way of money, but in the way of *talent*. Magical talent."

I stared down at him like a hog looking at a wristwatch, utterly confused. "Come again?"

He didn't seem to hear me. "I got invited, just like everyone in my family did, but . . ." His head drooped. "I didn't have what it took. I was a null. A magical nothing . . . should have had more to me, but didn't."

"A . . . *magical* . . . nothing," I repeated. We'd circled back to nonsense words.

"Your mother, though . . . she was exceptional," he gushed. "So talented. So beautiful, like you, with that long dark hair and amber gold eyes. She was the belle of any ball. And of course, she was the top of her class, just like Thomas. I couldn't go to the academy with her—I didn't pass the trials—but I stayed close to support her. I worked the grounds." He put up his hands. "She didn't talk about it much, but she left because of some family curse. She swore off the magical world and wanted her children to do the same." He shook his head. "And you should've. Thomas should've. I let him go. It was my fault—"

Dad's voice was slurring slightly and I wondered how much moonshine he'd had, but it was clear he believed what he was saying. These fantasy ideas to him were real. At least they were right now when the alcohol was affecting his brain.

"He wanted to go," I said, trying to soak his words up, to hold them close so I could make sense of them. I put a hand on his too-thin shoulder. "He probably would've pushed to get his way. He would've thought it was the right thing to do. All that money, a good education leading to a good job—you couldn't have stopped him. None of us could have, even if we'd known."

Maybe Rory could have, though, I thought whimsically. Tommy had turned to Rory more than once for advice and had always taken it to heart.

Dad sighed and rubbed a hand over the back of his neck. "I suppose you're right." He paused and shook his head. "I thought maybe the neighbor kid and him could watch over each other, like they did growing up."

Confusion smacked me yet again like a two by four to the back of the head. "Wait, you mean Rory?"

Dad swayed. "We all used to have such a great time, us and Pam Wilson. Pam and your mother were thick as thieves. They were in school together for a while. But then your mother died, and well, that mean ol' codger got heavy into the sauce. He was always bad news. I told her to leave, that I'd help somehow, but what could I do, really? And then there was Emelia in town. She and your mom were good friends too—"

"Dad." I leaned forward and put my hand on his arm, trying to jog him out of the past. I remembered Rory's mom and mine laughing over their glasses of sherry at the kitchen table, but that had been a long time ago when my mother was young and full of life, and my father hadn't been riddled with sickness. "What about Rory? Rory went to that school?"

"That mean old bastard gave me a split lip, do you remember that?" Dad ran his hand over his face. "He was as fast as I ever saw."

Dad meant Buck, Rory's father. Buck had never needed much of a reason to throw a punch. But given that I'd been asking about Buck's son, it meant my dad's grasp on timelines and people were getting confused. I didn't have time to straighten it all out, not that it would've mattered if I had. I'd gotten a couple postcards from Rory from Nevada, the other side of the country from the school Tommy went to. Besides that, Rory had never lied to me. That was one thing we'd promised each other—we'd always held stock in honesty.

I sat heavily in the chair opposite my dad, my hand sliding from his shoulder. Truth rang in his words, but so did alcohol. There was no telling what was fantasy and what was reality. Not when he was this deep in the moonshine.

"This is the contract, then?" I flipped the pages of the packet, and in a moment, I had my answer. A section at the back laid it all out, right down to the nitty-gritty.

If Billy showed up to the trials, he could keep the money in the welcome packet, and if he was offered a place in the academy, he could apply for financial aid. We were all bound to silence, and our lives would be forfeit if we breathed a word about any of this. Then, at the very bottom, almost like an afterthought, was the line, "If APPLICANT fails to appear at the Culling Trials, APPLICANT stands in breach of contract, and APPLICANT's family will be destroyed."

"It doesn't even make sense," I said softly, reading it again. "At the top it says *if* Billy shows up at the trials. Then at the bottom, it's clear he doesn't have a choice."

I threw the contract down, the papers fanning out.

"They can't make this stick. None of this is legal. They sound like the freaking mafia, not a school for the . . . privileged." I shook my head. "He's not going. There's no conceivable way they can make him. He's still a minor, for criminy sakes. I'll call the police tomorrow and file a harassment report. I'll turn the money over to them." I flung up my hand, anger eating through me. "If they think we can be bullied into doing what they want, they are sorely mistaken."

My father clasped his hands, staring at the packet with tight, worried eyes. "I tried to call the police after your brother died. I tried to get someone to properly investigate." He swallowed hard. "I should've known better. These people, magical people, have their own laws. Their own set of guidelines. They don't play by the rule book you and I know, Wild, and they don't have to. They have an understanding with certain powerful world leaders. It's been years since I was part of it, but none of that has changed."

There was that word again. *Magical.* Uttered in complete seriousness as though it wasn't straight out of a children's story written by someone with a crazy imagination.

Not something I could focus on at the moment, so I didn't. I ran my hand down my face. "So . . . what are you saying? What are our options?"

"I don't know. We have to run, maybe. Take the money and try to find someone to hide us."

He was saying that these people—this school for the . . . talented—would absolutely kill us to get what they wanted. And what they wanted now was Billy.

My little brother with the dimples and the out-of-control hair, the little boy that I'd rocked to sleep more than once when we were little, when Mom was too busy. I wasn't that much older than him, but he . . . he was mine to protect. Just like Sam was.

I sagged in my seat. I'd never felt so old or so alone, and for the first time in a long while, I desperately wanted my mother. I wanted to lean my head against her shoulder and breathe in the smell of talcum powder and lilacs that was uniquely her. To feel her arms around me and know that she would somehow make it right.

Out of a distant memory, but as if spoken right next to my ear, I heard her say, *"Take the risk no one else is willing to take. You were born for it, my love."*

My father's voice drifted over the moment. "I thought for sure you'd be next," he said. "I worried I'd have to tie you to your chair to keep you from going. You have less sense than Thomas in that way. But Billy?" He looked up at me, his face stripped of its vitality and the dashing good looks that adorned the pictures on the mantelpiece. "Billy is not even a man yet. And he doesn't have the survival instinct needed for this. Not him."

"I told you, Dad, Billy isn't going." I knew what I had to do, the plan forming quickly in my mind. I could pull it off. I had years of prep in my own way.

"Wild girl of mine. You follow the wind like you always do," my mother used to say. *"The wind and the wild go together, hand in hand."*

My eyes prickled with a rush of emotion and I dashed any tears before they could fall.

"And tying me to my chair won't work. If they're expecting a boy to fill their ranks—well, then, I need to get a haircut and a sports bra. Instead of Billy, they will get a wolf in sheep's clothing. Let's see how they like that."

CHAPTER 4

I stood in the tiny bathroom of our rundown house, staring at myself in the mirror. The thick, pre-dawn morning air raised goose bumps on my bare arms and across my exposed shoulders. A small tank top hugged my chest over an even tighter sports bra that flattened my already on the small side breasts.

To help Billy, to save him from being forced to go, I'd have to present myself as a boy. Given that he was only sixteen, still fighting his way through puberty, I had a shot.

But I'd have to cut my hair.

I fingered the ends of my thick brown locks, tracing the soft curls that ran to my mid-back. There weren't many things about me that were girly—there weren't many occasions for pretty dresses and makeup in farm life—but my hair was high on that short list. It softened my sharp cheekbones and severe jaw line. It made the tiny cleft my chin seem feminine and less like Clark Kent's. Without it, my resting bitchface would be boosted to epic proportions, intense enough to make people jump ship in a raging storm to escape me.

I sighed and gingerly picked up the scissors. With this hair, I'd be pegged for a girl, identified as easily as Ronald McDonald in a lineup of hard thugs. It had to go. I had to set the bitchface free.

Heart racing and palms sweaty, I pulled one strand of hair away from my face and opened the blades of the scissors. The first cut was the hardest. After that, it would be easier. It had to, or I'd be sitting here all morning instead of getting on the road, trying to get to upstate New York before my father could pry himself from his chair in the living room and stop me.

"We'll find another way, Wild," he said the night before. "We can take the money and hire someone to hide us. I still have a few connections from my school days—I'm sure one of them will help us."

I'd always thought my father was a terrible liar, the odd one in a family surprisingly great at manipulations and half-truths, although now, I wasn't so sure. While I still didn't know what to make of this magic business, he'd kept information about the academy from us for years. Maybe his fear of the place, or of Mom, had kept him quiet. Because I knew one thing for sure: he was lying through his teeth now.

None of his "connections" would help us. No one would shelter us from this particular storm. Someone had to go and pull out the threat by the root, and it most certainly wouldn't be the little boy I'd cared for over the years. He was too pure of heart—too good. He was too much like Tommy.

No, it had to be me. I had the skills to make it, the ability to adapt in pressured situations. I'd tried to remind my dad of all that. *I* was the one who'd brought home Whiskers, the bull that would keep our farm going a little longer. A few years ago, he had been the pride of the livestock auction, anticipated to demand a fat price. But with my fast tongue and an ability to read and manipulate people, I'd gotten him for a fraction of the cost.

I could use that in this school. I knew I could. And a part of me looked forward to duping the people who'd killed my brother.

But to do all that, I had to cut this danged hair.

"I can do this," I whispered, steeling my courage. I took a deep breath and moved my shaking hand to the dark strand of hair.

"What are you—" Sam's voice went straight through me.

"Ah!" My fingers convulsed and the scissors' sharp edges cut through a chunk of hair.

I sucked in a breath as my sister moved closer. She'd walked up without me hearing her. The little fart was getting really good at sneaking around.

"Here," Sam said, reaching for the scissors. "I'll help. You need to get going, you're running out of time."

Her lack of surprise was more than telling.

"You listened through the vent, didn't you?" I accused, letting her take the objects of my hair's soon-to-be destruction. She pointed to the small stool and I sat. "Was it just you, or did Billy listen, too?"

"Just me. I remembered that envelope from when Tommy got it. Dad hid it in his normal hiding place that time, and I looked through it. It was the same one, right? With all the money?"

"Yes. This one was meant for Billy." I stared at her in the mirror, seeing the same hard look I wore. Resting bitchface number two coming right up. The women in our family were if nothing else, survivors. I was proud of her for that, proud that she was hard like me. When I left, I knew she'd keep Billy and Dad safe. My heart gave a funny thump I didn't like. I rubbed at my chest, knowing it for what it was.

If I left them, and something bad happened, would they be okay? What if Dad got hurt again? What if the twins got sick? What if, what if, what if. They flowed through my mind, making my anxiety rise with each beat of my heart. They were all I had in this world worth fighting for—but that meant leaving them.

"Billy's too young for college," Sam said.

"I know."

"He's too nice. He believes me half the time when I tell him fibs." Her lips quirked upward.

I smiled back. "I know that too."

"He's too like Tommy." Her voice dipped low along with her brows as she snipped through the strands of my hair. I flinched as if I could feel each cut. "He wouldn't stand a chance at a college—special school or not."

I huffed out a laugh even though I agreed. "He's not as sweet as Tommy—he just seems like it because he uses his charisma and dimples to get what he wants. You'd probably get further if you tried that."

"I have. It's easier just to tell people what they want to hear. It saves time." She shrugged, unbothered by that fact.

I laughed again. Our mother would've been proud of the twins' ability to get out of trouble. I was pretty sure that was a parenting fail. Then again, when you were down on your luck and barely had two pennies to rub together, some careful and harmless manipulation wasn't the worst thing in the world if it got you an improved deal. It was better than taking Robin Hood's approach and flat-out stealing.

"Regardless," I said, worry eating my guts, "you're right. Billy is not old enough for this. Life has already steamrolled me. He's still too gullible. He'd believe they want the best for him."

"I know," she said softly, slicing through another sheet of my beloved hair.

"It'll be up to you to step in with the ranch. You're better at numbers and managing than Billy is. You've got to make that money last as long as you can."

"I know."

"You can make him cook, though. You're rubbish at that."

Another little smile lifted her lips. "I'm going to be a chef one day, just you watch."

"I believe it." The surest way to get any of us to do something was tell us we weren't capable, to dare us to show our ability. I closed my eyes, no longer able to bear the sight of my shortening locks. "Make sure everyone shares the duties. Don't just take it all on because they are lazy and give you flak. I learned that lesson the hard way with all of you. Don't let them sit in their own stink for too long. You have to yell at Dad sometimes to make him wash up. And he can help in little ways."

"I know."

"And don't lose your head and run off with whatever cute boy you have a crush on this week." I peeked at her in the mirror.

She laughed and shook her head. "Billy wouldn't let me, anyway. He threatens anyone who tries to get close. Not like I need the help."

I chuckled. Yeah, she was going to be more like me than she realized.

"He's protecting you. Tommy and Rory did that with me growing up."

"I don't need protecting. Guys think I'm weak 'cause I'm a girl. But I'll kick them in the balls and take all their money if they mess with me."

I burst out laughing and leaned forward till my forehead touched my knees. Sam swatted me and I sat up straight again.

"I never needed protecting either." The words felt ominous, almost like a jinx. I sure hoped I still didn't need protecting, but I was about to go into the snake pit of the unknown. If my father could be believed and magic did exist, I would be up against a whole lot more than a farmer with a set price for his livestock.

CHAPTER 5

P lease be safe, Wild," Sam said with tears in her eyes, standing with me at the door.

Light streaked across the sky in layers of yellow, orange, and pink. The sun wasn't far from making an appearance over our struggling farm. A mournful, deep moo sounded in the distance, almost like Bluebell knew I was leaving.

I'll be back, I thought. I wasn't going to end up like Tommy. I would fight as dirty as I had to, so I'd come home when this was done.

I tapped the handle of my knife in its sheath on one hip and then tapped the misshapen crossbody bag hanging over the other hip. The invitation, trinkets, contract, and some of the small fortune were tucked inside. I'd strapped the watch to my wrist.

My father had said that Tommy had gotten close to forty grand, half of which he'd taken with him, just in case.

Turned out my mental calculation had been off. Way off. They'd given Billy eighty grand.

Eighty thousand dollars!

I'd nearly passed out when we'd counted it and had made Dad count it again to be sure. I couldn't believe so much money was in a wad in a nondescript envelope on the table for anyone to open.

I'd left most of the money behind for the family with instructions on where it would help the most. Ten grand was plenty for me. Having spent my childhood trying to one-up Rory, Mr. Mischievous Bad Boy Lacking Morals, without my brother catching on and taking me to task for acting like a common thief or thug, I was good at getting what I needed when I absolutely had to have it.

"In a game of survival, there are no rules," my mother had always said. *"Play to your God-given strengths, Wild, and don't feel bad for it."*

I would live by that now. Mother said so.

First on the list: steal myself a ride to the airport. A couple days ago I couldn't get the truck to turn over and hadn't circled back to figure out the problem. My bad.

"Take care of everything," I said softly, hugging Sam tightly. "Make up a lie to appease Billy. Let Dad have some moonshine to ease the blow. And stay out of my room. I'm coming back to it."

A tear rolled down her still baby soft cheek. Her red hair flared around her head as the first rays of the sun hit it, a fiery halo. "I guess it's Billy's and my turn to grow up, huh?"

I gave her a sad smile. "That time has come and gone. Now it's time for you to stop being lazy and letting me handle everything."

Her surprised laughter sprayed spit across my face.

"Nice," I said, wiping it away, and with it, my own tears.

"Stay strong," she said, her large blue eyes tracking me as I walked toward the door. I knew she was quoting our mother just as I'd done in my thoughts. "But don't be afraid of your weaknesses. Take every opportunity to laugh. Let yourself cry. I'll hold this place together."

God, how many times had Mom said that? Too many to count. I brushed away more tears and turned away with a nod. I'd let myself cry later. Right now, I had to get going. My time was counting down.

The gravel crunched under my feet as I made my way past the cow paddock and down our long driveway, thinking of the stranger who'd shown up without a sound.

I still hadn't figured out where the hell he'd gone.

Magic, I heard my father's voice say.

But I swatted the thought away.

Near the junction of the main road and our driveway, I turned right at a packed-dirt path, one I'd taken a million times throughout my youth. But now weeds struggled through the hard crust, trying to reclaim the wildness of the land my two accomplices had pounded flat and clear, running to each other's houses in the long, lazy summer days, or in the wild, storm-thrashed winter evenings.

A strange tingling sensation between my shoulder blades interrupted my thoughts. Rory's parents' house loomed a quarter mile away, a decrepit, sagging structure that should've been condemned years ago. Only his father lived there now. Pam had taken off about when Rory did, leaving Buck with no one to pick on. Leaving him alone with his drinking.

The feeling of being watched coated my body in uncomfortable shivers, my skin twitching like a fly-stung horse. I kept at the same pace, careful not to look around. A predator would attack if they thought their prey had been alerted to their presence.

I nearly lifted my hand to flick my hair, intending to use the movement to covertly glance to the side—only to remember my hair was now cropped close, a shaggy sort of affair that I'd covered up with a dingy old ball cap. Sam had assured me that while the cut would work for a boy, it could be styled into something more feminine if I needed it. I doubted I would need it.

Left devoid of that crutch, I adjusted my bag and staged a trip, staggering off to the side and looking behind me at the offending clump of nothing. Trees lined both sides of the path and sprinkled the fields beyond, giving someone ample opportunity to hide. Birds chittered a chorus of warning, alerting their fold that a human walked in their midst. The still morning air left leaves and grasses unmolested. No movement caught my notice.

In a measured pace, I kept going, focused on my surroundings, ears strained for any sound.

Because something or someone was there. I was sure of it. Silently stalking me. Mountain lions weren't as common in our part of Texas, but it was a possibility, and they were incredible hunters.

And yet, I knew this was no animal. Humans and animals had always triggered different anticipations and expectations under my skin. Essentially, they read differently when it came to how dangerous they felt. I'd played some intense hide-and-seek with Rory and Tommy when we were kids—to get caught would've meant a pummeling.

Something about the way an animal stalked its prey felt straightforward to me. Scary, but logical. Their motivations were as predictable as their approach. The opposite was true of human hunters. Their style of stalking changed with their mood and emotions, and their ability to stay hidden was enhanced by their increased intelligence.

Humans were the most dangerous predators.

The hairs on my arms twitched, a low level of warning rolling through me that had nothing to do with being eaten, and everything to do with being in far more danger than any animal could bring to the table.

A human, then. An expert with a higher-level intelligence. Apparently, he could move without a sound, hide without disturbing the still foliage, and likely pounce when I was least expecting it.

A pair of dark sideburns and a condensed body of muscle flashed in my mind's eye. I increased my pace. At some point, prey was prey, and it needed to scamper off before the predator took it down. If I was up against the man who'd brought me the envelope, I had no illusions about my role in this game of cat and canary.

I made it to Rory's old house as quickly as I could without looking like I was hurrying.

The same old Chevy sat in the gravel driveway, hardly used anymore by the look of it—cobwebs woven between the mirrors and the body, leaves collecting on the cracked wipers. Buck, Rory's dad, didn't work, preferring to live off of the state, and had no friends to visit. He'd be inside, sleeping off his nightly alcohol binge.

I slipped beyond the brown, scraggly hedge and tiptoed along the side of the house to Rory's old bedroom window. At the base, I paused as a memory from the past assaulted me—Rory clutching my arm, asking Tommy and me not to leave him. I'd been nine at the time, too young to recognize my friend was a scared kid afraid to be alone with the monsters that made up his world. Rory's dad had started shouting then. The shouts had grown louder, accompanied by the soft sound of his mother's sobbing. Tommy was the one who'd known what to do. "Come on," he'd said. "You can stay with us tonight, Rory. They won't miss you."

And they hadn't. Not that night, or the dozens of others he'd spent with us.

That was the first time it had occurred to me that, unlike me, Rory couldn't seek shelter at home. If he did, he'd only find more nightmares. It was why I hadn't batted an eye when he'd said he was leaving this town. And why I would beat the snot out of him if he'd lied to me. You didn't lie to people you shared trust and history with. You just didn't.

I lightly pushed on the window, hearing the soft click that released the broken lock, and flattened my palms so I could slide the window open. A soft squeal made me pause for a moment. An intense itch flared between my shoulder blades.

The stranger was here, watching. I was sure of it. Sideburns, or one of his minions, was watching me break into this house.

My breath turned shallow, but I didn't stop. He'd basically threatened Billy. I doubted he'd be calling the cops. Besides, we didn't have a working truck and Billy had a deadline—he could do the math.

Trying to ignore the eyes digging into my back, I gritted my teeth against the next squeal and slid the window the rest of the way open. That done, I paused, listening.

A soft rhythmic ticking caught my notice. A clock. Nothing else permeated the thick, gooey silence.

In one swift movement, I pulled myself through the window, stepping onto the strategically placed dresser and the stool beyond it, evidence of Rory's habit of sneaking in and out. In near silence, I tiptoed out of his room, skipping the loose board below the dingy, rust-colored carpet, and paused at the edge of the living room.

No head crested the faded green recliner with the back torn out of it. Leaning to the side, I looked around the chair facing the rabbit-eared TV and spied the couch. Buck's body lay across it, his shoulders as broad as ever and his belly bigger than when I'd last seen him. Crumpled beer cans littered the floor next to an empty vodka bottle on its side.

The expectation of danger slid across my skin as I crossed the threshold into the living room. That was the thing about Buck, he could be blind, passed-out drunk, but if someone messed with his stuff, he could still spring to attention. I'd never understood it. I didn't trust that he'd changed.

I had no choice but to find out.

Silent as the grave, I slipped along the wall to the counter that separated the kitchen from the living area. A badly damaged basket held a pile of junk topped with keys, where they'd always been. Holding my breath, I gingerly lifted them from the mess.

Two keys scraped against each other, a mournful metallic melody. I paused, my heart in my throat.

Rhythmic breathing gently filled the space. Tremors of warning screamed through my gut.

I needed to get out of here.

I eyed the front door beyond the living room. Chances were Buck hadn't kept the hinges greased. That, teamed with his unreal ability to detect when people were messing with his space or his things, meant I would have to head out the way I had come in. Not even Rory had risked taking any of Buck's things out of the front door. That was a dead man's game.

Moving as fast as I could while still being silent, I ducked through Rory's window and slowly closed it behind me. Eyes dug into my back again, almost a physical feeling. I half wanted to turn and sarcastically thank the stranger for waiting. Instead, I jogged toward the truck, time ticking.

It wasn't the watch or deadline that had me moving. It was that miserable sonuvabitch whose property I was still in the process of stealing. He may have lost some of his killer instinct, but I wasn't counting on it. Adrenaline pumping, memories of the fear he'd inspired in my youth battering me, I reached the truck and eased the door open. A loud groan ripped through the silence.

"Crap on a cracker," I muttered as I jumped into the seat and fumbled for the right key. Rookie mistake—I should've plucked out the correct key when I was jogging closer.

I left the door open. The less noise the better. I'd close it when I flung dirt at that bastard's house, not before.

The key clinked as I fit it into the ignition, and I chewed my lip as I turned it. The truck turned over . . . and over, and over, the engine struggling. When had it last been used? My plan suddenly didn't look so good.

"Come on," I muttered, giving the gas pedal a push before trying again. "C'mon, c'mon . . ."

The truck cranked to a slow, coughing start.

I heaved a sigh and reached out for the door, chancing a glance at the house as I did so.

The front door stood open.

"Whuddya think yer doin'?" Buck roared as he stepped around the side of the truck. His huge hand wrapped around the edge of the driver's side door. "Tryin' to steal my truck, you stupid—"

He reached in to grab me with his other massive, scarred hand.

The old coot would beat me bloody without shame.

Terror flooded me, and I reacted without thinking.

I jammed my fingers into that ol' bear's beady little eyes before hammering a fist into his throat. Before he could react, I flung off his reaching hand, and he fell backward with a strangled shout.

I slammed the truck in gear and jammed my foot onto the gas pedal.

The truck coughed and sputtered but caught, slowly rolling forward.

"You filthy, thieving whore," Buck yelled, his voice raspy. He lurched for me again with one eye closed, his reflexes dulled with age and lingering drink. He wasn't giving up though. And neither was I.

I leaned to the side and yanked my arm away. His long fingernails raked across my skin, tearing it open. The truck jerked forward and the door swung shut, catching Buck's body.

He grunted, and I swerved the truck to the right, the quick motion finally wresting his hand from the side of the door. An elbow hit the fender and his body fell away. I yanked the wheel, swerving the truck in the opposite direction before skidding onto the road. Buck's body rolled in the dust and flying gravel behind me.

"Serves you right," I muttered as I left him behind.

I guess there wouldn't be a question of who stole his truck. Thank God my siblings knew how to work the shotgun. I had less than forty-eight hours at this point—I didn't have time for a nap in a jail cell.

CHAPTER 6

I gripped the steering wheel of Buck's crappy old truck as I wrestled to keep the entire hunk of junk on the hard curve of the on-ramp. Clearly, it hadn't been left to the spiders just because Buck lacked gas money. The power steering was completely shot.

The brakes squealed like a pair of pigs caught in a noose, and I was pretty sure the signal lights were out, given the level of honking from my lane change. Still, it was better than walking.

With one last crank of the wheel, I was on the highway. "Almost as bad as holding Bluebell," I muttered as I shifted up, the gears grinding.

Foot on the gas, I pushed it to the floorboard in a vain effort to get up to highway speed. The body of the truck shook and rumbled under me, and what was left of the muffler clattered before screeching against cement and falling off—freaking falling off! It tumbled off the road in a shower of sparks that lit up my side mirror.

When I was fairly certain nothing else would fall off, yet, I rolled the window down and let the fresh morning air blow out the stench of old man and sour beer. A deep breath in and out and my heart rate finally slowed. I was on my way to these Culling Trials, and I had time to spare. Once there, I could convince them that Billy would never be a good fit. That he would be terrible at . . . whatever they wanted him for.

I lifted my eyes to the rearview mirror and the blood cooled in my veins, sending a shiver right down to my tailbone.

A sleek black sedan, gleaming in the morning sun, pulled into my lane about three cars behind me. The cars between us, annoyed with my lack of speed, passed one by one, but that sedan hung back, allowing others to cut in front.

"Dumber than a box of rocks if they think I don't see them," I murmured, adrenaline racing through me. Nothing that new and shiny would loiter around these parts, happy to go slower than the speed limit. They were here for me.

There was no way I could outrun a slick new sedan, not in Buck's truck.

Fear mingled with the adrenaline and I chewed the inside of my cheek, my mind running through the possibilities. The next exit led into a series of suburbs, schools, and small parks. I could turn off, see if they followed and try to lose them. But if they were aggressive . . . I'd have no choice but to abandon the truck and lose them on foot.

That would slow me down, and time was not something I'd been allotted a great deal of to get to upstate New York.

I turned my right wrist up to see the face of my new watch. Thirty hours, fifteen minutes, and four seconds left. The flight would take four hours or so, I guessed. The drive to upstate New York maybe another two. I wasn't sure it would work, but I had a crazy idea that might get rid of this tail.

Crazy was my only option at this point.

"I've got time." I cranked the wheel hard to the right and shifted the truck into a lower gear, letting the engine slow the speed rather than the squealing brakes. It clunked along unhappily, but at least it was quieter than the alternative.

I coasted down the off-ramp, wrestling with the steering wheel again as I went around the curve. A glance in the rearview showed me all I needed to know. The sedan had followed me, closing the distance between us, and the sensation of being watched crawled over my skin again.

The difference was this time there was no doubt someone was on my butt.

A part of me was so scared, I couldn't think. Not just any predator was tracking me, but the ultimate predator, pushing me toward a dangerous future from which I might not escape. Another part of me, however, flared to life, the part that had raced through the fields with Tommy and Rory and broken into abandoned houses. The part that had earned me my nickname.

"I can do this." I shifted down again, and again, until the truck was all but crawling in first gear, the engine grumbling unhappily, chugging and jerking along. I didn't have the vehicle to outrun them. But that didn't mean I couldn't outsmart them.

I rolled the truck to a stop at the bottom of the off-ramp, stuck my arm out the window and waved them by me. Anyone trying to keep their anonymity would surely comply and pick up the tail later.

The black sedan crept forward, closing the distance between our bumpers. It stopped just shy of bumping me, waiting patiently, applying pressure to hurry me along. In the rearview mirror was a stern face wearing aviators and sporting some serious sideburns.

A grin I couldn't control budded on my lips even as warning tingles washed through my body. That man was dangerous. I knew it in every fiber of my being. But he was hounding me, and I didn't take well to that kind of treatment. There were times to back off and times to fight back. My gut told me this was one of the latter.

Here's to hoping that Buck's back-up lights don't work any better than his turn signals.

I shifted into reverse and hit the gas. The engine growled, and the truck shot backward far more efficiently than it moved forward, slamming hard into the hood of the black car. I didn't take my foot off the gas.

"Take that, Sideburns."

The tires of the sedan shrieked on the pavement, but Buck's truck was heavy and made for hauling weight. It shoved the smaller vehicle backward, smoke curling up around it as Sideburns worked the brakes. But I wasn't done yet. Grinning, staring out the back window, I cranked the wheel hard, turning the truck and forcing the sedan into the ditch on the side.

Gravity helped me out and the black car rolled down the steep slope, tires spinning in the dry grass until it bottomed out. There would be no getting out of that without a tow truck.

Still grinning maniacally, I put the truck into first gear and drove forward. One last glimpse in my rearview mirror showed me a single person standing at the top of the ditch. The sunlight flared off his aviator glasses and those sideburns.

My grin slid away at the look on his face, which those glasses did little to hide.

That lone wolf I'd killed, the one with a taste for cattle, had looked at me like this, with glittering eyes and lips curled over teeth that wanted to tear me apart. I knew without a shadow of a doubt I'd made an enemy that didn't take well to being bested.

As surely as the sky was blue above me, one day, this moment would cost me.

I pressed the gas pedal to the floor and got back on the highway as quickly as I could, fear pricking at me to move faster. To get clear of that wolf's gaze.

The drive was long enough that I had plenty of time to stew, even as I constantly checked my mirrors. I was going to a school where students died and their deaths went uninvestigated. A school for *magically* talented people.

I snorted to myself. If there were real magic in the world, like it was in fantasy books, I would've known about it before now. That was too big of a secret to keep. Maybe my dad had exaggerated, and the school was for kids with exceptional skills in certain areas, more than book smarts.

This time I frowned. As much as I hated it, I could understand why they'd wanted Tommy. He was good at everything he touched. The consummate golden boy who made friends easily and charmed the teachers and got good grades. But Rory had a rap sheet with the local police a mile long for fighting, and his only skills were five-fingered discounts and a knack for shifting the blame to others. None of it made sense.

I sighed to myself as the sign for the airport came up. The answers would come, but I doubted they would just land in my lap. I'd have to hunt for them. At least that was one skill I had under my belt.

I merged into the airport traffic, working to keep the truck from lurching forward into one of the nicer vehicles. Traffic slowed to a stop, caging me in as we approached short term parking.

The engine growled and lurched forward, nearly kissing the shiny red Porsche in front of me.

"Total pig of a truck!" I muttered as I hit the brake hard.

I leaned and craned my head, trying to figure out the hold up. I knew cities were crowded and busy, but with so many people coming and going out of this place, I would've thought they'd have traffic under control.

An SUV inched forward in the right lane, giving me a glimpse of the terminal. My breath caught. Two black sedans glimmered in the morning light. Waiting for someone.

I jerked my head straight and inched forward behind the Porsche. My heart picked up speed, hammering away in my chest so loudly, I couldn't hear the honking around me.

Sideburns apparently had more friends than I did. I watched them from the corner of my eye. Both sedans were new and undented, so neither of them belonged to Sideburns. I swallowed hard, a litany of curses flowing under my breath as I tried to figure out what to do. How did I get out of this pickle?

Buck's truck wasn't exactly what I'd call inconspicuous with its peeling paint, louder than a shotgun blast engine, and the smell of the exhaust rolling out past its non-existent muffler. Then again, I wasn't in the only rust bucket in the airport either. Given that they hadn't climbed into their car or jogged into traffic, I was good for the moment. As long as I kept things calm.

A few more minutes, I checked the time on my watch. Twenty-eight hours, forty minutes, and eighteen seconds to go. Plenty of time.

The numbers shivered as I stared at it, as it went foggy, and then jumbled up like a snow globe being shaken.

"What the hell?" I tapped the screen with one finger. What a junky piece of crap they'd given me . . . and then the worst thing that could happen did.

The time changed.

And not in my favor.

Six hours left, and counting.

"You piece of donkey crap," I snapped, anger flaring. "Whoever is tinkering with my watch is begging for a shortened life span."

Gritting my teeth, I craned in my seat, seeing a man a few cars up directing traffic into the parking garage. A sidelong glance told me the black sedans were still there.

The minutes ticked by. The truck fought my maneuvering. I kept from looking at the watch, terrified the time would change again.

The airport staff at the mouth of the parking garage waved me to a stop, redundant given the lowered wooden arm next to the ticketing kiosk.

"How long ya gonna be?" he called.

I fought past my heart lodged in my throat. "No time at all. Short. Short time." I grimaced. When had I forgotten how to talk to people? "Just real quick."

"Yup." He waved me on. "Second level. First level's all full up."

I grabbed a ticket, nearly took out the wooden arm as the truck lurched forward too quickly, and parked in a no parking zone on the second floor that was faster than finding a spot big enough to easily fit the badly maneuvering truck. I left the truck running. Maybe someone would steal it. Again.

I bolted for the stairs. I needed to figure out a way past those sedans or I needed to head to the next terminal.

Movement too close behind me fired through my senses. On pure instinct, I dodged right, putting distance between us. A brick of a man pivoted, not thrown off for long. Another from the other side ran between two parked cars.

The first man lunged for me, nearly grabbing me. I danced away and clipped a car with my hip. The car alarm blared and lights strobed in the dim interior of the garage. My blood pumped through my veins as I spun and landed in a crouch in front of my assailants, two men in suits identical to the one Sideburns wore. They had the same look going on—military short haircuts, aviator sunglasses, and jackets bearing the red Web of Wyrd patch— except these men were both clean-shaven. Apparently, terrible facial hair wasn't standard issue.

The man on the left smiled, but it was cold and reptilian. "Billy. Don't make this harder on yourself."

Billy. They knew who "I" was.

I stayed crouched but scooted backward, feeling my way with one hand. I tried to deepen my voice. "I got a flight to catch, boys."

The two men smiled in tandem and a prickle of a warning snapped me around. A couple of additional men had crowded in behind me and one had what looked like a black canvas sack aimed for my head. I came up with an uppercut that snapped his head back so hard, his sunglasses flew off as he fell backward. My clenched fingers throbbed from the contact. That was going to hurt tomorrow but more for him than me.

I didn't stick around to watch the fallout. I put on a burst of speed as I raced through the parking garage, once more using the cars as leverage, setting off alarms left and right.

I didn't care. Down the stairs and I could see the doors to the airport. I was almost there. Though it wasn't exactly like I'd be home free. They were audacious enough that they'd attacked me in a packed parking garage—why stop?

I dared a glance at the stairwell behind me. Empty.

But that one look back was my undoing. I turned forward to face the main doors as a black bag settled over my head and tightened around my neck.

"Tie him up good. He's a slippery brat."

Hands grabbed at my limbs, pinning me down, and my panic ratcheted into the stratosphere. What the hell was happening? Sideburns had brought the manila envelope that had started this whole mess. Presuming these guys were with him, shouldn't they want me to go to the school?

Suddenly, I was thinking they didn't.

I kicked out, snapping my booted feet free of their hands and driving them into anything I could reach. I connected twice, one blow right after the other. Score one for the girl with long legs.

"He's a big bastard for fifteen!" one of them grunted.

He was an even bigger bastard for a girl, I supposed. Amazons didn't make for easy kidnapping.

I bucked and rolled to the side, getting another shot in on a joint. A knee. Cartilage cracked. Someone swore.

I rolled to the side and broke free, pulling my hands in front of me in time to smack against the hard ground. I was reaching up to rip the sack off my head when coarse, ridiculously strong hands grabbed me again. These fellers were strong and fast, experienced, and there were too many of them.

I knew when to give quarter to a bigger beast. Just like Whiskers. You had to know when to smack him with a two by four, and when to offer him his favorite treat.

For now, I would give them a mint and let them think they'd won.

Because if I couldn't outfight them, I'd have to outsmart them. I'd have to outwait them.

And then I'd bust their balls when my moment came.

CHAPTER 7

I'm done," I said, my breath heating up the space inside the bag they'd stuffed my head into. "I won't fight."

"Got some sense in you at least," one of the men growled.

I slumped in their hands, letting them take my weight. The bag over my head stunk like a hippie's armpit and my nostrils flared as I clamped my mouth shut. My wrists were still held out in front of me. I wanted to ask what they were doing but I resisted the urge. I could have fought and yelled, maybe gotten the attention of the other people at the airport, but I had a strong feeling it wouldn't have helped. Which meant silence was going to be my friend.

"Hold him tight," one of them said and I tensed as my wrists were squeezed so hard, the tendons rubbed over the bones. With the blood flow to my hands constricted, I barely felt the prick of a blade on my right hand, right in the center of my palm. There was pressure, and then a faint warmth.

I kept my mouth clamped shut, but my eyes caught a glimmer of light from a small hole in the bag. Twisting my head slightly—not enough to alert them but enough to shift the bag—I lined up my left eye with the opening. Through it, I watched as a paper was brought up to my right hand. A contract if I ever saw one.

On impulse, I jerked backward, straining away, but they were ready for me. My body was thrown to the ground. What felt like two guys crouched to either side of me and a knee found the center of my back, pinning me hard. My palms were twisted up painfully, at the edge of breaking, and the brush of parchment paper against my right palm said it all.

I'd signed something, even if I hadn't wanted to.

"Got him. Let's load him up so we can get this run over with."

"No shit, I need a drink and a healer," another guy grumbled.

I was pulled to my feet and my wrists were shoved together as a hard piece of plastic was set around them. Zip ties. Until now, I'd only seen them used on captives in movies.

I strained my wrists apart, to give me space to wiggle if I had to. I was going to be fighting my way out of this as soon as I could, zip ties or not.

The only good thing regarding the bag over my head was it helped me hide the fact that I was a girl. And my sports bra was doing its job seeing as no one had noticed anything in all the wrestling.

I was marched along after that, my feet barely touching the ground, the men around me talking to one another as if I weren't even there.

"Where to next?"

"Arkansas, Missouri, Illinois, Indiana, and Ohio."

"No Kentucky? I thought that was part of our run."

"No."

"Do we need to give Shamus a minute to fix his nose?"

"We're running late. He can do it on the flight. He should've known better than to underestimate one of these kids."

I frowned and sweat beaded up again, sliding down the sides of my cheeks.

One of these kids?

Did that mean I wasn't the only one they were intercepting? What did they want with us?

I pushed the questions from my head. I could ponder them later. The bigger problem was that all those stops would take time. Time I didn't have.

I wasn't going to make my new deadline if I didn't do something.

My mother's voice seemed to float on the air, whispering to me words she'd spoken long ago. I'd been complaining about Rory and Tommy out-fighting me. *"Patience. Wait for the moment to strike. If you hurry the blows, you'll be stuck chasing your prey. You need them to step into your fists."*

At the time, I'd been learning to hunt, but the advice seemed a better fit for this situation. It struck me that a lot of my mother's advice had been . . . well, let's call it more violent than motherly. Maybe she'd suspected all along that the academy wouldn't leave us alone.

As I was hiked along, a whiff of something tugged at my nose, even through the bag. The new scent was a smell of home, of the farm and something else I couldn't quite put my finger on. A scent of spice and vanilla, easing my fears.

I relaxed, really relaxed, and waited for my moment to come. I had to believe it would show up, and when it did, I would have to be ready to grab it with both hands.

The distant sound of thumping reached my ears, like the rotors of those big helicopters in the war movies Dad and Tommy loved. No, strike that, these *were* helicopter rotors, and I was being led toward them.

If I'd been sweating before, it was nothing to the droplets that slid down my body now. Heights I could do if I kept my concentration on the task at hand, but the idea of being in the air with what equated to a giant food processor above me was not on my bucket list. It was far too easy to imagine being pushed into those blades. Or to remember how easily helicopters crashed in those war movies.

I wasn't sure I could stay relaxed for this part. I slowed my feet, digging my heels into the ground, but I was picked up the minute I put on the brakes, hands on either side of me digging into my biceps and under my armpits.

"Jesus, he's slim but solid," one of my lifters grumbled, and I swung my boot out, catching him in the thigh. He yelped but didn't set me down.

"Knock it off, kid, or we'll throw you out once we're in the air," the man on the other side of me said.

"Yeah, right," I snapped. They would not go to all this trouble just to throw me out. Hopefully.

The spinning rotors were going harder now and the wind that washed off them blew the bag tight to my face. The little hole gave me a quick glimpse of the interior of the helicopter, and the sight made my blood run cold.

A dozen other kids lay on their sides within the flat deck of the enormous helicopter, many in the fetal position. All had their hands tied behind their backs and bags over their heads, just like me. They lay free in the middle of the cleared space, without straps to keep them put or handles to awkwardly grab. As if they might indeed be thrown out for causing trouble.

I did not like this and couldn't think of a way to get out of it.

"Drop him there, next to the girl on the end."

I was boosted into the helicopter and dropped like a bag of grain, left without any restraints like the other kids. The helicopter rotors picked up more speed and then we were moving, lifting into the air. The doors were still open.

This was insane.

"Are you serious?" I yelled as I flattened, the lift of the helicopter making my stomach roll as we rose rapidly.

"You must be from Texas. I can hear it in your accent," the girl next to me said over the din, something that should've been impossible for me to hear without headgear. "You know in Texas, there are places where the number of alligators outnumber the number of people?"

I did a slow turn of my bagged head toward her. Was she serious? We'd been tagged and bagged and left for luggage in a moving helicopter, and she wanted to talk about alligators?

Through my little peephole, I saw her nod as if hearing me. "Death by alligator is a terrible way to go. Not quick at all. First, they pull you under the water, usually clamping down on a hand or foot, which will give you the impression you might be able to escape. Of course, you probably won't. Very few people do, you know."

Good God, how did I get her to shut up? And how was I hearing this over the wash of the rotors?

Magic. The single word whispered through my mind in my dad's voice. No, it couldn't be—

The girl went on, oblivious. "Once they have you under the water, they begin to roll, twisting around and around so they can ideally rip off your limb and bleed you out while at the same time drowning you. Rather effectively called a death roll."

I turned my head away from her, trying to see if there was something within reach I could use to cut through the zip ties. I tried reaching for the knife on my hip, but wasn't flexible enough.

"Then, usually while you're still alive," the girl continued, "they stuff you into their underwater food stash. They prefer their food to be marinated in swamp water and mostly rotted. I think it would make the flesh taste better, to be honest."

"Shut the hell up!" I snapped. "Nobody wants to hear about how alligators eat people!" What in the world was wrong with her?

"I don't want to die!" someone down the line yelled, a guy, I thought, but it was hard to tell with how high pitched his voice was, drunk on panic. "Please. I don't want to die!"

I lowered my head to the floor, pressing my forehead to the only solid thing around, and breathed carefully through my nose. Why had the doors been left open? To scare us? Or did they really intend to throw us out like they'd threatened?

I shivered and found myself thinking about how long it would take to hit the ground, wondering if the bag would come off my head first for one last look at the world. Crap, that girl's death babble had gotten to me after all.

"Death can come in many forms," the girl next to me said, her voice dipping into a monotone that reminded me strangely of Walter Cronkite. "But it is up to us if we embrace it or fight it. I suggest embracing it. We all die. But do we all truly live?"

"Shut up, Wally!" I yelled. "Just shut up!"

"My name isn't Wally—"

"You sound like Walter Cronkite," I said and promptly burst out laughing. Hysterical, hyena-like laughter that ripped out of me. I was in a helicopter with a bag over my head, and the girl next to me was obsessed with death and sounded like flipping Walter Cronkite. This was not real; it couldn't be.

There was only one thing I was sure of. I was going to die.

The laughter cut off as suddenly as if I'd flipped a switch. "I'm not going to die."

"Of course not," Wally said. "And I like that name. I think that will be my nickname from now on. Thank you."

"I don't want to die!" the other fellow yelled again as the helicopter tipped to the side, aiming us toward the open door. I rolled and shimmied, ending up on my ass as I dug my boots into the slick metal for traction. Wally began to slide next to me, the sound of her body scooting across the floor tipping me off.

I stuck my leg out, catching her against my thigh.

"Thanks," she said, as calmly as if I'd offered to hold a door open for her. "Splatting from this great of fall would end my life, I'm quite sure."

Laughter bubbled up again, anxiety-driven and incredulous. Walter Cronkite meets Professor Obvious, this chick couldn't be for real.

"Oh no! Oh no!" the guy from earlier yelled over the sound of a body sliding. "Oh no! Noooo!" His voice reached an octave I hadn't thought possible for a boy of any age before the sound drifted away, along with, apparently, his body. "I'm falling!"

"Oh my God," I whispered. "He fell out. Holy—he really fell out!"

His screams echoed through the space around us, fading, disappearing, and then weirdly returning, louder and louder. As if he were above us now, still falling. Falling toward us.

"Noooo!" A thud rocked the helicopter, followed by a grunt. "Holy cats!"

It was the guy who'd just fallen out! Was I on drugs? Had they pricked me with a needle when they'd taken my blood?

"Holy cats," he repeated, out of breath. "Am I dead?" The sound of rolling preceded a body knocking into mine. "It doesn't hurt. Oh no, it doesn't hurt. Does this mean I'm dead?" His voice crested to a high soprano. "AM I DEAD?"

Wally laughed. "The dead tell no tales. So you are not dead. It's a miracle, too, given your level of hysteria. I'm surprised your heart didn't stop. You must have a strong ticker. Now, if you'd kept falling and had reached terminal velocity by the time you hit the ground, your bones would have cut through your organs as you would've literally exploded on impact. Messy, but effective in terms of making sure that someone dies. There isn't much that can bring you back from that kind of injury. The body is all but useless at that stage."

"Whu . . . what?" the guy stammered. "WHAT? WHAT'S HAP—"

There was a thud, and I wiggled my hood to see that one of the men with the aviators and a black jumpsuit loomed behind him with a billy club.

"What happened?" Wally asked.

"He got knocked out. One of the guards whacked him," I said.

"Too bad. I found his fear fascinating."

I shook my head slowly. "You are seriously weird."

"Of course, I am. So are you. We all are."

"Weird or not, I'm not falling out." I lowered myself to my belly, flattening to the floor as best I could. Behind me, I found a seat leg and I tucked the toes of my boot around it. I didn't know how they'd brought the soprano guy back, but I didn't want to assume they'd do the same for me. I was pretty sure I was on their black list, and maybe letting me fall would be an easy way out.

The sudden pressure on my side said Wally was following my example. "I like you," she said.

"Thanks?"

"I'm going to stick close to you, I think. I have a good feeling that you'll be strong."

I grimaced. "Lucky me." But the strange thing was, something about Wally was calming. Her knowledge of how people could die was nothing short of morbid, and yet the more she talked, the less it bothered me. I didn't mind. Not really. Maybe she wasn't so bad. At least her babbling helped distract me as we landed and picked up someone else, also in a black hood from what I could see through my peephole. Unlike me, though, the other kids weren't fighting the men. Why not? What did they know that I didn't?

Time. Which I had to be nearly out of, although I had no way to check with my hands zip tied behind me.

Through Wally's ongoing chatter, one thought kept cycling through my head—an apology to Dad. To Sam and Billy. *I'm so sorry. I screwed this up. I'm so sorry.*

We stopped five times in total after my pick up. I rolled the states through my mind. Arkansas, Missouri, Illinois, Indiana, and Ohio. We were getting closer to New York at least, but how close? Could I find a way out of this mess?

After the third stop, I stopped thinking about anything but getting the zip ties off and having a pee. My wrists were numb, but my bladder surely was not and each bump and drop of the helicopter made the urge worse.

"I think we're almost there," Wally said, breaking off her monologue about paper cuts getting infected and going gangrene in a rather small number of people—a freak occurrence, but an unfortunate way to go. Hardly heroic.

"Almost where?"

"You don't know?" She sounded genuinely surprised. "I mean, you *really* don't know?"

The helicopter began to descend rapidly, throwing us all into the air for a split second, the lack of gravity making my belly roll. As we dropped and hit the floor once more, my heart rate skyrocketed. There was no time to ask Wally what she meant, and really, I didn't need to. I'd been a fool not to figure it out earlier. Anyone who threatened a family would do something this insane and violent.

They'd given me a ride. How sweet of them to wrap me up like a present.

And now, we'd arrived at the Culling Trials.

CHAPTER 8

A popping sound filled the interior of the helicopter as if a balloon had been burst, and the steady drum of rotor blades assaulted my senses. Something had definitely been hampering the sound so we could all hear one another speaking without headsets. Now, there was nothing but noise and darkness, mitigated only by that one tiny peephole that had become my salvation for the ride.

Something hard brushed against my back. A knee. The bag was ripped off my head, and light bit into my eyeballs, as jolting as the onslaught of sound. I ducked my head and squinted as my wrists were tugged. My hands came free, tingling and numb as strong fingers curled around my upper arm.

"Time to show us what you're made of." I heard the words still audible over the helicopter as though they'd been delivered right to my ear. The familiar voice sent shivers down my spine.

I blinked my eyes opened, forcing myself to acclimate to the sound and light. Shorter than me still and built stockier with a hand that seemed made out of pure metal was my old friend.

Sideburns.

"What are you doing here?" I asked, sounding as lame as someone could. It was all I could think to say. This was obviously his gig, and my rough handling was likely by his instruction.

Sideburns jerked me past the bodies of other kids in the helicopter, my feet catching on limbs and my weight tipping forward. Shouts and yelps were reduced to muffled cries by the helicopter's noise. He held me up and all but dragged me to the edge, my feet edging out into space as we started to land.

My jaw dropped. Five other large army helicopters had landed ahead of us, with three more still in the air waiting to touch down. Before us loomed an enormous twenty-foot-high stone wall covered in ivy. The wall stretched in both directions, broken only by thick metal gates, five in all, that looked like they'd been there a very long time. Sentries lurked atop each gate, looking down on the strip of land before them, their bodies poised and hands holding guns or nothing at all. They each looked to be assigned to certain portions of the ivy wall.

More shivers attacked me. For some reason, those sentries without weapons made me the most nervous.

Kids tumbled out of helicopters that had already landed, falling into the dirt and scrambling to get up and wipe their eyes or rub their wrists. Others stood in lines or clustered in groups, occasionally shoved this way or that by handsy men or women dressed like Sideburns.

All of that paled with the realization that the sun had hardly moved from when I'd been grabbed at the airport. I felt like I'd spent a whole day traveling, but the position of the sun said it must've been no more than a couple hours.

Magic.

I didn't get a chance to dwell. In the distance, rising above the cacophony of sound, roared an enormous beast.

"What is this place?" I asked quietly as the helicopter bumped down.

"Your future. Or your grave," Sideburns said, somehow hearing me. He jerked me to the right. "The choice is yours."

"Clearly it isn't, since you kidnapped me and brought me here." I resisted him slightly, just to make him work for it. What could he do, kidnap me again?

"The most important lesson one of your kind needs to learn is how to adapt." He directed me off the helicopter and toward a table surrounded by wide-eyed kids who all blinked in a daze.

"One of my *kind*?"

He shoved a girl with straight blonde hair to the side before grabbing the shirt of a tall lanky kid and ripping him the other way, making a path for us. The kids from my helicopter were just now tumbling from its belly, landing on the dusty ground. Apparently, Sideburns holding a grudge meant I got preferential treatment. Yay me.

"Time to wizen up, or you'll get dead faster than you can cry for your mama," he growled.

"Ah." I nodded as he pushed me against the table. "You have superior linguistics. Quite the professor."

He reached around to a large pocket on his side and pulled out a hat—my hat! I didn't even remember losing it. He slapped it onto my head and pulled it down taut. A cold feeling washed through me, wondering if he knew exactly who I was. How couldn't he? But if he did, why would he be playing along?

"Johnson, Billy," Sideburns barked at the table attendant, an equally hard-faced woman with a jaw that could chop boards.

She glanced at me then down at her computer, her fingers tapping the keys with a staccato that blurred her surprisingly bright red nails. The kids around us pushed away, their tight-eyed gazes flicking to Sideburns and then quickly away. He clearly made people nervous.

"He's young for the trials. Have you got the appropriate permissions?" she said without inflection.

No kidding, "Billy" was too young. All of the kids crowding into the strip between the helicopters and the imposing walls looked like recent high school graduates. My age. The same age Tommy had been when he'd left. I didn't know what was in store for us, but it was clear that it was dangerous, and my younger brother wouldn't have stood a chance.

"That has been cleared, all permissions granted," he replied, lying with ease.

"What do you have against my family?" I asked without meaning to.

The woman's eyes flicked up as a handheld machine resting on the table beside her computer bleeped blue lights. She pointedly looked down at her computer.

"Not me," Sideburns said in a low voice, for my ears alone. "But our world? That's a whole other issue with you and your family."

I didn't have time to process that statement. The woman ripped off a piece of paper that had emerged from the machine and handed it across the table. A name tag with Billy's name and the word "Shade" under it.

Sideburns snatched it up before grabbing the wrist with the watch and pulling it out over the table for the woman, forcing me to bend over or lose an arm. He peeled the backing off before slapping it onto my chest, his hand briefly covering my breast before pulling away.

I froze for one heart-stopping moment, staring at myself in his aviators, knowing that he was looking at me from behind them. A tense beat passed in which I wondered if he'd felt my flattened boob. I was skinny by boy standards even though I was all lean muscle—no way could that little squishy area pass as a pec. The sports bra had it smooshed tightly to my chest, but it was still a breast, and they felt different than anything on a man's body. A guy like Sideburns would know that. Despite the bad choice of facial hair and the hard lines etched into his face from constant scowling, he was a looker. He would know his way around a female's anatomy, or a man's, if that was his thing.

The thought rose up again: If he knew who I really was, why was he playing along?

Uncertainty churned my gut.

The beat lengthened as a machine beeped in the background. My watch vibrated against my wrist. In the distance, three helicopters lifted into the air, leaving their human cargo behind.

"All set," the woman said.

Sideburns turned, and my exhale gushed out of me. If he knew—and how could he not—he didn't plan to reveal me. He grabbed me by the arm again and yanked, taking me back in the direction of the helicopter that had dropped me off, its interior empty now. It shuddered before lifting into the air.

"Watch yourself," Sideburns said, pulling me past a gate where a group of kids with name tags waited, shifting and fidgeting with nervousness or maybe anticipation. A few of them were grinning, which seemed out of place after a ride like that. What the hell was going on?

He walked me toward the last gate, and as we neared it, I saw that the ivy covering the wall wasn't the lovely docile plant I'd originally thought. Inch-long barbs covered the vines, and the leaves had fully serrated edges, scratching in warning against the concrete wall. Like nails on a chalkboard, the sound made my teeth clench.

Sideburns finally stopped, but he didn't back away. "Your strength has always been in adapting. This is no different. Adapt and follow your gut instincts. Don't question your intuition, and don't shy away from your nature. Do whatever it takes to stay alive. Always. That is your only chance."

I stared at him, mute, as he let go of my arm. Kids shied away from us, their widening eyes following him like they were sheep staring at a wolf in their midst. His advice made it sound like he knew me. Like he was a coach who needed to remind his star player of her training before a big match.

Her, because he surely knew, I realized that now. He knew and he let me stay anyway. Why?

Strangely, his words hit a primal place deep inside me. I felt their rightness. Their poignancy. Something within me responded to his suggestion.

"Stay strong," he said before glancing at the huge iron gate in front of us. "And stay here. This will be the easiest course for you to get through while your mind is spinning."

He nodded, as though I'd agreed, before striding away, his shoulders straight and head high, parting the anxious students.

"What just happened?" I muttered to myself.

I barely noticed the slight girl with large brown eyes and heavy black lashes drift in beside me, her gaze fixated on Sideburns.

In her strangely deep voice, the one that reminded me of Walter Cronkite and his nightly news specials, Wally said, "Life is eternal, when you know the right people."

Movement at the top of the wall caught my attention as more kids filed in around me. A huge wolf prowled near the edge, looking down at the kids gathered in front of the gate. It passed in front of a stoic individual with a large knife attached to a belt around her black clad hips. A sword scabbard jutted out behind her on the other side, the weapon attached to her back within easy reach. The wolf didn't react to her presence. She didn't appear to notice it stalking along.

"What is happening?" I breathed, my heart ratcheting up. Wolves did not ignore humans like that.

"Hello." The slight girl stepped in front of me and stuck out her hand. Her head barely reached my chin. "I'm Drexia," she said in a squeaky voice, drastically different from the deeper one she adopted when delivering odd statistics that had little relevance. "I'm named after my beloved Nana, God rest her soul. My friends call me Wally."

I couldn't help a smile. "I'm the one that called you Wally, actually. In the helicopter."

"Yes," she said.

Okay. I guess that meant we were friends now.

I lifted my eyebrows, not really sure where to go from there. To say she was an odd duck would be a bit of an understatement.

The last of the helicopters lifted from the ground, showing the natural land behind them, covered in dense foliage and gently rolling hills. The helicopters hadn't been for show—I could feel it. There wouldn't be civilization for miles. We were at the mercy of whoever ran this show.

"What's your name?" Wally asked, holding her hand out to me.

"Wild." I grimaced, quickly deepening my voice to cover my mistake. "Billy, actually. It's Billy."

"Wild. I like that better. Hi, Wild." She didn't lower her hand.

"Hey." I took her hand in a sure grip, not having to pretend to have a strong handshake. Running a farm, you dealt with men a lot, and a handshake said a lot about a person. I had learned quickly to make it firm. No limp handshakes were allowed in Texas.

The deep roar I'd heard earlier shook the ground and clattered my teeth, still way in the distance but no less potent. The wolf from before passed along the wall in the opposite direction, and though I couldn't see for sure, it felt like its eyes were beating down into me.

"The Tyrannosaurus Rex, often referred to as the T-Rex, lived around sixty-eight to sixty-six million years ago in what is now western North America," Wally said as she stepped in beside me.

A red-headed kid I immediately named Freckles pushed his way to my other side. "Why'd the Sandman bring you over here?" Freckles asked over Wally droning on about T-Rexes and their eating habits.

"The Sandman?" I asked, watching that wolf make its way past us yet again. "How is . . . Why . . . Am I seeing things?"

"To date, in this century, there has never been a death by mauling as it pertains to the T-Rex," Wally said within the ebb and flow of nervous chatter around us.

"Yeah, the Sandman," Freckles said, apparently not realizing that someone else was also talking to me. It was a miracle I could focus on anything outside of a massive predator walking the walls of some sort of death compound. "He has the most career kills of anyone of his kind. Rumor is he's a millionaire from all the high-dollar contracts he's taken, but he doesn't do too many anymore because he's bored. He needs a bigger challenge. That's why he became a teacher in the House of Shade. Rumor is he's creating his own army. This is his first year of recruiting. Did he say anything to you?"

"To date," Wally said, fingering a button on her sweater as she watched the top of the wall, "in this century, the Sandman has laid to rest over one thousand people that we know of, the most lethal in the House of Shade, driving fear into the hearts of the students, and creating discourse between the faculty and the school headmaster."

"Yeah. Him," Freckles said. "Do you know him?"

"He threatened my family if I didn't show up." I glanced down the wall before pushing up onto my tiptoes. Six feet might not have set any records for height, even for a girl, but it was usually tall enough to see over a crowd of people.

More groups of people waited down the way, each clustered in front of one of the gates. A few people stood closer to the wall, but most were pushed back in a big horde, shifting and fidgeting in a way that indicated they weren't excited about what lay beyond. It spoke of the unknown. Of nasty surprises.

"Oh." Freckles nodded like my answer made all sorts of sense. "You must've been on the 'hard case' roster and gotten unlucky with him. A lot of people didn't think he'd do well as a recruiter for the House of Shade because he's lacking in his manipulation techniques. Clearly he found another way that suited him better."

I frowned as I looked down on Freckles, seeing the logic in what he was saying, but bewildered all the same by the lingo. "Huh?" was about all I could muster.

"Yeah, he probably brought you up personally to prove a point. Man, that sucks." Freckles shook his head and shifted to the side. A lithe and beautiful woman walked along the edge of the wall, a serene smile on her face and a stick in her hand. "This place is scary enough. I can't imagine dealing with his threats on top of it."

"The House of Wonder." Wally's voice dropped. "Beware that which beguiles and delights, for a blade is hidden under the mage's robe."

"What is this place?" I asked as the beautiful woman passed in front of the black-clad woman, who was so still, I almost lost track of her presence. Almost.

Wally turned her gaze to my face. "Did your parents not tell you of this place? I wondered about that in the helicopter, a metal beast not meant to fly."

I shook my head. "No, they must have forgotten to include it in their bedtime stories."

"They didn't tell you anything?" Freckles asked, turning to survey me as well. "Why not?" He tilted his head in commiseration. "Did they think it was cheating? Yeah, my dad said I should experience it blind, like he did. That it would make a man out of me. But my mom walked me through everything I might face. Don't worry, I'll help you, man."

"Attention, everyone." The speaker was the beautiful woman who'd walked past us, and although I could barely see her now, her voice rang out with perfect clarity. "Attention, please."

The noise and chatter from the ground died down. A few fingers came up to point.

The woman continued to make her way along the wall until she stood in what I assumed was the center above the middle iron gate.

"Welcome to the annual Culling Trials." She lifted her hands to the sky and a cheer rose from around me and on down the way from all the other kids. "Here is where we will test your mettle. Your strength. Your speed. Your know-how. Here is where you will learn if you have what it takes to advance into the Academy of Shadowspell, or if you'll be doomed to a life . . . of *lesser.*"

A wave of chatter followed her pronouncement. Feet shifted and scraped against the dirt. Bodies pressed in tighter, the anxiety and excitement palpable.

"I really hope I make it through," Freckles said softly. "My dad said he would disown me if I didn't. I mean, he was joking, but . . ." Freckles's voice reduced down to a soft mutter. "I'm pretty sure he was joking . . ."

"Eight out of ten make it through the first stage of the Culling Trials," Wally said, still worrying that top button of her sweater as she watched the woman on the wall. "Nulls and those not physically capable often drop away, leaving able-bodied magical types to advance to the academy, a cutthroat smorgasbord of treachery and betrayal. The academy is what squeezes you. Bends you. Finally, breaks you. One in eleven of those who leave the trials ring the bell and excuse themselves, hanging their heads in shame. The rest are forced to leave, unfit and destitute, for a half-life with the Norms. Forever known as dropouts and failures. Lesser."

"Wow. She's a real downer," Freckles murmured. "Who can even do all that math?"

Wally's voice dropped. "You do not choose the academy. The academy chooses you."

"What the hell?" Freckles leaned around me to get a better look at Wally.

As Sideburns—the Sandman was too cool of a name for that guy—had predicted, my mind spun. A magical academy? Assassins? Wall-walking super wolves? Even though my dad had told me about some of it, I hadn't believed him.

But seeing what was in front of me now . . . how could I not?

I wasn't up for any of this. Hell, I *was* an ordinary person. I'd always been.

My mother's voice rose up out of nowhere, taking over my thoughts.

"There is magic all around us, Wild. Everywhere. In everything. In you. You gather people to you like moths to a flame. You were built to ride the wind, my love. So ride it. Your time will come."

Very little of that had made sense at the time. I'd been in the middle of getting in trouble for convincing my brother and Rory to follow me into the neighbor's bullpen, sure we could tame the mean old bugger with the single horn and a seriously bad attitude. I'd nearly gotten us killed. Dad had been too livid to deal with me, so he'd passed me off to my mother to finish the tongue lashing and decide on a punishment.

She'd decided on no punishment. Tommy had fumed and even Rory had been disappointed, both wanting me to get my butt whooped for convincing them to take the risk. Instead, no one had been blamed, not even them for going along with it.

When mom had said all that about magic, I'd never, in my wildest dreams, thought she was talking about real magic, the kind in children's books. Yet here I stood with a bunch of people who'd apparently been raised on this stuff along with their Wheaties.

"Say goodbye to your contact with the outside world," the woman continued, her hair dramatically blowing behind her as if she were a model across from a fan, and even though I couldn't see it from the distance, I knew she had a sweet smile on her face. A fake smile that hid a gleaming blade, like Wally had said. "Cell phones are useless. There will be no computers, no social media, no GPS. There will only be your courage and your mettle. Your watch will help us monitor your progress through each trial. If you take it off, your time here will be forfeit. Make it to the end for full points. Grab the gold for a bonus. And, as always, keep your friends close, and your enemies closer. I will see you on the other side."

She sauntered off to the side and held her stick high. With a flick of the wrist, the heavy metal gates that stretched out down the wall clunked before us, shuddering. They opened, little by little. The creaking sound of metal riding the roar of what Wally seemed to think was a freaking T-Rex. People pushed in behind me, but no one attempted to get ahead. A quick look down the line showed the same thing at each gate. Groups of people, no one stepping forward.

That faint smell I'd caught earlier rode the moment. Dirt and sweat and spicy vanilla. A smell of home and comfort. Of kicking ass and causing mayhem.

A slow grin slid over my lips and I clung to the words of my mother.

"You were born to ride the wind, Wild."

CHAPTER 9

What's the strategy?" I grabbed Wally on one side, Freckles on the other, and stepped toward the gate in front of us. I'd be damned if I was doing this alone, and they seemed to know what to expect. We'd be stronger together, something I'd learned from my childhood with Tommy and Rory.

"Okay." Freckles hurried beside me, jogging to keep up with my longer legs. "The person on top of this section obviously belongs to the House of Shade, which is what this stretch will be dedicated to. If the Sandman was your recruiter, then you're probably in your element."

"You said they kill people. You think that's my specialty?" I asked incredulously.

"Creating walking memory banks, that's mine," Wally said.

"Oh gross, you're not a necromancer, are you?" Freckles groaned at Wally. "That's the type of thing one of them would say. Dead people shouldn't be used for information recall. It isn't right. It just isn't."

"There is comfort in rising from the dead," Wally replied as the gate in front of us opened wider. We were nearly there, leading the pack of not-so-eager participants.

"No, that's *not* comfortable," Freckles said as a warning blared through my mind and ran all the way down my spine. "Coming back as a rotting corpse after dying is *not at all comfortable!*"

"Wait," I said, slowing as we reached the now-open gate. I grabbed Wally and stepped to the side. Freckles fell in behind us.

"What's the matter?" Wally whispered.

A narrow path led from the gate into a forest of dense redwood trees. Green grass filled in between artfully tangled weeds and the occasional shrub that would easily tangle a foot should someone go running through them.

The pack of kids behind us slowed, and I knew without knowing how that everyone was waiting for someone else to go first. Why wouldn't they? We were walking into a house of freaking predators who were known for killing people. Even if this was some elaborate joke that I would not find funny, Sideburns was part of it, and his sense of humor was obviously dangerous. Boogeymen lurked in this place, and they had the upper hand.

I took Wally's wrist for the same reasons I would've taken Tommy's back in the day—half for comfort, half to get the show on the road. A sudden pang of loss hit me. Had he paused at this gate like I was doing? Had he waited for someone to grab his wrist like I'd always done in potentially dangerous situations?

"Go through or go around?" I asked quietly, walking forward slowly. This wasn't unlike walking through the wilds after an animal had gotten onto our lands and killed livestock. I needed the same awareness. The readiness to act.

"My mom said that most people went around, but she'd wished she'd gone through," Freckles said. "But she never talked to anyone from this house."

"In the academy's history, three percent of those who have gone through the middle have died," Wally whispered. "Sixty-five percent made it to the end."

"How many people died the other way?" Freckles asked.

"None," she replied as a group of tough-looking boys broke from the pack. They went right, avoiding the path, at a slow walk. "But only fifty percent of them made it through."

"So we have a better chance of making it through if we go through the middle, but we might die?" Freckles's voice increased in pitch. "What kind of odds are those?"

"Better odds than hang-gliding in a hurricane," Wally replied, cool as a cucumber.

"Why are you so good at math and so stinking bad at social skills?" he screeched, bringing his voice up a few octaves, and I was suddenly pretty sure he was the screecher from the helicopter. "It's not natural."

A group of five girls dressed all in black, down to the painted fingernails they held near their chests, walked around us toward the path, giggling as they did so. Outwardly they looked nervous and silly. They looked like they'd get taken down, no problem. But the fluidity in their gait and the seriousness in their eyes told a different story.

A story I had no trouble reading.

If I'd seen this group slip into the park in town at night in my hometown, I would have instantly known they were up to no good, that this wasn't their first rodeo, and any attempt to follow them, even out of curiosity, would lead to retaliation.

Something within me clicked into place. A strange understanding.

"They belong here," I said, marveling. "Wally, of the sixty-five percent who make it through, how many end up in this house?"

"Yes. Good question." She paused. "Eighty percent of the sixty-five percent, I believe. A larger percentage of the ones who make it through the other way are not native to this house."

"It's unnatural what she's doing," Freckles repeated. "It is literally another language, and only the criminally insane speak it."

A short guy with a stick, much like the woman on the wall had used, strutted forward, leading the way. Dumb as a post, I could tell. He grinned for the people behind him, his audience, and gave a mocking half bow before stepping onto the path.

I knew what he was thinking: If a bunch of silly girls can do this, obviously I can.

A grin crept up my face.

Those girls were luring the over-confident morons after them. They felt confident in these surroundings, and their intent was to do harm to those that didn't understand what they were up against.

"Fascinating," I said, my heart quickening even as my stomach pinched. "I mean, super messed up, but . . . wow."

The Bro glanced at his watch, gave his fan club a grin, and walked forward. Immediately, a small crowd hurried to follow, the guys all bravado and the girls twittering and laughing nervously.

Hook, line, and sinker, the dumb fish were caught.

"Let's go," I said, grabbing the two by my side and hurrying after the Bro Pack.

"Okay, that was a lot of math back there, but isn't this the bad way for people like us?" Freckles said, trotting beside me, his round face already sweating.

"For us, yes," Wally said, not needing my tug to stay with me. "For him?" She nodded to me. "We shall see."

Releasing their arms, I said, "It's a bad way for all of us, yes," forcing myself to slow as we neared the path. I needed to think this through.

Logic said to go around. Hell, statistics said go around. No one had died the other way. Sideburns might've thought I'd do well in the House of Shade, and someone obviously thought this was my—strike that, Billy's—place, but I didn't know about that. I didn't know about any of this. We should take the easier approach, the one favored by those who didn't belong in the house.

Except . . .

Something about the girls' approach pulled at me. Dragged me behind them. And it wasn't just a sick fascination, or the weird heaviness in the pit of my stomach that said their actions fit with the danger of this place. They were taking others along this path for a purpose. In this game of survival, they'd thought it necessary to bring bait. They knew what they were doing. It made sense to tag along and ride their coattails, so long as the Bro Pack stayed between us.

Don't shy away from your nature. Do whatever it takes to stay alive. Always.

"Okay, Sideburns," I said under my breath, stopping just before the path. "You win."

I stepped onto the center path with one foot, then the other. My watch vibrated and a message flashed across the screen.

You've chosen. Good luck.

Something bumped my back, pushing me forward, but a quick backward glance showed me nothing was there.

I spun, wide-eyed, and put out a hand. My palm found a hard nothingness separating me from the path, or lack of a path, I hadn't taken. Like plexiglass, only it wasn't glass and it wasn't visible.

Wally and Freckles stood side by side, staring at me on the other side of the invisible barrier while the Bro Pack's loud talking and laughing echoed as though we were locked in the same ethereal chamber.

My chest constricted and I struggled to breathe.

Magic. Real, honest-to-God magic had trapped me on this path. The small hold-out part of me that still hadn't believed could no longer deny the truth. "What's your name?" I called to Freckles, not sure why that should be so important right then but needing to know. Maybe just in case we all ended up dead.

His brow creased and he leaned forward a little. His lips soundlessly formed the word *what?*

"What's your name?" I said again, knowing I needed to turn and hurry to catch up with the Bro Pack, but feeling the urgency here, as well.

He frowned and shook his head a little before stepping forward.

"What?" he asked, placing his second foot, his voice now loud and clear.

I sucked in a breath, guilt tearing through me as I looked down at his feet, both firmly on the path. His watch vibrated. After he'd read it, his eyes hit mine.

I'd just accidentally lured him in. I'd learned from those girls and immediately applied the lesson without intending to.

"What's your name?" I asked softly, an apology under my words, cursing the Sandman for dragging me into this. Cursing my parents for never explaining what I might someday be forced into.

"Oh. Pete. Just don't call me Peter. My brothers always tease me about Peter. I mean, it's a person's name, not just a dick's name." He rolled his eyes—"Anyway"—and put out a fist.

Handshakes I had. Fist bumps weren't part of the old farmer language. They made me feel awkward for reasons unknown.

"I'm . . . Billy." I caught myself just in time. "Sorry, Pete, if you didn't want to come this way," I said, feeling like it was my duty to clear the air. Then, remembering that the guys I knew didn't usually apologize—they were more apt to find someone else to blame—I amended, "But you did step through, so . . . your bad."

Wally pushed up behind us, shoving Pete out of the way. "I couldn't hear you guys. What'd I miss?"

"That's Pete." I hooked a thumb at him.

"Hello, Peter," Wally said professionally, putting out her hand for a handshake, same as she'd done for me.

Pete scowled at her. He hurried after me. "Of course, I was going to come. The Sandman ushered you over here. He only pays attention to the best. My best shot of getting through is to hang with you, man."

I laughed sardonically. They couldn't possibly know that my brother was the one Sideburns had attempted to lure here and got me in his place. I didn't understand his game, but he hadn't denied my family was a target and he hadn't cared that I'd shown up instead of Billy. Good thing I knew something Tommy didn't.

I knew how to fight dirty.

CHAPTER 10

The Bro Pack meandered along ahead of us, through the tall trees, reaching out and touching them here and there. I resisted the urge to do the same. Whatever this place was, I wasn't trusting it and that meant no touching if I didn't have to. The two girls at the back hung onto each other, looking to either side fearfully. They were way out of their element in this trial if their balayage hair and designer clothes were any indication. Both of those things were great for us. Whatever beasties lurked in this place would pick off the weakest prey first. Which was most certainly them.

"We're going to use them as chasers," I said, keeping my voice just low enough for Wally and Pete.

"What?" He frowned up at me, brow crinkling.

"A chaser," I repeated, somewhat surprised that he didn't know. "A car ahead of you on the road that's speeding. You tail them, and if a cop is waiting in a speed trap, they'll get the chaser car first. What kind of dude doesn't know that? It's like Driving 101."

He flushed and I almost felt bad. "I don't have my license yet," he mumbled. "But I played Gran Turismo a lot."

That had to be a video game, something I'd never played. Growing up, I'd considered myself lucky if I got a turn to pick what was on TV a couple times a week.

I held up both hands, feeling the need to get moving. "Let's push in close to them. We need to follow closely enough to see what comes at them, but not so close that we get caught up in it. Got it?"

I started forward and they fell in beside me. Wally clasped her hands in front of her.

"Two miles of No Man's Land is the typical length of each of the trials," she said. "Though those that run them often claim they're far longer."

"I can't run one mile, never mind two!" Pete's face bloomed a bright pink as if he were already running.

I spared him a glance. "If we do this right, we won't be running."

We'd taken no more than a few steps when the light around us dimmed to an unnatural twilight. Deep shadows pooled between the trunks of the trees and hid the path ahead.

Then the entire scene shifted right in front of us.

"Holy cats," Pete whispered.

That wasn't the word that went through my mind.

The trees shifted and spun, dizzying me. Then they grew, their limbs shooting up and out, changing color and appearance as they did until we were surrounded by towering buildings. The ground below us hardened rapidly, turning from dirt to concrete. In the distance, the sound of traffic cut through the night instead of the birds and soft rustling of leaves.

"We're in a city," Pete said.

"Nothing gets past you," I muttered.

Dead ahead was an alley that cut between a series of buildings. At what had to be the end, I could see a sign blinking in the distance, well above our heads. Exit.

"Here we go," I said. The anticipation of our first challenge intensified in me until I was wound tighter than a dollar-store guitar.

Wally crowded in on my one side and tried to slip an arm through mine. I shook her off.

I needed my hands free for what was coming.

"Can you see those idiots that were ahead of us?" I asked.

"No," they chimed in unison.

Well, that settled that. "Sorry, Pete, I lied," I said as I broke into a jog, heading deeper into the alley.

Pete groaned. "I knew I should have cut out the Snickers bars. I should have gone to the gym."

"Every year, thirty-five to fifty-six people die from ingesting peanut-laden chocolate bars, not realizing they are allergic to the peanuts. Even more people die from cardiac arrest while attempting to get into shape. Fifty-year-olds drop dead from running on a non-regular basis. You should be grateful—you dodged two deaths."

"Except now I'm running," he wheezed.

"Yes. Your odds of making it through this are dropping dramatically," Wally said solemnly. "Good luck."

My lips twitched. I wasn't even sure she knew she was being funny, which only made her funnier.

The alley was easy going, smooth with no visible obstacles—and *that* made me nervous. There was a sudden shout up ahead, then a series of shouts that turned into screams. A normal person would have stopped, maybe turned and made a run for it.

I picked up speed, following instincts hammered into me my whole life. If someone screamed, you hurried to help.

Pete and Wally hissed at me to slow down, to stay back, to take it easy, but I kept running until the alley came to a T-intersection. I paused there, waiting for a noise to pull me in one direction or the other.

A whimper, barely above a whisper, drew me to the left. I crouched, pressing my hip against the building as my hand slid to the knife sheath on my other hip. I pulled the homemade blade free.

Just in case.

A small part of my brain tried to point out the insanity of what was happening, which didn't follow any pattern I'd learned over the last eighteen years of life. The voice was only trying to keep me safe, but I'd gotten good at telling it to shut up.

A light above a doorway on the other side of the alley flickered to life. At the base of the entrance lay a crumpled figure, blood clearly visible against his hair. I'd seen him with the Bro Pack at the beginning. The smallest of the bunch, he was fair-haired to the point of being white blond and slight, barely five feet, if that. Sam would have outweighed him, and she was a waif.

The shuffle of boots on the pavement.

"Don't leave me," the crouched figure whimpered, curling tighter around himself.

"Kill the goblin, we don't need him," a voice shouted from the other side of the light. Highbrow, cultured, and cruel, the voice was the epitome of good breeding gone terribly wrong. My lips curled. And then my brain tried to linger on the goblin bit. Nope, not going there, I didn't have time to process it.

A spatter of laughter followed the Bro's pronouncement, followed by the sound of feet running from the scene. Four hulking figures stepped out of the shadows, surrounding the kid on the ground. These were not eighteen-year-old students—the maze had revealed its first challenge.

I smelled Pete before he reached me, a faint musk. I crinkled my nose. A heavy breath escaped him. "That's a goblin," he whisper-gasped. "The thugs there can deal with him. We can slip by, use him for distraction like the others did."

Wally—only a second behind Pete—nodded. "That plan will give us the best chances of survival, easily increasing our odds by seventy-five percent."

Sure, if we wanted to sacrifice someone to save ourselves.

I didn't work like that. I wasn't leaving the kid to those thugs. Goblin or not, he didn't deserve this. "You two slip by first, I'll follow and cover the rear." They didn't have to know what I was planning.

Wally crept ahead, pinning her back to the side of the building. Her eyes widened as she hit the edge of the light thrown by that single flickering lamp. Her entire body was visible to the thugs, but their eyes were on the small kid who'd tucked his body around himself, pressing against the wall like he hoped to disappear into it.

No doubt he'd thought he'd be safe going in with a big group of guys. But they hadn't lured their bait in the same way the girls ahead of them had. They'd flat out taken him with them, promising him safety in numbers.

Anger snapped up and through me. It was one thing to lure stupids after you, another to make a false promise of safety to someone who trusted you.

I motioned for Freckles to go, and he stepped surprisingly light on his feet, following Wally.

There was a thud of a boot hitting a body. I couldn't wait for Pete to get all the way across.

Sorry, bud.

I stepped into the light. "Y'all are pretty tough, huh, beating up on one kid? Four against, one? Really?" Pete squeaked, clearly visible to the four oversized thugs as they did a slow turn in unison.

I'd like to say in that moment I wasn't afraid, that I didn't take half a step back, that I didn't consider my poor life choices, including that one, in a single flash, but that would be a lie. The thugs . . . they didn't have faces. I mean like nothing. No eyes. No lips. Nothing, just a blank canvas of pasty white with weird stringy hair that hung past where ears should be. These creatures were not people, not even close to human.

Terror tripped along my spine and it made my mouth do terrible things.

"You got a felt marker? I could draw you in some eyebrows. Nice big bushy ones." I grinned through the fear, feeling the wild in me surge up and out.

Reckless, I know.

The one *thing* closest to me lifted a hand that held a short knife. I mimicked him. "You'd make amazing mimes. Like fantastic. Probably make a lot of money if you took your show on the road. You'd conquer one curb at a time."

"I'm going to pee my pants," Pete squeaked.

The knife-wielding faceless *thing* lunged at me, knife in a straight thrust for my guts. I danced to the side and swung a slice of my own with my blade, cutting across its arm. I grimaced as the blade dug into bone. A spurt of blood was sure to follow with a blow. Great gushes of it. Or something, there should have been something.

I yanked my knife back and the thug didn't slow, not for a split second, nor was there a single splatter of red.

Another of the hulking creatures went for Pete. I cut the thing off, knifing it where the kidney *should* be. It swung to face me, and I dropped to a knee, rolling out of the way.

Pete—bless his stupid heart—jumped into the fray. With their backs to him, the creatures didn't see him coming.

"I'll get this one, Billy!" he yelled as he *climbed* up the back of the brute closest to him. I couldn't help but stare.

How in the heck had he done that? Like he'd had handholds on the back of the—thing. I needed to understand what I was dealing with if I was going to beat them.

"Wally, what are they?" I yelled as I stepped closer to one of the creatures and kicked out, smashing my boot into the inside of its knee. The crunch was solid, and on a person would have shattered the bones, displacing the knee cap and rendering them pretty much useless. Not so much here. The beastie barely bobbled on its legs.

"Golems," Wally called out. "Anthropomorphic creatures made entirely from inanimate matter. They are controlled by their creator from a safe distance. Less than point-zero-zero-one percent of deaths have been caused by golems. But, to be fair, all of those deaths occurred within the Culling Trials."

Of course, they had.

Wally paused. "They are Jewish of origin if that helps."

"It does *not*!" I yelled as I ducked a knife swipe at my head. "Unless one of you is Jewish and knows what to do?"

Neither of them answered, which said it all.

"I got this one!" Pete yelped as he wrapped his arms around the neck of the golem he'd climbed, letting his legs swing out wide.

It was quite the sight. The rodeos at home had nothing on this.

"Fantastic info, Wally, but how do we stop them?" I dodged a big boot coming my way, straight for my head. They were bendy bastards for being so big. The blow meant for my face missed so narrowly I could feel the wind slap my cheek.

"You don't kill them," the goblin kid on the ground said. "You leave them someone to torment while you continue on. That is how this works."

"Not today it doesn't," I said as I slid between the golems, keeping them swinging, arms and feet going in all directions. If I got close enough, maybe I could get them to smash into each other. "Pete, get ready to bail."

I put myself between two of the golems, keeping my hands at my sides. "Come on, ugly boys, let's see what you've got."

They swung for my head at the same time, one from the right, one from the left, and I dropped to the ground just before they struck flesh. They crashed into each other with an enormous cracking bang, like Humpty Dumpty having a really bad day, and I scrambled across the ground to the kid still crouched against the wall. I glanced behind me. The two golems now lay on the ground flat on their backs, blocking the paths of the other two. Beautiful.

Pete had bailed and was nowhere to be seen. For the moment, we were good, but it wouldn't last. "Time to move."

The kid's eyes lifted to mine—huge, round eyes that were totally out of proportion with the rest of his face. "Why are you doing this? Nobody helps in the Culling Trials."

I wasn't about to tell him that he reminded me of Billy. That if my little brother had come instead of me, he probably would have made the same mistake as this kid—he would have hooked up with the big boys, thinking he'd be safe with them.

No one would have saved Billy, but I could save this kid.

"Not the time." I grabbed him by the arm and swung him up onto my back. How many times had I done this same move with Sam? Hundreds. And he was far lighter than she was even now.

I dodged the now stumbling golems, driving a foot into the knees of the two still standing, slowing them down. They were freaky to look at, but slow and dumb. Not much of a challenge if you asked me.

"Run," I said to Pete and Wally as I took off, the new kid clinging to my back like an oversized monkey.

"They'll track us," Pete said. "Golems don't give up their prey easily."

"Doubt it." I shot back. "If this is a trial, then there will be something else up ahead of us. The golems," cripes, I could not believe I was saying that word as if it were real, "won't follow us far. Otherwise, there wouldn't be anything left here for the kids who come after us. We just have to get to the next obstacle as quickly as we can."

"That seems like a bad idea," the kid on my back said. "Quick is death in the Culling Trials."

"Well, moving slow wasn't doing you any good," I pointed out.

"Touché," he said. "My name is Gregory."

"Gregory Goblin?" Pete snickered. "Did your parents think you were going to end up in a comic book?"

Gregory's hands drifted to the top of my collarbone as I jogged along, precariously close to the girls. That was not happening.

"Okay, ride's over." I let go of him, dropping him to the ground abruptly.

He yelped as he hit the pavement, rolled, and came to his feet.

"Dumb jerk," he snapped up at me as he dusted off clothes that were nicer than anything I'd ever had in my closet. Did goblins have money? Or style for that matter? Apparently so.

"Yeah, well, this jerk just saved your butt, *Gregory Goblin*," I said. I checked my ball cap, tugging the rim to make sure it was on good and tight. This whole acting, looking, and talking like a guy thing was a lot of work. And I kept forgetting about the part I was supposed to be playing, which didn't help.

"Um, Billy?" Pete said.

"Call me Wild," I replied without thinking.

"I think we have a new problem."

Of course, we did. I made a slow turn and let out a big breath as I took in the scene ahead of us. "Jesus Murphy on a limping donkey, do we ever."

CHAPTER 11

S creams erupted back the way we'd come, followed by the sound of distant thumps. The golems had forgotten about us, just as I'd predicted.

A whole new problem lay ahead in this city of death we were trapped in. My eyes locked on what I could only see as a wall of death and dismemberment.

I didn't mean figuratively either. The ground dipped easily ten feet into a hole that stretched the width of the alley from building to building. The ditch, if it could be called that, was six feet wide, and ended in a metal wall stretching up and out of sight into a bank of fog. It resembled an oversized chicken wire fence with large blades jutting out at random intervals, which would force an intrepid climber along a particular path. I blinked and the blades closest to the ground drew back and popped out somewhere else on the wall. A faint dusting of rain pattered down around us. Not fog, then. Clouds. Wet metal was a right bitch to climb, slippery and cold. I flexed my hands, already sizing up the best path to take, timing the emergence of the blades.

"Okay, so I've seen worse," I said.

The buzz of electricity cut through the air, and the hair along my arms stood as parts of the wall glowed blue, sizzling against the rain.

"Really?" Gregory said beside me, rubbing his arms. "You've seen worse?"

I was going to answer but was interrupted by a bellow of pain somewhere above us. Way above us.

Pete swallowed hard enough that it was audible.

"Falls equate for a sum total of over six hundred fifty thousand, five hundred twenty deaths a year. Globally, that is," Wally said softly, the fear in her voice palpable.

"I've seen worse. We can do this," I repeated, more for myself than the others. "If those ladies in black ahead of us could get through, then so can we."

"Those ladies in black," Gregory said, "are from some of the longest lines of assassins this world has ever seen."

"Then we need to figure out how they did it." I took a few steps toward the ditch. The marks on the edge showed fresh scuffs left by the Bros who'd jumped across, pushing hard to make the full six-foot leap. I frowned as I lowered my gaze to the base of the ditch. I crouched and put my hands on the lip of the ditch, feeling the marks, seeing others that weren't immediately visible if you were, say, running from the golems.

This challenge was like going through the most violent haunted house I'd ever thought possible. But it was a puzzle too—one with deadly stakes.

I wasn't about to tell the others that I kinda liked it.

My wrist vibrated and I glanced at the watch as a message flashed across it.

Getting passed is bad for your health.

"Did you just get that message too?" I looked up at the other three and they nodded in unison.

Which meant we had to go.

Gregory launched across the open space, covering it easily, and began to climb the wall, his words echoing my thoughts. "We have to move!"

Only we didn't have to move, at least, not in the direction he was going. Not if the marks under my hands were any indication. "That's not the way."

Pete all but danced at my side, his feet tapping out a rhythm.

"You gotta pee still?" I asked.

"Yeah, when I get nervous." And he just whipped it out and started to whizz right in front of me. Like I was one of the guys. Which, of course, I was supposed to be. Wally squeaked and spun her back to him.

"Not in the ditch, you idiot!" I shoved him on the hip, turning him away from the hole.

"Why not?" He looked over his shoulder at me.

I lowered myself along the edge of the ditch, avoiding the splash of piss. "Because it's where we're going."

Wally nodded and sidestepped him. "That's good. I don't think anyone has died in a ditch. At least, not that I know of."

I wanted to ask her about the first two world wars but refrained.

My feet landed on much softer ground, boots sinking down with my weight. Mud, liquid mud. It had better just be mud seeing as there were no cows around. Wally slid down the side of the ditch and landed with a sloppy splash, Pete next, and remarkably enough, even Gregory.

"Change your mind?"

"I hate climbing." He wouldn't make eye contact with me, which was fine. Let him keep his pride.

Pete grabbed my arm. "I can smell cotton candy perfume. One of the girls was wearing that. They did come down this way. But how did you know?"

I pointed at the faint depressions in the soft ground, wondering how he'd smelled anything over the heavy scent of earth . . .

and urine. But he was right—now that he'd pointed it out, I could pick up a faint cotton candy scent.

"Footprints," I said. I'd only seen them once I'd crouched. Even then, if I hadn't taken a moment to process what I was seeing, I would have missed them. Just like everyone who'd leapt at the obvious path. "Let's go. I don't want anyone else figuring this out if we can help it. Gregory, give me your coat."

"What are you going to do with it? You're too big," Gregory said, but he did hand it over.

I pushed the three of them ahead of me and then used his coat to brush away the footprints we left behind as best I could. "Covering our tracks." It wasn't as good as tree branch, but it would do the job.

They stepped ahead as I swept the area. I had to trust that they wouldn't go too far—and they didn't. I bumped into them as I reached the end of my sweeping job. They'd gathered under an overhang of street that hid us from the open mouth of the ditch. Again, you wouldn't have seen the overhang or the tunnel until you were in the ditch. "What are you waiting for?"

"It's locked." Pete jangled something metallic.

I turned to see a five-foot-tall gate that led underground, and by the initial direction, under all the buildings. From the gate hung a brand new lock. Too fresh, too new. I would have laid money that the ladies in black ahead of us had locked the gate. I sighed. "Any of you picked locks before?" I had, but I felt someone else needed to step up and show off their skills. That's what this place was about, right?

Gregory nodded. "I have." He held up his hands, showing off long, almost delicate looking fingers. "I'm quite good at it actually. I just need something to work with."

"Would a bobby pin work?" Wally asked.

Gregory nodded, and she pulled one from her hair. I wasn't sure it was even holding anything up. Almost like she'd decided to put a few bobby pins in for an emergency. Which, given how much she and Pete knew about the trials, was a distinct possibility.

"While Gregory works, tell me what you know about this school," I said.

Wally's eyes widened and the telltale spitting of electricity made me grab Gregory and pull him back as the blue light flickered across the metal gate. "Thanks."

"No problem." I let him go but didn't take my eyes from Wally. "Talk to me, Wally. And not about death."

She shrugged. "That will be difficult because the Academy of Shadowspell is death incarnate in many ways. There are five houses within the school. From top to bottom in terms of standing amongst the world and magical community, it is the House of Wonder, where magic and power are held as the highest objectives first. The House of Night, where darkness and the undead rule, second. The House of Claw, where animals and their masters stand shoulder to shoulder, third. The House of Shade, where the shadows cover those who deal in death, fourth. And the final house—"

"The House of Unmentionables," Gregory said as he flourished his hands at the now-open gate. "Of which goblins and other unmentionables are a part."

I eyed him up. "You don't look much like a goblin. More like an undersized Justin Bieber."

Gregory's lips curled upward. "We get uglier as we get older. And ugliness is prized in our culture. We leave beauty to those who would be blinded by it."

Pete leaned in to me. "So, you just insulted him."

I opened my mouth to apologize and then clamped it shut. That was not what a guy would do. No, a guy would rub that insult in.

"Well, Biebs, you're one cute little runt, aren't you?"

He opened his mouth, showing off rather sharp teeth and emitting an even sharper hiss, when the sound of voices reached us. The group behind us had almost caught up.

Without a word, the four of us hurried through the open gate and closed it softly behind us. I thought about locking the gate as those ahead of us had, but I wasn't that much of a jerk. If the others behind us figured out to get into the ditch, I wasn't going to slow them down. I left the padlock hanging so that it appeared to be locked but wasn't fully engaged.

I turned away to see Gregory watching me. Pete had his nose in the air as he stepped farther into the underground tunnel.

"This way, I can smell that perfume. It makes me hungry," he said. Wally was next to him and I thought I heard her say something about death by perfume causing lungs to collapse.

A few steps in and my shoulders itched, right down the middle, a warning if ever I'd felt one. I turned to see Gregory watching me closely.

"What?" I asked.

"You are not . . . what I expect from a Shade," he said.

A frown pulled my lips down. "A shade?"

He pointed at my nametag. "They think you'll end up in the House of Shade based on your ancestry, though no one can be certain until after the sorting at the end of the Culling Trials." He shrugged. "No one else could have dodged the speed of those golems. Except maybe a vampire, but you're definitely not one of those."

There was a scuff behind us and I spun. Nothing but shadows. Still . . . maybe something was stalking us, even if I wasn't picking up any danger from that direction.

My frown deepened as I kept pace with Gregory in the rounded-out tunnel. Water sloshed under our feet and the faint scent of shit curled around us. Like we'd stepped into the sewer system under a big city. "The golems weren't that fast."

"They were a blur to me." Gregory said softly. "I could not have avoided them on my own."

That made no sense. "They were slow as turtles in molasses come February."

Gregory snorted. "That's my point. I couldn't see *you* either. The ability to move at speeds that can only be matched or beaten by a full vampire is the House of Shade personified."

I glanced at him then down at the tag on my chest. "And you're not just saying that because of this?"

Under my name was a single word. Shade.

Gregory looked ahead. "Even without it, I would know what you are. Your kind and mine often work closely, as we are considered . . . less than those with true magic."

I shrugged. "And if I am a Shade?"

"Then you are the only reason the other three of us will make it out of this trial alive and with any standing," he said.

"No pressure at all, right?" A dry laugh escaped me.

A moment later, we caught up with Pete and Wally, who'd stopped walking. It wasn't hard to see why—the tunnel bucketed out into open space. Wally had pressed herself against the rounded curve of the wall, and Pete leaned out over the opening on his hands and knees. "Holy cats, Wild. Check this out."

As Gregory and I stepped up to the lip of the tunnel, I got my first look at the next challenge.

"It looks like a video game," Pete said. "All those platforms, ladders, ropes, and lots and lots of places to fall. And how is it that tall? We aren't that far underground, are we?"

He wasn't wrong, but something wasn't right. "We've been walking downhill the last ten minutes, so yeah, it is possible." I thought for a moment. "Wally or Biebs, either of you get a feel for this place?"

Sure, Gregory thought I was made for this place, but that didn't mean I believed him. Even if I felt a flash of recognition deep in my belly that he was *not* wrong. Even if the emotion that coursed through me was nothing short of adrenaline-fueled excitement.

Gregory tipped his head. "Why are you asking me? Us?"

"It's smarter, that's why. The group as a whole is greater than its individual parts," I said. "So you got anything?"

Gregory wiggled his fingers and closed his eyes. Like he was communing with the dead or something, which at this point in my day I would not be surprised about. He gave a full body shiver and then nodded. "There's gold nearby. It's . . ." He pointed upward and vaguely ahead of us. "It's somewhere . . . above us. Other than that, I cannot be sure."

"My mother said that only the House of Shade people go for the gold," Pete said, shaking his head. "It's really hard to get. She said just to get through as fast as possible without taking any detours, but . . . I don't see a set path, do you?"

"What do you mean gold? The lady in the beginning said it was a bonus. Is it . . . like a medal?" I stared up at the oversized death trap, a plethora of circular platforms separated by empty space, connected by ropes or ladders here and there, although not enough of them.

"No, in each trial there is the opportunity to set yourself apart from the others," Gregory said. "You can complete the trial, or you can test yourself against a harder challenge and be rewarded financially. There is only one chance at the bonus per trial, so if one group gets it now, no one else will today. Then they ante-up another trunk of gold for the next run-through, so for each run, everyone has a chance. The actual amount of the bonus is determined by the house and can change. The shifters tend to put up more gold to *encourage* people, for example."

My eyes tracked along the bits and pieces as I considered what he was saying.

"Would the gold be on the way out, do you think?" I asked.

"It should be," Wally answered, "But it's got to be protected by something. They won't just hand you gold to keep. We'd have to fight for it."

"They handed us a bunch of cash to come here," I said.

"Yeah . . . but you *had* to come here," Pete said.

Touché.

A flash of movement up on the course caught my attention.

One of the ladies in black who'd entered the trial ahead of us leapt from one platform to another, her long blonde hair floating behind her. She was aiming for a smaller platform diagonally right, in the general direction Gregory had pointed.

"How would she know where the gold is?" I said softly, scanning the course again, trying to discern any identifying markers. Because it was clear she was purposefully heading to a rope leading into the mists. She didn't have a goblin on her back, so something in the course must've clued her in.

"You get more points if you get the gold," Wally said.

"Wait." I held up my hand. "There's a point system for the trials?"

"Yes," she answered like I was dense.

I grinned. "So if we get all the gold, and those ladies in black don't, we win?"

"Well, yes . . . or we die trying. Which isn't a great option," Pete said.

"We also get to keep the gold," Gregory said with a hunger in his voice that I understood. Growing up poor, the pull of money was strong. The ability to send it home to my dad and the twins was worth the chance.

"No one outside of the House of Shade has ever walked away with the gold," Wally said. "Those that try usually fail the whole course."

I rubbed my hands together, something in me feeling the challenge and wanting to meet it head on. Percentages meant nothing to me. "First time for everything, Wally. First time for everything. Besides, it's a sure way out."

Pete sighed like a man completely spent. "I should've never followed you in here. It's going to get me killed."

Why I grinned, I couldn't say.

I leapt out from the lip of the tunnel onto the floating platform closest to me.

CHAPTER 12

I have to admit, there was a large part of me that was worried about this next part of the trial. What if I was leading the others the wrong way? What if I was wrong? It would not be the first time I'd led others into danger—I'd done it before with Tommy and Rory. Anxiety rocketed through me, but it was too late, I was already in the air.

The platform swayed under my feet, jarred from my sudden transfer of weight. I moved to the edge and turned, bracing as Wally jumped after me. The woman had no fear, though muttering to herself was certainly an issue. She was probably recounting the likelihood of her imminent death.

"Running, jumping, math—this has become my personal Vietnam," Pete said before gearing up and taking a running start. When his jump peaked too far away from the platform, his eyes rounded.

He wasn't going to make it.

"Hold my legs, Wally." I pushed forward and stretched out a hand.

Pete's arms windmilled like he was a cartoon character. "I'm going to die!" he screeched.

"Reach out, you blockhead," I hollered, straining forward.

The fingers on his right hand brushed mine. His left hand swung around as he lost altitude. "I'M FALLING! I'M FALLING!"

Adrenaline and fear dumped into my body, the space below us sucking up my focus. If he missed, he'd have a long fall before he went splat.

His palm slapped my wrist and slid. I curled my fingers, dimpling his skin so I wouldn't lose hold of him, and slammed my other hand down on his forearm.

"Don't . . . go into . . . hysterics, just hang on," I said in a series of grunts, my body sliding toward the edge with the weight.

Wally's fingers, stronger than I would've expected, tightened on my ankles and anchored me to the platform. My forward progress halted, but Pete's weight tore at me and I fought to hang on to him. He swung under the platform before slamming into something solid.

"Ow," he said.

"You would not believe the amount of deaths that occur each year from blunt force trauma," Wally mumbled. I needed to find her off switch.

"Hang on, buddy," I said, pulling on his arm with all my strength. "I got you."

"Don't drop me." Pete reached up with his other arm, grasping both of mine.

Gregory flew through the air, his feet *thunking* down next to me, too close for comfort. He dropped and rolled past before springing up and crawling back.

"I guess if you're hellbent on saving him, I can help," Gregory drawled before crowding in.

"Yes. Please. Be hellbent on saving me. Please," Pete said in a high-pitched, terrified voice. He wasn't great at staying calm in near-death situations.

Gregory reached down over the platform and took hold of Pete's arms. He pulled with me, our combined strength enough to drag Pete over the lip of the platform.

"Holy cats," Pete said as he scrambled up. "That was close."

"One of many close calls to come," Wally said. I sure hoped that wasn't her idea of comfort.

Breathing heavily, confident that Pete would be fine, I dusted myself off and turned to survey the way ahead. In the distance, four lithe shapes, dressed in black, climbed a rope from the target platform before disappearing into the swirling mists above.

"One is missing," I said quietly, searching the platforms for any other movement. "Five set out, but only four are up there." The Bro Pack was nowhere to be seen. Across from us was an opening in the wall, and I suspected they'd taken the easy way out.

"Maybe she fell," Pete said, stepping up beside me. "Though the rest of them are getting up that rope really fast."

"Forget them, how are we going to get to that platform?" Gregory said, his tone dubious. "It's a maze, only instead of walls, it has huge gaps. We can't jump a ton of those."

I turned my focus to the course, taking stock of the layout, the various sized platforms, and most importantly, the gaps. Almost immediately, it became apparent that there was only one manageable path to the target platform and it was long, complex, and windy. More than one jump gave me pause, a few platforms looked like they might not be stationary, and the swinging rope near the end almost made me throw in the towel and aim for the easier exit point.

But those girls had made it. Clearly, it was possible.

"I can get us there," I said confidently.

"Are you sure?" Pete said. "Every path I pick out ends in a ginormous gap."

"He's a Shade," Wally replied. "He's good at strategy and puzzles and stuff. We follow him, and we'll make it."

It's true. I was good at puzzles. The best in my family actually. No one would play chess with me anymore.

"I can get us there, but there will be a couple hairy spots." I chewed my lip, cutting my eyes to Pete. "This will need to be a group effort. I need you all to commit."

Wally and Gregory joined me in looking at Pete, clearly the weak link when it came to jumping the gaps. Pete nodded, either not catching our dubious looks or finding his courage within them.

"I can do it," Pete said, determination overshadowing the uncertainty in his voice.

I nodded once, no more than a jerk of my head, and jogged forward before leaping to the next platform. Once I touched down, I turned and pointed. "Wally, you next. Then Gregory. Brace yourself near the edge and wait for Pete. Good?"

"Okay," Wally called mid-jump, landing in the center of the platform and bumping into me. Gregory landed without a hitch this time, careful not to touch us, before Pete flung himself in with wide eyes and wildly swinging arms.

Thankfully, Pete did get better as we made our way, and amazingly, handled the swinging rope like a champ, only bungling his landing on the small platform.

All of us breathing heavy, we congregated two platforms away from the target, the others quietly letting me assess where to go next. They'd only questioned me once on the way up, Gregory thinking one of the chosen platforms would lead us to a dead end. My explanation had been quick and distracted as I recalled the way forward, but strangely, it had been enough to appease them all. After that, they'd followed blindly. We were making good time, so I wasn't complaining.

A strange feeling washed over me. Shivers of warning coated my skin and cold crept up my spine. I glanced around, trying to pierce the darkening haze suddenly pressing in on us with my gaze. Something was out there, waiting. Watching. It wasn't the something that had been dogging me either. Whatever this was, it meant us harm.

A new urgency pushing me on, I leapt to the next platform. The wood under my feet swung forward with my weight. I windmilled my arms with the sudden shift in balance and barely kept from toppling backward into open air. This hadn't looked like a swinging platform.

"Careful on this one," I said with a shaking voice, crouching to stabilize.

"Wow." Wally let out a breath and clutched her chest. "That was a close one. I thought you were going over."

So had I.

"It's too far now," Pete called as I surveyed the swirling mists rolling and drifting above the knotted rope hanging down to the target platform.

A glance back said he was right. The platform wasn't a swinging platform after all. It had shifted under my weight, and it hadn't drifted back. Which meant . . .

"You're all on your own on this one," I said, making the easy leap to the target platform. As expected, the platform I'd been on drifted back to its default position, close enough for one of the others to jump. "There is no safety net."

"It's like watching a master at work," Wally said, a cockeyed grin on her face. "Isn't it? I mean, wow."

"That's why the Sandman was escorting him, I told you," Pete replied. "I really hope I don't fall. My worst fear is falling like this. I thought I was a goner when I fell out of the chopper earlier. That was a mean trick to just let students slide out."

My talent with strategy and life-sized puzzle games wasn't why the Sandman had taken an interest in me, but I let it lie. The less they knew about why I was there, the better.

The warning from a moment ago intensified until a feeling of dread seeped into my bones. My chest tightened and heart sped up. Something was coming. Something dangerous to all of us.

I shifted my weight back and forth, needing to move. To run or fight. But I didn't know what form the threat would take. And there was nowhere to run *to*.

"Let's get going," I called out as Wally made the jump. "Fast as we can."

Pete rolled his shoulders and looked around him, standing next to Gregory. "Do you feel that?" he asked Gregory as an itch manifested right between my shoulder blades.

Gregory ignored him, watching as Wally made the final leap to me and the target platform, graceful now that she knew the platform moved. Moments later, she landed next to me.

"Eyes." Pete turned in a circle. "It feels like we're being watched." He lifted his nose, sniffing the air.

Sweat broke out on my forehead and I turned to the rope, knotted for ease of climbing, leading up into those dark gray, almost black, swirling mists.

"What do you think is up there?" Wally asked quietly.

"Trouble," I said, yanking on the rope a little, just to make sure it was really attached to something.

Gregory jumped onto the target platform with us, leaving the other one to drift back to hopefully collect Pete.

"Careful, it moves," Wally reminded him.

"This rope is too easy to climb," I said softly, thinking through all of this. "The path here was complex. Getting here was physically taxing. And now, at the endgame, it's a knotted rope? Why not just make it a ladder?"

"How else would we get up?" Wally asked, confused.

"He means it's too easy," Gregory said, quickly drowned out by a screaming Pete.

"Made it," Pete yelled, squatting like an attack spider. "I made it."

"It's too easy," I agreed.

"I smell the gold," Gregory said, his gaze arcing skyward. "It's faint and kind of fluctuating, like it's being carried on a breeze, but it's closer now."

"I really wish I could smell gold," Wally said wistfully. "But I don't feel a breeze."

I shook my head. Neither did I.

"Easy or not, this is the way up." I curled my fingers around the rope.

Pete yelled out a curse when his platform stopped moving, but thankfully didn't pitch off the edge. Shaky, he jumped to meet us.

"Bad news, Pete," I said, not able to tear my eyes away from those swirling mists. Everything in me said the danger lay up there. That to climb this rope would put our lives at stake. But hadn't that been the case with the other challenges thus far? In jumping across the large gaps?

No. This is different.

I pushed my strange certainty away. It wasn't helping. But I knew without a doubt that I needed to send the others up first—I just didn't know why.

"You should go first," I said to Pete. "That mist up there is probably fifty feet up, and who knows what's beyond it. If you suddenly lose your grip, we should probably have someone to stop you from going splat. Besides, you seem to have a knack for climbing."

"I hate this," Pete said, ambling over.

"Yes, but when we get to your house's trial, we'll all probably hate that." Wally patted Pete on the back. "It'll be even then."

Pete gave a little hop, hefting himself up onto the rope. A strange vibration drifted through me, like ripples in a dark pond.

You don't belong here, it seemed to say. *You will go no farther.*

I hadn't felt that when I'd touched the rope, only when Pete had.

I ripped my gaze higher, the itch between my shoulder blades turning into claws scratching and digging in deep. The angry mists swirled above. Something unseen looked down through them. I was certain.

"Watch yourself on the other side of those mists," I said to Pete, stepping closer. "Get up, fast as possible, but keep your eyes peeled." I dragged my bottom lip through my teeth. "This might've been a bad idea."

"These are the Culling Trials," Wally said, pushing in behind me. "You'd be hard pressed to find a good idea if it means staying out of danger."

Hand over hand, Pete pulled himself up, his feet finding awkward placement about as often as they missed.

"Wally, you next. Go." I shoved her at the rope, not waiting for Pete to get too far.

Gregory didn't wait for my direction. He must've sensed I'd want to go last, to catch anyone who fell.

A scream rent the vast silence of the platform area behind us. I spun around as the rest of the crew stopped climbing, craning their necks to look over their shoulders.

Four people scattered from the lip of the tunnel, rushing for the sides, hands reaching for something to hang on to so they didn't join their friend.

"He was pushed," one of them shouted, looking behind him. "I swear to Christ, he was pushed!"

"Go." I shoved at Gregory's butt. "Go!"

"Colt, did you see who did it?" one of the other guys asked.

Another said, "Better him than us."

Light flared from the end of a stick in a muscular guy's hand. It shot into the air, illuminating the area in hazy red light.

I used the opportunity to look up through the swirling dark mists at the top of the rope. There, just above Pete, lying on her stomach with her upper body slung over the side of a platform was the lady in black with blonde hair. Her hand moved in a sawing motion and the knife she held glinted in the throbbing reddish light.

"She's cutting the rope," I yelled, helplessly throwing up my finger.

Her gaze flicked from her task to me, and in that look, I saw sparkling cunning. She was enjoying the game, and sabotaging fellow trial goers was part of the fun.

"Climb faster than you've ever climbed before," I yelled at Pete even as someone from the tunnel shouted, "That black widow is trying to throw the trial!"

I turned in time to see a blast shoot out from the guy's stick, what I had to finally admit was a wand capable of real magic. A jet of bright blue light streaked through the air. It passed within feet of the girl cutting the rope and she jerked away, rolling to the side.

I looked for something to throw. Anything.

"Go, Pete," Wally yelled. "Go, Pete!"

"I'm hurrying," he said, his movements jerky and his breath short. "I'm hurrying." Another jet of light cut through the air, screaming by me. The heat coated my arm.

"It's not us," I yelled, taking hold of the rope as my crew labored up. "We're not—"

A dark shape moved behind one of the guys at the lip of the tunnel.

"Look out—" I screamed, but it was too late. He pitched forward, his hands clutching the air as his feet left solid ground. Although he had a wand, it didn't help him any. Light erupted from the end, slicing through the air and exploding against the earth ceiling far above our heads. He screamed, reaching for a platform that was too far away, but gravity took hold, and his body dropped from view.

"Hurry up," one of the guys shouted, an attractive man with confidence and swagger in spades.

Soft laughter echoed down in the failing red light, and I could just barely see the blonde girl, still leaning out over my crew. She winked, setting off warning bells . . . and then she was gone.

"This is what happens when the mean girls get free reign," I said through suddenly numb lips, grabbing the rope.

"The mean girls are nothing," Wally said as Pete ascended through the fog. "It's the murderous bastards you have to look out for. In the Culling Trials, they don't have leashes."

"Clearly."

Down to three, the guys behind us took to the platforms. The muscular one, tall and broad, with a wave of dirty blond hair, swept his wand in front of him. Footprints shimmered into existence on three of the platforms—the first three we'd taken. He followed in our footsteps, literally, leading the other guys. When he got to the furthermost one, he stopped and waved his wand again.

"Cheater," I grumbled. "Let's hustle, everyone. They're able-bodied. They'll be here in no time."

"I'm surprised he doesn't have a map," Pete said in a strained voice, clearly recognizing the guy. "Crap. Oh crap, what's that . . . It sounds like something is groaning."

"It's the rope," Wally said, fear riding her words. "It's the rope. The rope is going to break. Hurry up, Pete. And no more Snickers bars. No more. You're officially cut off."

"I'm at the top," Pete yelled a moment later. "I'm there!"

"Then pull yourself up," Gregory shouted.

The guys behind us were only a few platforms away by the time I reached the deep cut in the rope. As I pulled myself over it, a second strand broke free, pulling hard on the remaining strand. I doubted it would hold strong for the copycats, at least not all three.

"It's that way," Gregory was saying as I heaved myself up over the lip of the wooden platform at the top.

On the left, a shaky looking suspension bridge hung over nothingness, leading to another tunnel. Gregory pointed in the opposite direction, across a log with no handrails suspended over a sea of spikes. The end of the log disappeared into more dark, swirling mists, this trial clearly using the unknown to spark fear into our hearts.

A small table on the log side of the platform held three pairs of binoculars and large metallic discs that I figured were shields.

"Those spikes are an illusion," Pete said, drifting closer. "Right? Or else there would've been a strip of roof above some of the platforms, and there wasn't. It was all one big, open cavern."

"So, it's an illusion, so what?" Gregory picked a set of the binoculars. "If we don't fall on spikes, we'll bust our heads on the platforms way below. Not a big difference."

"The number of people—"

"No." Pete held his hand up for Wally. "Don't say it. Whatever horrible stat it is, don't say it. I don't want to know."

The rope groaned behind me. The dirty blond, muscular guy had just started up, one of his friends joining him a moment later.

"We're out of time."

Gregory sucked in a breath through his teeth. "There it is," he said, cutting me off. "Holy shi—"

"Lemme see." Pete grabbed a set of the binoculars. "Oh f— I changed my mind. I'm in. Gold. I choose gold."

I took the two quick steps and grabbed the last pair of binoculars. They cut through the mist, revealing a doorway and a room beyond it. I sucked in my own breath as an enormous pile of gleaming gold caught my attention. It sat atop a stout table in front of the rear door, spilling down onto the floor there was so much of it.

"Holy crap," I said softly, but I couldn't let the gold blind me to the danger. There was a reason they'd provided shields. I swung the binoculars to the right, at the ivy-covered wall in the distance. There, on a wide platform with a door at his back, a bow in his lap and a quiver of arrows at his side, sat none other than Sideburns, his own binoculars pressed to his eyes.

I gave him a wave featuring one of my fingers. He'd gotten me into all this, he deserved a little shade thrown his way. Pun intended.

On the other side, much closer, a woman leaned against the cavern wall. A metal stand with six holes, each filled with long sticks, took up a large portion of her deep platform.

"Silly, rabbit," I muttered to myself, zooming in on the stand beside her. Then I chuckled to myself, because what the hell else could I do? "Those aren't sticks, they're spears."

"What's that?" Gregory said.

Something snapped and a scream filled the air. A loud *thunk* cut off the sound.

I spun, finding the dirty blond man just climbing over the wooden platform. Once up, he took a quick look down, his demeanor unaffected by whatever he saw.

"Did that rope snap?" I asked, hurrying over.

"You don't want to see." Wally held up her hand to stop me, looking over the edge. "Unless you like a leg bent the wrong way. Then you do want to see."

"Colt is tough; he'll be fine." The blond guy stepped away from the edge, giving Wally a wide berth. The untrustworthy rarely trusted those around them. "This is it, then? This is the path to the Shade treasure? How much are they offering?"

Gregory and Pete backed away as the blond guy sauntered toward the log, his eyes scanning the shields before he reached out for the binoculars.

I held onto them. He hadn't said please.

"What have we got?" the guy said, looking my way when his hand wasn't immediately filled with the binoculars.

"A party crasher," I growled low, my guard up. I tugged my hat a little lower, and wiped a hand across my cheek, smearing sweat and a good amount of mud still there from the ditch.

The dirty blond guy turned toward me, his eyes bluer than any eyes had a right to be. He took my measure for one solid beat, but this wasn't the way a man would usually size up a woman, analyzing her face for beauty before looking at her body—he puffed up slightly, pushing out his chest and leaning in just a little, a play for dominance.

Because, of course, I was a dude.

I liked this far better. Beauty I couldn't control, but kicking him in the head to prove my dominance was well within my skill level.

Stare hard and body loose, I met his gaze and held it. I didn't want to care what he looked like, but there was nothing wrong with my eyesight. His face was classically handsome—straight nose, defined jaw, and high cheekbones. The set of his robust body and broad shoulders denoted a level of confidence above average, and the upward tilt of his face and superior air led me to believe he'd grown up affluent, not rough and tumble like I had. I hadn't met many people like that, but there was no mistaking the cloud of entitlement.

That meant he hadn't learned street smarts the hard way. He hadn't needed to. That gave me an edge he would never understand.

I smirked and handed over the binoculars, secure in my place at the top of the pile. In response, his brow lowered in obvious confusion. He'd catch on sooner or later. In the meantime, we could use him. He was good with that wand, even if his aim could use some work.

"Arrows on the right, spears to the left," I said, turning toward the log. "At the end is a plain room that surely houses all sorts of nightmares. There's no way they'd be content to give away all that gold to someone with good balance and quick feet."

Mr. Peepers lifted the binoculars to his eyes, checking my findings. A moment later, he blew out a breath. "Crap. That's the Sandman."

"Oh, you recognize the sideburns, do you?"

"Good balance and quick feet won't be enough against him," he said.

"That's why they've given us shields, I'd imagine." I dragged my lip through my teeth and glanced back at the suspension bridge. "Did those girls try their hand, do you think?"

"Which girls?" Peepers rolled his finger across the top of the binoculars, zooming in as he looked at the room across the way.

"The five girls that went down the path first. I saw four of them make it to this platform."

Peepers took the binoculars away and studied me for a moment. "Did one of the girls cut the rope, or did you stage that?"

"Hard to cut a rope when you're still climbing it."

His brows lowered. "For a no magic hack, yeah, I guess." The binoculars clattered across the table—he clearly had no respect for someone else's property. "If they went this way, they didn't make it far, being that the gold is still there. The spikes are an illusion. If they fell, they landed wherever the losers go. The arrows and spears are real, though. Those'll hurt. They won't aim to kill, so the worst thing you'll face is falling or pain." He glanced around at our motley crew. "Only one question left. Who's going first?"

CHAPTER 13

A log over an open chasm, spikes waiting to stick you from below, and two shooters working to knock you into said spikes. This was not a good idea.

"Wait, wait, wait." I held up both hands, connecting eyes with Wally, Pete, and then Gregory. Whatever my own inclinations, I had to consider their safety—no different than if it were Billy and Sam with me. "Look, this is incredibly dangerous. What are the chances we'll get that gold?"

Pete looked at Wally. "Well?"

"I . . ." She put out her hands. "I don't have enough information to calculate that. Not good?"

"Oh sure. When we really need it, where are you?" Pete asked.

"What are you, chicken?" Peepers taunted me, and I got the feeling that line was supposed to pack more punch than it did.

I ignored him. "Crossing that log will be hard enough, but whatever's in that room will probably be nuts. Or we could just take the suspension bridge out of here. With the rope cut, no one else will get that gold. We'll still get a win, the ladies in black didn't take the gold, that much is obvious. We'll get out of this trial. I know it."

"I'll get that gold," Peepers said confidently.

I waved my hand at the log. "Well then, be my—"

"No, wait." Pete stepped forward. "Bi—Wild, wait. You go. You go first."

"What?" I widened my eyes. Talk about throwing someone to the wolves.

Wally's voice took on the tone that had earned her the nickname. "Cheaters never prosper unless those cheaters are from the Helix family."

Peepers huffed out a laugh. "What sort of freak show did I walk into? Look, are you going to go, or what? It might be helpful to see how you're taken out. Otherwise, step aside."

Pete skulked over to me, his back bowed and head low, showing submission, though not to me. To Peepers.

"He gets everything handed to him, Wild," Pete said quietly. "His dad probably told him exactly how to beat this challenge. What spells to use, who to follow, who to knock out first. We can't let him have it. You can do it. You don't even have to cheat, you're so dang good. You should get the money, not him."

"What happened to 'we'?" I mumbled as Peepers bent for a closer look at the log, pushing it with one toe.

"We'll keep him from taking you out when you reach for the gold," Pete said out of the side of his mouth. He jerked his head, and I saw that Gregory was eyeing Peepers in obvious disdain.

"Who is he?" I asked as a shock of anxiety rolled through me, followed by a surge of excitement. Crossing that log would be no problem—I'd crossed the creek on our property via logs, rocks, and any manner of bridge more times than I could count, in all sorts of conditions. Being shot at was one of those conditions if you counted rocks, sling shots, paintballs, and once a dead possum. As the youngest of our crew growing up, and the only girl, I was often the odd man out. I'd always been elected to play the role of the enemy—I got good at avoiding rapid fire.

But none of that would help me with whatever waited in the room at the end. That was a giant blind spot. Despite the obvious danger, I was eager to test myself against it. If I didn't have to drag the others into my bad decisions with me, I could do so guilt-free.

"He's Ethan Helix, Bruce Helix's son," Pete said, then waited expectantly.

My shaking head wasn't what he was looking for.

"*Bruce* Helix." Another expectant pause and wide eyes. "Cripes, do you know anything about the magical world?"

"I didn't even know there was one," I said.

He rolled his eyes in disbelief. "He runs the North American branch of Shadowlight. Super powerful, connected, rich, and his family goes back centuries in the magical world. He's a big deal. Like *the* big deal."

"Usually, the big deals are the biggest blowhards."

Pete leaned in close. "He's a blow hard with a lot of clout. Helix always wins, Wild. His family, I mean. They are always on top. If just once, someone else . . ." His words trailed away, and I heard him loud and clear.

Just once it would be nice if the little guy won. If the underdog took home the prize.

I nodded, determination raging through me. "Let's see how a farm gi—boy—from Nowhere, Texas stacks up against the big dog, shall we?"

Pete's smile stretched from ear to ear.

"Ladies and gentlemen," Wally said in her strangely deep voice. "Hold onto your seats. The show is about to begin."

"What is with that voice?" Ethan said, looking at Wally.

"I'll go first." I strutted up to the table beside the log, letting the thrill of the moment energize me. If I hurried, I wouldn't have time to think about the obvious differences between the creek at home and this log suspended above either sharp spikes or absolutely nothing for hundreds of feet, depending on how you looked at it. I wouldn't reflect on the vastly different pain potential of a well-placed arrow or spear versus a paintball or roadkill. And I certainly wouldn't think about the death trap at the other end with its hidden dangers just waiting to snap closed on me.

Nope, best to just keep moving.

I hefted a shield, gauging the weight. Not terribly heavy, and while I held it, it also seemed to lighten a little. I grabbed another, knowing I'd need two. There was no way I could pivot and turn to use only one shield on the log—I'd need to brace with a shield on each side.

Adrenaline coursed through me as I eyed the log again.

"Fortune favors the brave," I mumbled, using Rory's favorite catchphrase growing up.

"What a circus," Ethan mumbled.

I placed one foot solidly on the log and shifted my weight. No give. I slid it out a little farther. Still nothing. The log was solid.

"Here we go." I stepped out with the second foot as Wally put the binoculars to her eyes.

"Our hero steps onto the log," she said in her newsroom voice.

"Don't look down," Pete called out.

I gritted my teeth, ignoring the urge to do just that.

Eyes straight, I let my mind relax and focused on feeling the log under my feet. Trusting its solidity and my balance. A slight breeze slid across my skin before a prickle of warning brushed down my right side.

Wally's voice drifted into my calm, announcing an incoming arrow from the right.

I took a step to align my body before bending, ducking down between the shields. As tall as I was, they didn't cover everything. The arrow sliced through the air right behind my head. Had I not taken that step and ducked, it would've given me a new ear hole.

Apparently killing was a *go*. Sideburns didn't pull any punches. I guess his pep talk didn't prevent him from going for the jugular. Then again, had he pulled any so far? Not really. Besides, there was that incident with me shoving him and his car in the ditch. Probably made him look bad.

"Wally," I called out as a trickle of warning slid down my left. "I need you to announce kill zones. Head height, chest height, stomach, so on."

"You got it, boss—"

"Chest, chest, chest, chest, *chest*!" Pete called out.

I held firm and a spear clanged off of my shield, pushing my weight too far right. I surged up and pushed forward, needing movement to regain my balance. Another warning lit up my right side.

"Right. Legs," Wally called out as Pete sounded the same alarm in a much higher pitch.

I took two fast steps, focusing again on the solid log beneath my feet. On my balance. On sensing which sides the blows would come from. Having regained my focus, I crouched between the shields. The arrow zipped past me. Sideburns hadn't expected my movements and he was too far away to react in time to erratic changes. Good news for me.

"Left, chest," Pete called out.

I pushed to walking, his warning—and a prickle from the left—giving me enough time to brace for impact. As expected, the spear rammed into my shield, mighty in power. I faltered, my weight thrown, needing a moment to get my bearings. But a new threat was already coming in.

"Right, legs," Wally called urgently. "Right, head. Right, arm. *Run!*"

On impulse, I spun and took two fast steps—back the way I'd come. Shield at body height, an arrow clipped the very edge. The others missed, but not by much. I swiveled back around. Hurrying now, I kept my focus on the solid log. On my balance. Trusting in my ability. Staying calm.

"Good one," Pete called.

"She's readying two," Gregory hollered. "Left. She's readying two."

"The Sandman has his bow lowered," Wally said. "Not sure why."

"He's watching his prey, that's why," I said to myself, not wanting to advertise. Then, louder, "Keep me updated on what they're doing."

"Roger," Wally called.

"She's throwing," Pete said. "Two, one in each hand. Holy crap, is she ambidextrous?"

"Body, body," Gregory called.

I put on more speed, nearing the center of the log at a fast walk.

"Impact!" Pete shouted.

The spears hit the edge of my shield—the first with the expected force, and the second compounding it.

I swore under my breath and, not hearing Wally, took a second to pause and regain my headspace. I let out a slow breath, but before I could fully release it, Wally was announcing, "He's getting ready—rapid-fire, rapid-fire!"

"Where?" I shouted, but it was too late. The first arrow whistled an inch from the tip of my nose as I dropped down, crouching between my shields. Another sliced across the back of my neck. Pain blossomed, and I grimaced as a third arrow sailed overhead and a fourth struck my shield.

He was covering all his bases, forcing me down.

As if hearing my thoughts, Gregory yelled, "Go, go, go, go!"

I didn't wait to be told twice.

"Here comes another one," Pete shouted. "Left! Left! I mean, body!"

That's all she did, the spear thrower—her might was the weapon. Her might made me go into defense mode, where Mr. Sunshine and his barrage of arrows could pick me off.

"Adapt, damn it," I scolded myself. "You know what they're doing. Adapt and get off this log!"

I walked at a fast clip, steady, seeing the blur from the left out of the corner of my eye. As the spear neared, I turned just a little and angled the shield. The spear ricocheted off, some of the impact deflected.

"Rapid-fire, rapid-fire," Wally shouted. "All over. Up, down—"

I hurried forward, half running, my gaze on the log and the shield covering my vitals. Searing pain sliced through my calf before vibrating up my body. Metal arrow tips clattered off the shield.

The mist cleared slowly as I neared the end, the door jiggling in my vision. An arrow point jostled my hat and I jerked, lifting the shield. My balance wavered. I crouched and took a deep breath to stabilize myself, thinking of the spikes below me. Thinking of the long plummet after they dissipated to nothingness.

"Left. Wait, she—left! She's throwing!" Pete shouted.

I surged up, my heart in my throat, not completely balanced but clearly out of time. The spear smacked the shield, the impact vibrating my arm but not shoving me as hard. I was farther away now, she'd missed her chance. The arrow-slinging lunatic, however, was plenty close.

"Rapid-fire, rapid-fire," Wally shouted again, and I swung my left shield to my right side, stacking them on top of each other to cover my whole body. The weight of the two compounded, dragging me close to the edge. I breathed as slowly as I could and focused on the log under my feet. On balance.

Metal dinged off metal, the arrows smacking the shields so fast, my mouth dropped open. I couldn't believe someone could shoot and reload that quickly, from that distance, and continuously hit their mark.

"Left," Pete yelled. "Body."

I switched the left shield back with effort. My breath coming in fast in gulps as my stamina was tested. An arrow smacked into my boot, not forceful enough to pierce the leather. Pain flared across my knee and I sucked in a surprised gasp. Another arrow sliced through my pants, opening a gash in the back of my thigh. I staggered as yet another spear smashed into the left shield, throwing my weight too far right.

I tried to windmill my arms, so close to the edge I could almost jump. But the shields hampered me and the pain shooting up my leg stopped me from dancing forward to get my bearings.

Pete yelled, Wally screamed, but I couldn't get straight. I couldn't regain my balance.

My feet slipped.

I was falling.

CHAPTER 14

As I slid sideways off the log, my balance shot, I pushed off with everything I had, the spikes below swimming in my panicked vision. Shields falling away, I reached out, stretching to grab the platform on the other side holding the gold. My palm hit the edge. I clutched it in a death grip, the weight of my body trying to rip my fingers away, and then grasped it desperately with my other hand.

An arrow now and I'd be done. But no arrow drove into my flank. No spear struck my back.

Gritting my teeth, I pulled myself up by my fingertips. Chin above the platform, I threw my arms over the edge one at a time. Body shaking, various points throbbing in agony, I pulled up a knee. Slowly but surely, I rolled myself onto the platform.

Only my rapid breathing and the thrumming of my heart in my ears interrupted the vast silence.

"Am I dead?" I asked myself, closing my eyes for a brief moment. That had to be the mantra of these trials, and now I'd taken it up. *Am I dead?* I almost laughed. Almost. There was no point in scrambling for cover. If Mr. Sunshine had wanted to kill me, he'd had his opening.

Pete's voice drifted across the space. "I literally *cannot* believe it. Do you see? Didn't I tell you he was good? He's so dang good! This is why the Sandman showed an interest. See?"

Pete clearly had low expectations. I was bleeding from multiple places, dog tired, and I'd nearly fallen to my death. This, when I'd had a team of people to help me. I wasn't expecting an award for brilliance, that was for sure. Still, I had made it. That counted for something. And we were one step closer to the gold.

I slowly rolled onto my stomach and shoved onto my hands and knees.

The spear thrower stood without a spear in hand, watching me. On the other side, I barely made out Mr. Sunshine (I still couldn't bring myself to call him what everyone else did) sitting in his chair, just watching. This leg of the challenge was complete.

I really hoped I hadn't just gotten through the easy part, but I had a feeling that might very well be the case.

Ethan stood at the beginning of the log, his expression curious, his body poised and ready. He didn't intend to let me take that gold without him. The others fanned out around him, grinning at me. Wally put up a thumb, smiling wide.

"Next," I said softly, no longer excited for the challenge to come. No longer feeling the confidence in the pit of my stomach. The struggle to survive the log challenge had exhausted me.

The sliding glass door slid open before me, and I crossed the threshold into the circular white room beyond. The gleaming floor squeaked under my soles. The mountain of gold glittered in the harsh light—and so did the metal weapons of all shapes and sizes that hung on hooks and rested on cloth-covered tables throughout the room.

Another step inside and it was like someone had flicked a switch. The feeling went from stagnant to expectant.

I cupped my knee, applying a little pressure to the throbbing wound before rubbing the back of my neck. My fingers came away red. Super, I was in tiptop shape for some sort of weap-on-loving nutcase to come at me for dirtying their white room. At least, I figured that's what was about to happen.

But as I stood there, the pregnant pause intensified. The pres-sure increased. Danger lurked, waiting for its moment to attack. The feeling of dread from earlier strengthened, overwhelming and suffocating.

"Come at me then," I said softly, taking a step closer to the gold. "You're there, somewhere. I know it, you know it, and you know I know it. So *come at me.*"

One more step toward the gold. That would be the trigger, I knew, but then what? Where would the jack jump out and with what weapon?

My knife hung heavy at my side, a dwarf compared to some of those hanging on the wall. I took another step. Then another—ten feet away now, and I could barely breathe over the tension. One more step and a scraping sound from behind me rang out in the silence.

Instead of spinning around and showing my back to the closed inner door, a potentially lethal mistake, I stepped diag-onally and cocked my head, using peripheral vision. The door I'd come through slid shut and a sheen—a see-through wall—dropped down from the sky, trapping me in. My watch vibrated against my wrist. I'd expected no less. What I didn't understand, however, was where the sound had come from.

The gold shimmered, twinkling even without extra light from outside, before blinking out. Another illusion. There wasn't a single coin left.

"Nice," I said sarcastically, backing up to the side of the glass door, my back to a solid wall.

I touched it to be sure.

The door behind the fake pile of gold slid open, revealing a slender woman with blonde hair, most recently seen cutting the rope while Pete was climbing up. I'd assumed she was with the other girls.

I stopped myself from saying, "*You!*"

She grinned as though she guessed at my restraint. Then she winked at me, mischievousness twinkling in her eyes.

"Welcome to the Culling Trials," she said in a mid-range voice with no defining characteristics. "I am a sophomore student in the House of Shade. One year ago, I beat this trial and claimed the gold. This year, I was hand selected to usher the new students in should any actually make it this far."

"And kill them where appropriate?"

She smiled. "Maim only, of course." She stepped forward and the door slid shut behind her.

"So how does this work?" I asked, feeling a strange tingle through my body. "You try to maim me, and I try to . . . what? Maim you?"

Her smile increased in wattage. "Take me down, of course. If you can get me to yield, you can have the gold. Fail, and you will go to the healers."

Healers. That was good news.

A throwing star sailed toward my face. I hadn't even seen her move!

"Holy—" I just barely dove out of the way, rolling across the white floor. Another sawed the air after me, tugging at my shirt as it zipped by. Best to keep moving.

I scrambled up as a third throwing star skittered against the ground where I'd just been. The woman had great aim, but she was slow at anticipating my movements. I had to use that to my advantage.

Similar weapons littered the table two feet away. I snatched up a throwing star, larger and with more prongs than the ones she was using, twisted and threw. I expected a wobbling mess that would buy me only a little time. Instead, the weapon flew fast and true, spinning through the air perfectly, directly toward her stomach.

Her eyes widened minutely, and she dodged out of the way, her fluid movements speaking of natural skill honed with training. I grabbed a mace from a nearby shelf, having absolutely no intention of getting closer to her and swinging the thing. No, I just threw it, my aim good and my expectations low.

She pivoted and dodged, easily evading, before dodging again, this time barely getting out of the way of a really neat ax that would've struck her with its handle. I wasn't an experienced ax thrower.

"You are a mess," she said, grabbing an army knife with a wicked serrated edge from the nearest table.

"That's Hot Mess to you, sweet cheeks." I snatched up a whip, wanting something long that could keep her at a distance. I needed a plan of attack, and until I had it, I intended to stall. As tired as I was, I was used to long, hard days. I would have bet my last dollar she'd never wrestled a cow in her life, let alone a bull the size of Whiskers for hours on end.

She ran forward, her knife held by the hilt, the business end pointed to the side. It was clear she knew how to use the thing.

I flicked the whip, once again not expecting much. The tip flew out and snapped viciously, right next to her head. The sound reverberated through the room.

Her eyes widened again, larger this time, and she changed direction, heading for the other side. Behind her, through the sheen of hardened air, I caught a glimpse of Ethan in the middle of the log, the end of his wand glowing as arrows bounced off of some sort of magical shield. That sure would've been helpful to me. Wally stood behind him and Gregory behind her. In front of all of them, keeping Ethan put despite his magic, was what looked like a badger.

Where the hell had the badger come from?

A knife flew out of nowhere, dragging my focus back into the room. I jerked to the right and it flew past my head. I flicked the whip again, the handle strangely comfortable in my grip, like shaking hands with a long-lost friend. It cracked against her forearm, opening a three-inch-long gash.

"How did someone so young master such a weapon?" she asked, frustration ringing in her voice.

I had no idea, so I just grinned at her. "Natural talent."

Her left hand zipped past her hip and a knife blossomed out of nowhere. It turned through the air, end over end, passing my face in crystal clarity.

I snapped the whip. The end slashed across her upper arm, slicing through fabric and skin. Blood welled up.

She dove, tucking into a somersault at the last minute. I readied the whip, but she was too quick, already inside my strike zone. I threw the whole thing at her and picked up a dagger with a long blade.

She popped up like she was on springs. Her fist, lightning fast, connected with my nose. My head snapped back and my eyes watered. I dodged a hook, staggering out of the way.

Terrible idea.

In a fluid movement, she swung her foot around, striking my chest. The breath left my lungs and I flew backward, knocked into a table full of weapons and dragged the whole lot down on top of me. A blade cut my arm and a knife point jabbed my leg. Pain screamed through me as I climbed to my feet.

She danced toward me, lovely and graceful, horribly lethal. Her knife slashed the air.

I stopped improvising. Time to use what I knew.

I ripped my knife from my hip, comfortable and familiar in a way none of these other weapons could be. I dodged her knife thrust and countered with one of my own, raking the short but sharp blade across her skin.

She sucked in a breath and tried to pivot, but I was on her, jabbing, not worried about doing her harm. I was sure a healer could take care of her as easily as he or she could me.

She dove, rolled, bounced up, and a throwing knife sailed through the air. I smacked it away, hitting the handle and shocking the hell out of myself. I hadn't meant to do that, hadn't even thought it was possible!

She stepped closer, struck at me with her knife, missed, and punched me in the face. Blood leaked down my mouth and my eye started to swell, but I didn't stop. Couldn't. I'd come too far to get knocked down in the final hour.

I pushed forward, topping her by six inches and having a much longer reach. I jabbed her side with my knife, ignoring the part of my mind that quailed at assaulting someone with a deadly weapon. If I'd learned anything, it was that there would be no jail time here. No repercussions.

She let out a pain-filled grunt but didn't slow.

I dodged her strike, staying outside of her arm span, before striking again. She blocked and sliced across my arm. Pain bit deep with jagged claws, weakening my knees, but I blocked it out and slid my blade home, punching a hole in her other side. She staggered like a drunk, holding one arm tightly with the other.

Seizing my advantage, and putting my long legs to good use, I kicked out at her shin, missed, stepped back, and raked my other leg across her thigh. Her legs flew out from under her, taking her to the ground.

Snarling and shouts filled the room. Light blared.

Ethan.

Throwing knives flew from god knew where, one sinking into his leg.

Acting fast, I bent to finish the job, clunking the handle of my knife against the woman's forehead. Her lights went out, and she went limp. The headache when she awoke would be immense, and that was strangely satisfying.

When I sat back, panting, multiple places aching or on fire with pain, Ethan shot a jet of light at the woman's chest as she lay there. Her body shook with whatever he'd done.

"No," I said, waving him away. "I already did it. I—"

The gold shimmered back into the room, as solid as when I'd first seen it. The door at the back slid open and colored lights glowed down from the ceiling. Grinning faces filed in even as the badger took up a post in front of the gold, snarling at a red-faced Ethan.

"You did it," a dark-skinned man said with a gleaming, white-toothed smile, clapping as he positioned himself next to the table of gold. "I think this might be the first time someone other than the House of Shade passed the final challenge in this trial."

"Wild did it," Wally said in frustration, her fists balled up. "Billy, I mean. Billy did it, and he didn't need to cheat."

"Will someone get that badger out of here?" the man said, not hearing Wally.

"*I* did it," I said, rising from the ground. Blood dripped from my chin. "I was the one that knocked her out."

The man paused, his smile slipping. His gaze roamed my various wounds.

Ethan laughed to cover the moment. "You fought the good fight, surely," he said, all ease and confidence. His charisma filled the room and then some, ever the handsome trust fund baby who would rule the world one day. "But we both know it was my spell work that actually took her out. Look at you. You wouldn't have lasted much longer. If I hadn't finished her off, we'd have lost."

"He shouldn't know those spells." Wally flung a finger at Ethan. "Someone prepared him for this course. That's against the rules! His spell work is too advanced for someone his age."

"There's no rule against spell work once you're in the trials," Ethan said with a million-dollar smile, walking over to shake hands with the dark-skinned man. "I'm ahead of my class. What can I say?"

The man's brow furrowed. "It does seem that there was more than one player in this challenge. That is a first, too, I believe."

"Ethan just waited until Wild did all the hard stuff," Gregory said from the corner. "He didn't do anything. Billy, I mean."

If the man's eyebrows lowered any more, they'd become a mustache. "You're . . . Billy?" he asked me.

I realized with a start that somewhere along the way, I'd lost my hat. I plucked at my shirt to make sure no breast definition showed, then smoothed my hair back. Blood continued to drip from my nose and I pinched it shut, half to hide my face.

Maybe I *should* give Ethan the limelight. I couldn't have the scrutiny. I didn't need anyone realizing I wasn't who I claimed to be.

I shrugged. "Ethan did make his way in here," I finally said.

Wally sagged and the badger—Pete??—snarled louder and kicked with his back feet, claws scratching across the floor. A distinct smell of rank musk floated off him. Gregory looked at the ground in the corner, his shoulders drooping.

I was letting my crew down by giving way to the rich, handsome kid that had it all, but I didn't have any choice. Not if I wanted to keep my anonymity. Stick to the middle, that's what I needed to do. My whole family's safety depended on it. And they meant more to me than any bunch of kids I'd only just met.

"Yes, well, we'll get it sorted out." The man smiled and gestured Ethan toward the door. "Come on, let's introduce you around. Or do you know everyone already?"

The two of them laughed, already as thick as thieves, leaving us all in their wake.

CHAPTER 15

The white room slowly emptied of everyone but Wally, Pete—okay, assuming the badger was Pete—Gregory, and me, still kneeling in a growing puddle of blood. I'd never been so sore in my life, not even after Mr. Whiskers had first come home and run me over.

"Why would you let him take it?" Wally asked. "The officials would most likely believe you, you know. No one outside of the House of Shade ever gets the gold in this trial."

I tipped my head back and struggled to breathe around the blood sliding down my throat. "Some things aren't worth the fight. Gregory, explain to her why we never would have gotten that gold."

He snorted. "We are lesser than them, girl," he said, his tone bitter. "They would have found a reason to not believe us even if Ethan hadn't made it across. Had we all been from the House of Shade, sure, but with Ethan Helix here? Well, that gives them another thing to take from us. Another thing to lord over us."

I waved a hand in the air. "See?"

The badger let out a snarl, followed by a groan. I made myself watch as Pete shifted back to human right in front of me. His body kind of twisted in on itself, there was a moment where the air around him shimmered, and then it was just him on the floor.

Buck naked.

I jerked my head away. "Welcome back, Freckles. A badger, huh?"

"How could you do it, Wild? How could you let him win after everything? And I'm a honey badger." He stood and I closed my one eye that wasn't swelling shut.

"Because, she knows when to let them win, so that there can be a bigger pay off later. That is the proper way to play the long game," a new voice said softly, like a whispered hiss that crawled along my spine.

I spun on my knees, hands going for the weapons closest to me. There, standing just behind Wally, was a kid about our age, his skin so pale, it was near translucent in spots, showing the veins in his face and neck. Dressed all in black, he would have blended into the shadows easily.

"He," I snapped. "I'm a guy, goth boy. Who the hell are you and how did you get in here?"

His eyes fluttered to half-mast. "I am one of your crew. I followed you into the trial, though you did not see me, and followed the others on the log bridge to this place."

"Vampire," Pete said. "That's what he is. Creepy buggers. They might as well be in the House of Shade for how blinking sneaky they are. Sneaky sneakers!"

I kept my eyes on the—Jesus, vampires were real? I'd thought Gregory had been joking—new guy. There was an edge to him. Like one of the young bull calves at home who hadn't yet figured out they could be stronger than the rest of us. One day he'd be dangerous—deadly even. The possibility was there at least.

"What's your name?" I asked, pushing to my feet slowly, painfully.

"Orin," he said softly, his eyes dilating as he eyed me up. No, not me.

The blood dripping off me. His gaze tracked the drops as they fell and a pink blush covered his high cheekbones.

I arched an eyebrow with serious difficulty. "Come at me now, Orin, and we are going to have a seriously bad start to our relationship. I've had a crappy day, and you do not want to be the next person in line for a butt kicking."

I spat to the side for good, masculine effect, a gob of blood and saliva that hit with a thick thud. Vampires could smell really well, right? Was that why he'd called me 'she'? Could he know I was a girl? Morning crap on toast, I did not need him spilling the beans about my own little illusion.

"I can control the blood lust," he said, though the strain in his voice said otherwise. "I could not have come to the trials if I was not capable of that much. I would come with you, all of you. If your . . . crew . . . will have me as a companion."

"No," Pete said. "Not a good idea, Wild. In fact, a very bad idea."

I kept my good eye on Orin. "Why should we let you in?"

"Because I was following you all along and none of you noticed," he said. There was not an ounce of smugness to him. He was just stating facts.

So that's what I had been picking up in the tunnel.

"Not good enough," Gregory said. "We'll be housed together and—"

"I despise Ethan Helix," Orin said. "We went to school together. I know his style."

Silence hung for a single beat, then Pete and Gregory all but jumped on each other to speak first.

"He's in."

"Yup, let's take him."

Orin and I continued to eye each other up. He twitched under my gaze and shrunk a little inside his black clothes. "You don't like me."

"I don't know you enough to not like you," I said.

But if I kept him close, there was less chance he'd rat me out to the officials. You didn't rat out part of your team—that was how the guy code worked, even I knew that much.

He bobbed his head like a bird of prey and then wrapped his arms around his upper body. "Fair enough. I will be sure to prove my worth. To all of you."

Part of me wondered how he'd gotten to the top platform after the rope was cut. But if Pete was right, and Orin was a master of sneaking, he could have even taken a different path. Hell, he could have flown up here for all that I knew about vampires.

I sighed and turned as a new someone stepped into the doorway that led out of the white room.

"Excuse me, does anyone have need of a healer?" The newcomer was a stunningly handsome man in his early thirties. From the corner of my good eye, I watched with faint amusement as Wally swooned a little, her eyelashes fluttering. I couldn't blame her, not really. He was quite the package with jet black hair and deep, bottomless brown eyes. His frame was lean, cut hard, and he was one of the few people I'd seen so far who was taller than me. A smile crossed his perfect lips and two fangs peeked out on either side. I steeled myself to keep from stepping back.

Another vampire. Was it coincidence?

He had a pair of sweatpants in his hand and he tossed them at Pete, who grabbed them in mid-air and yanked them on. Apparently, he could move fast when motivated.

"I am Jared," the older vampire said. "Supervisor of the Culling Trials. I see you've got one of mine with you." He glanced at Orin. Tension rose between them, taut, and behind me, I could feel Orin cringe under his gaze. I stepped sideways, cutting him from view. Orin was with us now, and that meant nobody was picking on him, not while I was around.

"Yeah, about that healer? Think you can take me there? I got a scratch or two," I said.

Jared snorted. "You Shades are all the same. Tough as nails and about as smart. Follow me."

I didn't let myself react, which was surely what he wanted.

He didn't turn, didn't walk away. He was just there one second and gone the next. I blinked my one good eye through the smudge of blood. "Am I seeing things?"

"Full vampires are extremely fast," Gregory said and then shook his head. "I seriously cannot understand how you don't know anything about our world and still . . ." he waved his ridiculously skinny fingers back the way we'd come, ". . . have done all that. And won. Despite what Ethan said, we all know that you won this trial, Wild."

"Sheltered. *He* has been sheltered and that makes *his* fear less," Orin whisper-hissed. I turned to give him a glare. Yeah, he knew I was a girl.

I blinked and he was gone too. Just like that Jared dude. I narrowed my eyes until I could pick out the subtle outline of his head in the single solid shadow at the back of the room. "I can see you, Orin."

Hide and seek was going to get old fast, but I didn't have the energy to do anything about it at the moment. The cuts all over me throbbed, making themselves well known now that the adrenaline had faded. I blew out a breath, only able to breathe through my mouth. "Let's get out of here."

Wally stepped up beside me and tucked herself under my arm. "Lean on me. You know that sepsis can set in within hours of a cut and it causes thousands of deaths a year. That would go poorly on all of us."

Pete stepped up on the other side and I dropped an arm across his shoulders. "You're a real downer, Wally."

"I know," she said with a small smile. "It's what I do. You'll be glad for it one day though."

"Doubtful," Pete muttered.

Gregory rolled his eyes as he passed us and took the lead. I assumed Orin fell in behind us but didn't bother to check.

The hall that led out of the white room was serviceable solid concrete and blessedly short seeing as each step sent new shock-waves of pain up through my body until Wally and Pete were all but carrying me. I almost apologized to them. But that's something Wild the girl would do, not Wild the boy.

I clamped my jaw shut and just worked on breathing through the pain and not passing out. Head down, I put one foot in front of the other. Thank God this was over.

We stepped out of a final door and into the bright sunlight of a late summer day in upstate New York.

The sudden change in scenery threw me for a loop and I took a minute to breathe it all in, to taste it on the back of my tongue.

We were at the end of the trial. I'd made it.

A white tent with a red cross emblazoned on it was set up in the grass ahead of us. All of the flaps to the tents were pulled wide, allowing medical staff to easily go between them. A few of the guys from the Bro Pack were being treated by what looked like doctors. One of the guys had burns all over his hands, and I had no doubt he'd been caught by a blast of electricity while climbing the metal wall. The blonde chick I'd fought in the white room was there too, stretched out on her back on one of cots.

I did a slow turn of my head. This wasn't the only tent. There were more tents to either side of us, at what had to be the exits for the other trials, and each was overflowing with patients.

Crying, whimpering, yelps of pain echoed through the air.

"Is he missing an arm?" Wally asked.

"Holy cats." Pete gulped heavily, "that one's belly is sliced open."

"Keep walking," I said, and they stumbled forward, jarring me. For just a second, I thought I was going to vomit, the pain was so bad. Surely the cuts I'd gotten couldn't be this bad?

I swallowed the nausea down with difficulty and closed my eyes. Two sets of hands gripped me, pulling me forward the second my eyes drifted shut. I snapped an arm up, breaking away, and opened my good eye.

"Easy. We're going to help you out here. My name is Mara. I'll be your healer today." The voice was soft and soothing, and it belonged to a woman who looked equally soft. Her body was all curves and there would have been no hiding her as a boy at any point in her life. Her kind, gentle smile calmed me enough that I let her guide me to one of the beds. "You Shades, always so defensive."

There it was again. Shade. I'd been well and truly labelled. I doubted I'd even need the sticker name tag any longer.

I lay on the bed, unable to hold back a groan. I wanted to make a smartass comment, but I decided to leave that up to someone else for once.

The woman—Mara—put a hand on my forehead and then one on my belly. "Dirty tricks in this trial, the blades were edged with a nerve-damaging agent to make the pain worse. I bet you're feeling pretty low right now."

I opened my mouth to answer and ended up rolling to the side, puking into a bucket that had been strategically placed. I gagged and spat, my nose plugged with blood and my throat clogged with puke.

"Don't you worry. I'll get you all fixed up and then you can have your banquet." She leaned into me, her hands pressing hard against both head and belly.

I groaned, sucked in a slow breath, and my body heaved as if I were going to puke again.

"Hold on, this will be uncomfortable," Mara said with that gentle voice. My skin tingled under her touch, like her flesh was covered in tiny hot pokers that went from being warm and soothing to so hot they burned. But I held still, shaking so hard the table rattled and my feet banged against the foot of the gurney.

Wally and Pete were close to my head, and I focused on their voices as Mara did her thing.

"Wally," Pete whispered, "are they pulling a blanket over that kid's head? Is he dead?"

"Yes, he is," she said. "I see his spirit leaving him. Sad, he fell and snapped his neck when he landed."

I shuddered and was going to open my eyes, but Mara slid her hand over them. "Let's get these fixed up for you. And that nose. It would be awful to have it set crooked."

"Why? Chicks dig scars," Pete said. "Let him keep his crooked nose."

Mara's hands tensed at that word—*him*.

Oh. She was a healer, trained in the human body, of course she would know I was a girl. Probably when her magic delved me, she could tell the difference. I was a fool. How was I going to keep this up?

I reached up and pulled her hands from my eyes. "Leave the nose."

I put all the pleading I could into my eyes, begging her not to give up my secret. She frowned, her cupid's bow mouth curving downward. "All right. For now, I'll heal it as it is. But if you change your mind, we can fix it later."

"Thanks."

"You might have residual pain through tomorrow, and your appetite will be huge, but don't overdo it in one go. Small meals, spaced out if you can. You'll be ready in no time for the next trial." Mara stepped back and I found myself staring at her, still flat on my back. Her words rang in my ears as though they'd been spoken in another language.

"How many of these trials are there again?" I asked with numb lips. "Also, can we skip any?"

Mara's eyes were a little amused. "Five. You've successfully made it through your first trial, plus the bonus. You're off to a great start. But you'll have to run all five, young . . . man. One for each house, to be sure you are placed right."

All . . . five.

My jaw dropped and I spluttered, at a loss for words. Or maybe not. "Are you yanking my chain?"

"Texan," Wally muttered.

Gregory cleared his throat. "We need to have a discussion, Wild. We are a crew now and—"

I waved my hands across my body, cutting him off. "Not here." I couldn't say why, but I wanted to keep my lack of knowledge as close to the chest as possible.

Before I could even leave the cot, my most favorite of favorite people arrived on scene.

Mr. Sunshine. Sideburns himself.

And he wasn't alone.

The world dropped away, dizzying, flipping everything inside me upside down. A rush of relief and comfort washed over me, bathing me.

I'm not alone.

A moment later, though, a newfound rage burned me through.

I stared, unable to believe who stood in front of me. Unable to believe that he had really come here, despite all we'd been through, and not said a word.

There, in the flesh, standing in front of me with a bloody blank face on his fool head was Rory Wilson.

I hadn't wanted to believe this moment would come. I hadn't wanted to believe my father. Rory should've had a better life in Nevada. He should've found a calm woman who never caused trouble and started a family.

Instead, he'd run full steam into more danger than he'd left.

He'd been here when my brother had died.

I could barely speak, I was so angry, and I completely ignored the traitorous memories of what he'd been to me. He'd been my protector when I'd been up to my eyeballs in bad decisions, my watchdog when I hadn't needed protecting, and my partner in crime when I'd wanted to have a little fun. He'd been part of my world.

But he'd lied. Pushed me away. Left a note and snuck off in the night like a coward.

He had let my brother die.

My childhood buddy and fellow heathen was my soon-to-be nemesis.

CHAPTER 16

I was up and off the table in the medic tent in a flash, stomping my way across the small space between Rory and me. In those few seconds, I took him in, my first look after two years of nothing but memories.

He'd grown in the time we'd spent apart, muscling up, hardening into a man. Sure, he was still Rory, but . . . not. He no longer looked like the boy who'd left rural Texas for a better life. His hair was shorter, he had a new scar along the side of his jaw, and there was an aura of danger rolling around him.

Sideburns held up a hand. "I need to speak with you, *Billy.*"

I smacked his hand out of the way and kept moving until I was nose to neck with Rory. "You have some nerve showing up here, Wilson. You couldn't be bothered to even come to Tommy's funeral. You lied about where you were going and now you show up with this cuntasaurus rex at your side? What the ever-living hell?"

His smell permeated my world, and my stomach fluttered. Clean cotton, spice, and a hint of vanilla. Home. He smelled like home, and good memories and nostalgia rolled me like a wave.

My mouth dropped open. I hadn't realized that smell was his until this moment. That smell had been there when I was at the airport getting mugged. "You helped them kidnap me, too, you sick sonuvabitch? Wow, you've sure changed. From a cool guy I used to know to a real sack of crap."

Pete groaned. "He's going to get us all killed."

"He's definitely getting closer to death, I'll give you that," Wally said quietly. "Be careful, Wild."

Rory jerked a little when Wally used my nickname. He stared down at me. "Nice to see you too Johnson. Your brother's death was a shame, but that's what you get when you aren't cut out for the academy. You die. You'd best remember that."

I sucked in a sharp breath, his words worse than any blow from any weapon. I snapped a fist out in a hard hook, directly into his left side, driving it as hard as I could. He bent at the waist as he took the blow, a whoosh of air escaping him. I stepped back and he slowly straightened, face pale. I tipped my chin up, anger making my traitorous eyeballs water.

Damn him, he could always bring out the worst in me as well as the best. I could feel the angry tears pooling in the corners of my eyes. Definitely not a manly trait to cry when you were angry. I sucked in a slow breath, pushing the emotions down. "You were always sloppy on the left. Nice to see *one* thing hasn't changed."

His face tightened, jaw clamped, and eyes narrowed.

Sideburns stepped between us. "Enough." His voice cracked through the air and more than a few people straightened as if he'd snapped them in the ass with a whip.

I turned my glare on him. "What? You going to try and knife me here, in front of everyone?"

He grabbed my arm and dragged me through the tent as though he were pulling a child along with him. "You will listen to me now, *Billy*, or you are going to get yourself killed." He took something from his back pocket—the hat I'd lost—and jammed it on my head with enough force to make me wince.

"Now you want to act like you're trying to help me? That's a pile of horse crap, and I know horse crap, Sunshine. I used to shovel it—"

He came to a dead stop. "What. Did. You. Call. Me?"

Oops.

I hadn't meant for that to slip out. "Sideburns," I quickly amended, followed by a pronounced wince. Worse still!

He pulled off his aviators and his eyes were as dangerous and dark as I'd imagined, darker because I could see death in the black pools. He was a killer through and through, of that there was zero doubt. "There are more forces at play here than you realize. At some point, it will make sense. But for now, keep your head down and your hands clean. Stay out of the limelight." I couldn't help but glare. Anger at Rory still coursed through me and made me stupidly bold. "You threatened my family, so I'm here. You know—"

He jerked me closer so we were nose to nose, forcing me to stoop just a little. Strangely, though, he seemed bigger even though I looked down on him. "I know what you are, *Billy*. Let's keep it to only me knowing. And stick to the middle ground, you idiot. You stand out, and what do you think is going to happen? People are going to notice you. You don't want that, not here."

There was an unspoken threat there. But I wasn't one for unspoken anything.

"Or what?"

His hand tightened on me. "You'll have to watch your siblings come through the trials and see them die firsthand. You might survive here, but do you think they will?" he growled. "Right now, you being here can protect them. Just like you wanted. But only if you keep the illusion up as long as possible."

He let me go, shoving me a little so I stumbled back. "I've got my eye on you, *Billy*. Don't fuck up."

With a snap of his fingers, he turned to leave. Rory studied me for a silent beat before turning without a word and following his new bestie. But I'd seen the flash of mirth in his eyes. The twinkle of excitement. That look had always meant we were about to get into something incredibly foolhardy and dangerous. I hardly knew the guy I'd grown up with anymore while still knowing him like the back of my hand.

First, he'd lied to me, then dismissed my brother's death, and now he was helping Sideburns?

Fire burned through me even as my heart cracked.

I gritted my teeth to prevent myself from going after him. He'd get his; I'd make sure of it. But right now, I had to look after me. Me and my new crew. He wasn't the only one with a new bunch around him.

I slapped away a trail of hot tears down my face. They had no place in this setting, especially with the image I needed to maintain.

I fisted my hands at my sides and turned away from them to see Gregory, Pete, Wally and Orin watching me with wide eyes.

"Did you . . . talk back to the Sandman?" Pete whispered. "You've got to have the biggest balls of any guy I know! You're my freaking hero!" He clapped a hand on my back and tried to get me in a half hug, which I slid out of. Just in case.

"I hope you live long enough for the next trial," Wally said, all seriousness.

Orin snorted and covered his lips with a hand. I glared at him until he withered under my gaze. Look at me making friends wherever I went.

"Where do we go from here?" I asked. I needed to change the subject. I needed to protect Sam and Billy with everything I had and that meant pulling my crap together.

"You follow me. As it should be."

The five of us turned to see the blond pretty boy, Ethan, standing there, his wand tucked through a loop on his belt, hands on his hips. Like a wannabe Peter Pan if I ever saw one.

"We aren't going anywhere with you," Pete snapped.

I nodded. "What he said." Tipping my head, I added, "And where's your Tinker Bell?"

Ethan glared at me, his face going slightly pink. "Just what are you implying?"

"That you look like Peter Pan, idiot," Gregory said. "The stupidity of the House of Wonder truly mystifies me. How in the world you got to the top of the food chain is beyond my ken."

I pointed at the goblin. "What he said."

"You don't have a choice," Ethan said, ignoring us. "We finished our first trial together, which means we are a unit in each subsequent trial whether any of us like it or not. Assuming you all survive, that is."

He walked toward me, bumping me with his shoulder as he went by. Or trying to. I didn't so much as budge an inch and I watched with amusement as he lifted a hand to rub his own shoulder. "They are announcing the winners of today's trials. Then we eat and get tomorrow off."

I didn't want to follow Ethan, but . . . I needed to keep a low profile, and Peter Pan would clearly steal any spotlight he caught a glimmer of. Maybe staying around him wasn't such a bad idea.

I glanced at my . . . friends? Were they friends? Yeah, they were. "Come on, we're with stupid."

Pete's face said it all, he did not want to do this. And I didn't blame him. "Seriously? After the stunt he pulled?"

I shrugged. "If he dies in the next round, we're done with him. That's got to give you hope."

Wally hurried up next to me. "Depending on the trial we face, that is highly plausible. Though, with him being a Helix, I suppose those numbers drop. Likely he will have some superior training to help him survive." Her lips pursed and I could almost see her working the odds out in her head.

The group of us followed Ethan like a flock of sheep to a shepherd. He never once looked back, as though he was so sure we'd follow.

Lambs to the slaughter.

"Let's see how we can make it work to our advantage," I said to the others in an undertone. "If he has knowledge about what's coming, then all the better."

Gregory was the first to nod his agreement. "We will all be more likely to survive with him in our group, that is true. Being a Helix will give him special privileges."

They were quiet a moment, and surprisingly it was Orin who spoke next. "I'll keep an eye on him. Like I mentioned, I know his style. He'll play us like a fiddle if we let him."

Gregory waved a hand. "No need. We will be dorming together. With the exception of our necromancer. No girls allowed. She might peek at us in the shower."

Necromancer. I whipped my head around to stare at Wally, remembering the comment before the trial about walking memory banks. It made more sense now. But her name tag didn't have a designation under it like mine did. Like Gregory's did. Pete's had fallen off, but there was no doubt about Orin. "You can raise the dead?"

She shrugged. "Maybe. I won't know until all my training is done. But my chance of ending up in the House of Night is close to ninety-nine percent seeing as my entire family has trained there on both sides, going back four generations."

And then the rest of what Gregory had said slipped into my brain. "Wait, we'll *dorm* together?"

"Yes, the five guys will dorm together. And Wally will be put into the girls' dorm. Maybe in another group." Gregory rubbed at his pointed nose. "I smell roast beef."

"I smell it too," Pete said, grabbing at his flabby stomach as it let out a loud growl.

With the guys following their noses—and Ethan—I let myself drop back a few steps.

Orin fell in beside me. He said nothing for a moment and then spoke quietly. "I won't tell."

"Why?"

The question I asked was just as quiet, Sideburns's warning still ringing through me. "You don't even know me."

He tucked his hands into the bottoms of his long sleeves so they disappeared. "You drew me to this group . . . my mother was a seer and I have a little of her talent. I need to be here, with you and the others. Besides, you let me into this group without much hesitation. Which, considering what I am, is saying something."

I frowned. "Somehow a vampire is worse than a goblin?"

His lips twitched upward. "Depends on who you ask. But most would not sleep in a dorm with a vampire. I don't believe that Ethan even realizes I am part of this group. He won't like it when he does."

"That's going to matter why?" I frowned as I worked through everything he was saying. He thought he was meant to be here, which was fine—weird, but fine—but he also thought I'd drawn him to the group. I'd done nothing but do my thing. Run across a log. Beat up a girl. Dodge electricity. Outpace some golems.

Right?

"It's going to matter because he is terrified of vampires." Orin grinned then, showing off the tiniest set of fangs I'd ever seen. Smaller than the barn cats at home.

"I've seen housecats with bigger teeth," I muttered.

His grin slid. "They get bigger when I am inducted as a full vampire."

"I bet all the guys say that."

Orin laughed. "Your secret is safe with me. Be careful though. I do not know if the others would feel the same way. And there is a chance they'll be able to figure it out. If Pete figures out his sniffer. If Gregory looks too close."

I nodded, not because I didn't trust the others but because it seemed like the thing to do. I would do the best I could with what I had, and hope it was enough.

We followed Ethan across an open field and up a slight incline. At the top of the slope, the view spread in front of us like a scene straight out of a fairy tale. A mansion sprawled in the shallow of the valley below. Five floors of brick and ivy and dormer windows. The grounds were immaculate and movement drew my eye to the side. A caretaker walked with a pair of shears, cutting and trimming, his back bent, movements slow.

Pete, Wally, Gregory, and even Orin gasped a little and excitement bubbled out of them. "The mansion is bigger than I expected!"

"It's every bit as plush; you can tell from here."

"Brilliant!"

Call me a pessimist, but with my luck and the Grim Reaper aka Sideburns as my guardian angel, there wasn't a hope in hell we'd be staying in luxury. "Don't get your hopes up. The job here is to break us, I think. Giving us a cushy mansion dorm would not fit with that," I said.

Ethan snorted and smirked. "Please. I'm a Helix. We'll have the best rooms. You can thank me later."

I wanted to bet him that he was wrong. But I had nothing to bet but . . . the money in my backpack that awaited me when I left the medical tent. A flush of excitement cut through the worry.

I held out a hand. "What do you want to bet we get shoved into a grimy little nothing of a hole?"

A slow grin spread across his face. "How about a portion of that gold *I won* back there?"

Pete was all but vibrating, but he held it together. Kind of. "You're a nasty piece of work, aren't you? Slimy House of Wonder crap."

I nodded but kept my eyes on Ethan. "And if I lose, I'll give you the cash I have in my backpack."

I thought he'd tell me I'd have to leave the trials. It's what I would have asked from him.

His grin widened. "Done."

I turned my palm up and he slapped his hand into it. A burst of sparkles erupted from the connection that seemed to surprise even Ethan, though he covered it up quickly.

I pulled my hand back and waved him forward. "Lead on, mighty Helix. Let's see where you can take us." I already knew though, and if Ethan was going to be dumb as a post, I'd happily take his gold. Seeing as it was really my gold in the first place, I didn't feel bad, not one bit.

He strode forward down the hill, arms swinging like he was the king of the world.

And maybe he was with all his magic and money. But that didn't mean I couldn't take him down a peg or two. I grinned as I watched him stride away.

Maybe this would be a little fun after all.

CHAPTER 17

B ut *how* did you know?" Gregory insisted as we stepped up to the rundown portable housing off to the side of the mansion. The siding had come off in places and the screens on the windows had been torn away from the inside going out, which was less than comforting. The stairs leading up to the one door were barely twelve inches across and looked to be held up by chunks of rotting wood.

I'd won the bet, sure, but we were the losers no matter how you looked at it.

The best part of the whole situation? Not all the teams got shafted. Some of them did end up in the mansion in the lap of luxury, but not us. And that had chafed Ethan's chaps like nothing else could have. All his friends got to stay in the mansion.

He was the only kid from the House of Wonder who had been shoved out here with the riffraff in one of the rundown portables. That was enough to make me grin.

Gregory danced in front of me, barely dodging my feet as I strode along. "How could you have possibly guessed? Even the necromancer thought there was no way you'd win that bet against a Helix."

Speaking of . . . Ethan was way behind us, still arguing with one of the school officials—one who happened to be his father. I slowed enough that I could overhear them.

"Why you would bet any of your portion of the gold is beyond me. Especially up against a Shade—you know how devious they are." Mr. Helix sighed heavily. "You can never trust the other houses, Ethan. This is a lesson for you, frustrating as it may be. One that would have come at some point or another."

I fought the urge to turn around and glare at the older Helix. Instead I spoke just loud enough that everyone could hear me. "Mr. Helix says we each get a cut of the gold. Ethan was wrong about taking it all. How magnanimous of him." There, let them chew on that big word.

Pete and Gregory did a fist bump, and Pete tried to follow it up with a chest bump that ended with him banging into Gregory in a rather awkward way. Gregory shook his head. "Beast shifters, seriously."

Orin pushed the door open and we all stared into the space that would be our home for however long we lasted here. Three sets of bunkbeds stared back at us. Nothing fancy, they could have been pulled out of the barracks of any army. Thin blankets, thinner pillows, and bedsprings that looked like they'd been completely stretched out.

It was the table of food laid out in between them that had my attention.

"Oh. My. Holy. Cats." Pete breathed out. "I *knew* I could smell roast beef."

He shoved past us as a tingle of warning slid down my spine. I hurried after him as he stared down at the food, literally drooling. His hand shot out, faster than I'd ever seen him move, and he had a handful of roast beef lifting to his mouth when I smacked it down.

"What the hell, Wild?" He stared up at me like I'd just told him Santa wasn't real. "I'm starving!"

"Just . . . wait a second." I frowned at the food as if glaring at it could make it give up its secrets. The enticing smells warred with the tingle of warning that still ran up and down my back. How many times had I kept Rory and my brother from eating the wrong mushrooms?

Ethan shoved between us. "It's a *banquet*, Johnson. I don't suppose you, in your piss-poor hovel of a town, would have ever been to one. But this is it. Copious amounts of food that has been cooked to be eaten."

He grabbed a tart and brought it to his mouth. I could have let him eat it.

But I wasn't sure it wouldn't kill him. I snapped a fist out and knocked it out of his hands.

"Something's wrong with it," I said. "Poison maybe."

My explanation seemed to have come a smidge too late. Ethan jumped at me, his hand going for his wand. I sidestepped and stuck a foot out, tripping him easily. He might have magic on his side, but he was no fighter. He crashed to the floor, where he immediately turned toward me and pointed his wand at my head. "There is nothing wrong with it. You stupid, vile, ignorant—"

"Umm, guys?" Pete waved a hand between us. "Some of the food is burning through the table."

We all whipped around to see the center section of tarts *melting* the plate and table below them. I backed up. "See? No *bueno*. No damn *bueno*."

"See, he's amazing! Wild knew. He knew this would kill us. Holy cats, you saved me. And . . ." Pete grimaced. "You saved Ethan? Why in the world would you do that?"

I didn't look at Ethan. "What does it matter? He's on our team. I don't have to like him to know that we have to work together to get through this." I stared at the food, stomach rumbling. Pete wasn't the only one starving.

Orin whispered from the shadows in the corner of the room. "You think they'll bring us more food? I'm getting awfully hungry."

"Shut up, vampire!" Ethan shouted, and for just a second, I thought I saw a glimmer of tears in those baby blues. Fear. He really was afraid of the vampire.

I frowned. "What are you so worked up about anyway? We aren't going to starve."

"This isn't how it's supposed to be! I am a Helix!" he roared, and with that he stomped out of the portable, slamming the rickety door behind him.

"Think he's going to get help?" Pete asked.

I nodded. "And complain. And somehow make it like we're to blame and he's the hero."

Gregory laughed, though it was a bitter laugh. "So, the usual?"

I gave him a half grin and nodded. "Yeah, the usual."

Using a couple of folding chairs as scrapers and a blanket as a catch all, we managed to get the food out of the portable and off to the side, away from our rickety stairs. The tarts were still smoking and something else was glowing a pale green in the dusky night.

"What if it was just the tarts that were bad?" Pete moaned, his stomach echoing him.

"You want to take that chance?" I asked.

He sighed. "No. But I'm *starving*. I'm going to fade away to nothing."

I tapped my fingers on my chin, thinking. "This was a final challenge for us, because of the trial we went through, right?" I looked to Gregory.

The small goblin nodded. "It would seem that way. Poison is one of the assassin's deadliest tools."

"Right, so here's the plan." I drew them in close and gave them the rundown quickly, simply. The teams who'd gone through trials for the other houses would not have poison in their food, but they also likely wouldn't share. Which meant we were going to have to work for our supper.

The next closest portable was nearly pushed against us, but no way were we robbing our neighbors. No, we needed to venture further out and put enough portables between our target and us that they couldn't know who the culprit was.

"Orin, you think that you can take the lights out?" I directed as we jogged behind the row of portables.

"Yes, I'm adept at killing light sources." He jogged too, but made it look like floating, which was both creepy and cool.

"Pete?"

"Yup, I've got them." He held up two pillow cases, tossing one to me, and one to Gregory. As if we were going trick or treating. Only we weren't going to ask nicely for the food. More of a trick than a treat for those in the portable.

Gregory shook his head as he caught the pillow case. "This place is not supposed to be fun. Why does this feel like fun?"

I grinned at him.

Pete pointed a finger. "It's his fault. I don't know how, but I know it's because of Wild."

Gregory didn't want to like me. I'd known that from the first moment I'd picked him up off that alley floor. He didn't want to like anyone. I'd known people like him growing up—the world treated them like dirt and they responded as though they didn't care. Rory had been like that when we'd first met.

Gregory didn't want to trust me, but I was winning him over.

I shrugged. "I'm hungry. You guys are hungry. What else is there? Let's get some grub."

God, I sounded like Rory in that moment. He'd said something like that to me to convince me to steal from the general store. I'd been caught with a bunch of bananas in my shirt. Rory had escaped unscathed as usual.

The four of us took up our positions. We'd start by knocking the lights out. Orin was on the roof and pulled the lines, a pop of wires letting go the only sound.

The portable went dark and a volley of shouts went up inside.

Next came Pete's job. He shifted into his honey badger shape and went crazy digging at the base of the portable, snarling and freaking out the entire time, his claws louder against the wood and metal than I would have thought possible. He sounded like a monster, and his efforts shook the portable. Gregory and I leaned in on the other side, shoving the building on its foundation. I glanced over to see him grinning from ear to ear. And I do mean ear to ear.

"Fun, right?" I whispered.

He snickered. "Way too much fun."

The shouting inside intensified and from the rooftop came a loud snarl and the sound of tin being ripped off. Orin was adding a nice touch.

A split second later, the door busted open and the guys from inside piled out on top of one another, racing straight for the mansion without looking back.

"Hurry! They won't take long to bring an official back," I picked up the pillow case and ran for the door. Orin re-attached the wiring and the lights popped back on in a blinding flash. I held up my hand a moment and then took a look at the food. They'd barely touched it.

Better than that, there was no warning tingle. No intuition that the food was off.

"It's good," I said, and we started stacking containers in the pillow cases. Under a minute and we had them both full and were making our way out of the portable.

"Hurry, they're coming back and they've got help!" Orin whisper-hissed as he dropped down from the roof. We bolted, heading toward the tree line that wrapped around the sides of the mansion. It would take us longer to get back to our own portable, but we'd have a better chance of keeping our food.

Pete caught up, still on four legs, still snarling and snapping. Gregory pulled a tart out and tossed it to him. "Shut your trap, Pete."

Pete. The first time he'd used his name. Maybe I wasn't the only one winning the goblin over.

We crouched in the shadows and watched as the five members of the group led someone toward the portable we'd just abandoned, and the official that followed was . . . "Oh, crap, that's—"

"The Sandman," Orin said ominously.

At least he wasn't wearing his sunglasses at night. That would have just made me ridicule him harder.

He took a quick look at the portable. "The lights are on."

"No, you don't understand, we were under attack!" one of the guys said, his voice so high-pitched he could have fit into the girls' dorms.

"Yeah, it was bad. Stuff was breaking, the lights went out, and I swear one of the beasts followed us out of the trial. I could hear it."

I held out a fist and Pete shifted to two legs and fist bumped me back. Score for our team.

The group circled away from us to look at the far side of the portable, and I tipped my head. "Let's go."

We hurried along the edge of the trees, and only once did I look back, a tingle along my spine tipping me off. Sideburns stood outside of their portable, staring into the trees. His eyes swept over us, but they didn't slow. But he knew. I don't know how I knew, but I knew that he knew it was me.

I shuddered and hurried the guys along. Promises of food and a warm bed were all it took to make my feet move . . . until I remembered that I was covered in my own blood, sweat, and filth and could smell myself a mile off.

How was I going to shower with a room full of guys and not get caught?

CHAPTER 18

The food was gone faster than I'd thought possible, despite the healer's warnings not to eat too fast. But that brought me to my more pressing issue of just how to get clean when I was sharing such a small space with four guys. "Who wants first shower?" I asked, noticing the large trunks to either side of each set of bunk beds.

"You can go, if you want," Pete said, rolling into one of the bottom bunks. After his bellyaching about heights, it wasn't a surprising choice.

"Nah." I knelt beside one of the trunks, slipped the open padlock out of the metal hook, and flipped up the clasp. "I need a minute to let my food settle. You can go."

"I'm first." Ethan pushed open a trunk on the other side of the room before extracting plain gray sweats and a plain white T-shirt.

"Of course, you are," Pete mumbled as Gregory and Orin checked the trunks near their chosen beds.

What had just become my trunk held the same items as Ethan's, and shockingly, the pants went all the way to my ankles even though I was the tallest in the room. Had I gotten lucky with my trunk choice, or did these sweats somehow alter to fit the wearer? More magic, that was the only answer.

A feeling of vertigo washed over me. I braced against the wall. "This magic stuff is blowing my mind," I said as Ethan pulled off his shirt, revealing a toned chest that under other circumstances would have had me staring. "Magic is supposed to be made up. It isn't supposed to be real. Vampires, goblins, shifters, *wands* . . ." I rubbed my temples. "This can't be real life."

Ethan stalled at the bathroom door. "Looks like a communal shower." He turned back with a hard stare. "Four shower heads does not mean four people need to be crowding in. I don't need your hairy asses that close."

Pete groaned. "Could this place get any worse?"

"At least there's a door on the toilet," Orin said, peering in behind Ethan.

Ethan rolled his shoulders and flared his elbows. "Dude. Back your creepiness off."

Orin's blank stare took Ethan's measure before he slowly took one step back. "I wax."

"That's—" Ethan blew out a breath through his nose and shook his head, confusion and disgust radiating from him.

"What the hell have I gotten stuck with . . ." He continued into the bathroom.

"Don't your parents have magic? I mean, I assume one of them is a Shade," Pete asked me, scooting to the edge of his mattress so he could see me.

I pulled out a shirt and a pair of tighty-whities. "I honestly have no idea." I draped them over the bar of the bunk above Pete. Orin slipped into the bathroom. "But now that I'm here, some of the things my mother said throughout my childhood make me think she knew about all this. She must've, right?"

"Unless her parents excused her from the academy for some reason," Pete said. A squeak preceded the sound of running water from the bathroom. He must've read the confusion in my expression. "You can request to be pardoned from the Culling Trials, which then means you don't go to the academy. You'd go to normal school and live your life like someone without magic." He shivered. "I have no idea why someone would want that for their kid. It's no life, not when you could have this."

I snorted. This. Like the Culling Trials were some great opportunity?

Like the academy where Tommy had died was an even better place to be?

I fingered the hem of my sweats, my mind whirling. That was the life we'd lived on the farm. No magic. No talk of magic. Why would my parents willingly choose that for themselves and their kids if it was *lesser* in the magical society's mindset? Why would they hide all of this from us? It didn't make sense. I was missing something, I had to be.

I hated that she had to give it up because of a rumor about that curse.

My father had said that, muttered to himself after too much moonshine.

"What about your dad?" Gregory asked, cutting through my thoughts.

I shook my head slowly as Ethan's voice drifted out of the bathroom. "Dude, back off. I'm not going to tell you again." Apparently, Orin was taking his Ethan watching to a higher level.

"Dad never said anything. Until Sideburns showed up, he never once mentioned magic to me. But . . ." I thought back to what he'd said about Tommy coming here. About wanting to live through his son. I shook my head again. I didn't want to admit that he'd been a null. I didn't want the chance that they'd turn their noses up at my dad.

"Maybe they got kicked out of the Culling Trials," Gregory said as the water in the bathroom turned off.

I just grunted, thinking about what my dad had said. Wondering if it was true. Had my mom known Tommy's life would be in more jeopardy than the other students?

"That's why they have people like the Sandman," Pete said. "Well . . . not him specifically, but people that visit the worried parents. The recruiters almost always talk the parents around. It's really not *that* dangerous here."

"Dude. People *died* today," I said as Ethan emerged from the bathroom with a towel wrapped around his hips. Steam billowed around him and I had to rip my eyes away from the droplets of water clinging to his muscular chest. Yup, not looking, not looking at all.

"Yeah, but that hardly ever happens." Pete shrugged.

"Wild is right," Ethan said at his trunk. He pulled off his towel and I jumped, jerking my gaze to the metal bed frame in front of my face. Things were getting awkward. "Today's challenges had a record high death rate. Someone is going to get fired for that. I can guarantee it."

Pete rolled out of his bed and grabbed some sweats before hugging them to his chest and heading for the bathroom. Hopefully that meant stripping down in front of everyone and drying your balls wasn't common practice among men bunking together. At least not for everyone. Thank God, since I had no balls to dry.

"You coming?" Pete asked.

I jerked my head at Gregory, who was staring at me. "You go. I want to look and see if there are any boxers in here. I'd rather . . . freeball it."

"Spoken like a guy who's never played any sports," Ethan said, stepping into his underwear.

Now would've been a great time to take up smoking and excuse myself outside.

"What's next for tomorrow?" I asked, digging through my trunk to keep from peeking at a truly well-formed rear end. Not that I should know that about him or even notice it.

The water turned on again and I breathed a small sigh of relief when Gregory skulked into the bathroom.

"Should be a free day." Ethan shrugged into a shirt before climbing to the top bunk with his phone. "One day on, one day off. Tomorrow, we can explore the mansion and meet up with other people."

"And after that?" I pulled my hat down a little more and headed toward the door that led out of the portable. Maybe I'd just take a walk around the small domicile in the guise of securing our sleeping area. After lights out, I'd sneak in and take a quick shower by myself.

"Another trial. We're stuck together in a team now, so you bastards better not blow it."

I huffed. "You didn't seem too worried about your buddies in the last trial."

I barely saw him shrug as I turned the door handle. "I'm no one's caretaker. If people can't keep up, that's their problem."

"Where are you going?" Orin asked from the far corner, staring at me with his deep, solemn eyes.

"Just to . . ." I made a circle with my finger. "Just to make sure things are good. Go ahead and hit the hay. I won't be long."

An hour later, after I'd made a million laps around the portable, I finally snuck back in, my limbs sore and my eyes drooping. I was exhausted, mentally and physically. I needed a good sleep and to wake up from this terrible nightmare. What I wouldn't give to be back home, to be in my own bed and to hear the twins snoring on the floor below me.

Deep shadows pooled in the corners of the room and a small slice of light cut across the middle of the floor from the bathroom. Rhythmic, deep breathing indicated the guys were sound asleep, the mounds of bodies snuggled into the crappy lumpy mattresses.

I quietly grabbed the sweats and underwear I'd set out and slipped into the bathroom, closing the door behind me. A square area with four shower heads was stationed in the corner, the heads definitely too close together for comfort. Green tile stretched from the shower area to under a urinal, and two toilet stalls were tucked in behind that. One sink with ample counter space stretched away with a large mirror hanging over it.

Unable to help it, I curled my lip at the setup. I bet the ladies' dorms and bathrooms were nicer. Girls' stuff was always nicer. And we didn't pee on the floor.

The shower spray was hard and warm, pelting my skin and melting away all the stress and worry. I hoped my dad was taking my leaving okay, and that Buck hadn't stormed to the farm demanding my head.

Homesickness pinched my gut as I shut off the water, a quick clean all I could afford under the circumstances. I turned, reaching for a towel on the stand next to the shower, when the door swung open and a sleepy, puffy-eyed Pete trudged in.

I froze.

He froze, his gaze rooted to my chest.

"Boobs?" he said in a hasty release of breath. He jolted and his eyes flicked downward, but I was already moving.

I'd been caught out as a girl, and on my first damn day.

BOOK TWO

CHAPTER 1

S tanding in a shower, buck naked, in a crappy little portable sometime after midnight, being caught out as a girl by one of my teammates was the last place I wanted to be. Check that, the last place I wanted to be was here in the Culling Trials at all.

I grabbed a towel and wrapped it around my middle, realizing belatedly that guys didn't cover their chests, but what else was I supposed to do? Let the girls hang out? Yeah, that was not happening. Besides, maybe the towel thing didn't matter—that ship had sailed.

"Crap," I muttered, grabbing another towel and draping it over my shoulders in an even more awkward arrangement.

"I just saw boobs," Pete whispered, his face bright red and his eyes wide. "Why do you have boobs?"

A disembodied voice cut through the air. "You'll want to watch who you tell—"

I startled at the unexpected, if familiar, voice and Pete shrieked.

Orin stood in the far corner, his face blank and eyes piercing as he stared at Pete.

"How long have you been there?" I gasped, pulling the towels tighter around me and scooting into one of the toilet stalls.

"I was keeping watch," Orin said as I locked the stall door.

"On what, the door or my ass? Because you didn't do a bang-up job on the former."

"I was distracted by your neck. You have a strong heart. Your blood pulses in a very nice rhythm—"

"Did I just see boobs?" Pete mumbled, clearly to himself. "I couldn't have. I'm dreaming. Sleepwalking. But dang what a dream!"

"Close the damn door, Orin," I ground out between clenched teeth. "We don't need the whole place hearing this conversation."

The door clicked as I hurried to dress, donning a sports bra before pulling on my T-shirt and boxers. The cloth stuck to my damp skin as I wrestled it into place, all the while listening to Pete's mumbling.

"They were perfect," he said, whispering. "Round and perky with pink nipples. That isn't right. Right? He's a . . . he. Guys don't have . . ."

I unlocked the door and pushed out of the stall, grabbed Pete by the front of his shirt and slammed him against the wall. I leaned into his face, schooling my expression into a hard mask.

"You didn't see boobs, got it?"

His widened eyes stared at me, but it wasn't because of my thinly veiled threat. He was still lost in the vortex of female anatomy that had interrupted his midnight pee.

"Shake it off, man." I slapped him across the face, just hard enough. "They are for feeding kids, for cripes' sakes. Every second adult has them."

He blinked slowly before his eyebrows pinched above his nose. "You have boobs?"

"He's not the brightest crayon in the box," Orin said with an eye roll.

I curled my fingers around Pete's neck. "As far as you are concerned, no, I do not. I am a guy. I have a dick and a flat chest. Got it?"

Understanding lit Pete's face, and a grin twisted his lips. "I saw your boo—"

I increased the pressure on his neck, willing him to understand. I didn't want to hurt Pete. I liked him.

"It is really surprising human males are tolerated with this type of behavior," Orin drawled.

"They aren't all like this," I said, remembering when Rory, that lying bastard, saw me naked by accident once. He'd walked into the bathroom while I was showering, thinking it was Tommy. When I'd unknowingly flashed him, he'd simply apologized, turned his back, and asked if we needed anything from the store. He hadn't said a word about it ever again, not even to tease me in front of my brother.

Pete needed to grow up.

I was about to help him.

"If you mention this to anyone, I will kill you," I said, low and rough. "I will slit your throat in your sleep and let you bleed out in that cozy little bed out there. You saw me in the final trial—you know I'm not bluffing. I could do it."

I was totally bluffing. But he didn't know that.

His face paled as he wheezed around my fingers. He nodded his head adamantly, fear finally cutting through his confusion and humor.

"I am pretending to be a boy to save my brother," I went on. "I'm here in his stead. He's not even sixteen—he never would've made it this far. If you mess with me, you are messing with my family, do I make myself clear? I will kill for my family."

A strange sensation pulled at my stomach. An assurance. A confidence in what I'd said. That primal part of me *wasn't* bluffing. I would do what it took to save my family, and this place would give me the tools to protect them. I felt that as surely as I felt the ground under my feet. And to keep Billy and maybe eventually Sam out of this, I would use those tools violently if need be.

"They don't bring people in that young," Pete struggled to say through his squeezed windpipe. "It's against the rules."

"He is incapable of focusing on the threat to his life," Orin said. "Fascinating. That or he trusts you implicitly."

I released my hand and stepped back before pointing at myself. "Boy. I am a boy."

Pete rubbed his throat. "Yes, fine, I won't tell. But . . ." His brow furrowed. "They don't even take geniuses below the age of seventeen. The academy isn't just about academics—people have to be a certain age to properly control their magic before they can be tested."

I ran my fingers through my hair. "Mr. Sunshine said he got it cleared."

"Who?" they asked in unison.

"The Sandman. Sideburns. My own personal Grim Reaper. When he checked me in, he said he'd gotten Billy cleared. It was pretty clear then that he knew I wasn't Billy. I assumed he didn't say anything because it would look bad on him if he showed up with the wrong kid."

"Why not just bring in you?" Orin asked. "You're the right age, aren't you?"

"He said something about my electing not to come. But I never saw a letter or anything."

"Oh. One of your parents must've filled out the form," Pete said. "Though why would they opt out for you and not your brother?"

I wondered the same thing, though a larger issue nagged at me. "It wouldn't have been my parents to fill out that form." I couldn't bear to elaborate. I didn't want to talk about my mother dying early, or the role my father might've inadvertently played in my other brother's death.

Thinking of Tommy—

"Could a sibling have filled out the form?" I asked.

Pete shook his head. "It has to be a legal guardian."

"Then who would've—"

"Hey!"

We all jumped. Ethan stood in the doorway with a glower. "Can you guys shut up? It's late and I'm tired."

"Sorry," Pete nudged me with his elbow, "I was just talking with my bro here."

I rolled my eyes and made my way out of the bathroom, thinking on what Sideburns had said. Wondering why the school had gone after Billy so aggressively, well before it was prudent, even if I was mysteriously excused. Something wasn't adding up. Or, I should say, *another* something wasn't adding up. I needed to know why my family was a target—why my mother had tried to keep us out of this life.

There was someone I could ask who might know. Rory. And tomorrow, a rest day, I'd find that miserable, two-faced, cowardly sonuvabitch and force information out of him.

One way or another.

CHAPTER 2

Asiren blared through the crappy little portable, echoing in the small, close space. I startled awake, sitting up on my top bunk and smashing my head on the ceiling.

"Owww." I pressed my palm to my forehead.

The lights flicked on, dim, showing that it was still not quite light outside.

"Let's go, let's go, let's go," someone shouted in at us.

An object clattered across the floor. A moment later, small blasts filled the space, crackling and popping. Someone shouted outside.

"What's going on?" Pete thudded against the floor below me as I scrambled to the bunk ladder.

Ethan threw his legs over the railing of his top bunk and leapt to the ground, landing in a half crouch.

"He's a douche, but he's an agile douche," I said, attempting the same thing and half sliding, half falling from mine. Amazing that I could run across a log while being pummeled with arrows and spears, but could barely manage dropping out of bed. Then again, there was no adrenaline pumping despite all the noise. These theatrics were irritating, certainly, but not dangerous.

Another set of mini-explosions drowned out the shouts and yells from outside—fire crackers meant to scare and drive us out.

The door burst open, and a woman with short platinum hair and thin lips stepped in. Her clothing style said she was part of the program. "Get moving! Let's *go*, slugs!"

"What's going on?" Ethan yelled over the blaring siren.

"Your second trial starts in half an hour. Get to the gate or get a ticket home. Let's go!" The woman peeled away from the doorway as we staggered forward, sleep drunk.

"Today is supposed to be a day off," Ethan called after her as she strutted down the narrow lane leading to the other portables. People waited in their clusters, their crews, rubbing their eyes and huddling together against the early morning chill. More kids surged out of the mansion, their movements jerky from the shock of being woken up just after the butt crack of dawn.

Pete stretched and then groaned. "I'm still sore from yesterday."

"We all are. That's why we're supposed to get a break," Ethan groused.

"Head to the buses." The woman stalked toward us, motioning us to the buses. "Load up."

"When was the last time the academy changed stuff up like this? They've always had a day of rest between each trial," Gregory asked Pete.

He shook his head. "Wally would know." He pointed. "There she is!"

Wally broke away from a group of girls and jogged toward us across a broad stretch of lawn, waving her hand like she was stranded and flagging down a rescue plane.

"She's not supposed to leave her group, I don't think," Pete said softly.

Ethan rolled his eyes and shoved me forward before grabbing Pete by the shirt and yanking him after me. "Hurry up. They've been known to leave without people."

"Suddenly the team player?" I asked Ethan dryly as Wally caught up to us.

"I need someone to trip if we're being chased by beasts," he replied. Funny enough, I didn't think Ethan was kidding, not for a second.

"Only three times in the history of the Culling Trials have they altered the format," Wally said breathlessly. "This is very exciting."

"Why do you think they're changing things?" Gregory asked. "Do they want to hurry us into school, maybe? But really, what's an extra few days?"

A line of chartered buses waited for us in the mansion parking lot, the doors open and an attendant standing by each. I didn't see Sunshine or Rory anywhere.

"Which one should we choose?" Pete asked.

"Follow me." Ethan cut through the crowd.

At the fourth bus from the end, the attendant held up her hand. "Room for one more group. Let's go."

"That's us." Ethan put out his hand to stop another group of five guys who stood much closer to the bus. "Find another bus," he told them with a haughtiness that seemed as grotesque as it was useful, given they all deflated and backed away. He glanced back at us. "Come on."

"Why this bus?" I asked, seeing no distinction between this one and the rest.

He didn't answer, only strode past the empty seats at the front. Near the back of the bus, he stopped next to a seemingly random seat and jerked his head at the occupants. "You're in my seat. Move."

The two starry-eyed girls fell over themselves to get out of his way, batting their lashes and showering him in sweet smiles.

I scowled at them. "Grow a spine, ladies."

"You too. And you." Ethan motioned for more seats to be vacated, this time by equally starry-eyed guys before taking his seat and nodding for me to sit with him. The way both genders reacted to him was unreal.

"People just do what he says?" I asked Wally as the displaced kids found new seats and the bus door slid shut.

"He's a Helix." She shrugged and sat.

Apparently, that was answer enough.

I slid in beside Ethan as he pulled a square of thicker type paper from his pocket. After a cursory look around, he peeled the corners away and read the sheet. His hand slid to his belt where his wand stuck out of a canvas holster.

"Do you have your cell phone on the other side, nerd?" I asked with some snark. I didn't plan to mention that I was so poor, I neither had a phone nor a belt to put it on. "You should at least get a leather belt. It's way cooler."

The bus shimmied to a start, following behind those in front. The sun lit the interior and a few people started chattering.

"Did I hear right that you don't know anything about magic?" Ethan asked, refolding the paper and tucking it into his pocket.

"Yes, you heard right. This is all new to me."

"But you made it to the end of that Shade trial."

"Teamwork. You should look into it." I looked out the window as we rode. The scenery was all trees and bushes in full summer bloom. The heat wasn't too bad, at least, especially not this early in the morning. If this trial was as physical as the last, we were going to be hurting in a few hours.

"The others in the crew, they're useless. You're . . ." A small crease formed between his brows as he studied me. "Odd."

"Great. Good observation." I turned away, nervous about how he was studying me. He was the last person I wanted to know my secret. His kind would sell secrets to the highest bidder and laugh when "Billy" ended up paying the price.

"You know Rory Wilson?" he asked.

The change in his conversation threw me and I paused before answering. Until yesterday, I would have said we were friends. Not anymore. "We grew up together."

"He's trouble."

"Always has been, yes."

"He's the best Shade in his class. Nearly the best in the school, though he's only a third year. Well, fourth year coming this year."

"He's a lying blockhead that's going to get a thump as soon as I get a chance, so help me God."

"What's he doing here though, at the trials?" Ethan asked.

I paused again, having no idea where the conversation was going, but still not expecting it to end up where it had.

"I have no idea," I said honestly. The bus turned down a small dirt road. Dust flew past the windows, fogging the view. Anticipation quickened my heart. "He didn't tell me he was coming here. I thought he was in Nevada. He sent me a postcard from *Nevada*."

Ethan didn't say anything for a long time. A quick glance told me he was staring at the side of my head.

"Is there a problem?" I asked

Ethan's eyes bored into me. "Rory Wilson doesn't have friends."

"As of yesterday, I know why. Where are you going with this?"

The bus came to a stop, and Ethan pushed me to get out of the seat.

"He's an enigma. People wonder what side he is on," Ethan said.

"Side of what?" I moved in line as everyone exited the bus. He didn't answer. Great, another question to add to the pile.

The five gates stood in front of us once more, sentinels lined up at the top, same as the day before.

Ethan blew air from his nose, and I got the distinct impression it was supposed to be a laugh of derision. He motioned me to a gate with a sparse crowd waiting in front. Our crew followed behind.

"You better hope you keep being useful," Ethan said, "or someday soon you'll be crushed by your lack of knowledge."

"You should get a side job writing for fortune cookies. You'd be a smash hit."

"This is the House of Unmentionables," Pete said, interrupting us. "Why are we doing this one?"

"We have to do them all, and we have to do them all together. I've got a pattern we need to follow." Ethan shifted as the same beautiful woman from the day before walked along the edge of the wall.

"Welcome, everyone," she began.

Ethan didn't stop to listen. "This is one of the easiest. All we have to do is beat the simpleton creatures and find the gold. I know where it'll be . . . mostly . . . and the basic spells I'll need. With you guys to run interference, it shouldn't be a big deal. Hopefully by the next trial we'll be used to working together and you won't drag me down."

Wally's voice dropped low. "This cheater always prospers."

The gates shimmied open and Ethan gestured us on ahead of him.

"Go back with your team. You're going to get in trouble. You're going to get us in trouble!" Pete tried to shoo Wally away, like a wayward dog.

"You're my team. They are just my dorm mates," she replied. "The school will catch on eventually. That's how this works, you know."

As we crossed the threshold into the trial, bare dirt was all that was in front of us. A few scraggly bushes dotted the way and one lonely tree reached into the sky, its branches bare and trunk gnarled and hunched. Gradually, a hush pressed in around us, unnatural for so large of a place. The wall behind us melted away, and the desolate land stretched out to infinity.

"This stuff trips me out," I said as Ethan found a path on the cracked earth and followed it without hesitation.

"Did you memorize all the right paths or something?" I asked, scanning the way for any sign of danger. A warning vibrated through my body, but it didn't take a form or indicate a direction. We were in the thick of danger without any indication where it might come from.

Giddyup.

"Yes. It's good to have friends in high places." Ethan stopped at a fork, looked each way, then went right. "Except I don't remember that fork."

"Super," I glanced back at the others. "Thoughts?"

"He's the one cheating. We're just playing follow the leader," Pete said. "We can claim we didn't know."

"I agree. This is the best-case scenario at the moment." Wally turned in a circle while walking. "When he doesn't need us anymore, that's when we will need a plan B."

"Wise woman," Ethan said.

I gritted my teeth. His overconfidence that we were all idiots or incompetent would be the ruin of him. I'd make sure of it. But right now, Sunshine's words burned through my brain. I needed to stick to the middle of the pack. To let Ethan take the heat off me so I'd go unnoticed.

"We're about there, I think," Ethan said, hitting a three-way stop and choosing the far right path. He'd clearly made the correct choice at the previous fork.

"Where is there?" I asked, winding toward the left before Ethan took yet another right turn. Then another. My brain said we were going in a circle, but my sense of direction said we were still winding our way east. The path was a mind bender for sure.

"The bridge. It's the easiest crossing place," Ethan said.

The roar of water grew louder as we walked. Ahead, I could barely see the rolling, boiling, white water of a large chasm. Foam floated up, creating a rainbow in the strengthening sun rays, then cut off abruptly as if tumbling off a cliff. The oddity was the land was flat. There was no actual cliff, no natural drop off. The chasm cinched into little more than a stream.

"I do not like this," I grumbled as Ethan pointed right.

"There," he said, picking up the pace.

"We have all day. We don't have to hurry," Pete groaned, jogging to keep up.

"I'm not the only one with connections," Ethan said, not slowing. "The first one to the gold takes it all. I want to be the first."

"Don't you have enough money?" Orin asked, drifting along behind us, in no apparent hurry.

"You can never have enough money," Ethan replied. "And this isn't about the money. Not really. It's about taking all the glory. It's about winning."

A stone bridge was built into the side of the river, leading over the thinnest part of the water. The drop from the bridge was plenty steep, I had to admit, but only a trickle of muddy water flowed through, probably knee high at best.

"What's the task?" Wally asked.

"Simple, we have to get across the bridge," Pete replied as we all slowed near the stone steps.

"It won't be simple," Gregory said quietly. "I can guarantee that."

A deep growl issued from somewhere. At first, I couldn't figure out the source, but the growl rose in strength until a deep, booming roar reverberated from under the bridge.

"No," I said, shaking my head, knowing exactly what was coming. Mom had read me enough fairy tales for me to know what lived under bridges. "No freaking way."

Another roar like a garbled "ahhhhhh" followed, shaking the ground and sending my senses into overdrive. Everything in me said to run. To get away. Fighting whatever was under that bridge was absolute madness. You didn't slap a lion on the nose and then put up your dukes. No. You climbed a tree and hid like a coward. Right?

My laughter rang out, a reflex I couldn't control, as a huge green head poked out from under the bridge. Warty and hideous, it had a wide nose with big nostrils dripping thick yellow goo. An enormous hand grabbed the edge of the bridge, its thick fingernails chipped and deeply lined with the color of dried blood.

"Who's going first?" Ethan asked, taking his wand out of its canvas holder.

Almost as one, everyone looked at me.

CHAPTER 3

I shook my head as the others backed away from the bridge and the oversized deep green troll climbing out from under it, which effectively put me out in front. I stood sideways so I could keep an eye on both the troll and the traitors.

"Some friends you all are," I said.

"You're the quickest of us," Wally said, her eyes glued to the troll. "If you can get the troll to follow you, then maybe the rest of us can get by with minimal fighting."

"Basically, what she's saying is, you first, Shade," Ethan said. "I've got your back, but we all know you move like lightning."

I turned a look on him. "Really? Compliments now?"

Pete snorted but didn't step up. "He's trying to sweet talk you into going. You know, as if you were just as dumb as he is."

A bellowing roar snapped my head around and I took a few steps back. I couldn't help it. I might be braver than I was smart, but even I could see this was far from a slam dunk.

The troll now stood fully exposed in the center of the bridge, flexing his big hands with those disgusting cracked nails. His feet and toes matched his hands, right down to the chips in the nails and the junk jammed under them.

But to be fair, that was not what had my attention. I blinked and shook my head. When I said he was fully exposed, I do mean *fully* exposed. The big bastard was over eight feet tall and his hands, feet, and . . . other appendages . . . were about three sizes too big for his body.

"How does he not step on it?" Pete wondered out loud. I had the same question, but I was as irritated as a cat who'd been thrown into bathwater. The irritation kept me from freaking out and letting fear control me.

"Put some clothes on!" I snapped and pointed a finger at the troll. "Ain't nobody got time for that."

The troll bent at the waist and roared in my direction, showing off cracked and broken teeth, a tongue split in three and a maw big enough to stuff my entire head in and bite down.

Fear tickled at me, working its way down my spine. I fought it hard. Pushing it away as it fought to take me over. "You look ridiculous. Like an oversized Shrek, you know that?"

"Yelling at him won't work," Gregory said behind me.

"Really? What are you going to tell me next? That the pope is Catholic?" I brushed the hair from my eyes and adjusted my hat. "So what *will* work?"

"Why are you asking him?" Ethan barked. "Get moving!"

I rolled my eyes and held my ground. "Gregory?"

"His sensitive spot is not what you might think. Trolls are capable of—"

A crack behind us preceded a burst of light as though a series of fireworks had been let off. Gregory yelped, and something snapped my ass like a metal-tipped whip on steroids.

"Ah, what the hell?" I jumped forward as heat and pain sliced through my right butt cheek, making me gasp. Cold washed over my body. The troll startled as though I'd snagged my foot on a trip wire.

"Ethan!" Wally gasped. "How could you do that? He's on our team!"

"We need him to move. He's the bait today."

As if I needed any confirmation of who'd just shot me and with what. I put a hand to my butt, but my rear end was far from my biggest problem.

Apparently, there was an invisible line I'd just crossed—a line that Ethan had known about and pushed me over on purpose.

And now the troll was coming for me full tilt, mouth wide, hands outstretched as it made grabby motions with those wretched fingers.

I darted to the right, drawing the troll back to the bridge. If I could get him to follow me to the other side, then my crew would be free to cross. Maybe this was like those golems from the Shade trial, and we could leave the troll behind to terrorize the next set of kids.

I ran up onto the edge of the bridge, climbing the stone railing so that I was almost as tall as the troll. "No questions? Isn't that how the fairy tales work? Shouldn't you ask me questions before you go crazy and try to kill me?"

"No, don't engage him! Keep moving! He'll overwhelm you!" Gregory yelled.

The troll curled his lips and rolled his wide shoulders as he slowed his advance. "You wanna question, little duck? How about a rhyme? Do you think you can outsmart me?" The troll's lips curled and pulled wide, a grotesque sort of smile if I'd ever seen one. "Give me a moment, and I'll have you."

He wiggled the index and middle fingers on his left hand, and a strange sizzling feeling rolled over my skin—his magic, if I had to guess. Trolls clearly had magic.

I worked to brush it off, but a scene interrupted my vision. The troll stood over me as I lay with my limbs bent at strange angles, my eyes wide and pleading.

I blinked my eyes then rubbed them, trying to clear away the image. Trying to root myself in reality and shake the visual he was forcing on me. I couldn't quite do it, but it no longer commanded my attention. Pain throbbed through my body as though his huge, meaty foot had stomped on me.

My legs shook from the visceral reaction, so badly I had to lock them to keep standing.

"See?" the troll breathed the word, hissing it. "Now you see. You see what I will do to you. What I will enjoy doing over and over again."

Gregory groaned. "It isn't real, Wild! None of what he will show you is real—ignore it and *fight!*"

I gave a slow nod and breathed through the washes of fear coming at me, like breakers in the ocean. I squinted through the double vision. "Try again, dumb ass." I gritted my teeth as I made myself grin at him.

His bulbous eyes bugged out even farther. "Not possible! You *will* fear me!"

I couldn't stop myself from flipping him off, even though the effort left me shaking. I forced my frown into a grin. "So much eloquence coming out of a big, dumb-looking, booger-riddled creature. Why is that? What do you have? Some smarty-pants magic user feeding you lines?" I adjusted my stance on the thick stone railing of the bridge. Or tried to. I fought to lift a foot, but I was stuck to the stone. The troll's smile widened and the bugger winked at me.

Oh crap.

"*Six little ducks went out one day.*" He took a step toward me.

"Get ready to run. He's about to be very distracted," Ethan barked, but I didn't think it was at me. No, *I* was the distraction here. My crew would run to safety, leaving me to handle the troll.

The troll took another step and the image it was taunting me with shifted again, showing my intestines spilled out into the water below the bridge, the water turning pinkish red. I blinked it away and fought to keep my balance as vertigo hit me hard and left me swaying.

"*Over the bridge and far away.*" The troll took another step and I tried again to yank my feet off the stone. Glued, I was damn well glued to it with some sort of troll magic.

"Boots, get them off!" Gregory yelled.

I bent and ripped frantically at the laces. Got one of them off.

"*Mother duck called quack, quack, quack.*" The troll reached for me before I could free my foot from the other boot. "*But only five little ducks came limping back.*"

That big paw of a hand swept toward my head and I did the limbo backward on pure instinct, my one foot stuck in the boot that was still attached to the stone. I yelled as I swung down, the force wrenching my knee before that foot came loose at the last second.

I tumbled through the air, landing in the water below with a sickening thud. Not enough water to cushion my fall, not enough mud to sink under me. I groaned as I rolled onto my belly and feet, soaked through.

"Hurry!" Wally said. "Trolls are known to eat as many as ten people per annum."

I lurched toward the far side of the creek, the cold water soaking my clothes and chilling me despite the warm weather. A huge splash behind me told me all I needed to know. My new friend had followed me, allowing the others to cross.

I spun, reaching for my knife as I whipped around.

The troll was a hell of a lot bigger than I'd thought, that or he'd grown in the last few seconds.

"Little duck, you are going to die. Better that I do it now than you see what is coming for you. What is coming for you, oh, that is much worse than anything I could do." He grinned and pointed a finger at me. A magic finger that could make me see horrible things.

Well, that was enough of that garbage.

I lunged toward him and slashed with my knife, aiming for that finger. He was far too slow, and I took the finger off at the second knuckle before he could so much as blink.

We both stared as the digit fell into the water. *Bloop.* For just a split second, there was nothing, no noise, no drop of blood, and then it all went to hell.

The troll fell backward, swinging up his hand, and in the process, spraying me with blood the color of a grapefruit's innards. Pale pink splattered over me—the smell of it not that far off citrus either—and I pushed my back against the solid ditch behind me as the troll wailed at the top of his lungs.

The fear was gone as were the visions he'd superimposed on my sight. But for how long?

"My fingy, my fingy, she took my fingy! You said I wouldn't get hurt. You said I'd scare them and get to eat them, but none were mean enough to hurt me! Oh, I'm going to tear this bitch apart." He roared the words as he straightened himself up, his eyes coming back to find me on the far side of the ditch.

Time to go.

Panic clawed at me. I had no boots, a single knife, and a troll that had just decided I needed my body parts rearranged.

"I need help!" I yelled up at my team, hoping they hadn't gone far.

"Here, I have a stick," Pete called from above me. I spun and reached my hands up to see he'd oversold it—it wasn't a stick but a twig that was thin and wobbling even as he stretched down to me. I spread my hands wide.

"That isn't a stick, Pete! Find a branch, not a sliver!"

His shoulders slumped. "Sorry." And then he slunk back, leaving me there.

"Damn it, I still need help!" I yelled.

"Oh, the humanity! I'm going to tear her a new hole!" the troll hollered. He slammed into me again, but his eyes were rolling as though the pain in his finger was nothing short of incapacitating and it made him super sloppy.

Score one for me.

I spun with him, like some sort of horrible tango. His snot slapped onto my face. He gripped at me with his good hand and *something* bumped my leg.

"Get off me, you freakshow!" I yelled and shoved him away. Shockingly, he fell backward, right onto his butt into the water, still holding his hand, still crying massive crocodile tears as he spewed obscenities.

"Pain in his hands is his downfall. It steals his magic!" Gregory leaned over. "You did good. That injury will keep him occupied for at least a few minutes."

"I'm coming, Wild!" Pete yelled from above.

I stared at the wall of dirt and stones that comprised the ditch, able to see some handholds now that the troll's magic had diminished. "I can climb out, just warn me if he's coming."

Only Pete didn't wait for me. No, Pete was in what I like to call white-knight mode. Was it because he knew I was a girl now? Yeah, most likely.

A new snarl from above cut through the air and then a honey badger came flying down.

A furry Pete—in full on honey badger form—landed between me and the still inconsolably sobbing troll.

Gregory groaned. "He will be far deadlier once he snaps out of the shock. You two need to get out of there!"

A snarl of serious ferocity ripped out of Pete and the troll opened his eyes.

"Oh, no." Gregory said. "Get out of there!"

"Trying!" I yelled back, only now I couldn't leave. Not without Pete.

He snarled and lunged at the troll's foot, snagging a big toe in his mouth and flipping his head back and forth so hard his body was a blur.

The troll bellowed bloody murder as Pete put the toe hold on him. "I'm eating badger for breakfast!" he roared.

His hand shot for Pete and I lunged forward without thinking, knowing only that Pete was one of mine to protect. I slashed with my blade, catching two more of the troll's grasping fingers.

They plopped into the water and the troll lurched to the side and puked as his newly cut fingers bled pink into the churned-up water.

A gargled *ahhhhhhh* ripped out of the troll. "Imma kill her ten ways to the solstice and back!"

Jesus Murphy, he was going to unmask me if I didn't get my ass out of here.

"Come on, Pete!" I grabbed his stubby tail and pulled him backward while he fought to get closer to the troll, clawing at the ground, muddying up the waters even more as he went.

"No, we have to go!" I snapped at him. We did, although I still had to figure out how to get us both out of the ditch. Although we hadn't noticed the ditch's walls as we approached, they now appeared never ending.

This place was such a mind trip, I literally couldn't grasp what the hell was going on with the landscape. But one challenge at a time. Still dragging Pete back by his tail, I got us to the wall of the ditch.

"Look out!" Wally yelled from above. I swung sideways, and by virtue of my farm muscles, swung Pete up as a kind of honey badger weapon.

He snarled as I turned, his claws outstretched for the troll's very wide eyes. He would have gotten them, too, except that big maw had also opened. I pulled Pete back just as the troll's teeth snapped shut, but I kept swinging, throwing Pete, sending him up and over the edge of the ditch.

There was a yelp from one of the others and then another body tumbled into the ditch with me.

It was like we were in some sort of deadly comedy. I was just waiting for a pie in the face to mark the end of the scene.

A flash of dirty blond hair, and then Ethan hit the water beside me. The troll didn't so much as turn toward him. Not even a glance.

"Go on, go after him a minute. He's an ass. Nobody likes him." I made a quick shooing motion, like I would have done with a badly-behaved cow.

The troll tipped his head and squinted an eye at Ethan before turning back to me with a wide grin. "Not allowed. That one has protection on him. You, little duck, do not. And you have seriously pissed me off."

"What the hell?" I yelled. Ethan stood as if nothing had happened, took his wand from his pouch and made a lazy swirling motion with it. The wall of the ditch shifted, changing into a set of stairs that led up and out of the water.

"You dirty son of a bitch, you could have helped all along!" I snarled.

But I got no more than that because I'd been stupid. I'd taken my attention off the troll, which was the only opening he needed to wrap his remaining fingers on one hand around my neck.

"Got ya," he whispered.

CHAPTER 4

From above me, stuck in the ditch with a troll's one good hand wrapped around my neck, Ethan hollered to the others. "Let's go. We're down a Shade, but we don't need him now that we finished his house trial."

He was just going to leave me here?

Anger burned in my gut—not at the troll, but at Ethan—strong enough to shatter whatever remaining hold the troll had on me. Well, minus the hand around my neck.

He squeezed my neck as he grinned. "Imma pop you like a daisy."

I lifted my hand, still holding my knife, and laid the razor-sharp blade against the back of his remaining knuckles. I breathed out—or should say I tried to—and let all the anger swell in me, let it bleed into my eyes until there was nothing there but the urge to finish the troll off. I'd fight like a rabid wolf if he forced my hand. Maybe I'd die, but I'd take him with me.

For a split second, his magic rose around us, dark green and misty, and I . . . breathed it in? Was that right? No, maybe I absorbed it somehow. It soaked through my skin, and I *owned it*. I held it tightly for a beat before it flowed out through my eyes.

The world around us flickered and changed, but this time it wasn't a misty image or a disorienting overlay on our world. It seemed entirely real.

The troll was drawn and quartered, tied under the bridge by his feet like a cow carcass hung to tenderize, the pink blood dripping slowly into the water below, dead eyes glazed with a white film. All ten fingers missing.

"No." The troll let me go, turned and touched his own image. The flesh moved and he howled, and bolted away from me at top speed. I went to my knees as the troll raced away down river, his body jiggling like a bowl of jelly. But I couldn't laugh. I could barely breathe and I'll admit a large part of that was straight up fear catching me.

That troll meant to kill me, and I didn't see any teacher showing up to stop him, no supervisor of the Culling Trials making sure I didn't indeed have my head popped off like a daisy.

"Let me go!" Gregory yelled, and then the little goblin was running down the stairs that Ethan had cut into the side of the ditch. He looked at me on my knees in the water and then at the retreating figure of the troll. He said nothing but hurried to my side and helped me to my feet.

"You okay, Wild?"

I swallowed hard, coughed a few times, and finally nodded. "Thanks for the advice. Helped."

"You . . . handled him well." We slowly made our way up the stairs. At the top, Pete was still in honey badger form, being held by Wally as though he were a fat house cat and not a snarling twisting maniac of a badger.

Ethan raised his eyebrows.

"Boots," Orin said, thrusting my boots at me. I bent and yanked them back on, lacing them up quickly. Behind us was the next group of kids. I could just hear their voices, and I knew we had to get going. Being passed was bad. Even if my heart was still racing, even if I wasn't entirely sure just what had happened here.

Because part of my brain said I'd somehow sucked in the troll's magic and spat it back at him, using his own gift against him.

I swallowed hard. "So, we're done now, right?"

Wally shook her head slowly. "Three challenges for each house. We have two more. The final one will be where the gold is, assuming we chose the paths correctly."

I rubbed my head. That couldn't be the full story. There was something missing. There was no way that a place like this used the exact pattern for each trial. The trial for the House of Shade had been all about strength, speed, and predicting your enemy's moves. Made sense if they were badass assassins. But the House of Unmentionables was not the House of Shade.

If my childhood fairy tales had taught me anything, trolls and goblins hoarded things.

Ethan was already partway down the path, eyeing up his piece of paper. Out of earshot. Still, I bent and spoke quietly into the goblin's ear.

"Gregory, do trolls have any sort of talisman?"

His eyebrows rose and he slowly nodded. "Usually they bury something close to where they haunt. A trinket they love."

I ran down the stairs into the ditch and did a slow circle through the muddy water, ignoring the sloshing inside my boots. "Would it be precious metal or something else?" I couldn't explain what was driving me other than this challenge's lack of complexity. Getting past a troll had been physically hard for me, not having done it before, but for Ethan, it would've been a cakewalk. There had to be something more.

Gregory hurried down the stairs and took a big snort of air, his eyelids fluttering. "A ruby. There's a ruby buried in the creek."

With Gregory helping as a magical treasure detector, we pinpointed a slight depression in the ground in under a minute. I started clearing away the wet rocks and mud.

"Stop messing around and get out of there!" Ethan snapped from the top of the stairs, then disappeared again. Thankfully, he wasn't the suspicious type, just impatient.

My fingers slid over a smooth surface, different in look and texture than the rocks around it. In fact, it was a perfect square, strange to exist out in nature. I pulled it out and rinsed it in the water. Vivid red. I'd found a gemstone. A ruby.

I handed it to Gregory. "Hang on to it."

"Why me?"

"I don't know, just hang on to it. And keep it from Wonder Bread."

He snorted. "No problem."

We ran up the stairs and reached the top just as voices filtered to us from the opposite bank.

I looked over my shoulder at the approaching kids. "We'd better move. That troll isn't coming back anytime soon to slow down the next group."

Ethan looked past me and waved his wand with a sharp stabbing motion. A circular bubble shot out of the tip, wrapped around the stone bridge and vibrated.

"What—"

The bridge erupted, stones flinging every which way, the noise cutting through the air and making my ears ring.

"That will slow them down." Ethan snorted.

Pete snarled and lunged out of Wally's arms, going straight for Ethan.

"No, Pete. Leave him." Much as I wanted to see the honey badger take a piece out of Ethan, I knew in my gut we still needed him.

Why, I wasn't sure, but I was a pro at listening to my instincts, and I wasn't about to stop now just because Ethan was a giant douche canoe who deserved to have his head bashed in.

Ethan waved a hand for us to follow him, and I fell in behind him even though I was struggling with what all had just happened. Gregory dropped back beside me, Pete and Wally stayed to the middle, and Orin was off to the side.

Gregory was the first to speak. "We can't trust him, Wild. He would have let you die in there. If Pete hadn't shoved him in, he would never have created those stairs."

"I know," I said. But if Ethan hadn't fallen—or been pushed—in, I wouldn't have been caught in an inescapable situation, and whatever . . . thing I'd done wouldn't have happened, either. I was pretty sure I needed to figure out that piece of the puzzle. Maybe they'd given me the wrong designation?

"Then why follow him?"

"Can a person be in more than one house?" I asked.

Gregory looked up at me. "What?" I'd given him conversational whiplash.

"Can you be in more than one house?" I repeated slower. "Like, say your mom was magical like Ethan and your dad was a shifter like Pete. Could you be in more than one house?"

Wally dropped back to walk with us. "Yes and no."

Gregory started. "What?"

She shrugged. "There are very rare cases where an individual carries the genetics of multiple gifts. One gift will always be dominant, but you could have secondary traits. Say you favor shifting but can still manage a wand to some degree. Less than one in a hundred have this magical quirk. And usually it is trained out of them in the academy. The trait that is considered of higher quality is cultivated, and the lesser talent is ignored and ultimately unused and considered dormant."

"I didn't know that," Gregory said softly, touching the tips of his ears.

Wally turned her head to look at me, long black eyelashes fluttering a little. "Why do you ask, Wild?"

Her explanation, funnily enough, didn't make me feel any better. Did that mean I wasn't a Shade? Weird that I could be bothered by the thought of not being trained as an assassin so quickly after learning it was a possibility. I was cracked.

I frowned and rubbed at my head, worry prickling at me. "It's just that—" Hell, I didn't even know how to explain to them what had happened back there because I didn't understand it myself.

And I didn't get a chance to say more than that.

"Look sharp!" Ethan snapped. "We're at the second challenge."

"Not it," I responded just as sharply. "You first, Wonder Bread. I'm tired of being the one to test the waters."

Something bumped against my leg and I looked down. Pete looked up at me, still a honey badger.

I sighed. "Sorry, we forgot to bring extra pants."

He shrugged and chattered his teeth, and I could almost hear him say, *Pants-shmants, this way I can pretend I don't understand all of you.*

"That's cheating, Freckles," I said softly.

His head whipped around and he stared at me, slack jawed. I stared back, my own jaw dropping wide.

"What is happening?" I whispered. I was not hearing a honey badger talk, was I? I was not like Pete. I was no shifter.

"What's happening is we have to get our asses up that tower," Ethan said. The dubious quality to his voice snapped my focus back to the moment.

I tilted my head, looking up at a massive tower that appeared out of nowhere, reaching a good hundred feet into the sky, flat on top. Large blocks, nearly my height, made up a few rows along the base, but above that, the wall seemed to even out, nothing but divots and small ledges to the top. There weren't even windows or doors—it was basically a massive climbing rock.

"Where the hell did that come from?" I asked, daunted.

"Looks easy, but there are bound to be nasty surprises," Ethan said softly.

I huffed out a laugh. "Climbing that looks easy?"

"Goblin, you go first, seeing as this is your house," Ethan barked.

"This tower will be protected by gargoyles," Gregory said, analyzing it. "They're as dumb as the rocks they're made from, but they are vicious. They'll try to pick us off as we climb. See them there, at the top?"

I squinted, as though that would help my vision. It didn't, of course, but I still saw what he'd spotted. Three oversized stone gargoyles perched at the top. One of them had wings, two were without. All resembled mishmashes of creatures—lions, dragons, crocodiles— the bits and pieces jammed together to make horrible stone beasts.

One of them moved—the dragon-headed one with the set of wings peered down the back side of the tower. Another chill of warning made my breathing shallow, and my body flooded with adrenaline, prepped for anything. Sort of.

Figures gathered at the bottom of the tower caught my gaze. I didn't know how a team had gotten ahead of us, but clearly one had. Maybe the troll bridge they'd crossed was easier. Maybe they hadn't faced a troll at all. Regardless, this was an opportunity that we hadn't had yet, to see how another team fared at a challenge.

Ethan and Gregory made to pass in front of me and I grabbed them both, one in each hand. "Watch."

Ethan and Gregory both went still as the scene played out in front of us.

There was a moment of silence as the kids started to climb the tower. They'd made it twenty feet up when a sudden movement caught my notice. A creature—a gargoyle—I hadn't seen, stretched to life, much smaller than those perched higher and nearly matching the color of the stone under its feet. It shot down, moving like a spider on a wall, heading straight for the kids.

"It'll be like this all the way around," Ethan said, stepping to the side as if that would get him a better look.

A sudden high-pitched scream cut the air, and a winged gargoyle flew straight into the air behind the tower. As it rose, it circled closer to us, clutching a student in its talons. The kid's legs kicked in panic.

I grabbed Ethan's shoulder. "Save him!"

Ethan huffed. He didn't move a muscle.

"Ethan, save—" The screaming kid's flailing body disappeared from the sky.

"If they killed everyone, there would be no one left for the academy," Ethan said dryly. I caught a whiff of *you're an idiot* in his tone.

"No time like the present." Ethan shoved Gregory in front of him. "Go."

"You're a real class act, Wonder Bread. A real stand-up guy," I said, stepping forward with Gregory.

"And you're white trash," he replied, following behind us. "Just be glad you're not also useless."

Any other time, he'd be flat on his back with a split lip. This time, though, I figured we needed his wand. Assuming, of course, he'd actually use it.

I directed the others. "Gregory, stick close to me. Orin and Wally, you take the rear. These suckers move fast—yell out if they get in behind us."

I was at the base of the tower and Pete was still beside me.

"You, my fat little friend, are getting a boost."

He chattered his sharp teeth. *Can't climb. I could hook my claws in, but I can't—*

I grabbed him around the belly and tossed him against the wall as high as I could. "Then hook in, buddy. I have a feeling we're going to need some honey badger badassery."

He screeched until he hit the wall and his claws dug in. He glanced down at me, teeth chattering rapidly.

"Rude, so rude." I grinned up at him. "Now, move your furry little butt. We have a tower to climb."

And another token to find. I was sure there'd be treasure here, just like the ruby we'd found at the troll's bridge. Call it intuition, or maybe just plain logic, but each challenge would have a talisman.

He curled his lips up and snapped his teeth once more, but then he did start climbing, contrary to what he'd said about his capabilities. Given that his claws were scraping against stone, and the divots had been designed for hands, I was mighty impressed.

Magic.

I took a deep breath. I'd need to get used to this new reality that defied the logic with which I'd lived my life, and soon.

I jumped up, catching a handhold just above my head, and hung there a moment while I searched for another. "Come on, everybody, this will be easy. Ethan said so."

"Any idiot can climb a wall," Ethan said as he started up to my right.

"You'll be proof," I bit out with a grin.

"Incoming!" Wally shouted, and I looked up as one of the wingless gargoyles skittered down the wall at us like a lizard.

It blinked rapidly a few times, swaying from side to side, a long tongue flicking out to taste the air.

"It can't see," Gregory whispered. "But it can feel us move."

I lifted a foot and dug it into another hold, a few rocks falling.

I grimaced and looked up as the gargoyle came straight at me.

CHAPTER 5

C rap stains on white jeans," I spat out, my heart rate ramping up. "How the hell am I supposed to fight a freaking nightmare?"

The gargoyle was coming straight for me as I hung by my fingers and toes on the side of a stone block tower. This did not bode well.

I scanned the immediate area for all available divots and handholds, lodging them into my brain. I needed a strategy. If these suckers were made of stone, jabbing them with a knife wouldn't do me a whole lotta good.

"You better react, or you'll go flying," Ethan warned.

"Very helpful," I grunted.

The gargoyle closed the distance with lightning speed, shimmying down the flat surface as though its feet had suction cups on them. Rather than strike out, I let the stone creature keep its momentum. When it was just two feet away, I threw myself sideways, heart in my throat, and grabbed a new handhold with my right hand.

The fingers on my left hand just barely scraped against the other hold I'd targeted, but my own momentum swung my body past it and to the right, leaving all my weight pulling on one precarious hold. My jaw clenched and I let out a groan as my fingertips tore into the stone, one nail bending back. That was going to hurt later.

The gargoyle zipped past me, right into the rest of my crew. Wally screeched and Gregory hissed and pulled back, skittering across the stone like it was second nature to him. The gargoyle slowed and turned, focused on its target—me. But between us was Ethan, stuck to the wall with one hand and one foot, his wand out and his baby blues wide. I knew that look. He'd frozen in panic.

"Do a spell," I hollered, reaching with my left hand to secure my position before starting back up. "Hurry! Anything!"

Growls and hisses drew my attention upward. I fully expected another gargoyle to launch into us. Instead, surprise stopped me cold as an incensed honey badger dropped through the air, all four legs spread out like a flying squirrel. Pete landed on the gargoyle's shoulder and scrambled to get purchase, claws digging in, tiny pebbles dropping from the stone beast.

The gargoyle made an ear-splitting sound, a cross between a shriek and a high-pitched baby's cry. Pete, incredibly ferocious in this form, ripped and tore with his mouth and claws, biting off chunks of the gargoyle and throwing them into the air. Rocks shed from the creature and it shuddered. It reached up to slap at Pete, making him slip and scramble to stay on its back.

"Help him!" I yelled, nearly there but blocked by Orin.

Ethan started out of his stupor, closer than any of us to Pete.

Lightning fast in a way only someone from this house could be, Gregory crawled across the wall with ease. Long and incredibly strong fingers fit into tiny pockmarks and divots no normal human could use. He pulled himself up to just below the shrieking and distracted gargoyle before reaching in and raking his fingers across the stone beast's belly.

The gargoyle froze, its face twisted into a mask of agony. Its limbs slowed and hardened.

"Grab Pete," Gregory called, raking his fingers across the stone creature again for good measure.

Ethan, finally reacting, stowed his wand and reached out, grabbing the spitting and growling honey badger by the tail. He flung Pete upward, just barely getting him onto a ledge jutting out the side of the tower, startling a kid standing on it. The other kid fell backward, arms windmilling as he went down.

"Hang on, buddy," I called out as Pete hunkered against the wall, teeth chattering away with enough profanities that I was shocked the others couldn't hear him.

"Clearly, we'll need to head in that direction," Wally mumbled.

The gargoyle finished its metamorphosis back into a statue, stuck on the side of the stone wall like it was glued there.

"Knowing how to disable them would've been nice," I grumbled, heading in Pete's direction.

"You need claws, and the more blows the better," Gregory said, following me. "Let's hurry. It will only stay immobile for a little while."

"You don't have claws." Wally grunted as she found the next handhold.

"My nails are as hard as claws, if not as sharp quite yet. They will be, though. Eventually," he answered. "Wild, your magical knife will probably work. Ethan's magic would too, if he'd use it."

I said, "My knife isn't magical—"

"Yeah, nice reaction time, Helix," Orin said below everyone and apparently not at all remorseful about it. "Daddy can give you the winning magical spell, but Daddy can't teach you courage, can he?"

"I saved the badger, didn't I?" Ethan ground out. "Besides, I didn't see you do anything, blood sucker."

Orin didn't miss a beat. "This is not my house. I expect to fail here. It will hinder neither my transformation into full vampire nor my eventual acceptance into the academy."

"Ten percent of vampiric recruits are not accepted into the fold because of their inability to work with others, and of that ten percent, ninety percent are eventually staked by fearful magical folk afraid the vampire will go rogue," Wally said, relaying the stats in her perfect monotone as she climbed. Her voice dropped to that of her namesake. "There is a fine line between confidence and delusion. One will help, and the other will hinder."

"Fascinating," Ethan said, sarcasm dripping from the word.

A yell caught my attention, to the right. Someone else fell from higher up, his arms swinging through in the empty air. Another scream on the distant left, a girl plummeting to the ground.

I pulled myself up, my hands and muscles screaming. "A lot of people got here before us."

"Doesn't mean they'll finish," Ethan said, strain in his voice. "Now move it. Let's get to the top."

Reaching Pete, I grabbed a hold of him and swung him up. Unfortunately, I botched the release and he sailed out too far right, hitting the wall and sliding until a small ledge stopped his fall.

Several feet above him, just below the lip surrounding the top of the building, the three stone creatures perched on the large overhang shuddered. One by one, their limbs stretched away from the wall, no longer stone. And one by one, they all turned their stone heads to look at Pete, clinging to the tiny ledge above a whole lot of empty air.

"Hurry, hurry, hurry!" I said, reaching for the next hold, pulling myself up as fast as I could.

"That was a terrible throw," Ethan chuckled. He didn't follow me. Instead, he climbed straight up where the coast was clear. He was going to let us be the distraction so he could get to safety.

"You filthy, stinking . . ." I gritted my teeth.

"Cheat. Hoodwinker. Scam artist," Wally finished, thankfully heading toward Pete. "Deceiver. Liar. User. Jerk."

"Okay. We get it," I said.

"Morally bankrupt whoreson—"

"Wow. We get it."

All three gargoyles started down the tower, each larger than the previous. My heart rate increased and adrenaline buzzed through my veins. This was about to get hairy.

Gregory skittered below me, moving nearly as well as the gargoyles on the rough stone wall. He reached Pete and climbed onto the tiny ledge beside him, positioning himself between the honey badger and the monsters.

"There are too many for just me," he called out, watching the creatures slowly move toward him.

"I'm coming," I said, out of breath, arm muscles screaming for more oxygen. "I'm coming."

Fingers starting to cramp, I grabbed another handhold. I braced the blunt toes of my boots, horrible for climbing, against another too small hold. My leg shook with the effort. The creatures descended, speeding up. Their eyes were all on Gregory, who clung to the wall, braced for action.

Understanding dawned, cutting through the lack of oxygen.

"They sense that you're one of their kind, in a way," I said while reaching up. My fingertips brushed the edge of a hold and slipped. My weight shifted and I slid, my cheek scraping against stone. I just barely caught the next hold, my weight pulling on my grip, my fingers threatening to give out.

"Yes," Gregory said. "They're making it harder for me. Testing me. Which means . . ."

"You're . . . worthy," Wally finished. I could hear the approval in her strained and tired voice. "Congratulations. I hope you don't mess up."

I chanced a look down. Sweat dripped off of my face and sailed into the nothingness below. Down the way, bodies clung to the wall. They looked awfully small way down near the bottom. As I watched, someone peeled away from the sheer face, falling back with slack arms. They hadn't been thrown, they'd simply given up.

My stomach flipped. While heights didn't scare me, falling did. While other students might be magically saved from their doom, my family seemed to be targeted for death. I had to assume that everything I did here was life or death. It had been for Tommy, after all. And it would've been for Billy.

More adrenaline coursed through my blood, giving me a boost. The gargoyles sped up, their feet and arms churning over the stone. I grabbed the next hold, and the next, putting everything I had into getting to that ledge.

Gregory surged up for the first gargoyle. It swiped out with a claw. He ducked out of the way and then lashed out, nearly scoring a blow of his own. I reached the ledge and pulled myself up beside Pete, shaking with exhaustion but knowing I couldn't stop now. Gargoyle number two picked up speed, passing Gregory and the first gargoyle before working back around, ignoring me and the others.

I let it pass, getting in position to flank Gregory before balancing my weight on the ledge and snatching out my knife. It might not be magical, no matter what Gregory said, but it was sharp and currently all I had to fight these creatures.

Gregory scraped gargoyle number one along the side, but he hadn't gotten deep enough. The gargoyle slashed out, opening up four parallel red lines on Gregory's shoulder.

Gregory sucked in a breath and pulled back, the pain clearly acute. He balanced on his toes at the very edge of our landing. I grabbed his arm and pulled him back without taking my eyes off gargoyle number one.

The stone muscles on gargoyle number two bunched in preparation to strike. I stretched, using my long reach to my advantage, and quickly jabbed my knife into it.

The creature shuddered as I dragged my blade across its hard-stone underbelly. Its lunge cut short before it had even began, it slowed and then turned back to stone.

"Huh," I said, jamming my knife into the sheath before changing my position. "Guess it doesn't need to be magical after all."

"It does," Gregory grunted as he crawled along the wall, drawing the first gargoyle with him. "I felt it when I first met you. It smells like magic. I assumed you knew."

I didn't have time to argue. The third gargoyle had honed in on me, realizing Gregory wasn't the only threat. It zoomed down the wall so fast, I could barely focus on it. Bracing my legs as wide as they'd go, I yanked out my knife again, my mobility drastically cut down now.

Gregory slashed out before moving up the wall. I lost sight of him as the huge stone gargoyle bore down on me, the big lion head at odds with its lizard-like body. A claw shot out, slashing straight at me, a blow I couldn't avoid. Blistering pain seared the skin on my arm.

I jabbed forward. My knife clinked against the thing's side. It slashed again, barely missing me, before changing position. I cut off a curse. With only one good hand, needing to hold on to the wall, I was stuck. The gargoyle had the high ground, literally.

The hissing and spitting increased in volume, and Pete leapt up to latch on to the creature's hind leg. It squealed and jerked away. I used the distraction, stretching as much as I dared, but my angle was off. I slashed under the thing's arm, not far enough in.

Ignoring Pete for the moment, gargoyle number three pushed forward and struck out. My eyes widened as the claws, aiming directly for my neck, whipped through the air. I jerked my knife up, but it wouldn't help. My fingers slipped as I shifted, trying to brace myself for those stone claws to tear into my neck.

CHAPTER 6

The gargoyle had me dead to rights, and there was nothing I could do about it but try and stare it down and pray someone saved me.

Orin's body popped into my line of sight. He pushed up in front of me and stuck out a forearm, taking the blow meant for me. The gargoyle's claws raked across his arm, but the injury didn't stop him. His fingers elongated into nasty, grayish-black claws, and he darted forward and slashed the underbelly of the gargoyle in one weirdly graceful movement.

Sparks flew and the creature's face closed down in pain, eyes shutting tightly. It immediately began to slow, the stone hardening into a statue.

"Wow," Wally said, poised on the tiny ledge next to me, her arms shaking as she clutched two handholds. "That was fast."

"My kind have no problem with these creatures," Orin said, and I could hear more than a trace of snootiness in his tone. It was clear why he hadn't bothered to get involved until now, thinking himself above gargoyles in the magical hierarchy. So then . . . what had changed? Why come to the rescue?

Panting, Gregory clung to the wall next to a slowing gargoyle, watching it return to a statue. Below us, a group of three people, all somewhat spaced out, worked up the wall unimpeded, the way cleared by us.

"Let's go." Gregory pointed up at Ethan reaching the topmost ledge. He doggedly pulled himself over. "All he'll have to do is find the treasure on top, if he knows to look."

"He didn't know last time." Orin grabbed Pete by the tail and abruptly flung him. Pete sailed up over the ledge and probably smashed painfully onto the roof. Orin pulled himself ahead of Wally and me, moving like an oversized spider with those long thin limbs of his.

"I guess we're lucky Ethan didn't memorize *all* the details," Gregory said dryly.

Utterly exhausted, arms and legs shaking, I pushed myself up the last ten feet. The guys reached the top edge and pulled themselves over. Wally labored beside me, working harder than she likely ever had in her life up to this point.

"You know . . . what I said about the percentage . . . of vampires being staked . . . for not working with others well? I made up . . . that fact . . . about them," she whispered, nearly at the top. "I'm sure . . . there is a stat . . . I just . . . don't know it."

"Why bother?" I asked, my foot slipping. I jammed it back into the closest divot.

"The trick . . . with a vampire . . . is to appeal to their . . . intellect and fear. Dying scares . . . them like it scares . . . anyone, and the ones who aren't . . . trained and don't find a faction, often turn . . . rogue and dangerous. Then they're . . . killed. He might not . . . totally believe me, but . . . it is just as easy . . . for him to help . . . us as to not. I gave . . . him incentive to do so."

I let out a tired laugh as I pulled myself up and over the top, spilling myself onto the glorious flatness of the roof. "Well done, Wally," I said, dropping my hands to my sides. "Well done."

She crashed down right next to me. "Thanks," she said sheepishly. "I'll have to look up . . . more stats in case he stops helping. I'm sure . . ." She gulped and sucked in a deep breath. "I'm sure there are many. I'm tired. So, so tired. I hate this challenge. I've never liked climbing."

I had to agree.

"Let's go," Gregory said urgently, reaching down and plucking at my arm.

"I've never seen . . . man boobs on a strong, skinny dude," Wally said randomly, looking at the sky. "Weird."

I froze for one moment before hopping up and tugging on my shirt, making sure it didn't cling. "We all have our genetic issues," I mumbled, glancing over the edge at the wall. One of the first gargoyles we'd shut down had reanimated. It slashed at the girl closest to it, claws sliding across her chest. She jerked back, screaming, lost her hold, and fell end over end. The other gargoyles slowly came to life as two more people climbed closer. But they were like the golems—we'd passed their territory, and they didn't seem to notice us any longer.

"I snore," Wally said, getting to her feet. "I get it from my dad. My mother always complains. Genetics are a funny thing. So don't feel bad. Not like you can control it."

I didn't respond, figuring it was best not to engage in discussing my "man boobs."

Instead, I focused on where we were going next. A free-standing door stood at the corner of the massive dirt and stone covered space. Two slouching, clearly exhausted people from the other team I guessed, reached it. One pulled the door open. Light glowed within, but nothing took shape beyond it. After both people passed through, a jacketed arm reached out, grabbed the handle, and pulled the door shut.

"Either they didn't know to look for the treasure, or we're too late," I said, rubbing at my eyes. Damn it, it frustrated the hell out of me to come so close only to lose. I wasn't going to bother commenting on the lack of a visible room beyond the door. Or the disembodied arm. Clearly the situation was magical, and everyone would just roll their eyes at my discomfort.

"They didn't know. But Ethan does. The trinket is gold. I can feel it over that way." Gregory nodded toward Ethan, who stood kitty-corner to the door. "He figured out that he has to find something up here."

Pete took off running toward Ethan, and we stumbled after him, limbs heavy. We reached Ethan as he bent down and started digging through the dirt and rock at his feet.

Pete sprung at Ethan—and slammed into an invisible wall. He rolled backward, shaking his head, growling and spitting, claws slashing at the empty air.

A wide grin spread across Ethan's face as he turned to face us, protected in his magical bubble. He fisted his hand and stood. My heart sank as he peeled back his fingers, showing us what lay on his palm. A chunk of gold in a perfect square. Like a Rubik's Cube only without the moving pieces.

"Dang it," Wally said, deflating.

Ethan's eyes narrowed at us, cutting between me and Gregory. "You found the treasure at the last challenge, didn't you? That's why you stayed behind. You found it, but you didn't say anything."

We all shifted in the following silence.

Ethan nodded like that was answer enough. He dropped his square chunk of gold into his pocket before waving his wand, taking away the magical barrier. Rather than stow the wand, he pointed it at Pete to keep him at bay.

Pete gave one last hissing snarl, turned and lifted his tail at Ethan. A distinct roll of stink filled the air, aimed at Ethan. His face turned green as he shot forward, through the cloud of stench and toward the doorway.

"I won't forget," Ethan said through clenched teeth, "but we may still need each other. For now."

The rest of us followed him to the door as two individuals on opposite sides of the tower crawled up over the ledge. Both looked a lot . . . well, more goblin-like than Gregory. They had large eyes, small, gangly bodies and knobby, curved fingers.

Wally's voice dipped. "Keep your enemies close, and your friends closer."

"You have that saying wrong," I said.

The six of us stepped through the door and shut it behind us.

Hands banged on it—the goblins who'd followed us.

We stood in a nondescript white room, empty but for a stooped figure in a suit with a huge, pointed nose and large, globe-like eyes. Obviously another goblin. His expression didn't change as we passed, though he seemed to watch us longer than was prudent.

The only way to go was through an empty white corridor. Our footsteps echoed and none of us spoke. We reached another white room devoid of furnishing, art, or any identifying marks whatsoever. A padded room wouldn't have been so uncomfortable—at least the upholstery wouldn't have had such a bright, punishing gleam. Three doors stood side by side, not labeled.

"I hate this place," I said, feeling a strange urge to drift toward the door on my right.

"We have that much in common," Ethan said, marching toward the door I would've picked. "We're almost done. The last challenge will be the easiest."

"Oh really? Fantastic. I could use a break," Wally said, starting off after him.

Ethan grabbed the door handle with the confidence born of a leader—or of a cheater who knew where he was going. As we shuffled in after him, my mouth dropped open.

An enormous field stretched out as far as the eye could see filled with nothing but row upon row of hay stacks. Equal distance apart, the same size and height, there was no telling them apart, and once the door behind us closed and disappeared, there were no doorways out.

"I think I'd rather be back in the white room," I muttered, now glad to follow Ethan. I had a feeling a person could walk for an eternity in these fields, the landscape never changing, the bright though sunless sky never dulling, and never find a way out.

"I thought you were a farmer," Wally said. "You should be familiar with hay."

"Being familiar with hay is vastly different than . . . this." I shook my head as we wound through the rows.

Ethan pulled out his paper and tapped it with his wand. Blue lines slowly soaked into the page, forming into a map, which then rose up as a 3D configuration of the area around us, including Ethan. A miniature figure bent over an even smaller piece of paper, appeared within the 3D map.

"Wow," I said, stepping closer. On the map, another figure popped into existence, standing beside the first—me, I was guessing—and circled in red. A warning. Someone was too close and would know what he was doing. "Your source is thorough with the details."

Ethan turned, getting his bearings before setting out, the rest of us in tow like the little ducklings the troll had thought us. "My family employs only the best," he said, stalling occasionally when he needed a prompt from his paper. The thing was idiot proof.

"But surely some other high-powered family who lacks morals also has a good insider," I said, grabbing a piece of hay and rolling it between my fingers. It didn't feel quite right, a little silkier than what I was used to—not scratchy enough to be real.

"We employ the best, because we *are* the best," Ethan answered. "There are others with similar information, sure, but as you've seen, they can't cut it in the trials. They aren't good enough, even with the guiding hand." He paused for a moment. "And it isn't a moral issue. These trials are rigged. They are geared toward those with the right magic. That's unfair for everyone else. I'm simply . . . making it fair."

"No." I smiled and shook my head. "You're not evening the playing field for everyone, just for yourself. Nice try, though, with the whole justification speech."

"The trials are supposed to sort people into houses, and the big prizes are intended for the best of each house," Wally said, "No one is good at all five houses. Except for the Shadowkiller, but he doesn't count. He was an anomaly. Basically, by trying to win a prize in the houses you're weak in, Ethan, you're stealing while also confusing the selection process. You don't want to be put in the same category as the Shadowkiller."

"Bull," Ethan said, winding ever closer to the glowing spot on the map. "I'll be in the House of Wonder. Everyone in my family history has been in that house. We only marry within the house to keep the magical lines pure. I use a wand, for Christ's sake. Finding the gold is just a boon, and why should it only go to someone from a specific house? How is that fair? It should be fair game for everyone."

"It is," Wally replied. "We work in groups so we can pool the strength of all the houses. We would not have done this well in this challenge without Gregory's help."

Ethan huffed, and I had the feeling he was rolling his eyes. "How many intact groups made it to the top of that tower?"

"One," Orin said. "And it is rather miraculous that we should have done so. The strategy of working in diversified groups has largely failed across magical society. Of course, that is why the trials are set up this way, to encourage groupings like ours."

"See?" Wally put her finger in the air in triumph. "Our success is what makes this setup fair."

"Except we're currently being led by a cheater because we don't know which way to go," I reminded them. "We're all cheating at this point. Which should probably make me feel bad."

Uncomfortably, it didn't. I didn't want to lose any more than Ethan did.

"I know the way," Gregory said quietly.

"What's that?" I asked, half turning back to look.

"We're getting closer. It's another gemstone. Sapphire, I think. I can feel it. I'd be able to find it. The proverbial needle in the haystack. That's the game here."

"There you go. See?" Ethan walked three-fourths of the way around a haystack before cutting between two others. "Not cheating. We could be using the goblin's cursed talents to win."

"Talking about morals with someone that has none is a journey of dead ends," Wally said and then sighed.

"Here." Ethan stopped in front of a haystack like any other. The 3D person projected above the paper stood next to the glowing treasure spot.

"No." I pointed to the haystack to his right. "There. Your figure on the map is next to it, not in front of it."

Gregory didn't wait for Ethan to figure it out. He circled the haystack, his focus totally engaged on the task at hand, and then stopped to face the pile. He ran his hand down the angled sides, barely touching the hay. A few seconds later, about halfway down the pile, he slowly pushed his fingers through the hay. His eyes were half closed, his head angled—he was feeling for the sapphire with his magic.

Ethan folded up the paper and tucked it back into his pocket.

"No, no." I pointed at it. "We need that to get back out of here."

He rolled his eyes but didn't comment. Clearly, I was incorrect.

Gregory leaned farther in, up to his elbow. Further still, nearly to his shoulder now. He closed his eyes fully and drew in deep breaths.

"No wonder the goblins have all the money," Wally said softly. "They can just wander around and collect it like in a video game."

"Precious gemstones don't just lie around in the world in perfect, ready-to-sell pieces," Orin said. "They are usually stripes in lesser rocks. They must be dug out, broken apart, harvested. Gold, as well, is not just found—there is more work to it."

Wally shrugged. "Same difference."

A muscle in Gregory's arm jumped, and he pulled back, faster now. Hand out of the haystack, he opened it. A perfect square sapphire, the same size and shape as both the ruby and Ethan's gold square.

"It's very pretty," I gushed as it caught the light. Ethan gave me a funny look.

Crap. Guys clearly didn't gush about gems. Or if they did, not in that way.

I had opened my mouth to fix the situation when the scene around us shivered, melting away. Haystacks wobbled, then spun through the air, sending straw whipping around us, like we were at the heart of a tornado.

I reached out and gripped Wally to steady myself, my stomach flipping with dizziness. Before I could adjust, smoke rose from below our feet and the spinning scene faded. The illusion dimmed. Darkness rushed in, muting our surroundings until a new scene presented itself.

Two or three torches were attached to each of the dark gray walls around us, which shimmered and danced as though wet. The room was triangular. In front of us, behind a heavy metal gate, sat a robust chest decked out in precious gems, overflowing with gold coins that sparkled in the glow of the room. This haul was definitely bigger than the last one—enough riches to buy my entire family a whole new life. Several lives maybe.

Staring at all that wealth, I let a breath slowly tumble out of my mouth. They were just giving it away. All these trials—this whole organization—clearly had more money than they knew what to do with.

"We just need to fit the pieces where they go," Ethan said, looking down at his square chunk of gold. "Put all the trinkets on the table so we can figure this out."

The table in front of us hadn't commanded my attention as much as the heap of gold behind it, but it was triangular, same as the room we stood in. An odd shape to say the least. There were three square openings embedded in it—one for each of the treasures.

Gregory hesitated, not that I blamed him. Arranging the pieces on the table would mean putting them within striking distance of Ethan.

"There's nowhere to go," I said, motioning for Gregory to comply. "We'll finish this one up together. We have to, or we won't be finishing it at all."

With all the square pieces on the table, Ethan put his hand over his pocket. He didn't pull out his paper, however, and after catching his eyes flicking around us, I knew why. He didn't want to get caught. This room was probably closely monitored, and while some cheating was allowed, if not condoned, it wouldn't be accepted here, not when there was so much money on the table.

"Puzzles. I can do a puzzle." I leaned forward, seeing each piece as it stood alone. All square, all cut exactly the same. I moved the pieces around, but each would fit into any of the openings on the table.

I frowned, trying to figure it out. I knew gold was a softer metal, and the two gemstones would be a fair bit harder, but that's about all I could come up with from my limited geology instruction in school. I thought of them as a whole. Given that there were only three of them, there were only six possible permutations. But which were they looking for?

I knew without asking that whatever I entered into the squares in the table would be our final answer. We'd need to sort this out before placing the stones.

"This wall is inlaid with rubies," Gregory said softly, turning to the wall on his right.

I reached over and ran my hand over it, feeling tiny little bumps against my palm, the source of the shimmering. A strange sensation washed over me, sliding along my skin before soaking down into me. Suddenly, the wall took on a different feel, impossible to describe, slight but persistent. Back at the table, the same feeling, though much more potent, throbbed along my skin.

The ruby. I was feeling the gem. Just like Gregory could.

I could *feel* the other squares we'd gathered too.

How the hell?

I didn't stop to question the how. I could mull over it later when I no longer needed to focus.

"Can you feel sapphires in one of the other walls, Gregory?" I asked.

He didn't even need to stop and consider it. "The wall behind us," he said, his ability to feel gems much stronger than my borrowed ability.

"Right, right," I said, my hands working, already connecting the dots. "And gold is to the left of us." The triangular room was set up just like the table.

Just. Like. The. Table.

I arranged the gems and gold beside the openings in the table, feeling the satisfying click as they fit together. I pointed at the red square "Ruby"—then the wall—"wall inlaid with rubies. Sapphire, wall inlaid with sapphires. Gold . . . with gold."

"So easy," Ethan murmured.

"Only easy for those who can feel it," I said, running the scenario through in my mind to make double sure I was right. "You wouldn't know gems made these walls shimmer. Even if you figured it out, there's no color to the shine. You would have gotten the gold right, sure, but you'd only have a fifty-fifty chance of choosing the gems correctly."

"I'm not sure I would've put two and two together," Gregory said, rubbing his nose. "I mean, it *is* easy now that I know, but . . . it hadn't occurred to me that the walls would be the hint."

"And that is why they want magical factions to work together. You see?" Wally braced her fists against her hips and nodded.

"I'm going with this, unless there's an argument . . ." I let the statement linger for a moment, and when I didn't get pushback, delicately placed the stones in the corresponding openings on the triangular table.

The squares sank into the stone table, and a flash of light made me stagger backward. The wall to our right glittered red. Blue twinkled behind us. The gold shimmered, and for a moment I thought it would all disappear just like the haystacks, but the metal gate shimmied upward instead.

We'd done it. We'd won!

As if on cue, Ethan stepped forward with his chest puffed out, and I knew he would try to claim the victory for himself, just like last time.

CHAPTER 7

N ot this time," I ground out before rushing forward and grabbing Ethan. There was no way he was going to claim this victory as his own. I flung him back with all my strength. His legs caught the edge of the table, which swept them out from under him. He dove, head first, onto the ground, skidding to a stop on his face. That was going to leave a mark.

Pete snarled and hissed before nipping Gregory's heels, clearly in agreement with what I was trying to do. Gregory shrieked and danced forward as a line of light traced a shape in the far wall behind the gold, outlining a hidden door

"It wasn't my win," Gregory said as the door slowly swung open, revealing a short, stooped figure with large, circular glasses over crazy big eyeballs.

"We did it together," Wally said, "especially you and Wild, except he's not supposed to win, since the Sandman and his really hot sidekick said so, so you need to be the frontman. You were the second most valuable player, not including the cheater, cheater, pumpkin eater."

"Shut up about the cheating," I grumbled through the side of my mouth as I fell back behind Wally and next to Orin.

Two other people, thin and slightly taller, flanked the lead figure as they all walked slowly through the door. The lead figure's large, slightly glassy brown eyes took us all in, shrewd and calculating. His gaze paused on me for a fraction of a second longer than the others, before flicking to Ethan getting up from the floor.

Busted.

Whatever. Knocking someone over wouldn't draw the same notice as claiming an enormous stack of gold from someone else's house.

"I am impressed," the lead figure said, stepping forward on his spindly legs. His clothes had to be made special—not even a master tailor could transform a regular suit to fit this creature's oddly shaped body with the long, swinging arms, and bowed legs. Was this what Gregory would eventually morph into? "No winner in our history has ever stood before us with their group intact, let alone with so many of you. You do realize that larger groups have a harder time going through? We rarely, if ever, see six team members."

Wally preened, and Pete looked up at me, chittering.

I'd really like to change back into my human form, but this would be an awkward time to stand around naked.

I suppressed a grin as Ethan threw back his wide shoulders and sauntered to the front of the group with Gregory. He clapped his hand on Gregory's shoulder, making the smaller guy jump.

"Gregory was integral to helping me find the hidden gemstones and solve the final puzzle. He really did our group proud."

Though he didn't say it outright, it was clear from Ethan's tone and manner that he was claiming the leadership role. He was magnanimously patting Gregory on the back for his role, while at the same time calling him a spoke in the wheel turned by Ethan.

I ground my teeth, and Pete growled.

Wally didn't seem troubled. "Yes, without Gregory, none of us would've gotten up that wall," she said. "Ethan had the right idea. I should've climbed straight up, away from the danger, like he did. It would've saved my arms. Gregory handled the danger like a pro. I believe he did his house rather proud."

I couldn't suppress a smile at Wally's less-than-subtle jab at Ethan. Pete's growl cut off and turned into a funny little snicker.

The authorities came to a stop behind the gold. No one else rushed in to congratulate us like they had in the last trial.

"We certainly saw some great leadership in this trial," the lead figure said, though he didn't look at any one person when he said it. "But you have claimed champion of the trial as a group, and therefore, the proceeds will be divided accordingly."

"Oh yes, of course," Ethan said, all ease and bravado. "It was a group win. That's the right thing to do."

The lead figure stared at Ethan silently for a moment. "Do any of you need healing?"

"I'll live," I said quickly, putting a hand to my throbbing arm where the gargoyle had slashed me. Maybe I could go to the healers later. Right now, I didn't want to chance a meeting with Sideburns and his lying jackass of a sidekick. I didn't want to upset Wally, who thought he was dreamy, when I had to rear-range Mr. Tall Drink of Water's face. "I'll just head back."

Through the door and beyond another of those strange, non-descript, white rooms, we found ourselves in a small, closed-in corridor that angled upward. At the end, the circular metal han-dle clunked after a quarter turn. The metal door swung inward.

"How the hell are we at ground level?" I asked as my mind dizzied again. "We just spent the last few minutes walking up a hill."

"Magic," Wally said as Ethan veered left, toward the back of the massive mansion hunkering in the distance. Shapes dotted the way, idly walking and occasionally limping. "That's why we're so close, too. We don't need the bus to bring us back."

Ethan didn't veer off to the portables or the healer tents. Instead, he kept on straight, unperturbed by the fact that we'd popped out of the ground like daisies. His destination appeared to be one of the grand, well-lit rear entrances of the mansion.

"Where are we going?" I asked, picking up speed to close the distance between Ethan and the group.

"You've lost your mind if you think I am going to stay in that *hovel* for another night." Ethan didn't notice the limpid, doe-eyed looks darted at him by a couple of girls. Nor did he notice a group of three guys puff up their chests and attempt to look important as he passed. The whole campus clearly knew Ethan by sight, and they were all trying to get into his good graces.

The whole thing irritated me. Ethan was the last person I wanted on my team.

"We don't get to choose where we stay." I followed him closely as we neared the back entrance, not sure if I should just break away now, maybe circle back to the healers, or see where this was going.

"*You* don't get to choose where we stay," he said, yanking the door open and shoving past someone trying to make their way out. He didn't apologize and the skinny boy with thick-rimmed glasses didn't seem to expect him to.

"I'd go with it," Wally whispered. "I've heard the portables aren't very nice. I got lucky and slipped into the twenty percent who get to stay in the mansion. I'd use his connections on this one."

Wally did have a point. The high, arched ceiling in the foyer stretched up to dizzying height, its gothic design allowing us to see all the way to the top of the building. The dark brown hardwood floor, polished to a high shine, stretched out before us, climbing up the large staircases we passed, of which there were many, and lining the balconies of the four floors above us. Huge paintings in gilded frames adorned the walls. The place was absolutely gorgeous, and just being in it gave me a soft, comfortable feeling.

The smell of something cooking floated on the air and my belly grumbled, reminding me that we hadn't even had breakfast yet.

Every so often, a crest with a strange symbol etched into metal took up wall space. One we passed gave me a shiver of recognition. The Web of Wyrd.

A series of three triangles interlocked.

A giant, multi-branched tree held within a circle.

A pair of back-to-back ravens, their heads tipped toward one another and holding a bone between them.

Finally, what looked like an unfinished figure eight, the ends of it curling in on itself in tiny flourishes.

My best guess was that the crests were the house symbols. Five houses, five crests.

The Web of Wyrd was the only one I knew by name.

I dragged my eyes away from the crests as Ethan hooked a left around an ornate banister and started up a wide staircase with a strip of fake gold on each stair.

I slowed and looked a little closer.

No, not fake gold. This was real.

"How much money does this school have?" I asked in wonder, lagging behind everyone else to stare.

"This place isn't just used for the Culling Trials," Wally whispered as we reached the landing and turned onto the next flight of stairs, curving up to the third floor. "The Culling Trials are only once a year for a week. Otherwise it's a training facility for the elite. It's like The Farm for the CIA. They're the very best students from the various academies. That's why there are portables for half the students—a lot of these rooms are taken. Only those that have graduated left an empty room."

"So . . . the elite are still here?" I asked as we hit the third staircase. "I haven't seen any of them."

"They get a couple weeks furlough," Gregory said, "but their stuff's still in their rooms. Which means someone has to be kicked out for us to get a room in here."

"It'll be others in the Culling Trials," Wally said as we reached the top of the first flight of stairs. After fighting a troll, climbing a tower, and wandering a field of magic haystacks, I was spent even with just one set of stairs. "No way are they kicking out the magical elite. If anyone is going to go, it'll be the dumb kids."

"That'll make us insanely popular," I stepped aside so Pete could file in. Ethan hit the last landing and headed down a grand hallway lined with an exquisitely designed rug.

"It will, actually. Anyone hanging out with Ethan gets preferential treatment," Wally said. "We'll be noticed wherever we go."

I chewed my lip, following Ethan to the last door in the corridor, painted red with a shining gold "1" affixed to the surface. Being noticed was the last thing I needed.

I shouldn't be in my animal form in here, I heard reverberate through my skull. *Naked would still be worse, right?*

If he didn't know, I certainly wouldn't, so I just shrugged.

Ethan reached the door and knocked twice. The sound, a great, booming noise, ricocheted off the walls and sank into the room beyond before echoing back to us. The effect explained the lack of door knockers.

The handle turned and the door swung open, revealing a burley looking man with a grim set to his mouth, shortly cropped brown hair, and a shiny black suit.

"Yes?" the man said in a deep baritone.

"Ethan Helix to see Director Frost. She should be expecting me."

"Yes. Of course." The man glanced behind Ethan, his gaze falling on each of us in turn. When it lingered on me, I felt as though I'd been put on a massive scale, each of my attributes weighed and measured. He stepped back, his gaze on Pete. "I will get you some sweats, shifter."

"There you go," I told him quietly as I followed the others into the large and plush waiting room. A few full bookshelves lined the back wall. To our right sat two empty overstuffed chairs. Next to them was a brown leather couch with a cat sitting on one of the cushions, its tail curled around its body, eyes at half-mast, watching us walk in like some sort of disapproving supervisor. "You're all set."

"Have a seat. She'll be with you in a moment," the man said, gesturing at the furniture.

"Oh look." Wally pulled out a book in the bookcase. "The latest Jack Reacher novel. I just love fantasy."

"That's a thriller," Orin said, standing in the corner with his hands at his sides and his face blank. The guy looked like he was at a funeral wherever he went.

Wally laughed, taking it to the couch. She gave the watchful cat plenty of space. "However you dress it up, it's still fantasy."

The tight-laced guy returned with a neat stack of folded sweats. He handed them off before directing Pete to the restroom where he could change, in both forms of the word. To the rest of us, he said, "Follow me. She'll see you now."

He led us down a small hallway ending in what looked like a reception area. A large black desk faced four chairs. A plant stood stationary in one corner, and the plant opposite it moved in a strange breeze I didn't feel. Next to the desk a door stood open, leading into a much larger office, full of deep oranges, yellows, and pinks, as if a sunset had been poured into the room.

"Ready?" Wally asked, plucking at my sleeve.

The man stood beside a desk, his dark eyes rooted to my face. I had the distinct feeling he didn't like me. But no warning blared along my skin, so I'd leave it alone for now.

"Yup." I scurried in past him, uncomfortable and not sure why, until I remembered I was supposed to be a guy, and they probably didn't scurry. A moment later, however, my fears were put to rest as Pete scurried in behind me.

"Madam Director," Ethan said, standing in front of a massive oak desk with two computer monitors on one side, and one of those padded calendar desk toppers on the other. Between them was a solid black box, like a jewelry box. The top of it had been shined to a perfect lustre. Something in me itched to flip it open and see what was inside.

A full-sized couch faced the desk with other chairs positioned in clusters around the room.

A petite woman in her late seventies stood behind the desk, a fitted suit hugging her small frame, thick glasses mostly obscuring her smoky gray eyes with pronounced crow's feet, and short-cropped gray hair in a style not unlike her assistant's. Aged, but aged well, she was calm, her demeanor one of faint amusement. The sensation of mirth was there and gone before I could be sure of what I'd sensed.

"Mr. Helix, how can I help you?" she asked tersely. If I didn't know better, I'd think she wasn't overly thrilled with Ethan. Clearly, she had more sense than the others if she recognized what a pain in the butt he was.

"My father should've touched base with you by now regarding our poor accommodations," he said without embarrassment. Boy, had we grown up differently.

The director's lips pursed, and her eyebrows lowered behind her large glasses. "Yes, he did. I do so apologize for the previous accommodations, Mr. Helix," she drawled, her tone so dry, a spark would light it on fire. "I would love to make your stay with us as comfortable as possible. I have taken the liberty of swapping your portable for one of our rooms within the manor. I merely had to displace other young people to do so. I'm sure they won't be put out at all. Hopefully that will be to your liking?"

"That will be fine, thank you," Ethan said matter-of-factly. He was ignoring her sarcastic tone with great aplomb.

"Fantastic." The director turned away to her monitors. "If there is anything else, just have your father let me know, and I'll do everything in my power to assist you. Or you can contact Adam here, and he will always do his best to fit you into my schedule. In the meantime, he'll show you to your room."

"Yes, perfect," Ethan said, still missing the overtones of sarcasm.

A grin worked up my face as I turned and followed Ethan out of the office. "That was some serious shade she was throwing," I whispered to Wally.

"It was embarrassing," Pete said softly, huddled next to me in sweats much too large.

"If you want what your station in life has promised, you must ask for it," Orin said loftily. "Those at your level will expect it. The rest don't matter, nor does what they think of you."

"Wow. You sure know your way around being a dickhead," I said. Wally laughed.

"I am a predator," Orin returned. "I have a fondness for those who think they are better than me. I will one day enjoy waking them up to the realization that they are not at the top of the food chain."

Ethan's back stiffened.

The memory of Orin in the shower, talking about the vein in my neck, dried up all the spit in my mouth. I really hoped I didn't end up on his bad side. I didn't want to have to fight him off. If his current speed was any indication of what was to come for him, I knew I'd never beat a full-fledged vampire.

On the second floor, way in the back near a rear stairwell that would be really handy for sneaking in and out without being seen, the director's assistant—Adam—stopped next to a door numbered 245. He didn't gesture or make any sound, just waited expectantly for us to disappear from his life.

"Right then. Here we go." I shooed everyone toward the door.

"Not her," the assistant said, looking directly at me.

My blood ran cold and a warning crept up my spine. My cover was about to be blown sky high.

CHAPTER 8

The group of us stood there on the second floor, staring at Adam—the director's assistant—as he stared right back at us. And the only thing I could think was that I was out—he knew I was a girl. I took a breath to defend myself, to beg if I had to.

"This floor is boys only," the man continued, his hard gaze cutting right through me. "Girls may visit, but they may not stay. If a girl is caught in a boy's room after dark, and vice versa, they will be kicked out of the program. Do you understand?"

"Pretty outdated," Wally said, stepping around me. "I mean, it's not like we're underage or anything. I'm eighteen. I can bang a whole room full of guys, and it's perfectly legal. Although, I have to own that more than half of the hopeful students in the Culling Trials have not yet turned eighteen. I suppose that could be an issue. I mean, it's not like I would I.D. everyone in the room before I—"

"Oh my God, Wally, stop," I said with a red face I couldn't help. Did she have any idea what she was even saying?

She blinked at me for a moment, shrugged, and then waved goodbye. "All right, then. See ya. I'll check back in tomorrow."

"That chick is seriously off," Ethan said as he disappeared into the room. Orin drifted in after him, much too close, with Gregory following at a normal distance.

Pete took a step toward the door and grabbed my arm. "Come on, buddy. Let's head in with the *rest of the guys*."

Adam's dark gaze rooted me to the spot, daring me to lie. But given he hadn't said anything direct thus far, I knew he wouldn't. Maybe not until he had proof, at any rate. Proof I'd make sure he didn't get.

"Yeah, sure," I said, making my tone as masculine as possible, and slipped over the door's threshold.

"Thanks again," Pete said, pushing the door closed on a still-staring Adam. With the door shut, he breathed a sigh of relief. "Holy cats. That guy is intense."

Unlike the hovel from the night before, this room was spacious with six separate beds, each wrapped in a canopy that could be closed for privacy. Each bed had its own nightstand, plus a trunk situated at the foot. I had a sneaking suspicion that we'd have perfectly fitting sweats in whichever setup we chose. A door between two of the beds led to a bathroom, and I barely stopped a sigh of relief when I realized it was a normal bathroom, with one toilet, no urinal, and one shower with a curtain. This setup would be *much* easier to navigate.

Without warning, Ethan rushed at me, grabbing my shirt at the chest, and slammed me against the wall. Without thinking, I lashed out, clipping his jaw with my right fist, following it up with a slam of my left fist into his stomach.

The breath gushed out of him and he bent double, ripping the neck of my shirt and tearing it down my side at the shoulder. He pushed forward, his thick shoulder hitting me center mass. I curled in on myself with the shock of pain before pushing through it. I drove three successive punches into his ribs, fast and furious, before angling my body, stepping into him, and throwing him over my hip, a move I'd learned from Rory.

Ethan grunted as his back hit the ground. I rammed a knee down on top of him, popped up, kicked his flailing hands out of the way, and rammed my knee down again, pounding his chest. That spot hurt, I knew from previous experience.

"Damn you," he shouted, reaching for his wand. I kicked, connecting with his wrist, which sent his hand flying above his head.

"Dude, sh-*he's* a Shade, you're physically outmatched," Pete hollered, dancing around us with his hands out. I couldn't tell if it was nervousness, a desire to join in, or he just didn't know how to break up a fight. "Just let it go, man."

Ethan shoved at my leg as I was coming down a third time, knocking my body to the side. I went with it, bringing my elbow down instead and smacking him across the face. He thrust a knee up between my legs, and it hit my thighs and just barely my crotch—a dull pain at best.

"Low blow, dude," Pete shouted. "That is a low blow."

"He's a coward. What did you expect?" Orin casually commented from the corner. "He'll probably have daddy sue for damages."

I flattened my forearm against Ethan's jaw and pinned his arms to his sides with my knees, a move that had worked on my brother and Rory countless times—until Rory grew to the size of a horse and could buck me off, which wouldn't be a problem here. Ethan was big, but not as big as Rory. With his upper body secured, I paused, waiting to see if he would use his lower half.

"Get the hell off of me," Ethan spat, tense but immobile.

"Are you going to throw another punch?" I asked.

He didn't say anything, so I held my position.

"Silence means no, usually," Pete said out of the side of his mouth.

Guy speak. Oops.

I gave a last little shove and pushed up off of him. I backed away, pulling at my shirt to make sure it still mostly covered my chest, and picked the closest bed.

"What the hell did you do that for?" I asked, flipping open the trunk and snatching out a shirt at random. I needed something to fling over my shoulder to cover the strap of my sports bra.

Ethan's eyes narrowed before his gaze drifted down my body. "What the hell do you think? You shoved me down at the end of that trial. That was a dick move, Johnson. But you . . . you don't have a dick, do you?"

My stomach clenched, and I schooled my face into an incredulous expression. "And you have balls the size of raisins. You constantly skirt by the danger, didn't do a damn thing yourself, and you thought I was going to let you claim *our* victory? You've lost your mind."

"If someone kneed me in the balls, I would've reacted," Ethan said with a glint to his eyes. "And you're not wearing a wife beater, are you? No, the straps are too thick for that." A grin curled his lips and he took a slinky step toward me, like he'd regained the role as predator even after getting his ass handed to him.

"Man boobs, thick strap, no dick—just look at that face. Awfully pretty, aren't you, Johnson? *Awfully* pretty. I'd thought maybe you were just waiting for your balls to drop—you're a big kid for fifteen, though that's not unusual in the House of Shade. But you haven't got any balls at all. What are you, a failure from a past year? A has-been who wants another chance?" He laughed. "Weird, choosing a young guy's identity to steal, but whatever. Regardless, the jig is up. Say goodbye to your share of the gold."

Fear ran through me. Possible options rolled through my head. But killing him and hiding the body wouldn't work. Even if the school didn't care—and that director might not—I knew his daddy would. He clearly had the power to call for a widespread investigation. I wouldn't have a chance.

The best I could do was plead for mercy.

But before I could, Gregory stepped forward with a photo held high.

"You give her away, and I give you away, old lady lover," he said, and chucked the picture onto the floor.

It fluttered to the ground, landing picture-side up. Ethan knelt beside an older woman, her hands cradling his face as their lips pressed together for what the angle indicated had been a deep kiss.

"Oh man, that is quite an age gap," I said without meaning to, grimacing. "She's old enough to be your grandmother. I'd make a lewd joke, but quite frankly, I don't want the image it'll bring."

"Where the fu—" Ethan bent and snatched up the picture. "It was nothing." His face turned bright red. "It's not what it looks like."

"You know that," Gregory said in a dangerous hiss. "But will all your elitist buddies know that?"

"It's my nana," Ethan spat, his hands balled up. "It was her eightieth birthday. It's just a bad angle."

"It sure looks like a bad angle," I said, doing what I could to hold back a snort.

Ethan scoffed. "That photo is, *at best*, embarrassing. I'll get razzed about it for a minute, big deal." He huffed out a laugh. "There's not a chance you can make anything out of this. You're a nobody goblin with nothing. After the next few trials, maybe you'll be a nobody goblin who has been handed his hat. You can't take any prize money if you don't stay in the trials. If you leave, that's a larger share for me. And let me assure you . . . I can *make* you leave."

"He might be expendable," Orin said, suddenly in the bathroom doorway. I hadn't noticed him move. "But the girl is not."

Ethan startled, and I realized Orin had caught him by surprise too. Ethan backed up a pace so he could see everyone.

"Even cheating, you wouldn't have finished the trials thus far," Orin went on, his face slack and hands at his sides, showing no emotion. "Wild has used the assets at her disposal, including you, to make us win. She has played this group like a fiddle, making it stronger than the sum of its parts. *She* is what they are looking for when they hope magical factions will work together, not you. Without her, you will not win all five trials. With her . . . we all have a better chance." He shrugged, unconcerned. "It would be in your best interest to help her keep her secret, to help her stay to the shadows, where her kind belong."

I shifted in thankful anticipation. Even if he'd jumped the gun a couple of times—I didn't belong in the shadows; that was where weirdos lurked—that was a really great argument. Better even than the blackmail photo.

Ethan hesitated, a flicker of fear in his eyes. "What's it to you, vampire? Everyone knows you *creatures* don't play well with others. You certainly never did in school."

Orin's eyes fluttered to half-mast while still pinning Ethan. "I need to join a faction, and if we win all the trials, I'll likely be courted by the best. I will have my choice, an enviable position. It will set me up well."

Ethan stared at Orin for a moment, and he was probably wondering what I was—if Orin felt that way, why had he been so blasé about the trials thus far? Still, the argument Orin had made for me stood.

"The vampires will eat you for lunch when you go through their house," Pete said, edging closer. "They're not fond of outsiders cheating in their domain, and trust me, they'll know. You'll need Orin, and he won't give you the time of day without Wild. And me. We haven't done my house trials yet, either. You don't stand a chance without me. Not a chance. Think the unicorns they bring in will be the docile creatures you've practiced on? They won't be."

I felt my mouth drop open, and suddenly I couldn't focus on anything beyond what Pete had just said. "Unicorns?" I turned toward him with palms out. "Unicorns are real?" Glee and stress made me giddy, and I had to fight to keep myself from clapping my hands together. "Oh my God, are you serious? Do we get to ride unicorns?"

"In the wild, they are ferocious beasts," Gregory said with distaste. "Even the docile ones have intense attitude."

I threw up my hands. "Do you honestly think I care? *Unicorns*, man!"

"If no one knew you were a girl before, you would've just outed yourself," Orin said, his voice dry.

Ethan took a step back, the wheels in his head nearly visible as they cranked and worked over the problem at hand. He knew Pete and Orin were right. Maybe he could have made it through the Shade trial by himself, but without Gregory, no way would he have gotten the gold in the last trial. He wouldn't have been able to find those gems, even with his maps and instructions.

"Face it, bro," I said mockingly, in a deeper voice, "you need us. All of us, the dick-less ones included."

He huffed out a breath, shaking his head, and pushed past me. He took the bed next to the window looking out at the rear grounds. The shoddy portables squatted across the large expanse of lawn, one of them housing a group of five liable to be in a very bad mood.

Thanks for the accommodations, guys.

"One wrong step, Johnson," Ethan said, pushing open his trunk and rooting around. "One wrong step . . ."

"And what?" I grinned with all the bravado I had left, trying to ignore the warning crawling up my spine. "You'll get rid of me and then start losing? Daddy won't be pleased if his golden son doesn't come home with the prize."

He grabbed a set of clean clothes and crossed to the bathroom, clearly intending to take the first shower. No one stopped him.

"Thanks, guys," I said as I grabbed my own set of clean clothes. Just like I'd figured, they were the right size. "I did not love the idea of begging for mercy from that guy."

"He's not capable of mercy," Pete said, collapsing onto his chosen bed on the other side of the bathroom. "That was bred out of his family generations ago."

I knew he was right, but I still would've tried. I had a way with words—most of my family did—I would've ridden that bicycle as hard as I could.

"How'd you get that picture?" I asked Gregory, who was looking out the window at the grounds. People milled around idly, probably to get away from their group mates. I could relate.

He didn't glance back. "Found the place he hides his phone and wallet. It wasn't hard. His magic is still rudimentary in many ways, and I've always had a gift for sniffing out secrets."

"You need to watch your back, Wild," Orin said, back in his corner. The guy was exceptionally weird. When he was older, he'd probably graduate to creepy. "Ethan won't like admitting that he needs someone. You're a threat, now."

Another mark on my head. Awesome.

"Oh shoot." Pete pushed up onto his elbows. "I probably am, too, then. Like you guys. Because we haven't done my trial . . ."

"You are not an alpha, so you are not a threat." Orin turned his attention to Gregory, ignoring Pete's sputtering. "Gregory is, though. A threat, I mean. He drew the notice of his house and took the glory today. They have their eye on him now."

"Yeah, but . . ." I scratched my nose. "It's not like Ethan wants the notice of that house."

"Ethan wants the notice of all houses, or else he wouldn't be his father's son." Orin took a small step back, and shadow draped across his face. *Exceptionally* weird. "You two need to watch your backs before someone sticks a knife in them."

CHAPTER 9

Sleep peeled away slowly, pulling me from a strange yet fantastic dream in which I was riding a sparkly unicorn within a herd of sparkly unicorns, running across the clouds and dodging massive spiked balls swinging at me.

It took me a moment to place what had stirred me. Everything seemed peaceful—stillness covered the room like a blanket, soft moonlight seeped through a crack in the curtains, and the only sound was soft, rhythmic breathing.

Then a prickle of warning ran down my spine.

Alertness chased away lingering sleep. My senses fired up, and I pushed up onto my elbows to take stock of the room. The lump that was Pete lay snugly within his blankets, curled up into a ball revealed by his open privacy curtains. Near the window, Ethan lay flat on his back, his face turned my way, his one visible eye closed. His privacy curtains were open, too, although they hadn't been when he'd gone to sleep.

Another warning fluttered my stomach, and I swung my legs over the edge of the mattress, bare feet on the cool hardwood floor. Orin lay on his back, too, his curtains open but his covers undisturbed. As if he weren't creepy enough, his alignment was that of a body in a coffin—arms tucked over his chest, legs pressed together, body straight.

I shook my head, peering into the other corner of the room at Gregory's setup. His curtains were still drawn. I tiptoed over, gritting my teeth against the cold floor on my bare feet. On the side of the bed facing the wall, his curtains had been pulled back. No head graced his pillow.

Darkness coated the open doorway of the bathroom, but on the off chance Gregory had dream-walked in to use the toilet, I peeked my head in and made a *psst* sound. "Girl needs to use the bathroom," I whispered. "Anyone in there?"

No slide of fabric or swish of movement answered me. I stepped farther in to make sure, relying on my better-than-average night vision. Shadows draped the interior, grays and blacks, and while I was pretty good in the dark, I wasn't nocturnal. I fumbled in and waved my arms around.

Nope, still empty.

Frowning, I backtracked and looked out the window at the empty expanse of grass, then the still portables beyond. Not a soul to be seen.

The alarm clock on Ethan's nightstand said eleven fifty-five, five minutes before curfew.

We'd learned of the curfew earlier, at the fabulous buffet dinner in the main cafeteria, a place all the trial-goers could now use. You could stay up as late as you wanted within your room—as long as you were respectful to your roommates—but you were forbidden to traverse the mansion or grounds after midnight, unless it was an emergency. To get caught would mean immediate expulsion from the trials.

The feeling of warning wiggled through my middle, demanding I take notice. But what could I do? I had no idea where

Gregory might've gone, and I couldn't risk getting caught wandering around.

Then again, I could always say I was worried about Gregory. His disappearance had to count as an emergency.

Of course, if he *was* sneaking around, he wouldn't appreciate me ratting him out.

I chewed on my bottom lip, antsy to get moving. To go looking. Something within me said he was in trouble. Orin's earlier words seemed to echo in my ears.

Watch your backs before someone sticks a knife in them.

I spun, my eyes narrowing. Ethan had connections. If he wanted someone to disappear, I had no doubt that he could make it happen, and Gregory had pissed him off with that photo. Not to mention the fact that Ethan's curtains were disturbed, too. Had he gotten up to do something—

No. Orin and Gregory could cross a floor without making a sound. Ethan thumped and tramped about, every move a call for attention. Stealth wasn't his style.

I put my boots on, telling myself I still hadn't decided. That maybe I was only putting them on for warmth. But by the time I finished, I knew better.

When it came down to it, Gregory had tried to save my ass. He'd fought to keep me in the game. It was my duty to do all I could to make sure he stayed in it too. I didn't know what his deal was, but I knew better than to ignore my gut. He was in trouble.

I rooted around in my trunk until I found a black sweat set, equipped with a black beanie. They were basically encouraging us to create mischief. Ready to go, I gently grabbed the door handle, being as quiet as I could.

"Where are you going?"

I jumped at Orin's whisper. He hadn't risen from his bed.

"Did you see Gregory leave?" I asked quietly. Pete shifted, rolled over, and sucked in a snore.

"Yes. About an hour ago. He probably couldn't sleep with your and Pete's chorus of snores."

I rolled my eyes. "Did he say where he was going?"

"No, because I didn't ask. I don't have that mothering gene you appear to have. But he did have his phone with him."

"I'm getting a bad feeling. It's almost curfew. This place seems pretty intolerant of wandering around when you're not supposed to."

"You're probably right in your bad feeling, but that was the chance he took. Now he is meat for the monsters."

I clutched the handle. "What monsters? What's out there?"

He chuckled softly and turned his gaze to the ceiling. "Just a figure of speech. They aren't monsters, they are simply highly-experienced authority figures who patrol the grounds looking for miscreants. I'm sure he's fine, though I doubt we'll ever see him again."

"These trials have turned you crazy," I said.

"No. I'm just now exposing this part of myself to you."

"Fabulous," I grumbled before taking a deep breath and turning the handle. Clearly Orin wasn't going to help, and though Pete would absolutely go with me, steadfast and loyal as he was, I didn't want to get him in trouble. No, I needed to do this alone or go down trying.

Sharp shadows sliced the hall. I drifted into it and hurried forward, using my intuition like I did when I went after predators on the farm. No sound of footsteps reached my ears, and no feeling of being watched tickled my shoulder blades. I was alone, for the moment.

I paused at the rear staircase, then turned to go down. Gregory wasn't a people person—if he'd wandered away on his own free will, I suspected he'd stayed to the sidelines.

Voices drifted through the air as I reached the first-floor landing. I slipped to the side into a pool of shadow.

"He's going to win every one, just you watch," a woman said, somewhere down the corridor. "His father told my father that he was confident Ethan would break the school record. All five hasn't been done before, you know."

"Yes, it has," another said, the voices not getting louder. They must've been stationary, somewhere down around the middle of the hall. "The Shadow Killer did it first, about twenty-five years ago."

The first sucked in a breath. "Don't talk about him here," she said, her volume dropping. "You don't know who could be listening."

"Who cares? I'm just stating a fact. He was the first ever to claim all five house prizes."

"That doesn't count. He's a . . . *you know*. Freak of nature. Ethan will be the first *normal* person to complete all five—"

I pushed off from the wall and hurried down the stairs. No way would Ethan be the first of anything. Somehow, I'd make sure of it.

The second my foot hit the ground floor, a huge *gong* reverberated through the floor and the walls, the sound pressurizing the air all around me. I paused, stricken, as the gong died away. Had I set off some alarm? The sound immediately repeated, and I realized it was issuing from the largest, loudest, most intense cuckoo clock I'd ever encountered. But no sooner had I realized that than I noticed a rhythmic tapping between each bong of the clock.

Footsteps.

I dashed behind a moving plant—though I wasn't sure what had moved it—before slipping behind a couple chairs farther down the way. The footsteps drew closer, the sound distinguishable over the deafening chimes in a way I didn't fully understand but greatly appreciated. The bottom half of a figure wearing tight black spandex came into view. A prominent hip suggested a female, and her wand stuck out from a cool leather holster with intricate stitching on it. Ethan needed to up his holster game.

The middle-aged woman who was clearly looking for delinquents started upstairs, footsteps increasing in speed. She'd probably heard the chatter of the other women in the hallway. Hopefully she had, at any rate.

As the lights around me dimmed, I popped out of my hiding place like a groundhog. Coast was clear, time to move.

Putting on speed and staying to the shadows, I turned a corner, intent on finding a back door. Loud shoe scuffling caught my attention as the hallway opened up. A muffled yell stopped my heart.

I slipped in beside a coat of arms that had clearly seen more polishing than an expensive car and peered around its arm.

Down the way, heading for a dimly lit double door leading out into the night, three figures dressed in dark clothes wrestled with a thin, bucking figure dressed in trial grays.

The expectation of danger flared up through me and adrenaline dumped into my bloodstream. I couldn't tell if that was Gregory from here, but whoever it was, they needed help.

Another muffled scream sent me out into the open.

"Help!" I yelled, sprinting down the corridor, hoping one of the security guards would hear me. If they cared so much about curfew, surely someone would be out enforcing it.

Two of the figures jerked, looking in my direction. One whipped out a wand as they neared the door. A blast of red zipped through the air, and I dove to the side, hitting one of those waving plants and sending it clattering across the floor.

"Wild! Help!"

My blood ran cold. I knew that voice. It was Gregory. They, whoever they were, were trying to take him.

"I'm coming," I yelled, climbing quickly to my feet and dodging another blast of magic.

Hands slapped the long metal handles on the double-door, shoving them down and the door open. Gregory tried to rip his arms free and spin away, but he was too small and they were too many. They held him fast and marshaled him through, aiming another blast at me.

I jumped to the side, kicked the plant, and plowed into an armchair. The door swung shut, but I was up and running again.

A slip of black caught my notice up the way, like a shape ducking out of sight. I wished with everything in me that I had a wand to brandish and a spell to cast. As it was, I'd have to hope it was a trick of my eye and not another bad guy trying to stay out of sight.

I jumped over a fallen vase that couldn't have been glass because it hadn't so much as cracked—or, well, magic—and shoved at the door handles. Crisp night air greeted me. The cluster of people moved away right, struggling behind a grouping of trees. Disturbed branches waved as they passed.

Another burst of speed, using the span of my long legs, and I was hot on their tail.

"Wild!" I heard Gregory yell from beyond the trees.

"I'm coming. Someone, help!" I called, really needing a little backup. This was an emergency if ever there was one. "Help me!"

I was nearing the trees when more footfalls registered right behind me. I didn't have time to look. I assumed someone had finally seen fit to answer me.

A solid, heavy mass hit me from behind. My front slammed into the ground and my face bounced off of the grass. The assailant landed on my left side, thankfully not center mass. Even still, the weight of solid muscle pushed the breath from my lungs. I gasped and threw an elbow back, hitting a hard slab of muscle. My attacker's arms tightened around my chest, and suddenly he was up, deadlifting me as though I weighed absolutely nothing and running me over to another grouping of pine trees.

"No . . . way," I ground out, and kicked behind me, trying to reach a shin. My foot sailed through dead air. I arched, punching back with my head, but barely managed to hit his shoulder. I spun and twisted, throwing my weight to loosen his grip. It did loosen, and I kicked again, but he'd already adjusted his hold, maneuvering me like a fussy baby, and handling me just as carefully.

His smell hit me like a Mack truck, even as branches *thwapped* my head. Warm spicy vanilla, pure comfort on a cold night.

My heart lodged in my throat, and I stilled for a moment. Sensing safety even though I'd just been tackled.

"Quiet now," Rory said urgently, his lips to the shell of my ear. "Really quiet. This is a bad night for you to be out snooping."

"But—"

His huge hand clamped down on my lips, muffling my protest.

"We have reason to suspect that the people being taken aren't being killed," he whispered, his hot breath dusting my face. "Your friend will be fine."

I peeled his fingers away from my mouth. "Don't you lie to me, Rory Wilson. What people?"

His sigh ruffled my hair. "Still able to see through my fibs, I see."

"It's not like it's hard. You're a horrible liar."

"You're the only one in the entire magical world who thinks so," he murmured before scooting away from me, farther against the tree.

I leaned forward to resume my chase, but Rory was faster than I remembered, and he'd always been damned fast. He grabbed me around the middle and hauled me back before crossing his legs over my lap. He hugged me tightly with his arms, keeping me put.

"Wild, help!" Gregory's shout was more distant, but the words were no less clear.

"Let. Go. Of. Me," I said through clenched teeth. "So help me God—"

"*Shhh!*"

The sound, his tone, and the sudden tension in his body dried up my protest. A moment later, warning flared through me again, this one so brightly hot and blinding that I couldn't think for wanting to run. Being stared down by a wolf, stalked by a mountain lion, kidnapped and tossed onto a magically enhanced chopper, even forced to endure the first two trials—nothing compared to the intense terror I felt in that moment.

Those other things had been dangerous, this was death incarnate. Someone was stalking us, and I knew this person was the reason I'd needed to take Billy's place. He—somehow I knew it was a man—was the reason Tommy had died.

Now he was coming for me.

CHAPTER 10

Below me the ground was hard and cold, and around me were Rory's arms—warm and solid, but neither of those helped ease the fear of knowing an assassin was only feet away and looking for me. "Easy, now," Rory whispered, his words barely riding his breath like he was talking to a spooked horse. "Easy, Belle."

Rory had made up his own nicknames for us when we were kids. I was Belle, the beautiful Maribel—his way of teasing me for the name I hated and for my appearance, which had never mattered to me. Tommy had been Tank, tough and stupid. Those names were Rory's way of claiming us and pushing everyone else away. Only those he trusted implicitly got nicknames. Only Tommy and me.

History was a hard thing to eradicate. Rory had always been my shield when I needed one, my fist when my own wasn't strong enough, and my tormentor when I wanted to get stronger. He'd been my rock through turbulent times, just as I'd been his. I'd always trusted him as hard as he'd trusted me.

No matter how angry I wanted to be, history made me trust him now.

I relaxed in his arms and let my head fall back against his shoulder, awaiting further instructions.

"Good," he said, just as softly. I could feel the fear in his words and knew instinctively that it wasn't fear for himself, but for me. "Now curl up your legs, real slow. Nice and quiet."

He lifted his legs to free mine, letting his thighs and calves hover in the air, a Pilates instructor's dream. I did as he said, closing my eyes in an attempt to regain focus. To ignore my pounding heart and my sweating palms. The desire to throw him off and sprint toward the mansion.

"Good, just like that." His volume dipped until I struggled to define the deep rumbling in his chest.

He lowered his legs back on top of mine.

"I'm not going to try to get away," I whispered, tilting my head back until my lips grazed the stubble along his jaw. He tensed, his hold on me tightening.

"You may have raw talent, but I have two years of training on you." His voice was strained. "I'll keep you alive. You'll get you dead."

"Taking vocabulary lessons from the Sandman, I see," I said beneath my breath, facing front again.

He must've heard because I felt his body shake with silent laughter.

The sense of warning outside the enclave of the tree sharpened, erasing any mirth until sweat coated my forehead. A presence lingered beyond the tree branches. I could feel it moving slowly out there. It was absolutely silent, which somehow made it worse. There were no footsteps this time. No swish of fabric. No padding of paws. No more cries from Gregory.

The night around us held its breath.

"Breathe deeply," Rory whispered. His arm shifted, a slow movement, and his fingertips touched down on the pulse in my neck, throbbing away as fast as a rabbit's feet. A strange little shock of electricity rolled through me, there and then gone. "Easy, Belle. Nice and easy. In just a moment, I'll need you to control your breathing. Feel my body. Do what I do."

I closed my eyes and sank into the strength and comfort surrounding me, feeling the slow rise and fall of Rory's hard chest. His smell tickled my senses, reminding me of home. Of safety, and a million close calls we'd braved together. His breaths were long and slow, as though we were napping in a meadow and not hunkered down next to some homicidal, magical maniac.

I can do this. Calm the eff down, you idiot!

The tiniest of sounds interrupted my focus. My eyes snapped open. I spotted it immediately.

Beyond the reach of the pine branches brushing the ground, movement cut through the static plane. A black boot stepped into view, polished to a high shine. Absolutely no sound accompanied the movement, though it was less than twenty feet away.

An explosion of fresh fear pounded through my body. No one had to tell me—the ultimate predator stood just outside our easily pregnable stronghold. His stealth was incredible, and I knew his strength and speed would match it.

House of Shade.

The thought bleeped into my mind, unbidden. *This* wasn't a student, either—this was a graduate, an expert. A killer.

And I knew without a shadow of a doubt he was stalking me.

My heart ramped up. My breathing turned shallow. I squeezed my eyes shut, trying to master the panic and return my focus to Rory's breathing, but only a fool turned a blind eye on a killer. I snapped my eyes open again in time to see the second shoe silently hit the grass.

There he paused. Listening.

Rory didn't whisper now, and thank God for that. He simply tapped my throbbing pulse and brushed his lips against the shell of my ear.

Memories washed over me, flushing away the worst of the panic. Hiding from shop owners. Causing trouble in the town green and then hiding in the shrubbery as the out-of-shape sheriff tramped around bellowing our names. Cowering in Rory's closet when his dad was on a drunken rampage. Rory had always shushed me in the same way: his lips against the shell of my ear, willing me, the younger, inexperienced troublemaker with a crooked angel's halo, not to give us away.

Shhhhh. Calm down.

I shut my eyes again, and this time I kept them shut, feeling the looseness of Rory's muscles around me. Energy coiled in his body, ready to be called into action, but he remained relaxed. I bet his heart rate was nice and slow. I doubted his shirt stuck to his back like mine did.

His lips pulled away a little in silent approval and I focused on my deep but silent breaths. Rory had always been good at stealth. At hiding and fighting. And, apparently, lying. He, too, was House of Shade. He clearly knew what he was up against, and if he thought he could hide us from it, I'd let him.

Sometimes history could save your life.

My eyes fluttered open as one of those black boots lifted off of the ground and turned in the air. It came back down softly. The other followed, until both toes were pointed right at us.

My breath caught. My heart ramped up again. Raw talent, my ass. I wasn't cut out for this.

Rory's fingers tapped the vein on my throat again. I wanted to slap his hand away. I wanted to grab the knife I'd stupidly left in the room. I wanted to throw a pinecone, *anything*.

The boots didn't move. They didn't even shift from side to side. How the hell could anyone stay so damn still? My whole body trembled.

Rory's fingers drummed on my neck, slower than my heartbeat. Strangely, with sweat pouring down my brow, I fell into that rhythm. Felt the comfort of it. When my heartrate eased, Rory's fingers slowed a little more. And a little more.

One of the boots lifted and it stepped to the side. The other followed. After a beat, the stalker side-stepped again. Then one more time. Down the way a little, the boots creased, the stalker probably bending forward. A moment later, they moved on.

Still Rory stayed firm, his arms not relenting, his fingers continuing their soft beat against my pulse point. Minutes passed, then more, until I lost track of time altogether. All I knew was his comfortable smell, reminding me of home, and the tap of his fingers against my throat.

Finally, after what felt like an eternity had passed, his chest rose in a deep, silent breath.

"We're good," he said, and his arms came away. His legs straightened and then bent off to the sides, leaving me ample room to crawl away. Cold rushed in to replace his warmth and I shivered.

"That was close, too close. You can't be wandering around alone. Not anywhere, and especially not at night, do you understand?"

His voice stayed even and calm, but I still heard the fear buried deep beneath the words. It set me on edge all over again. Which turned into an anger I couldn't control.

History also had a way of dredging up old wounds.

I pushed up onto my knees and spun to face him, flinging out my hand and slapping him across the face.

I hadn't meant to do that last bit.

His striking green eyes, the color just visible this close, surveyed me silently.

"I'm sorry for not telling you where I was going," he finally said.

I pulled back my hand to slap him again, but at the last moment he reached out and caught my wrist.

"You got the one, and I'll say I deserved it," he said, his eyes twinkling now. A little grin pulled at his full lips. "You have to earn the second."

Rory always could take me from spitting mad to giggling in a second, but I wrestled the smile off my face before it got very far. I couldn't let my guard down until I got to the bottom of this. I needed a real friend here. Someone I knew I could trust. I had to know if he was still that guy.

"Why didn't you tell me?" I asked

He shrugged with one broad shoulder, much more muscular than when I'd last seen him. "The letter I got said anyone I told would be in danger. My mom said that they were a brutal organization and were entirely serious. She went to the academy when she was younger, too, with your mom. When I got the envelope was the first I'd heard of it. I said she could have most of the money, and she was gone so fast out of the house I didn't hear much more about her past." He shrugged, and suddenly his mom taking off made all kinds of sense. "Your dad and Tank hadn't told you about the academy, and my mom said it was probably safer for you if you didn't know. I didn't want you to get hurt,

Belle, honest. I was thinking of you, otherwise I never would've lied about something like that."

My heart squished but we still had unfinished business.

"Fine. Then what about Tommy? You must've been there for that." Tears blinded me, the pain still so raw. It had never healed, not even with time. "You didn't come home for his funeral." The last was an accusation. A plea to help me forgive him.

He reached forward to touch my knee, then pulled back at the last moment. I couldn't have said why. He dropped both hands between his legs, hunching his shoulders, the picture of a man defeated.

"I wasn't there when Tank died, no. I should've been. I didn't want to go to this lousy school. Any lousy school. I'd always planned to stay in Texas with you guys and help out with the farm. But when the recruiter told me that Tank was here, I came for him. To watch his back. I figured, if I had this skill, I should use it to protect my family . . . my *real* family . . ." He lifted his hands for a moment, then dropped them again. "This magic I have, Tank had it, too. If he did, I knew you surely would. I figured you'd be here in no time, lighting the place up like you always do. But . . ." He shook his head. "Tank kept a lot to himself. I didn't know what kind of trouble was dogging his steps until it was too late. I came here to get his back, but when he needed me the most, I wasn't there. *I wasn't there.*" Those last three words were spoken so softly I wasn't sure he even knew he'd said them aloud.

His voice quavered and my heart broke for him. He blamed himself. Tommy had intentionally kept him in the dark, probably to keep him safe, but Rory still hated himself for not figuring it all out. His loyalty was like an oak: solid, strong, and with deep roots.

I'd been wrong to doubt him.

I lowered to sit cross-legged and let my knees rest on his shins.

He took a deep breath and let it out slowly. "I was at the funeral. Both of them—the one at school, and with you."

"No, you—"

"I'm a Shade, Maribel. My life exists in the shadows." His eyes pleaded with me. "I couldn't bear to look your old man in the eye and tell him that I let you guys down. That Tank got hit under my watch. It was bad enough to see you crying."

Despite what he'd said earlier, he let the slap land, and thankfully, he didn't ask why I'd thrown it. I didn't know myself. Raw grief ate at me, just as fresh as when I'd heard the news. I swiped my own tears away, but Rory let his fall, dripping from his strong jaw.

Needing more contact, I reached for him. He grabbed my wrist, pulling me into his arms, and held me tightly as he cried silently against my head. I clutched him, sharing his grief. Our grief.

"I miss him," I said, choking on a sob. "So much. Even more now that I'm here."

"I know." He pushed me back, holding me by the upper arms like I was a doll. "You won't be next. I've been training hard. I'm the best in my class. Nearly the best in my house. I'm ready this time, Belle. When he sends his minions, I'll take them out one by one. I was up tonight because I knew one of them was coming. I'd planned to go after him, but you had to get it in your fool head to go play cops and robbers."

Reality sobered me up and dried my eyes. "Gregory! Did the guy that came for us take Gregory?"

Rory stood and pulled me up beside him.

I really needed to lay down the law with this much stronger Rory, or I'd be manhandled the rest of my life.

Gesturing for me to follow him, he picked his way out of the tree before pausing at the tree line for a long moment. "No, the assassin doesn't care about your friend."

I choked on my spit. "Assassin?"

He started off toward the mansion, his black athletic sweats blending seamlessly with the shadows. A belt loaded with throwing knives circled his trim hips and a dagger was strapped to his broad back. A pouch of some sort hugged his ankle.

"Throwing stars," he said, catching me looking. "They're really common in my house—our house—and incredibly accurate. Anyway, a kid went missing at the first trial. No one can find her. Gregory is the second kid to disappear. Both outliers, so far. Loners. Easy pickings."

"Why?"

He shrugged. "Not my problem."

I frowned at him. Most things in life weren't Rory's problem, or so he'd always said—and yet he seemed to get tied up in them all the same.

"You're lying," I accused.

He huffed. "That's going to be annoying."

"Well, you should be used to it. I've been calling you out all your life, Rory Fenton Wilson."

He grimaced when I used his middle name, ushering me toward the mansion. "I know. I thought I'd gotten good enough to get past your natural lie detector test." He grinned down at me, and I could see the pride sparkling in his eyes. "You're going to be the best this damn house has ever seen, just you watch."

"Your cussing didn't get any better either."

"Not true. I'm much more colorful now. When I'm not worried about being slapped, that is. Anyway, listen. No one knows what's going on with the missing kids. But we're on it."

"We? Meaning you and Mr. Sunshine?"

Rory choked and then chuckled. "Yes. We think they're still alive, but we don't know why they're being taken. Or where they are being kept. I'm positive this is different than the assassin who's after you. You need to watch yourself, Belle—"

"After being a boy for a few days, I hate that nickname even more."

A grin tweaked his lips. "Like I said, you need to watch yourself, *Belle.*" He pulled the door to the mansion open, looking back at the grounds. Before he stepped out of the way for me to enter first, he placed his pointer finger against his lips. "I won't help you if you get caught."

He *could* help me but wouldn't. I frowned at him.

A smile lit up his face, clearly thinking that was a hilarious joke, before dying within the reality we now faced together.

"You felt the caliber of what you're up against. You cannot be caught alone. Ever. Do you hear what I am saying?" He lowered his gaze and leaned in, beating his stare into me. "Stay near the activity, always. Keep your classmates around. *Do not go running around after curfew.*"

I shook my head as he ushered me inside. "Why were they after Tank—I mean, Tommy—and now Billy? And who is the 'he' coming for me?"

His footfalls were deadly silent as he followed me down the hall. When I glanced back, his expression had completely closed down. It would take a crowbar to pry information out of him when he looked like this.

"Really?" I said quietly, stopping at the base of the stairs. The hush of my surroundings pressed down on me. "Still keeping secrets?"

Shadows draped across his high cheekbones and outlined his narrow nose, giving him a severe look. His eyes delved into me, piercing green. "Please trust me," he said softly. "And watch yourself. If there is one person in your family that can make it through this, that can *end* this, it's you. But the misconceptions about your magic won't fool him. He'll do everything he can to stop you. I know it in my blood. Trust no one, not even Rufus."

"Who's Rufus?" I asked.

"The Sandman. He's not what he seems. I can feel it. His position in the school is a cover. I haven't put all the pieces together yet, but you're in an incredible amount of danger from all sides, Belle. These aren't just trials for you. This isn't a game. This is life and death. Tank is proof."

Fear coursed through me, questions battered me, and all I could think to say was "His name is *Rufus*? No wonder he goes by Sandman."

Rory's grin was never far away, and I saw it now, even in the shadows. "Please take this seriously. Just this one thing—take this one thing seriously."

I started up the stairs, trying to get my questions in a row. My whole personality was a crowbar, and I would get my answers from Rory one way or another. He was talking about sides, but I didn't even know the players. He was talking about making it through *this*, but he obviously didn't mean the trials. And for the love of all that was holy, who was this *he*? What misconception could there be about my magic? Even saying *my magic* made my head spin.

"Don't get caught."

I glanced back to see what he was talking about now, and empty air greeted me.

My stomach flipped, and I stumbled to a stop.

It wasn't the speed with which he'd disappeared, which was beyond impressive. It was the speed . . . while silent. Moving that quietly should have made some noise. A scuff of his heavy boots. A swish of fabric. Something.

The House of Shade had clearly boosted Rory's natural attributes. He was broader, faster, stronger, and had unreal stealth. The boy had been sculpted into a man who excelled at his craft after just two years of training. And right now, he was showing off.

I let a smile bud.

I'll be better.

A little competition was good for the soul.

CHAPTER 11

Why don't you just admit it?" Pete said with spite in his voice as our crew climbed the stairs after breakfast.

I'd broken the news about Gregory to everyone this morning. Well, everyone except Orin, who I'd told last night, and who I was convinced never slept. The news hadn't set well with Pete. Ethan didn't seem to care overmuch, which only made Pete angrier.

"Admit what?" Ethan said.

"You ordered a hit on Gregory," Pete replied. "You threatened him. We all heard you. You hated him."

"If I'd wanted him gone, I would've gotten him expelled, genius. Hitmen and kidnappers cost money. Framing someone is free and much easier."

"He's got you there," Orin said.

This discussion had been going on some time, and my mind drifted back to my near miss with the assassin. In the moment, I'd been incapable of anything but fear, but it had struck me after the fact that Rory and I should have been in plain sight of my stalker. Or as good as . . . Where else would we have gone but the trees? The guy had basically stopped right next to us too. He'd even turned our way! But then . . . nothing. He'd moved on as soon as my pulse had slowed. He hadn't even stooped to peer into the shadows. It was like he'd been feeling out his prey—me—and lost the trail as soon as my panic faded. Almost as if Rory had somehow shielded our whereabouts.

"I know it was you," Pete grumbled, cresting the stairs and turning toward our rooms.

"Awesome. Let me know how that works out for you trying to pin something on me that I didn't do," Ethan said sarcastically, pulling me out of the residual tremors of fear from the night before.

Wally waited in front of our room, staring at the ceiling as if she could see right through it.

"She's like a bad smell," Ethan said as he brushed by her and opened the door.

"Hello, everyone. Ready to get going?" Wally said, as chipper as I'd seen her. "Nicer room, huh? Where's Gregory? I didn't see him at breakfast."

"I'm surprised I didn't see you at breakfast," Ethan said dryly, stopping by his bed and reaching for a note pinned to his pillow. A quick look around said we all had one, except Gregory.

"Oh, I thought it prudent to eat with my roommates like we're supposed to." Wally shadowed me to my bed. "You know, to ease the sting of leaving them high and dry for the trials. They could use my help."

"Are you serious?" Ethan read the note.

"Not again," Pete groaned. "I'm tired. When do we get a day off?"

I picked up my copy of the note.

You are hereby summoned. Your next trial awaits. You have one hours.

"Number one, there is a typo," I said blandly, not able to summon up the effort to feel outraged. "Number two, there's no time stamp. How are we supposed to know when the hour is up?"

My watch vibrated, and I glanced down at it. The face didn't give me the actual time, but a countdown that said we had fifty minutes and thirteen seconds left. Awesome.

"You guys should've taken a trip to the healer for more energy." Wally's mouth stretched with a smile. "I feel great. Excited, even. Which trial do you guys want to do next? By the way, where's Gregory? You didn't answer me."

"House of Claw," Ethan said, digging through his trunk. He pulled out wads of sweats and threw them onto the ground. His movements turned frantic, crazed almost, until he stood up so fast, I wondered how he didn't stagger with dizziness. "Where is it?" he demanded, his face red and his eyes ablaze. "What'd you jerk-offs do with it?"

I lifted my eyebrows and glanced at Pete, whose face was screwed up in confusion, nose wrinkled and lips tight. Orin stared out from a shadow in the corner that really shouldn't have been possible with all the light pouring into the room.

"Where is it?" Ethan demanded again, rushing across the room toward me.

I stepped forward, ready to meet him head-on. I didn't know why we were fighting, but that had never stopped me before. "Where is *what*?" I asked.

"You'll feel really silly if you *did* make the goblin disappear," Orin said with a small smile. "Since he was the one who took your . . . notes."

Ethan rounded on Orin, but the gesture was somewhat undermined by his unwillingness to get closer to him. "What'd you say?"

"Gregory disappeared?" Wally asked.

"Gregory took your cheat sheets?" Pete said, a smile working up his face, dispelling the confusion.

"Goblins are surprisingly adept at finding hidden treasure," Orin said, "whether it be gems . . . or personal items of interest. Such items might fetch a great price from the right bidder."

The whole room stilled, all of us wondering if Gregory had gone out last night to sell the cheat sheets, and if so, which of our competitors had bought them.

"Let's go," Ethan said, grabbing his sweatshirt and heading for the door. "If someone has those notes, I'll know it. And I'll take them back."

"Why would he sell those, though?" I asked, following along. "That puts him at a disadvantage. No, it makes more sense if he was keeping them for collateral. We should look to see if he hid them."

"He's a goblin," Ethan said, as though that explained everything.

My dumb look had Orin explaining, "Unlike a wand waver who thinks he's better than he is"—he pointedly looked at Ethan—"if a goblin hides something, you'd be hard pressed to find it. He's a novice, so a good magic user could probably figure out his hiding spot, but none of us are good magic users. We're all novices too. There's no point in looking."

"What happened to Gregory? Would one of you *please* fill me in?" Wally asked, trailing behind us. She shut the door as if taking ownership of the room.

I explained the situation to Wally as we joined other trial goers pouring out of the mansion. Buses waited for us in the same place as yesterday, and by the time we'd reached the boarding area, Wally was muttering to herself about statistics regarding abducted trial goers. "There have been a number of missing students over the years. First at the academy itself, but the security was improved as more Shades were used to guard the schools.

After that, there is a 2 to 3 percent chance of being abducted at the Culling Trials based on past history."

"How many were found?" I asked.

"None," she said. "No one abducted was ever seen again."

The odds weren't good that we'd see Gregory again.

"Wait," Ethan said, putting out his hand to stop my progress. Pete bumped into my back and stumbled to the side.

I followed Ethan's gaze to a cluster of students to our right. A few stood in a huddle, peering at something between them.

"Anyone who has any sort of leg up will pick the House of Claw today, I think," Ethan said, his gaze shrewd.

"How do you know that's the right trial to go to?" I got in front of Ethan, stopping his forward momentum.

He lifted an arm to push me away. I glared down at him. "How do you know it's *that* trial and not a different one?" I repeated the question, as if he were slow.

Wally once more took the lead. "There is no official route to take—the randomness and our choices of that randomness is part of the testing. To see where our instincts take us."

Ethan glared up at me, one eyebrow raised. "The shifters announced they've upped their prize money today because two of the first trials were won. By upping their prize, they're trying to lure in the top dogs."

"Looks like they know their prey well," Orin drawled. I had to agree.

Ethan's gaze swept the rest of the crowd, all moving in a steady flow. Only that one group had hesitated for more than a moment, and they were on the move again. One of the guys slipped a square of white into his pocket.

Ethan started forward.

"I still don't think Gregory would've sold the cheat sheet," I mumbled, though I had to concede I didn't know Gregory all that well; maybe he had planned on selling the sheets. Hell, I didn't know any of them that well.

"If he had it on him when he was taken, then someone else could have sold it," Wally said. "Given the size of the house prizes we've seen so far, any help would be worth a pretty penny."

"Best argument I've heard so far," Orin said.

I stepped up into the bus after Ethan, following the group of guys he was stalking.

"Did you hear?" a buck-toothed girl said to her seat mate. "Someone went missing last night. That goblin who won his house challenge."

"Ethan Helix won the challenge," her friend returned.

The buck-toothed girl rolled her eyes. "I meant his goblin teammate, obviously . . ." Her words drifted away, and her eyes rounded when she spotted the man of the hour walking past her.

A hush fell over the bus, though Ethan didn't seem to notice, his eyes locked on the other guys. He passed the group of boys from earlier without glancing their way and stopped at a random block of kids farther back. They all looked up at him, one girl's face reddening.

He jerked his head. "Get out."

"Wh-what?" one of the guys said, slim-faced with dark circles under his eyes.

Ethan stared him down. "Do you want me to repeat myself?" The threat in his tone was evident.

"This is getting awkward," I said quietly, inching backward a little as the kids he'd singled out pushed out of their seats.

"It's not awkward for anyone else," Orin said, although he'd made *our* situation awkward. He hadn't taken a step back when I had, and now he stood a little too close for comfort. I stepped forward again. "They expect this behavior from a Helix."

As Ethan waited, he nodded in a familiar way to a guy in the back.

The guy matched his nod, clearly douche-speak for *what's up, bro?* He looked familiar and I realized I'd seen him before. One of the guys who'd fallen in the first trial. What was his name?

Close up, I was able to get a better look at Ethan's friend. Given the stranger was smoking hot and had an air of confidence, I figured they were friendly because they were on a similar level. Pretty people always seemed to gravitate toward other pretty people.

"Why didn't we sit near the possible offenders?" Wally whispered, leaning around the side of the seat and looking down the center of the bus.

"We're sitting behind them," Ethan said quietly, dropping into the seat, with tense shoulders. I sat next to him.

"Yes, I am spatially aware, but why didn't we sit behind them, and also near them?" Wally pushed, sliding into the seat behind us with Orin. Pete, odd man out, shared with a red-headed girl behind them. "So we could hear their conversation. If I had a magic notebook, I'd want to talk about it with my friends."

"Cool people sit in the back," Orin said with a slight smile, looking out the window. "Social standing before stakeout. It is why the social elite don't do grunt work."

"No, it is because we can afford to hire people to do grunt work," Ethan replied without turning around.

"Yes." Orin's smile grew. I had no idea what point he thought he'd made, but I didn't care to dwell on it.

The bus traversed the usual path and came to a stop in front of the massive gates covered in the thorny ivy.

"Wait," Ethan said when we'd all disembarked, watching the guys he'd noticed earlier. They'd grouped together again, looking down at something between them.

"Welcome again," the usual stunning woman said, holding her wand high and smiling down at us from atop the stone and ivy wall. "Day three of the Culling Trials. Good luck to you and may it favor the trial you choose!"

"It almost seems like they are trying to rush us through all these," Pete said as he jogged after Ethan, who'd surged to a start, following that same cluster of guys. "But what's the hurry?"

"Oh . . . I don't know," Wally said, waving her hand. "Maybe all the political unrest in the magical world right now? They're sparing their resources for this. They probably want them back."

"Their resources are an elite school, and that school is on break," Pete returned as we hurried through the open gate. "The people running this thing are from one of the other schools, and *that* school is on break. No one gives two hoots about us."

A field spanned out in front of us, and when we stepped onto it, it morphed into a plain covered in tall yellow grasses waving in the light breeze. The scene was slightly familiar, although I wasn't sure why—there wasn't much to distinguish it from any other prairie, though for sure it wasn't Texas.

Night slowly fell the farther in we got, and a large crescent moon rose in the star-studded sky. The group we were following veered right, and soon their target became obvious: a lone tree bent over a small glistening pond.

No, wait . . . not just a pond. A watering hole.

It struck me why our surroundings looked so familiar. They reminded me of a documentary my dad had watched about the Serengeti in Africa.

Africa. Africa was full of things that could eat you. And I could bet I knew which of the big five it would be coming for us.

"We shouldn't go that way." I grabbed Ethan's arm. He flung me off. "Ethan, are you out of your mind? What better place to snatch prey if you're an alpha predator than at a freaking waterhole! We shouldn't go there."

"Oh," Pete said, like a tire losing air. He'd just honed in on our surroundings. "This is bad."

A look around said no other trial goers had followed our path. Still, we should have been able to see them—there were some dips and rises in the terrain, but not many. The only other people out here looked to be the kids ahead of us.

Pete shook his head. "They won't want us working with any other crews here. We'll all be kept separate this time—I'm sure of it."

"Well, that's just awesome," I muttered. It meant we wouldn't be able to use other crews for bait . . . or help.

The House of Claw had challenged their prey with a dinner bell, and we'd been stupid enough to answer.

CHAPTER 12

C ome on," Ethan said, no doubt realizing we were going to lose the guys in front of us. He jogged forward, closing in on the group nearing the waterhole, refusing to let the magic sweep them away.

"Ethan, seriously, notes or no, this is a terrible idea. Do you have no survival skills? No internal warning system that is telling you this is the wrong way?" I hastened after him, honestly wondering if I should bother. We were still on thin ice, he and I, and this would be a good way to get rid of him. Let him go down with those other guys.

And yet Rory thought I was in extreme danger, more so than I had gauged. I needed a front man who no one wanted to kill, a front man who had a father with power and connections. I might not want Ethan, but I still needed him.

"Forget survival skills, haven't you watched Discovery Kingdom?" Wally asked, looking behind her, those big eyes of hers wider than usual.

"Yes, that's a good idea." I pointed at her. "Watch our six. The big cats come out at night, and we're in the big cat freaking house. Pete—" I moved my finger to him as Ethan closed in on the cluster of guys, standing around like idiots, clearly trying to pretend they weren't about to do something wrong, like cheat. "You need to change, buddy. This is your world. We need that sniffer."

"Not to mention your honey badger rage. They face down lions on a regular basis," Orin said, facing out to our right. He didn't want to get mauled any more than the rest of us. I lifted an eyebrow at him and he shrugged.

"I watch the Discovery Channel from time to time. Honey badgers are known to attack lions. They have a great deal of attitude."

A vampire who liked animal shows. I shook my head and then nodded. "Yes, the rage will help." The terrain was uneven under the long grass and it made for slow going. The last thing we needed was a twisted ankle. The grasses brushed at my waist, easily long enough to hide a crouching, stalking predator. Or maybe a whole pride of them. "Good God, this is terrible. This whole place is terrible. And it goes on forever."

"It's just magic," Orin said. "Nothing is forever, not even magic."

"*Au contraire.* Your weirdness will be. I guarantee it." I caught up to Ethan on the sands of the watering hole, two paces from the cluster of guys.

"What do you have there?" Ethan asked, his snobby tone selling that line all wrong. He was not good at shakedowns, clearly.

Likely he was used to Daddy doing his dirty work for him.

"Wh-what?" The guy with an obvious secret took a step back, his eyes bugging out in an obvious tell.

Ethan jammed out his hand as Pete stripped. Wally and Orin stood with their backs to us, watching the gentle sway of the long grasses. A warning tickled the base of my spine—not like I needed it.

"Hand it over. It's mine!" Ethan shook his hand as he took another step forward.

Confusion stole over the guy's expression and he wiped at his pocket absentmindedly. "It's not . . . What's yours—"

"Oh, give me a break, this is taking forever." I pushed Ethan out of the way, grabbed the smaller guy by the shirt, and yanked him closer until I could see the individual pores in his face. "I will skin you alive if you don't pull that piece of paper out of your pocket right now and hand it over."

The guy's eyes were as big as the moon above us as he slapped and grabbed at himself. His pudgy hand finally made it to his pocket, and he pulled a creased page out with trembling fingers.

"Come on, man, hold it together," I muttered, snatching the page. "You're going to make me feel bad."

"Hand it over." Ethan took it from me and crinkled it open.

"My mom said everyone does it," the guy babbled. The cluster around him drifted away, giving him more space than he probably wanted. "It's not like I know exactly what's coming—it's just a little nudge—"

"This is garbage." Ethan threw the paper on the ground.

"At least give it back." I sighed, grabbing up the sheet. Slanted notes scrawled in a lazy hand covered the surface. Near the bottom was a hand-drawn picture of a unicorn head (third graders would be ashamed of the artistry) with an arrow to the tip of the horn, labeled "dangerous."

"Oh no, guys," I said, shaking my head. "This is . . . This isn't going to help you. I mean, hopefully it doesn't help you. If you need this to help you . . ." I was still shaking my head when I gave it back to the trembling kid. "Don't worry about cheating. Cheat all day long with this. Snobby McSnobberton over there cheated way harder. He's clearly got a more important daddy than you—"

"Damn it," Ethan swore, putting his hands to his hips and looking around, probably wondering what to do now that he had to actually use his brain. Now that he was marooned on a level playing field with the rest of us.

The trickle of warning turned into a flash flood, running through my body and pumping my heart into overdrive. My stomach flipped and the feeling of ants running across my skin made me dance into the cluster of idiots.

"Take cover, something is coming!" I yelled, shoving the guys around me into a human shield. It wasn't right, I knew that, but sometimes what wasn't right didn't line up with not being eaten by a lion.

"Movement," Orin said, taking a step back.

Pete hissed and spat, waddling toward Orin with his nose in the sky.

"I think . . ." Wally took a step back. "I think . . ." She hesitantly pointed in front of her.

"How many?" I yelled, my hands working, keeping the knuckleheads around me at a safe distance—safe for me, that was. I was *so* going to hell for this. "Wally, get over here!"

"What's . . ." Ethan's voice trailed away as he *finally* figured out what was happening. He drew out his wand.

"It would sure be great if you'd actually use that this time," I called.

A tiny crunch caught my attention on Wally's side of the waterhole. Like a light footstep on dirt.

Wally must've heard the noise, too, because she slid back toward me with her arms raised overhead. "Make yourself look bigger. Make yourself more intimidating."

"Bigger than a wild beast?" one of the knuckleheads asked. "How can we make ourselves—"

"Do not turn your back," Wally went on. "Often, their first volley is a mock charge. If you turn your back, you're done for. Ho!" Wally shouted, waving her arms. "*Hey! Ho!* Make loud sounds. Wave your hands. *Hey! Ho!*"

"They are freaking people, Wally, not real lions. They can understand everything you say." I pushed my group of bait toward the water, wanting a larger viewing area. My insides danced with anticipation. "They're close. They are right here."

"Where?" one of the knuckleheads asked.

"I can't see anything," Wally yelled.

"Neither can I," Orin said.

Five of them. Surrounding us.

"Five of them," I repeated, really digging the connection to Pete, though I did wonder why it didn't extend to the five shifters closing in on us. "All around. Get out your weapons."

"I can make their dead limbs dance again, but I cannot send them to the dance floor," Wally said in her Walter Cronkite voice.

"Why did I end up with the strangest people on the planet?" Ethan muttered, his arm shaking as he backed toward me.

"Good question, and get away from my shield," I said.

"What's going on?" one of the knuckleheads bleated, trying to drift toward the tree. I yanked him back into my shield formation.

"Five of what?" another asked.

The scene exploded before us. Sleek feline bodies leapt into the clearing, white teeth flashing in the moonlight. A massive lioness, larger than even those that were well fed in a zoo, sailed through the air straight for Wally.

She dodged to the side, but not fast enough. A body slammed into her at the last instant, rocketing her out of the way before the lioness's paws sunk into her. Orin, who'd tackled her so quickly, his movement hadn't registered, stood gracefully and looked my way.

One of the beasts launched at my cluster, followed by another. I shoved one of the knuckleheads at those reaching paws, a shameless act that would probably haunt me later. Or maybe not.

"Cheaters never prosper," I said to ease the blow, if not my conscience, before dodging to the side as the other lioness plowed down two of my human shields. "You'll thank me in the end," I said, dancing away behind Pete, whose growl and complete lack of fear was making a fourth lioness review her life choices. She backed up as he charged at her.

Animal kingdom for the win. Orin was right about the honey badger trumping a lion.

Ethan muttered something and a stream of magic erupted from his wand. It smashed full-scale into the fifth lioness. She roared and curled back on herself as Orin zoomed behind me, claws extended, and gouged one of the lionesses attacking my human shield.

Pete rushed forward, snarling and growling, no match for the beasts in size or strength, but plenty tough enough in attitude. The lioness he faced shoved backward and tripped over her own feet, rolling. Still roaring, two of the creatures took off, Orin and Ethan more than they'd bargained for. The third followed, not about to mess with a pissed-off honey badger.

The other two stalked at the edge of the sand. One, the larger of the two, flicked the end of her tail. Her blazing amber eyes focused on me, and a strange feeling crawled through my body.

Not warning, or danger. Something else—a promise of what was to come?

Then, without engaging us again, she turned away and loped through the grasses, disappearing into the night. Ethan shot off another spell, but the last lioness was already following, not ready to fight this crew of nutcases solo.

This was why they'd wanted distance between the crews. Not that the other crew had done much—the poor sots all lay bleeding and helpless in the sand—but we'd used them to help mitigate the attack. Instead of having to fight it all ourselves.

I heaved, trying to catch my breath from the rush and unpleasant exhilaration, but didn't want to wait around for hyenas, or wild dogs, or whatever other large creatures wanted a taste of our hides.

"Let's get on to the next challenge," I said, taking off at a jog. "We're flying blind."

One knucklehead groaned, another cried out in pain.

I grimaced. "Sorry! The healer will be along soon. Good work, though! Thanks for the help!"

"I didn't know you had it in you," Ethan said, catching up to me. By silent agreement, we ignored a pair of knuckleheads who popped up. They could follow if they liked—at a distance. We had enough weird in our crew, we didn't need to add stupid to the mix.

CHAPTER 13

I could feel Ethan staring at me as we walked away from the injured crew at the watering hole. "Please don't tell me that was good work back there. It's not a compliment coming from you."

"Good work," he said, and though I wouldn't look at his stupid face, I could tell he was smiling, could hear it in his voice.

"I have one tiny knife and no experience with lion taming," I muttered. "What else was I supposed to do?"

"Sacrifice yourself?" He laughed outright this time.

"Stop talking to me." I did not want to so much as twitch my mouth for fear he'd see the smile.

"Veer right," Orin said, suddenly next to me.

I jumped. I couldn't help it. "What do you know?"

"That the badger is headed that way, and he's not overly impressed by your lack of attention."

Pete was hard to see deep in the grasses, so when I stepped on him, I felt even worse than I had a moment before.

"Sorry," I said.

Idiots. You'd think they'd follow me here, in my own damn house.

"I said I was sorry!" I snapped.

Pete shot me a dirty look, then took off running. Orin followed directly behind him, somehow able to keep a better eye on him than we were.

"Where are my notes, do you think? And who would've taken Gregory? Was it because he stepped forward in that last challenge?" Ethan asked.

I wasn't sure if he was talking to me or himself, but I took it upon myself to answer.

"Honestly, Gregory probably hid the papers somewhere," I said, feeling a prickle of warning that didn't last long enough for me to pause. "Maybe he even hid them outside. I don't know, but I really don't think he would've traded them. Or sold them. To the group, they were worth more in your hands." I didn't answer the other question. I didn't know who'd taken the missing kids—I only knew that Rory and Sideburns were on the case, and that I intended to look for Gregory the first chance I got.

Another trickle of warning ran the length of my spine, but this one faded just as quickly as the first. There were watchers out here, but for whatever reason, they were deciding not to engage. Maybe one ambush was all you had to survive in this part of the challenge.

The landscape changed suddenly, the grass-swept prairie morphing into rock and dirt right under our feet. Pine trees rose up around us, bursting out of the ground, and the sweet scent of fresh sap tickled my nose. A deep rumble in the ground ahead made us all slow, the lay of the land suddenly rising with an incline as though the mountain was literally being created under us. Which at this point in the game would not surprise me in the least.

I looked behind us; the savannah had disappeared without a trace.

Pete led the way into a small clearing. Fresh grass sprigs shot up around our feet and a tall table stood off to the right next to a long, half cut log. On the log, five little bells were lined up in a perfect row beside a sheet of paper.

Ethan marched over to the log and I let him. He'd get the booby trap in the face if there was one.

"The next challenge is tracking," Ethan said with a sour expression, lifting the piece of paper.

"What's wrong with that?" I asked as Wally looked at her feet.

He crumpled up the paper and threw it into the log. "What's wrong with that?" He gestured at Pete, standing next to me. "He's not a tracking animal, and even if he were, we don't know *what* we're tracking. I don't have any notes. We're dead in the water."

I frowned at him, then at the rest of them when they didn't chuckle. "Are you guys serious? It's tracking." I lifted my hands, waiting for them to get a clue. "It's just tracking. Haven't you guys ever done that?"

"What would I track, pigeons? I live in New York City," Ethan said dryly.

"You could try tracking a better attitude, how about that?" I huffed, pushing my annoyance away. "Look, I grew up on a farm, not to mention hunting with my older brother. I know how to track. In regards to *what* we're tracking, well, let's figure it out, I guess. That paper didn't say anything else?"

I moved to fetch it but stalled near the bells. I still had ambushes and booby traps on the mind.

"What are the bells for?" I hovered my hand over the log setup.

Ethan snorted and turned away.

"The shifters are offering us a way out," Wally said. "They're taunting us."

"How so?" I asked, my mouth settling into a frown. "They're just a bunch of bells."

Wally tilted her head at me, and Orin turned to stare.

"It was in your contract," Wally said. "Didn't you read it before you signed it? Because you should always read contracts before you sign them."

"Or have your lawyer do it," Ethan said.

It was my turn to snort. "They forced me to sign the contract after I'd been tagged and bagged." The blank looks indicated they didn't have fathers who watched a lot of military flicks. I elaborated. "After they zap-strapped my hands behind my back and shoved a bag over my head, someone pushed the contract to my pricked thumb."

Orin's brows lowered over his eyes, something I hadn't seen before. It wasn't like him to show a reaction.

"That's . . . not right," Wally said. "They can't make you—"

"I had the Sandman," I said quickly, remembering Pete's reaction to him. He was currently at the edge of the clearing, sniffing a tree. "He's not very good at convincing. He's very good at threatening, though."

Wally still looked troubled, but Orin looked excited. Like I had more value to him than I'd had a few minutes before. The latter I really wasn't digging.

"Who cares about contracts and the Sandman," Ethan said, impatient. "There is a big bell at the front of the mansion grounds. When you ring the bell, you are removing yourself from the Culling Trials. You're quitting. The same goes for the elite who live at the academy. Ring the bell, and you're out. These bells are probably just for show. The shifters want to intimidate us. They think our submission will be funny."

"Yeah, that's kind of an animal's thing," I muttered, fetching the paper without disturbing the bells. "Dominance. Submission. Alphas and betas."

I read the type-written note.

Follow your nose and see with your eyes. Get to the end, and you'll be nearer the prize.

"Submission they've got—riddles, not so much." I shoved the paper into my pocket as Pete's fur and claws morphed into skin and a whole lotta Pete.

"I've got five smells around this clearing," he said without preamble.

"Cover your junk, man. We don't want to see it," I called out, turning away.

"The cold affects more than the harvest," Wally said, looking upward at the pale blue sky.

"Whoa, can't call the man out like that," Ethan said. "It isn't cool."

"You call out women for their breast size," Wally retorted. "I fail to see the difference."

"That's because you are socially awkward," Orin supplied. "There is a time and place. This is neither."

"Right. Okay. Pete, what'd you find?" I said too loudly, still staring out into the trees.

"Five smells, like I said." He pointed at five sections within the clearing. "Most of them are older scents, a day, maybe two since they were laid. One newer. A wolf, I think."

"Great. And their trails?"

"The wolf is all over this place but doesn't move past this clearing. Two of the other scents stay as well—a rabbit, I think, and something I can't quite place. Of the last two, the bear goes off that way"—he pointed to the left side of the clearing, which was mostly flat land—"and something else went that way." He pointed behind him, a graceful incline that might get treacherous later.

I snorted. A bunch of shifters intent on submission would not create a path through easy terrain. They'd say, "Follow this trail, I dare you."

"Clearly shifters think with their teeth, claws, and balls," I said to myself. "They don't put as much effort into the finer strokes of a challenge."

"Astute, and rather accurate," Orin said.

"Yes, thank you, peanut gallery." I shook my head, thinking back to the half-assed riddle. "So that's the nose portion. Now. I expect we'll see some or all of the tracks."

"Here. A rabbit." Wally pointed at a patch of cleared vegetation. "I've always loved rabbits. I used to stalk them through the fields behind our house, looking for their burrows. I wanted to trap one and take it home for a pet."

"We're looking at a future black widow here, folks," Ethan said softly, his eyes pointed downward.

"Oh no. I could never love people that much," Wally replied.

In a moment, we'd identified all five sets of prints, but none of the information matched. The rabbit's tracks told us it had left the clearing, but its scent didn't, and the bear's tracks indicated it had stayed, but its scent said it had left. Only the wolf had neither its scent nor its tracks leading out.

I rolled my eyes and headed up the steep incline leading straight up the mountain. It didn't take long to find a set of wolf tracks, clear as day.

"Here we go. This will be the trail we're meant to follow." I gestured everyone on. "If I'm wrong, I'll give you my portion of the winnings."

"If you're wrong, we won't get any winnings," Ethan replied.

"Look at you, finally using your brain. How does it feel? Rusty?" My double thumbs up earned me a scowl. "Pete, back into shifter form if you can handle another change so quickly. The note said eyes and nose, so we might need both to finish out the trail."

"Smaller animal forms can change faster and more frequently than the larger, deadlier forms," Pete explained proudly.

"Awesome, buddy. Keep up the good work." He *did* appreciate my thumbs up.

"Shifters are clearly no match for the House of Shade when it comes to mind teasers," Orin said as Pete led the way, sniffing out the trail that I followed by sight. Tracking an animal was pretty easy once you picked up the footprints. Rocky terrain and water posed different challenges, of course, but more often than not, wolves didn't spend too much time on those.

Then again, my experience was only with real wolves. Human wolves would change it up to confuse things, no doubt. I could only hope Pete's nose could plug up the holes in my experience.

"The House of Shade is no match for the House of Claw when it comes to brawn and power," Orin continued. "Shades hone their skills so as to become predators. Those of the claw are born predators, and they learn to hone their nature with their intellect."

"In other words, we are really hoping that Ethan won't crap himself in fear and freeze up when the wolves surround us later and try to tear us apart," I said, watching the subtle differences in the tracks as they made a straight shot up a gradually more horrible incline. The shifters were challenging our stamina right now. Four-legged animals would have an easier time of this than bi-pedal kids. I already wanted to give up.

"Rabbits aren't predators," Wally said, out of breath.

"Correct," Orin said, not out of breath.

"How do we even know we're going the right way?" Ethan asked, pulling off his sweatshirt and tying it around his waist. A whiff of masculine musk and Old Spice blasted me. If we had to run and hide, it wouldn't be hard to sniff us out. "We're probably doing all this for nothing."

"Are you always this much of a whiner when you're not cheating?" I asked through my gasps of progressively thinning air.

"'*The cat's in the cradle and the—*'"

"Knock it off with that weird-ass voice," Ethan said to Wally. "What is up with that?"

"Everyone needs a little charm in their lives," Wally retorted.

"Not that kind of charm," he bit back.

"Climbing a tower wasn't easy," I said as Pete slowed, and then stopped. "The fact that this is a similar level of difficulty should prove that we *are* going the right way. What is it, Pete?"

The scent is lost, I heard echo around my head. *Disappeared.*

I bent closer to the ground and waved my finger at the tracks, toes and claws indenting the dirt around pebbles and leaves. They'd become lighter as we climbed, more difficult to follow, but we hadn't lost the trail. "We're still good. See? It keeps on in the same direction, although no real wolf would weave this much. Someone had a little too much moonshine before they tackled this trail . . ."

"Moonshine, really?" Ethan tramped forward, leaning forward against the incline. "Country bumpkin much?"

"Moonshine, really," I said, pushing him to the side and taking the lead. "Hard core, always. It would knock you flat on your ass just from sniffing it."

"Like you would know."

"Wow, you really are dumb." I veered with the tracks, which became even lighter. In fairness, I'd only tried moonshine a few times, as all curious kids might, and only once, at the urging of my brother and Rory, did I push past the breathing fire stage and have enough to swirl my thoughts. We'd all thrown up quite a lot that time, and as far as I knew, none of us had touched it again.

The tracks cut right, went a ways, then stopped. Ahead, the mountain dropped away to a cliff face, that we'd have to navigate via a little tiny ledge that led to a thatch of trees and another upward slope on the other side.

Pete didn't move in front of me, which meant the scent trail didn't pick back up.

I braced my hands on my hips, looking back the way we'd come, thinking. Had we gone straight instead of cutting right at the last juncture, we would have hit a nearly solid patch of pines. The trees reached out to the path almost threateningly, as if daring someone to push their way into the shadows of their branches.

I pointed back that way. "Turn around and get going up. This is a test of our courage."

Ethan stared at me, his brows set low over his eyes. Orin stared as well, his eyes sparkling harder in a way that clenched my stomach, though I couldn't have said why.

"Don't magical people teach their kids that it's rude to stare?" I asked, stopping in front of them. "Move."

"How the hell do you know all this?" Ethan said accusingly. "You said you didn't know this world."

"I don't have your stupid notes, you turd." I shoved him out of the way. "Which should be clear since *I am not stopping to read anything*. It's common sense." I pointed back at the ledge. "No wolf is going to run across that. Give me a break. And again, these aren't real wolves. They are people, and this is a challenge. They're testing our mettle in the same way they would test one of their shifters. Strength, stamina, courage, fighting prowess . . ."

"If it were common sense, everyone would be able to do it," Orin said, his gaze boring into me as though he wanted to peel back my skull and have a look under the hood.

I shrugged and continued on, sensing the rightness of this decision. It felt . . . natural. Logical.

"If everyone would stay in their assigned groups, they probably *would* be able to do it." I hunted for more tracks as we continued up the mountain.

"You are wrong about that. No one gets assigned a group," Orin said. "Like choosing which trial to go to first, those you end up with in a group are randomly selected. We are very lucky to have one trial goer from every house."

"Says you," Ethan grumbled.

"It is a wonder they don't better mix the groups, instead of allowing us to choose for ourselves," Orin mused as Pete wobbled up in front of me and picked up the scent. Regardless of their rage, honey badgers were freaking cute. I wouldn't tell Pete that though.

I breathed a sigh of relief. I really hadn't wanted to be wrong.

"What do you mean?" I asked Orin as an impression in the soft dirt caught my eye. I found another paw mark, the nail indentations not as prominent as they'd be on a real wolf. That had to be because the shifter trimmed their fingernails.

"A mix of women and men, and not just houses. Often times, the different sexes bring something different to the table. Like a lion versus a lioness, for example. Same magical type, extremely different attributes."

"Less mixing in the social classes would be a nice change," Ethan said.

"For us, yeah," I replied.

"I'm happy to bring a bit of feminine energy to the group," Wally said, beaming. "And traditionally, the groups going through are not this well mixed. The school tried to enforce group selection a number of years ago, but the trial goers ended up fighting each other instead of completing the trials," she paused and then nodded, as if to herself, "like Orin, I am beginning to believe that our odds are better together."

Silence descended, everyone remembering she was the only one who didn't know I was also a girl. Although, she wasn't entirely wrong. I was hardly brimming with femininity.

The trees pressed in on us until we were forced into single file. Light filtered through the canopy in thin streams before diffusing into a soft glow. Shadows pooled in crevices and at the bases of trees, nearly thick enough to have substance. Cool air slid across my exposed skin and a warning skittered up my spine.

Here we go.

"Don't stop to put on a sweatshirt," I said in a hush. "That'll give you a moment of weakness, and a moment will be all they need." I reached down to flick Pete so he'd look back. Given his anatomy, he had to wiggle around so he could see. "You're the lead," I whispered, before falling back. "I'll take the rear."

"What's happening?" Ethan asked, putting his hand over his wand like Doc Holliday in the Wild West.

"We're coming up on the next battle," I said, feeling a strange presence throbbing from within the trees. A threatening presence, one that felt familiar—just like the wolf I'd faced at home. The itch of watching eyes flared between my shoulder blades.

This wasn't one wolf—it was a pack, and we were in their sights. Their strength was in their pack synchronicity. The pack would work in tandem, seamlessly.

Of all the times not to have a human shield.

CHAPTER 14

B ranches shook and shapes charged toward us from all
sides, graceful and deadly. Flashes of fur—gray, brown,
black, and even a brilliant white—cut between the pine
trees on this mountain slope, silent in their attack.

Rocks flew, one hitting a wolf square in the head and making
it stagger before falling. Another hit a body, eliciting a yelp. Wally
had a great arm and aim.

A jet of magic zipped right past a wolf, followed by another
blast, that one hitting home. The wolf yelped—and then yelped
again as Orin rushed forward, raking four deep red scores into
its furry side.

A large gray and white timber wolf lunged at me, snapping
my attention from the others' battles.

I yanked out my knife as I dodged to the side, fast and agile,
fueled by adrenaline and experience. I swung my knife around
and dug the business end of my short blade into the soft flank.
I yanked it back, pivoting as the wolf fell, and delivered another
puncture in its gut.

"I could gut you right now, but that would kill you," I said as
Orin zoomed around me and cut off another wolf running my
way. "If you continue in this fight, I will. Bow out, and you'll live."

I spun, catching a brown wolf mid-leap, its jaws lined up
with my face. A rock hit it square in the face, making it close

its eyes and rip its head away at the last moment. Its body was already committed, though, and I ducked, braced, and brought my knife up into its soft underbelly.

It yelped, its own momentum driving my blade lengthwise as it fell. I bent with the butt of my knife, knocking the beast in the chest above the heart and spinning away. Hopefully, it would get the gist, because I couldn't warn everyone.

Another stream of magic flew out, and a wolf sailed into the trees, blood dripping from a gash in its side. Honey badger snarls and spits toward the top of the line told me Pete was holding his own.

"Go," I shoved Wally forward, knowing Orin would run up behind her. "Go! They'll need to carry out some wounded. Orin, watch our six. Take down anyone that follows. Ethan, back them off our sides. Pete, lead the way!"

We made headway up the path as a unit, stepping over downed wolf bodies that were thankfully still breathing. I was immensely proud of our crew, and in the back of my mind, I took note of who was doing the most damage and how. I cataloged Ethan's spells and what they did, Orin's strength, speed, and fighting prowess, noticing how he moved and struck, and Wally's complete ease with wounds and possible death. Of course, there was Pete's determination and seeming lack of fear once he was in honey badger form. Most of all, I stored information about how the shifters had designed this trial, and what that said about their house.

I didn't know if I would ever need this information, but old habits die hard in a country girl. These silent calculations had helped guide me on the farm, telling me how to best wrangle certain animals and how to sweet talk the people into giving me a good deal. It had taken me a few trials in this crazy magical world to get back to basics, but now that I was a little more comfortable, I was there again. "They aren't following," Orin said a few minutes later, as calm as a spring day. I really wasn't looking forward to his house.

Without warning, for the second time, the scene changed dramatically. Trees dissolved and the slope of the mountain flattened out into a springtime field cut through by a sparkling stream. Breathing hard, still holding my now-bloody knife, I looked around and took stock of the new situation.

My stomach flipped in giddiness and a smile pressed up my cheeks.

"Yes!" I said, throwing a fist to the sky. I couldn't help it. This was what I'd been secretly hoping for all along.

Not far away grazed a herd of actual freaking unicorns, robust and all but shimmering with muscle, built just like normal horses with one important exception. A long horn protruded from each of their foreheads, colored a tarnished gold, just like in the fables. Their brown or black manes seemed pretty standard, but when their tails swished in the sunshine, the light caught a glimmer of gold.

"Ah-mazing," I said, excitement running through me.

"They fart rainbows," Ethan said dryly as he pushed toward the herd.

"Shut *up*! They do?" I practically danced after him.

"No."

"Your attitude is not going to ruin this for me," I said.

"I've never seen a guy react this way," Wally said, jogging after us. "It's refreshing that you are so secure in your masculinity as to be giddy over a unicorn."

"Wait, you guys."

Pete stood in the buff, pointing to a second herd behind us. Similar to the first, this group had two large differences: size . . . and wings!

"Ohmygod, ohmygod!" I jumped in place and clapped, not caring who saw me. "I didn't even know unicorns could have wings! This is such a great day. The best. I could die now and die happy!"

Wally's head tilted to the side as she looked at me, as though she were sussing out a secret.

I tried to tone it down. I did, but I just couldn't.

"Those are ten times harder to ride," Pete said. "Especially for me and Orin, since we smell like predators. We'd have to ride those to get the gold." He shrugged. "But we've already won two challenges. Just getting to the end, riding a plenty-hard-but-not-impossible unicorn will still be a win."

Ethan was already walking toward the winged unicorns, his expression set. I followed him without a second thought. This wasn't about the money. If I had a choice between riding and flying, it was flying all day long.

"Why ride a unicorn when you could ride a winged unicorn?" I said excitedly.

"Alicorn," Wally said, jogging to catch up to me. "The winged variety are called alicorn."

"Good to know." I sidestepped a pile of poop much like horse poop, but for one crucial difference. "Their poop glitters?!"

"Yeah. It's really annoying to clean up. If you get hit with it, the glitter sticks for days, then everyone knows you got hit with unicorn dung," Pete said dourly, looking between us. "Who grabbed my clothes?"

Ethan slowed about fifty paces from the alicorn herd, his focus intense. The rest of us swapped identical *oops* expressions.

"No one grabbed my clothes?" Pete demanded. "Seriously?"

"Do you always expect people to pick up after you?" Wally asked, no remorse.

"It's a fair question," Orin said. "I think your mother did you a disservice there."

Pete's mouth dropped open. He looked at me imploringly, and I barely kept from audibly siding with Wally and making him feel like everyone was ganging up on him. Pete's clothes had been the last thing on my mind when he'd changed, and he certainly hadn't mentioned it, either before he changed, or when in animal form.

I shrugged. "Sorry."

"Sorry? How the hell am I going to ride one of these *without* clothes?" Pete demanded. "I can barely ride a unicorn *with* clothes, and those were the tamed ones without wings!"

"This might be a little awkward for you, Pete, but I think you're about to find out how to ride one without clothes." I hurried forward. This time, the guilt was alive and well. He had handed me his sweats, but I'd dropped them back in the savannah.

"Approach slowly, but without fear," Ethan said softly, and I got the impression he was talking himself through it. "If the one you approach tries to nip or bite, dodge, back away, and give it another moment to adjust. Keep your hands out and up, showing them you are not trying to hurt them. If it tries to gore you with its horn, you've lost its trust. Choose another. Assuming you don't have a new hole in you."

"Are they as smart as horses?" I asked, sinking down into my game face. It was not easy. Glee kept bubbling up in my gut.

"Smarter. They can reason, to an extent. They have the intelligence of a chimpanzee," Wally said.

Chimps were smart enough to truly interact according to my education from the Animal Planet channel. "Do they know sign language?"

That question stumped Wally. "I don't think so? But I suppose it's possible."

"What would it take to have one of these as a pet?" I wondered out loud. I could already see an alicorn in our back field, giving Whiskers a run for his money. I didn't bother to suppress a grin.

"These aren't pets," Pete said, scratching his bare chest with one hand, his other hand covering his man bits. "Unicorns can be domesticated, but no one has ever domesticated an alicorn."

"But they've been ridden?" I asked as the danger of the situation finally began to seep in, dulling the previous joy and excitement.

"Yes," Ethan replied. "Rarely, but they have been ridden. It's why they're part of the trials."

"Fair enough." I pushed out a breath and shook out my hands. "If it's possible, it's worth a try."

"I vote we let the farm *boy* go first, seeing as he is rather overconfident," Orin said.

"You guys always vote that I go first, and it hasn't had anything to do with the farm before," I grumbled, not waiting for everyone to agree. They'd probably just shove me toward the herd, anyway.

Besides, this time, I wanted to go first. I wanted nothing more than to breathe in the smell of these fantastic creatures, to hop up and go for a ride.

Getting into the right mindset, I didn't approach the herd as slowly as Ethan might've, and I didn't keep my hands up and out like a teller in a bank robbery. Those two actions would've unconsciously relayed nervousness in the lines of my body, something an animal would pick up on immediately. Instead, I approached the fabulous horned creatures like I had Whiskers when I'd newly acquired him: with respect but no fear. The good news was, these creatures didn't weigh as much as the two-ton bull, and they had half the number of horns. I was already ahead of the game.

I approached the nearest of the alicorns, a smaller beast a little removed from the rest of the herd. Its head shot up and its eyes pinned to me, its white wings tucked into its sides. They'd have a whole language with those wings, I just knew it. Pity I didn't know the words that went with it.

"Easy now," I said, not unlike Rory had said to me the night before. I slowed my advance. "Easy."

It huffed through its nose and shook its head, its mane sparkling in the sun.

"Good lord, you are striking," I said, unable to help it. "Congratulations on being the most awesome of beasts. You won the genetic lottery."

It lowered its head minutely, tracking my advance as the other alicorns watched us.

"But I can tell you're not amused. Maybe you don't want to be here," I said softly, changing my trajectory. "I get it. I'm a stranger. A stinky stranger with blood and sweat and wolf smell on me. I think you're too low on the totem pole to take a chance on letting me ride you. I hear you."

I backed up and did a slow perusal of the herd. This time I chose the largest, an alicorn stallion, with a proud bearing, jet black coat, and light red eyes. With his solid frame, robust chest, and muscular physique, this animal would fetch a pretty penny at the livestock auction. Stud fees on him would be enormous. He held his wings a little looser than the first alicorn I'd approached, their tips at a slant from his body.

You need to learn their body language, I noted to myself.

"Hey," I said, and this time I did put out my hands, but not to demonstrate my lack of a weapon. In fact, I turned to show him the knife on my hip. An intelligent animal would know that humans were the top of the food chain. They wouldn't trust us. It was better to show you knew that.

At least, I hoped it was. I'd be shipped off to the unicorns if not.

I bowed my head a little, submitting. He was the boss here, and I respected that.

"I'd like to ride you," I said, knowing the intention of the words would color the positioning of my body. "My friends need a ride too. The shifters put you here. Hopefully with your blessing?" I paused, because that's what you did when you asked a question to an animal that couldn't understand you or answer, right?

My boot squished in sparkly poop as I continued my advance, and I wasn't even sad. The glittery residue would be a good conversation starter.

"If you didn't form some sort of peace treaty with them, you probably would've charged me already, I think." Two steps closer and the fantastic beast lifted his head. A tremor ran through his wings, and he held them a little away from his body, bristling. Another step, ten feet away now, and he lowered his head, pointing the foot-long weapon in the center of his forehead at my face.

"Yeah, I hear ya. That would hurt." I kept moving forward, moving through a small tingle of fear shaking my limbs. "But I'm not going to hurt you."

He stamped his foot, ears pinning back, and blew a loud snort that cut the air like a bugle, sharp and shocking. Challenge accepted.

"Only the biggest, baddest, assholes try to ride you, right? Try to force you into submission?"

I stepped forward again. And again, only five feet away now. The air sizzled with the pent-up energy rolling off him. I ignored another stamp of his hoof. The pressure of anticipation wound up my insides.

"But you only allow the alphas to ride. Not the assholes who call themselves alphas because of their fragile egos, but the real alphas, right?" I swallowed, wondering if I should step forward again, or wait for the alicorn to make his move. I kept talking to stall and a drip of sweat ran between my breasts. "Real alphas wouldn't force a creature like you to submit. Those guys garner respect through trust and level-headedness.

"They don't strive to be the loudest in the room—they can sit quietly in the back, confident in themselves and their abilities. I've always wanted to date one of those guys, but they are surprisingly hard to find. So often, *Mr. Alpha* is a big dickhead who would throw you to the gargoyles while he escaped another way."

"You'd salivate at the chance to be with me," Ethan called out from a safe distance away.

"So he's gay, then?" Wally asked. "That would explain the unicorn fetish."

I smiled, a soft laugh escaping me as I kept my hands wide, feeling as though I were standing on a knife's blade. One misstep, and I'd be dodging a horn thrust or a front kick.

"But that guy I described," I said, "doesn't have to be a guy."

The alicorn's wings snapped close to his body, and his head bobbed up, his mouth opening to expose some pearly white chompers. He reached forward, as I'd feared, intending to take a chunk out of my shoulder.

I reacted without thinking and dodged to the side. My right hook smashed into the sensitive if brutally hard-boned area just below his eye, a scary and painful spot on any creature who depended on sight for their safety and the safety of their herd. I grimaced and fought not to shake my hand. Damn it, that better have worked or I'd have a sore hand for nothing.

His head jerked up and he danced back. His eyes glowed crimson, and I nearly peed myself with fright. Two other alicorns bugled, the sound sharper and louder than the call of any natural horse. It resonated through the air, pushing against my chest and forcing me back a step. Another alicorn tossed its head, and a fourth pawed at the ground nervously. The whole herd's wings were pressed tightly to their bodies, like a boxer with his hands pulled in.

I put out my hands in a *well*? Smiling and not sure why. "We're even. Don't try to bite, and I won't punch you in the face."

He whinnied and bucked once, then struck out at the air with his front hooves, one at a time. His wings snapped out to the sides with a sound like a loose sail taking a gust of wind. My heart leapt, but I didn't so much as flinch. Instead of jogging backward and trying another approach like I would with a wild horse that needed to be gentled before it could be ridden, I stood my ground with grim determination. It took every ounce of courage I possessed.

The alicorn hopped, spun, and kicked out those two feet back again, the wind coming off them way too close for comfort. He pumped his wings, slapping me with a gust of air, and then rose and did it a second time.

I did not budge, but stood staring into his angry, glowing eyes, hoping I wasn't about to die with glittering unicorn poop on my shoes.

CHAPTER 15

Another of the creatures, at the far edge of the herd, whinnied and tossed its head before trotting our way. The alicorns parted way for the newcomer, almost reverently, as though this alicorn was something special. The male alicorn in front of me blew a loud snort but backed off a few feet, bobbing its head. One ear cocked forward, the other toward the newcomer, and his eyes no longer pinched at the edges with irritation.

I just barely kept myself from letting out a shaky sigh.

The smaller alicorn, a female, moved in beside the male, her movements lither than her counterpart's. With a gray coat covered in huge dapples and a dark mane and tail that shimmered with sparkles, she was stunning. But her wings were what truly drew my notice. The sunlight moved across them like a living thing, highlighting either a golden sheen or the colors of a rainbow depending on how the light touched the feathers. It was the most breathtakingly beautiful thing I'd ever seen.

I moved to her without thinking. Without hesitation. No bravado needed. I paused beside her flank and waited until she bent a front leg, just a little, before hopping up and onto her back, using her mane to steady me.

"Holy cats—"

Pete's words were lost in the snap of her wings spreading out, one side above the male. She pulled them back in and trotted a bit before turning, *allowing* me to be the passenger. I let her have all the control, not using my legs to steer like I would one of our old ponies back home. An expectant stillness rolled through the herd.

"She's waiting for you guys to pick, I think," I called out, totally guessing on that one. But why else would she be waiting? They must know why they were in these trials.

Ethan was the first to saunter forward with his shoulders swinging and his head high. As expected, he headed directly for the large male I'd just proven myself to. Not following his own advice from earlier, apparently thinking I had it all locked down and he could coast, like normal, he didn't slow in his approach or put out his hands. He just waltzed over and reached out to the alicorn.

The male pushed forward, fast and powerful, jutting out his wings and swinging his head low. His horn cut through the air, inches from Ethan's chest as Ethan backpedaled with comically rounded eyes. The alicorn tucked his wings back into his body, and the edge sliced across Ethan's skin.

"Walk away," I called out, fear churning low in my gut. My cockeyed grin didn't match my tone. Part of me couldn't help but cheer this creature for putting Ethan in his damn place. "He's not meant for you."

"I thought you said we could pick," Ethan yelled out, his face red.

"I said *I think* you can pick, moron. I don't speak their sign language, remember?"

Wally added, "Technically no one *speaks* sign language—"

"Just pick another," I yelled at Ethan, cutting her off.

Wally and Orin left Pete standing on his own, cupping his junk and staring at the herd. They each chose the closest alicorn to them. Orin approached his quarry with his head and body slightly bowed, the perfect posture for submission. The alicorn tried to gore him, flapping its wings and swinging its daunting horn. Without hesitation, he approached the next alicorn, which accepted him, and gracefully hopped onto its back, not blustering once.

Wally was easily accepted by the first one she approached. Her issue came with trying to get on. She jumped over and fell off the other side. Grabbed the mane and tried to scramble up, only to slip again. I was pretty sure her alicorn was laughing at her, tossing its head up and down and flapping its lips.

Ten minutes later, after Wally had finally managed to mount with an assist from one of her alicorn's wings, and Ethan had found an alicorn that would accept him, it was just Pete on his two feet in the field, staring at us with somber eyes.

"I'd be okay just calling it a day," he said in a low voice. "I've passed two trials—and I helped to get us here through the first two legs of the course. That oughta be plenty to get accepted into the academy. It would be more gold for you guys."

"Come on, Pete, this is your house. You need to finish strong," I said. "We all need to finish this, including your bare butt."

"Do you have any idea what it feels like to ride a horse bareback?" he demanded.

"Yes," I replied.

"With your balls hanging out?"

I grimaced. "Got me there."

"And horsehair up the crack of your ass?"

"Again, not a clue."

"Do you?" Wally asked seriously.

"Of course, I don't," he retorted, his face screwed up in anger.

"Sorry, it was just the way you were asking. I assumed—"

"And I'd rather not know!" he finished.

"Come on, Pete. Take one for the team, buddy," I called. "I got us in the door. You need to take us home."

"Dang it." He shook his head and shot a longing look at the unicorns.

"Those won't feel any better on your bells and whistle," I yelled. "Go big or go home, Pete!"

Grumbling the whole way, he walked into the alicorn herd and stopped by the first available alicorn. It pranced out of the way. The next did the same.

"Come on, buddy, put your best game face on," I said, holding down giggles. It was pretty funny to watch Pete's bare butt wiggle remarkably like it did in his honey badger form.

"Easy for you to say," he groused. "You have pants."

I barked out laughter, I couldn't help it.

"No one ever said winning these challenges would be easy," I called.

"No one ever said they'd be humiliating either," he grumbled, and I got the impression it was to himself. "They keep shying away, Wild," he said, louder, heading my way now.

I got the feeling Pete had stopped paying attention to which beast he was walking toward. That changed when he found himself standing in front of the large black stallion. His face went slack and his arms limp at his sides.

The stallion stared down at him with his red eyes, no longer glowing. He snorted, and I swear he might have winked.

Pete swallowed audibly. I could hear it even from several feet away. He lifted his hands, palms out. "I don't like this any more than you do. But I'd be honored if you'd let me ride."

The male blew through his nostrils and slightly lowered his head.

"I'm really starting to get the feeling they understand English," I whispered under my breath. "Right, then. Now where do we go?" I asked as Pete swung his leg up and over, seamlessly hopping onto the stallion's back. I barely stopped myself from considering the particulars of what would happen next.

My alicorn stretched out her wings and the rest followed suit, then all five of them pumped their wings in TANDEM, lifting us straight off the ground. No running leap, just straight up. The ground dropped away as we rose into the sky. Exhilaration such as I'd never known tore through me. My smile stretched across my face, growing even wider as the wind rushed around me and blew through the short ends of my hair.

"This is the best," I yelled, leaning forward like we were running across open land. "Let's show them all what it is to travel with speed!"

The large male was right on our heels, bigger and stronger but not sleeker. He also didn't have a rider who'd grown up riding.

"Come on, let's scare them senseless, Beauty," I shouted, laughing with glee as I held on to her sparkling mane.

We sailed over the land before banking hard and diving. I realized I was gently steering her with my knees, just like I'd always done with our mare at home. She let me, responding easily, and adding her own embellishes with her wings.

We climbed again, slowing a little, allowing the screaming crew behind us to catch up. The stallion came up on us again, his head and neck stretched out, that bastard wanting to take the lead, Pete clinging to his back.

"No way," I called out, urging her faster. She dove, almost a free fall, before tucking her wings in and spinning through the air three times in a perfect controlled maneuver.

"No!" I heard, high-pitched and terrified. "No! Not again. Never again. I don't want to die—"

And we did it again. And again. Climbing, banking, diving, climbing again, and rolling. My stomach did so many flips, I lost count. I was drunk on the moment, giddy with exhilaration, and couldn't stop laughing. I didn't even care if we were too late to get the prize—this was the highlight of my whole life, and I never wanted it to end.

Eventually, though, my alicorn leveled out, her wings stretched to the sides, gliding. The stallion finally caught up, his chest heaving, his coat glistening with sparkly sweat, and the look he shot us was pure pig-headedness. But he did give me a wink. Like he knew he'd been bested and almost admired us for it. I laughed again and leaned my head against my alicorn's mane, connected to her in a way I'd never been connected with my own horse. I'd found a horse just as wild as I was, and it made my heart sing.

We dropped altitude slowly before touching down into a large ring of robust men and women, hard-faced and tight-bodied. There was no doubt in my mind they were shifters.

"What's the deal here?" I said quietly to my alicorn, reluctant to slide to the ground. "Are they going to rush us? And if so, can we go at them as a unit?"

Her puff of air seemed like laughter, and that was good enough for me. I threw my leg over and hopped to the ground, walking to her head. After petting her nose and then up and around the base of her horn, I pressed my forehead to her nose.

"Good-bye. That was the best ride of my life, Beauty. Thank you." I kissed her nose, because it felt like the right thing to do, and took my place among the others—a little behind a green-faced Ethan and beside a pale-faced Wally.

"I will never forgive you for that ride. I'm beyond nauseous," Orin whispered from behind me.

It shouldn't have been as funny as it was. It really shouldn't have been. But I grinned, fighting the laughter. I mean, what wasn't funny about an airsick vampire?

A stocky man with compact muscle and a chiseled jaw approached us, and for the first time, I noticed the chest behind him, piled high with gold. As he neared us, he angled his walk so that he was looking directly at me, his stare hard but his eyes glittering with respect.

"To win the gold, contestants had to ride an alicorn into this area," he said, his voice raspy. "All of you accomplished that goal, despite the obstacles put in front of you." His gaze flicked to Pete and a half grin lifted one side of his mouth. "Gives a new definition to saddle sore, doesn't it?"

Pete reddened, and I didn't know if it was because he was star-struck, staring at the shifter in awe like he'd been, or embarrassed. More likely, it was a combination of the two.

The man chuckled, a hearty sound that loosened the muscles across my shoulders. "Been there, done that." His eyes came back to rest on me. "Amalthea, the matriarch of the herd, selects only exceptional individuals, ones with character above the rest. She doesn't often allow riders, but she chose you. For that, your team will get a boon."

My face turning red, I pointed at Pete. "His team. He's the shifter."

The man's eyes rooted to me unflinchingly. "It will be delivered to your rooms. Well done." He took a step back and lifted his arms. "My people will escort you out and see you back to campus.

Good work, all of you. Your combined efforts are a model for every team in this school."

As the others dispersed, each led away by someone different, the man who'd addressed us—the obvious alpha of the group— fell in beside me again, just for a moment.

"Amalthea has never, in all the time that I have known her, allowed someone to touch around her horn." He looked at me with serious, deep blue eyes. "She is a judge unlike any other. You have a friend for life in that alicorn, something no one I know can boast, not even me. You are special . . ." He paused expectantly.

"Wild," I supplied. "People call me Wild."

He nodded once, a curt movement. "You are special, Wild. I'll look out for you." He nodded again, moving away, his eyes lingering on me for a moment more. "I'll look out for you."

In theory, it couldn't be a bad thing to have a powerful alpha looking out for me. But it struck me that I wasn't doing a very good job of avoiding notoriety.

CHAPTER 16

Getting back to the mansion should have been as simple as boarding a bus, sitting down, and letting the driver take us there with no stops along the way. Of course, we weren't great at the simple way of doing things. Or maybe that was just me, maybe it was just my luck.

Ethan led us to the back of the bus, our usual station now that we were an unwilling part of the Helix cool crew. Ethan was on my left, head lolled back against the back of the seat, eyes at half-mast. Of course, he could totally relax. He didn't have some trained assassin on his tail.

I, on the other hand, was a mess of nerves. The glow of the alicorn ride had faded, and the longer we sat there on the bus, the tighter my anxiety wove around me. This wasn't a warning so much as a general realization that I was surrounded by people I wasn't sure I could trust. I needed some alone time, some space to think, but alone time was exactly what Rory had told me I couldn't have.

An all-male crew tromped in after us, covered in blood, busted lips, and some seriously wounded egos if their glowers were any indication. That drop-dead gorgeous guy—Colt, if I remembered his name right—was in the crew. He had a wand holster at his hip like Ethan and the other magic users carried. His dirty blond hair was just long enough to get messy, and he had a lean build like a swimmer or a runner, with a jaw line that begged to be touched. Not that I was that into pretty boys, but damn, he was the prettiest boy I'd seen in a long time. And I was far from blind.

Even if I was pretending to be a boy.

Wouldn't mind getting my hands on that—pouch. His dark eyes turned my way almost like he could hear my thoughts, and the slightest smile curved those lips I'd pay good money to kiss. The smile widened, almost like . . . no, there was no way he knew . . . and then he winked at me. A simple wink, so subtle I almost thought I'd imagined it. Only I hadn't.

Was he into dudes? I mean, it was possible, which was seriously a downer, much as it was another great win for the other team.

I leaned over to Ethan. "You know that guy there, right?"

He opened one eye. "Who? Colt? Yeah, we go way back." He settled himself deeper into the lackluster seat. "Went to grade school together."

"Is he into dudes?" I asked softly, not wanting to offend the hottest of hots.

Ethan burst into sudden loud laughter, but of course, he didn't let it end there. "Colt! You into dudes and didn't tell me?"

The bus erupted into immediate and intense howls from the guys who were with Colt, filling the small space even as the bus driver revved up the engine, normally loud enough to drown most noise. Apparently, we were abandoning the rest of the crews. Or maybe they hadn't made it through the trial.

Colt grinned as he leaned over a seat and stared back at us, flashing perfect teeth to go with his perfect everything else. "Last I checked, nope." And those eyes cut my way again. "I like my ladies with a bit of fire and a bit of badass, and a whole lotta legs."

The heat in my face was about as intense as the mirth unleashed in the bus. I turned to look out the window, staring hard at the scenery even though I didn't really see it.

Jesus Christ, he knew I was a girl! How did he know? And was he flirting with me?

Once the laughter settled, Ethan yawned and leaned back. "Why do you ask about his preference?" The way he posed the question, paired with the smug grin on his stupid donkey face, said it all.

The dirty tricksy bastard had spilled *my* secret to his friend. Any other time I'd welcome the attention from a guy like Colt, but not here, not now. Not when my siblings' lives were on the line.

I couldn't let Ethan stay so freaking smug. Sure, I didn't have the picture of him smooching his nana or his precious magical CliffsNotes, but that didn't mean there wasn't leverage to be had. Like all other magic users, he had something precious on his person. Something I could use against him.

Namely that boom stick of his.

As soon as Ethan closed his eyes, I drove my elbow into his solar plexus, pinning him back to the seat. With the other hand, I went for his wand holster. His fingers wrapped around mine, trying to stop their waist-ward trajectory, and I jerked away, twisting my wrist with a sharp movement while still pinning him down. The point of the elbow is a right brute when used properly, and I was using it for all I was worth.

He tried to get out from under me, gasping for air, but I leaned in hard, putting all my weight into the point of my elbow. His face twisted in pain as I drove it into him, scrabbling to get at his pouch. He was about to get a lesson in keeping his mouth shut.

"What's going on? Why are you two at it again?" Pete reached into the fray, then yelped as he caught the point of my other elbow as I jerked my action arm back before driving my fist into Ethan's gut. Under me, Ethan thrashed and fought to get his legs between us even as the last of the air whooshed out of him.

"He. Won't. Tell." He breathed out as my hands wrapped around the pouch and yanked it free from his belt. I stumbled back, knowing I held his most prized possession.

My breath came in gulps. My sister and brother would only be safe if I managed to pull off this cover for at least the rest of the week, if not longer. I stared down at him, keeping him pinned with my eyes as I opened the pouch. I lowered my voice, dropping the register as deep as I could.

"Listen here, numb nuts, you'd better hear me loud and clear."

From the front of the bus came a chorus of "oohs."

I ignored them as I pulled the wand from its pouch and held it between my two hands as if I would snap it in half. The wand was warm, tingling under my skin, but not in an unpleasant way. Ethan's eyes widened until I thought they'd fall out of his head. Part of me wished they would so I could kick them around the floor of the filthy bus.

I tightened my fingers around the wand. "I will snap this twig if you so much as breathe another word about me to anyone. Talk in your sleep? Snap. Spill under duress? Snap. Whisper it to your girlfriend? Snap. Do you finally understand the importance of this to me?"

Ethan sat there, shaking. He held out his hand. "Give it back to me."

This was not like him, but then I had just yanked his most precious item away from him and threatened to destroy it.

I narrowed my eyes. "Do you understand? Even with your skull as thick as a brick crap house? Do you get it?"

"I understand," he said, his jaw ticking with barely suppressed anger. "Now give it back to me."

I dropped the wand and he caught it midair and scooted over to the far side of the seat. I sat and faced the front only to see Colt watching us with eyes nearly as wide as Ethan's.

I tugged my hat down and slumped in my seat as if I were sleeping too. I wasn't.

Which meant I heard everything whispered between Pete and Wally.

"The odds of him being able to touch his wand without having a bad reaction are one in a thousand. More, actually, if you take into consideration the fact that he took it from him by force," Wally said.

"You mean if he'd handed it to him—"

"Yes, wands are tied to their owners, and while you can get a new one, if you touch someone else's, you're likely to get a burn, shock, or worse."

I swallowed hard and tried not to think about what that meant. That I was some sort of freakshow? Wally had said that you could have two abilities. Maybe I had more magic in me than even Dad and Mom thought. It was possible, I supposed.

I slowed my breathing. I'd absorbed the troll's magic and sent it back to him. I'd felt the stones like Gregory had. I'd connected with alicorns with a rare ease. I could understand Pete in his honey badger form, even if no one else realized it.

The whole concept of magic was still foreign to me, but I was no fool. I couldn't ignore what was happening in front of my face. Magic was what I'd been feeling all along. My ability to fight and track and all that came from growing up on the farm. From fighting with Rory and Tommy, living in a school of hard knocks and quick reflexes. Maybe I wasn't a Shade at all . . . because there was no explaining away the weird things I'd been able to do. The *magical* things. I tried to tell myself it didn't matter. Even if I was some kind of magical freak, the stakes remained the same for me. I was here fighting for Billy and Sam and my dad. Keeping them safe was the only thing that mattered.

Orin's voice tugged at my ears. "Sometimes when a wand doesn't like its user, it will be more lenient about outsiders touching it in the hopes that someone else will take it away. Perhaps that is the case here."

Pete sucked in a breath. "Really? You mean Wild could actually be a mage? Wow, that would be awesome."

I should have been excited about the possibility of having magic—real, honest-to-God magic. Even a week ago, if you'd told me I could wave a wand and make things explode, or use it to save people, I would have been over-the-moon excited. But . . . I'd gotten used to the idea of being a Shade.

It fit me in a way I hadn't expected.

So what would happen if I got stuck into another house, one with all the snobby highbrow bastards?

The bus jerked to a halt and everyone peeled out. Everyone but me, which meant that Ethan wasn't moving either.

"Get out of my way, Johnson." He growled, but there was very little heat in it. I lifted my head and tipped the brow of my hat up. The bus was empty—even the driver had left, and the two of us were completely alone.

I turned to Ethan, hating that I needed him to answer a question when I trusted him about as far as I could send him with a single kick to the butt.

"What are the chances that I'm being groomed for the wrong house?" I asked.

His eyes narrowed to the look of irritation he always bestowed on me. "What do you mean?"

"I held your wand," I shook my head. "And keep your mind out of the gutter, you know what I mean. I didn't explode. I didn't get more than a tingle. Could it be . . . that I'm being groomed for the wrong house?"

For the first time in our short, fraught acquaintance, I saw Ethan really listen to me, really consider what I was asking. A minute ticked by. His hand drifted to his pouch, and then he shrugged. "It is possible. As much as a filthy farm hand like you wouldn't deserve to be part of the House of Wonder . . . it is possible. A lot of what you've done so far—"

"Could be learned behavior," I said softly. I swallowed hard, suddenly needing to figure this out. "Who would be able to tell me?"

Ethan laughed and shook his head. "That's what you're here for. To be tested. You won't know for sure until you hit the final test, I guess. Until you face the House of Wonder."

I stood and started down the center aisle, my head spinning. My nametag on that first day had identified me as a Shade. A master of shadows and death. A killer in the making.

Now here I was doubting, wondering if there was more to me than even my father knew.

More than he or my mom, or even I could ever dream.

And it terrified the crap right out of me.

CHAPTER 17

I f you are still here, congratulations. You have survived the first three Culling Trials. You will now have a single day of rest. Be aware, curfew is now at 10 p.m. If you see any of the following students, immediately contact one of the academy supervisors, or Director Frost."

The booming voice cut through the really lovely, really hot and steamy shower I was having, and I stood there, water streaming off me, as the names were read through the PA system.

Heath Percival.

Gregory Goblin.

Lisa Danvers.

I toweled off quickly and pulled on my sports bra, wrestling the too tight material over my still damp body. I yanked my sweats on and all but tumbled out of the bathroom and into our dorm.

The three guys looked up, eyebrows raised. Pete shook his head. "Holy cats. I can't believe you got by even one day without anyone guessing."

"She didn't," Orin corrected him.

I shook my head, a plan already forming. "The names they called out. Do you guys know the others? I thought there were more missing the first day?"

Pete yawned and flopped into his bed. "Lisa was a shifter. A snake shifter to be exact. I think. I heard that the first kids 'missing,'" he made air quotes with his hands, "had just taken off from the trials and the supervisors found them on the nearest road hitchhiking out of here."

One shifter. One from the House of Unmentionables. "What do you want to bet that Heath was a future Shade?" All from the same house trials that we were doing at the time they went missing. My head was spinning with the possibilities. Someone was taking the kids, and Rory had said that as far as he knew, they weren't being killed. So why were they being taken?

"What does that matter?" Orin climbed into bed.

The pieces clicked inside my head, realigning themselves, trying to make sense of what was still missing. "Because it means that whoever is taking the kids is using the trials specifically to weed out the ones they want. And specifically, out of the trials that we are in at the same time."

I paced the room, thoughts whirling as fast as a hurricane, whipping up everything I'd learned so far. I could almost taste the answer. I clenched and unclenched my fingers as I walked.

"You're going to wear a hole in the floor," Pete said. "And even if you're right, what then?"

Before he could answer, the door swung open and Wally strolled in, pillow and bag in hand.

Pete jumped up. "Whoa, whoa, you can't be in here!"

Her eyes were puffy and red and her chest rose and fell at a speed that I knew all too well. She swept toward me first, then stumbled to a stop. "Wild. Are you a girl?"

"No one knows." I hurried past her to the door to make sure it was shut tight. "Please, my brother's life is on the line."

"You never asked me nicely," Ethan muttered to himself.

"Because you're a twat, and we only put up with you because we have to!" Wally snapped, shocking us all into silence, right before she burst into tears.

The guys all seemed to freeze, as if a girl's tears were more terrifying than any of the challenges they'd yet faced. I moved first, having spent more than my fair share of nights comforting Sam.

Wally leaned into me. "Those girls are awful, just awful."

I didn't ask her what the girls she was rooming with had done. It didn't really matter. That was the thing with mean girls; they were all the same, even if these mean girls were playing with a different bag of tricks.

"What did they do?" Pete asked.

"I smell blood," Orin whispered.

I shot him a look, but it was too late. Wally sniffed and swiped at her tears with both hands.

She shook her head. "I don't want to talk about it." She turned her head, and I saw the bruises on her neck. Finger marks tipped with claws.

"A vampire did that," Orin said, and I whipped around to face him as a white-hot burst of rage shot through me. A vampire had done this to Wally? Choked her and cut her, scared her to the point of tears?

"Oh crap," Pete said. "I see that look, Wild. That is not a good look. Do not take on a vampire. This is a very, very bad idea."

"And letting them think they can hurt Wally is a good idea?" I grabbed my clothes off the trunk, still covered in mud and blood from the last trial. I didn't even bother to go to the bathroom to change. I ripped off the sweats—wouldn't want to get blood on them—muttering as I went, "Nobody messes with my crew. Nobody."

And just like that, I claimed them as mine. My crew. Sure, Ethan was a bad apple, but he was our bad apple, and we never would have made it this far without his help.

"I'm coming with you." Orin ghosted to my side.

"Me too," Pete said, but I shook my head.

"Pete. You stay with Wally. I doubt Ethan has a sensitive bone in his body." I shot a look at Wonder Bread.

"You are insane." Ethan shook his head. "The next trial is the House of Night. We're going to get our fill of vampires there. Going after one of them now is just stupid."

I turned on him. "You want to look weak? Like our crew can't hold up under pressure? They're testing us, Ethan. Maybe this is even part of the next trial. Like the poisoned food that first night." I pointed a finger at him. "Without your cheat sheets, you don't know what this is, which means we deal with it."

"You can stay here," I said to Wally, "We have a spare bed with Gregory gone."

She sniffed. "Thanks. But I don't want to cause more trouble."

"She can't stay here. We'll all get thrown out!" Ethan roared.

Orin was on him in a flash, a cloak of black spilling out and around him like a shroud of darkness.

I'll admit it, I took a step back, dragging Wally with me. Ethan took several steps back. His face paling at a rate that made me think there would be no blood left in his head.

"She can stay here. She is part of our team. And if you haven't noticed, we already have a female in our midst, so what's one more?" His voice deepened with every word until the last was barely a growl.

"Fine, whatever." Ethan snorted as if he hadn't just about pissed his pants. Because as Orin ghosted backward, I was almost positive there was a wet spot at the front of his sweats. Ethan pushed past us and headed to the bathroom. "Idiots, my team is full of idiots and bleeding hearts." The bathroom door slammed behind him.

I made sure my knife was strapped into its belt sheath and went to the door.

"You have fifteen minutes before curfew," Pete said.

Wally shook her head. "Just let it go, Wild. They aren't worth it."

I shrugged. "Can't let it go. Where's your old room?"

She reluctantly told me.

This distraction was exactly what I needed. I couldn't figure out what was happening to the missing kids. But I could stop Wally from being picked on again.

I stepped out the door, Orin drifting silently beside me as I jogged down the long hallway. Fatigue and body aches rolled through me. The lineups at the healer had been long, and I'd thought to go in the morning when it was quieter.

"I don't understand you, Shade," Orin said. "You are protective of us in a way that is not normal, not even for a Shade bound to guard someone."

"Normal is boring." We rounded a corner, and the sound of talking reached us loud and clear.

Orin put a hand out carefully and laid it on my shoulder. "They are talking about Wally."

Shivers radiated out from his touch. My ears buzzed, the whispers becoming words.

"Who does she think she is? Telling us death stats like we need that?"

"Gods, she is so weird. I hate necromancers. Uppity bitch."

"I could have drained her right there, no one would have noticed. With the other students missing, we could have hidden the body."

Laughter flowed through my head, catty and cruel, and the anger it sparked in me was intense. Orin's hand slid off my arm and he shook his head. "They wanted to kill her and hide the body."

He could have downplayed the threat, pretending it was a joke, to protect the other vampire, but he hadn't. He'd stood by Wally.

Warm fuzzies tingled up my spine. "For a vampire, you're a pretty good guy, I think."

He shot me a look, eyebrows raised. "For a Shade, you aren't bad yourself. And I agree with you. This threat needs to be . . . handled . . . or they will come for her again."

I wanted to ask him why, but there wasn't a chance. A trio of girls hurried toward us, stepping out of the shadows. They weren't dressed all in black like Orin. There were no obvious tells other than the upside-down, bedazzled pink crosses on their sweats. No doubt they'd decorated those themselves.

I stepped fully into the light, and Orin stepped with me. The girls slowed, noses wrinkling in perfect unison. They were pretty, their faces done up with perfect black eyeliner and deep red lipstick even this late at night.

The lead girl curled a lip. "Oh, gross. Awful Orin, what are you doing here? And with that dirty Shade?"

I let a slow smile slip across my lips. "Oh, we're here to have a chat with you . . . bitches."

Orin chuckled. "That's so polite, Wild. I would have called them far worse. Rat drinkers. That's what they are. Especially Lucia there."

The trio of girls tensed and hissed as a unit. The lead girl, I was guessing Lucia, stepped forward. She could have given Ethan a run for his money with her ability to look down her nose at us. "Get out of our way. You aren't worth messing my hair over."

"You hurt our friend," I rolled my shoulders, loosening them. "There's a cost to that. A price you are going to pay."

There was no moment of tension like there'd be in a movie, only a blur as she came for me. Orin had moved so fast, I couldn't see him, but I had no trouble tracking her movements. I stepped back as she reached me, then grabbed her by the arms and jammed my foot into her gut. I flipped her over my head, and she sailed through the air, screeching as she plummeted over the stair rail and down into open space.

I didn't wait—I jumped up, grabbed the rail, and leapt after her, shouting as I went down. "You got the other two?"

"That I do," Orin shouted back as several screeches lit the air. I landed in a crouch two stories down, but the vampire was already up, her bedazzled pants catching the light. She sniffed the air, her eyes partially closing. Scenting me. Crap.

"You aren't what you—"

I shot forward, driving my fist into her nose, shattering it before she could get a bead on the fact that I was no boy. Damn it, I hadn't even thought of that before I'd decided to come after them.

It only meant I had to finish this fast for reasons other than our curfew.

She screeched and flailed backward, eyes rolling as the blood poured down her face. I blinked and stared as her eyes, which had been a light brown, darkened to a solid black, filling the entire orb. Like a cat seeing a Christmas tree for the first time.

Her fangs elongated.

Oh, crap on toast.

She shot forward, her extended claws coming straight for me as she lost control of her blood lust. I caught her by the wrists and stepped back, bracing against the force of her tackle. She snapped at me, hissing and spitting blood in my face.

"Gross." I tightened my fingers around her wrists and snapped one forward, catching her in the jaw. "Stop hitting yourself."

I drove her other fist up into an uppercut. She screeched, one fang piercing her tongue. "Stop hitting yourself."

God, how many times had Rory done this to me, if not with such vehemence? How enraged had I been as I'd tried to stop him but couldn't because he was so much bigger? Again and again, I drove her fists into her face until the rage slid from her, and the black of her eyes faded back to a light brown.

Not until she was on her knees and gasping for air did I stop.

My breath came in deep, slow takes. "You come near Wally, me, or any of my crew, and that threat you made? That will happen to you. Capiche, rat drinker?"

That sounded like something a guy would say, right? A quote from a movie. Maybe I should have said, "I'll be back."

Her head lolled.

"Say you understand." I gritted the words out as I tightened my fingers even more.

"I . . ." she spat to the side, a gob of blood. Disgusting. "Understand."

I let her go and took a step back, bumping into a body.

The smell of an open grave washed over my nose, and I knew in my belly it was a vampire. Orin had caught up to me.

Only it wasn't Orin.

A hand dropped onto my neck, fingers tightening with a power I knew could snap my spine in a second if he chose.

"Come with me," a male voice said,

He lifted me by my neck, and I could barely touch the floor with the tips of my toes. Panic sliced through me. He was behind me and I couldn't reach him with fists or boots. "Orin!"

"Coming!" he yelled back. There was no sound of him hurrying. But I could feel him getting closer, like a sense of pressure. And then it faded. "I . . . Wild . . ." He breathed the words. "I can't."

"I am his master," the voice said, and it struck me that I'd heard it before. This was the smiling vampire who'd escorted us out of the first trial.

"Jared." My head swam with the lack of oxygenated blood getting through, but at least I'd remembered his name. "They tried to kill—"

"Save it for Director Frost . . . girl," he said. There was no emotion behind his words, no anger, no nothing. And he knew. Knew I was a girl.

I was done.

The double doors of the director's office swam into view as the last of my vision faded. The next thing I knew, I was on the floor in the room, heaving for air on my hands and knees.

"Caught this one fighting in the halls," Jared said. "What do you want to do with her?"

Crap, had the director heard that last word?

"The same as the others," Director Frost said. I couldn't see her. I was still hanging on my hands and knees, knowing I was about to be kicked out.

The vampire's hand clamped on my neck again, and I was lifted as the doors burst open behind us. I was dropped to the floor for a second time. I rolled on my back to see Orin, Pete, Wally, and . . . Ethan sweep into the room. Mind you, Ethan looked like he'd just swallowed a shot of sour puss, but he was there.

"They threatened my life, Director," Wally said, turning her neck to show off the wounds. "And Orin heard them saying they should have killed me and used the missing students as a way to hide the body."

"I did hear that. Wild was protecting our team, making sure that no one tried to hurt Wally again," Orin said. "That is the sign of a true leader."

Pete nodded. My eyes went to Ethan. He was the one with the pull here, not us.

He grimaced. "Wild is part of our team. My father . . . would be very disappointed should we lose his help."

I rolled onto my belly and pushed onto my knees so that I could see the director's face. I expected her to look as pissed as a cat thrown into the bathtub. But her eyes crinkled at the edges as if she were holding back a smile.

"You make a fair point, young Helix, even though it surprises me that you would stick your neck out for someone else." She tapped the desk with a single finger. "Fine. But seeing as you have decided that you are a crew, you will all room together. Jared, make sure your student understands that should there be any trouble between the girl and her male roommates, he will be the one to bear the cost."

The cost. As in being kicked out. I can't say how, but I felt Orin straighten. "I accept that charge."

"Everyone, out." She clapped her hands together, ending what could have been a very bad scene for all of us. "Except you, *Mr. Johnson*. You and I are going to have a chat."

The others filed out of the room, eyes down. Jared paused at the door. "Do you wish me to stay?"

She smiled at him, but it was sharp, and predatory, and downright pissed. "Get out, Jared. I may be old, but I'm not dead."

He bowed at the waist and flashed her a big smile, going so far as to wink at her. "Not yet, you aren't." Damn, he was a mean flirt. Would Orin develop that wicked charm when he got his full fangs? Somehow, I doubted it.

I swallowed and faced the director, realizing that I'd lost my hat again. Damn it.

I lowered my eyes.

"We have a problem, you and I," she said.

"No problem, Director. It won't happen again." Keeping my voice low wasn't hard seeing as it was raspy from being partially choked.

She huffed a laugh. "Oh, I doubt that you will be able to keep that promise at all, *Ms. Johnson*."

CHAPTER 18

D irector Frost didn't move from behind her massive desk, and I didn't move from my spot in front of her on my knees. She knew I was a girl. I'd hoped her old lady ears would miss Jared's slip. But maybe she'd just looked past the sweat and blood splatter on my face and had known. Whatever the case, my secret was out, and Billy would pay the price.

"Please, my brother's life is on the line. I couldn't let him come, not when he's so young. He's not cut out for a place like this. He doesn't have any survival instinct. Please, please don't send for him." I was not above begging, not for Billy.

Her face didn't so much as twitch to telegraph her thoughts. "You have inspired loyalty in those I would never have put together in any sense of the word. Underdogs. Outcasts. The fact that the Helix boy spoke for you is truly amazing."

I blinked a couple of times. "Are you going to throw me out?"

She smiled then. "If a sharp tool is not in the right drawer, do you cast it into the garbage? Of course not. I have seen the reports on you, Ms. Johnson. I know very well who is leading your ragtag crew in the trials. And it is not the Helix boy." She leaned back in her chair. Yes, she was definitely not as old as I'd first thought. Her movements and face pegged her under fifty, not in her seventies like I'd first believed.

"We're working together," I said. "It's not just me doing all this. Isn't that what you want?"

"That is not normal for our world, even if it is what we strive for." She let out a sigh and spread out the papers on her desk. "I will not spill your secret, Ms. Johnson. Though I will tell you this, there will be no hiding behind a hat and a boy's name by the end of the Culling Trials. And the other directors will not be as lenient should you give them a reason to cast you out. Such as fighting in the halls. Or being out past curfew."

I stared down at my boots, a ridiculous urge to cry sweeping over me. A question burned its way to the tip of my tongue. "Why would they get rid of me when you can see I have value to this place?" I had to find a way to stay. For my family. And maybe a little bit for me too.

"Your family is well known, Ms. Johnson, and not, shall we say, well loved. Your father is a null. Your mother dropped out of the academy right before her fourth and last year. The time and expense put into her training was never recouped. So, any excuse to evict you early in the game . . . well, they will take it." She sighed again. "But . . . I will do what I can to protect you."

My head snapped up. "Why?"

Her smile was soft, genuine, and it soothed away some of my fears. "Because I have been on that side of the desk. In my day, women were not trained alongside the men, and we were seen as lesser because we had breasts instead of balls. You are strong, stronger than many of the men here, and that will make you a target and a threat."

Her words echoed the Sandman's, and a trickle of a warning slid down my spine.

She reached out and touched the black box on her desk that had drawn my attention on my first visit to her office. "Strength can be broken, Ms. Johnson. Even those who believe they are untouchable can be cast out." Her fingers flipped open the box, and I craned my neck to see inside it.

"Wands?" A stack of them lay in the box, at least a half dozen.

"Most of the students who have been kicked out of the academy under my watch were affiliated with the House of Wonder. Not the House of Shade as you might think. Arrogance was their downfall. Which is why I believe you will be safe. You're confident, yes, but arrogant you are not." She snapped the box shut and smiled at me again.

She scribbled something on a piece of paper then pushed it aside next to another stack. My eyes tracked it, latching onto the words even upside down on the further stack of papers.

Heath Percival.

Gregory Goblin.

Lisa Danvers.

Mason Whitehall.

Another kid had gone missing? I couldn't stop myself from saying something. She would know if there were any updates, and there had to be a reason she was working on sensitive information in front of me.

"Is there any word on Gregory? On any of the missing kids?"

Her eyes closed, and she leaned back in her chair, rubbed at her gray temples with her fingertips. "You need to go now, Ms. Johnson. That bastard Jared will escort you back to your room."

The door opened, and the handsome vampire held it wide for me, having obviously listened in to our whole conversation. He glared at the director but spoke to me. "Let's go, Johnson."

I wasn't sure that I wanted to be escorted by a vampire who could hold me up by one hand, but seeing as I didn't have a choice in the matter, I went along with him.

We had almost reached my dorm room before he spoke. "That was incredibly foolish what you did there with the girls. They could have killed you and been within their rights."

I looked him right in the eye. "And if I'd killed them?"

His lips twitched. "Should you have managed, yes, you would have been within your rights as well. They attacked your friend. You protected her."

"Then you can remind them of that fact,"—I put my hand on the doorknob—"because if it happens again, I'll bring a wooden stake with me."

He should have been pissed off at me for threatening his future students. But he smiled and laughed. "I'll do that. You are stronger than you look. That is excellent."

I opened the door and shut it behind me, leaning against it. I only had a second to take a deep breath before a blur of arms went around me. "They didn't kick you out?" Wally asked.

I pushed her off, gently. "Not today. But the director knows about me." I made eye contact with each of them in turn. "She let me stay because you all stood up for me. Because we're working together as a team."

Ethan grunted. "You mean because *I* stood up for you."

"That too." I nodded. "But I learned something while I was in there. I think another kid has gone missing."

There was a collective intake of air. "Who?" Pete asked.

"Someone named Mason Whitehall? Does that name ring a bell?" I asked. Wally answered slowly.

"He's a necromancer. Like me." Fear tracked across her features. I couldn't blame her. What if she'd been caught out on her own when she'd been on her way to our room? Would she have been taken instead?

I forced myself to look at Ethan. "Thanks. For what you said in there."

He shrugged. "I wasn't lying. My dad would be pissed if we lost you now. He's not stupid, and neither am I."

"Well, isn't that just a bucket full of love," Pete said.

I grabbed my clean sweats and made my way to the bathroom for a second shower to wash off the vampire blood.

The room was quiet as I tiptoed back to my bed only to find Wally in it. "I'm scared," she said.

God, I could already see how this was going. With a grimace, I climbed into the bed on the other side and turned my back to her. "Go to sleep."

She rolled over and threw an arm around me, spooning me. "Fifty percent of people who die in the night die in their sleep."

"Crap, not this all night," Ethan grumbled.

I patted Wally's hand. Just like Sam and her nightmares. How many times had she crawled into my bed in the middle of the night? Too many to count. I sighed. "Go to sleep, Wally."

I fell into a doze, but it was light. My eyes popped open at the soft thud of a mattress hitting the floor, followed by the shush of it being pushed across the floor. Pete positioned it next to my bed and flopped onto it. He held a hand up, and I took it without thought.

"They could take any one of us," he said.

He wasn't wrong.

I squeezed his hand. "No more losses from our group. Tomorrow, we find Gregory." I yawned and settled deeper into the mattress, my back warm from Wally and my hand tight in Pete's.

Home. I was home.

The next morning, I woke with an elbow in my neck and a heavy weight on my legs. I tried to sit up.

"What the hell?" I managed to prop myself up on my elbows enough to see the honey badger splayed across my legs on his back, pinning me and the sheets down. Orin lay on the mattress that Pete had pushed over, his head at my feet. Upside-down, Orin was not the way to wake up. His eyes locked on mine. "You did not wake up when something came by our door. It scared Pete."

The honey badger rolled over, still asleep, let out a fart that I swear lifted a green cloud around his butt, and kicked at the sheets with one foot.

"Jesus, Pete! That's awful!" I couldn't help the gag as I fell out of bed and onto the mattress beside us, scrambling over Orin to get away from the stench.

I crawled across the floor and finally stood ten feet away where the air wasn't so heavy.

Orin was already out of bed, as if he'd never been there. "How are we going to find Gregory?"

"Breakfast and healers first," I said, feeling the previous day's aches and pains come roaring back. I was not going to turn down the healers today. I'd aim to find Mara seeing as she likely already knew I was a girl and hadn't said anything. The last thing I needed was more people knowing my secret.

Ethan rolled onto his side. "And what if we find him and he's dead and they think we did it because we're standing over the body?"

I arched an eyebrow at him. "That's where you come in."

He arched an eyebrow right back at me. "You want me to use my pull if we get caught?"

"Bingo."

I was dressed in no time flat, my mind already working toward the goal of finding Gregory, where to start, who to talk to. Because even though Rory and Sideburns were on the case, I could no more leave this problem to someone else than I could leave Wally to have her ass kicked by a bunch of mean girls. Even if those mean girls were vampires.

The five of us ate breakfast by ourselves, and I was not the only one to notice. No one interacted with us, but to be fair, none of the other trial goers interacted with anyone outside their team, so it wasn't just us. Not even smoking hot Colt came over to chat with Ethan, though he did look my way more than once. I kept my head down and pretended not to notice him.

"The lines have been drawn," Orin said.

"Good." I swiped a hand across my mouth. "I'm going back to the room. Wally, come with me." Rory's warning pinged inside my head. "From here on out, we go out in groups of two. Even you, Ethan." I pointed at him as he opened his mouth, no doubt to protest. "No one gets left behind."

Pete grumbled something about being stuck with the dick of the group. Ethan shot him a look, and I snapped my fingers at both of them.

"We need to find out if anyone knows about this latest missing kid," I said. "Ask around, see if you can find any details. They may not have announced it yet, but someone has to know something."

I hurried away from the mess room, Wally at my side. The weight of many pairs of eyes was no small thing, but I did my best to ignore it.

"What are we going back to the room for?" Wally asked as we headed up the flight of stairs that led to the second-floor dorms.

"Gregory knew something was up. Whether it was because of the cheat sheets or something else, he knew."

She lowered her voice. "And you think he left a clue behind?"

"Maybe. It's worth checking out." The others had told me it was impossible to find what a goblin had hidden, but something had occurred to me between that bus ride yesterday and being called to task in the director's office. I had *felt* those gems in the House of Unmentionables challenge. Maybe I could use that same ability, whatever it was, to find a clue about Gregory's disappearance.

I reached the room first, and as soon as I lowered my hand to the handle, the slightest warning tingle cut across my palm. I put a finger to my lips and motioned for Wally to stay outside.

Someone was in our room.

There was no noise, but I felt it in my gut, alongside the warning that I was about to surprise someone who didn't want to be surprised.

I twisted the doorknob as slowly as I could, then slid through the narrowest opening I could manage.

A figure had his back to me, hunched at the window as he slipped out. I recognized that hair.

I slammed the door behind me, startling Rory.

He spun around, throwing stars in hand, and threw one on reflex. I ducked to the side and the star embedded in the door with a thud.

I glared at him and he glared back. *What the hell?* I mouthed the words.

"Everything okay?" Wally asked from outside.

"Fine, just bumped into the . . . door. Give me five minutes," I said.

"And they say I'm weird," she said.

Rory stalked across the room, silent even in his anger. He moved to grab my arm, but I was done being dragged around. I batted his hand away and pointed to the bathroom. Not the most glamorous place to chat, but it would work and give us a semblance of privacy.

I shut the door behind us and he rounded on me, not wasting a second. "What the hell indeed, Wild? Rumors are flying that you're a girl! And someone said you took on a trio of vamps last night *and* broke curfew? How in the hell is that flying under the radar?"

His words were like a bucket of ice, and I hated that part of me agreed with him. He wasn't wrong. But he wasn't right either. "They attacked Wally."

"Not your problem," he growled. "None of them are your problem. You look out for you, that's it in this world."

I lifted my chin. "No, not anymore. Director Frost knows. You're right about that. And she's backing me. So, no, I'm going to follow my gut."

He got right in my face, looming over me. "And what about Billy? What happens to him and Sam if you get booted out or killed? You think they won't come here the same way you did, looking for answers?" His words shot an arrow into my heart. He knew me enough to know how to hurt me. But that went both ways.

I curled my lip. "I see you have the same intimidation tactics your father taught you."

Rory grunted as if I'd booted him in the gut. Low blow, but I was done playing fair. No one else was, so why should I?

"I asked you to trust me." He stepped back, jaw muscles ticking.

"I do." I looked him straight in the eye. "Trust isn't the issue, Rory. You can't be here every second. Which means you have to trust me too. I'm doing what I need to do to survive. And my crew is part of that. They've helped me get this far."

He blew out a breath and closed his eyes, then shook his head and went for the bathroom door. "Stay clear of the vamps. They're in on this, on the missing kids. I don't know how yet, but . . ."

I grabbed his arm, stopping him. I knew already that someone from the House of Wonder was in on the kidnapping—I'd seen the wand myself in one of the kidnapper's hands. "What do you know?"

"Scent dogs were brought in. Cadaver dogs. They picked up on a vampire who shouldn't have been snooping around the mansion. It's all they've got so far, and I shouldn't have even told you that much." He put his hand over mine and leaned in closer, this time with none of the aggression. "Please be careful. I know you, Wild. A day off is the worst thing you could have right now."

"Why?"

"Because when you aren't kept busy, trouble finds you like a lemming finds a cliff." He grinned and then was gone, out of the bathroom and out of the window before I could ask him anything else.

"Okay, Wally, come on in," I said.

She opened the door, eyebrows lifted. "Did I hear you talking?"

"Um. Yeah. To myself."

"Oh, I do that all the time." She smiled and then did a slow circle. "So, you think Gregory hid something?"

I nodded. "Just a gut feeling." I thought about Gregory's connection to treasure, to gold and gems. A tiny pulse started in the tips of the fingers of my left hand. Quick experimentation indicated that the tingle dulled when I clenched them and deepened when I spread them wide. I followed the pull of that pulse to Gregory's bed.

"It seems too obvious," Wally said. "Statistics clearly show that goblins excel at hiding things. To put it near his sleeping area would be ridiculous."

I ran my fingers over the mattress, the sheets and the pillow, the pulse deepening as I got closer to the foot of the bed. "But he had nowhere else to hide anything. And if he left the room on his own, he might have thought he'd be coming back."

There was nothing in the sheets, but that pulse was still there. I pulled the mattress up—nothing. As I pulled my hand out from under it, my fingers slid against something like a flap. No, a slit had been cut into the underside of the mattress, almost imperceptible. "Bingo."

I reached in, felt paper, and pulled out a small bundle of pages, fanning them over the bed. "These are Ethan's cheat sheets!"

"We could use them," she whispered, as though someone might be listening in. Which I supposed was a distinct possibility.

I frowned. "But if Gregory wasn't taking these to sell them or turn Ethan in, what was he doing out the night he went missing?"

A booming announcement cut through the air, sudden enough that we both jumped.

"Mason Whitehall, report to Director Frost immediately."

I grabbed Wally's arm. "That's the missing kid. How can he be called to her office if he's missing?"

She frowned. "Could you have made a mistake?"

I'd been so sure his name was on the list of missing kids, but it struck me that there was a simple way of checking. We could watch her office, see if he showed up.

I tucked the cheat sheets back to where they'd been and let the mattress fall into place.

"Come on, we can see her doors from a spot down the hall."

I bolted from the room, Wally rushing to try and keep up with me, but I didn't slow, not for a second.

We covered the short distance in under a minute, skidding to a stop at the top of the stairs. The double door was shut and the director's thug, Adam, stood outside it, hidden in the shadows.

"Hey, did Mason show up?" I asked before I thought better of it.

Adam lifted his head, eyes narrowing as he looked our way. "No."

I nodded and slid down to sit at the top of the stairs, feet on the first step, watching the door.

"Wild?" Wally crouched down beside me.

"Why would they call him to the office if he's on the list of missing kids?" I asked again. Then a new possibility struck me. "Or are they worried about him being taken?"

My blood ran cold. The kidnappings seemed to take place after the trials. What if the director knew who was at risk?

We needed to see that paper with the list of kids on it. There could be more names added.

Which meant we were going to break into the director's office.

CHAPTER 19

We waited for over an hour, sitting at the top of the stairs watching the director's door for the boy to make an appearance. Mason was called twice more over the PA system, but he never showed. My skin prickled each time he was called. Every part of me knew he wasn't going to show, but I still waited. Just in case I was wrong. Finally, I turned away from the doors, Adam gave us a pointed glare from his spot in front of the director's door, and we headed back to our room.

Only Pete and Orin were there.

"Where's Ethan?" I asked as I shut the door.

"Where have you been?" Pete asked from the bed. "Did you go to the healers?"

I hadn't but felt remarkably okay. I'd take it as a win.

"Where is he?" I asked again, and Orin shook his head.

"He didn't want to wait for you. Said he had things to do."

I retrieved the sheets from Gregory's mattress and held them out to the others. "First thing's first. Wally and I found the cheat sheets."

Pete jumped up and I held them above his head. "Hey, let me see!"

When Orin took a step toward me, I pointed a finger at him. "Hear me out. If we got caught with these, what would happen?"

"Expelled," Wally said, her voice solemn. "It would be instant, there would be no recourse."

I took the papers and shoved them under Ethan's mattress. "He might be part of our crew, but if anyone is getting expelled, it can be him."

Pete grinned and spread his hands wide. "But can't we just look?"

"You want Ethan to—" I cut off as the door opened and Wonder Bread himself walked in. And he was not alone.

"You want Ethan to what?" Ethan put his hands on his hips. Colt stood to his left, a loose ease to his body. He was fit like Ethan, only not so bulky. Colt's body was leaner as if he'd actually trained for the physical strain of the trials and not just lifted weight to gain mass.

He held a hand up in a half wave. "Hey."

"What's he doing here?" Pete spluttered. "He's not part of our crew."

"Relax, he's here to help us find Gregory. Seeing as Wild here is *afraid* to be alone." The flash of heat that coursed through my cheeks was surely visible. The way that Colt was watching me was so not helping.

Pete nudged me. "Hey, does he know—"

"Yeah," I muttered. "Wonder Bread told him."

Pete let out a snarl. "What the hell, man? How are you going to pass the final tests if you can't keep a secret?"

It was Ethan's turn to flush. "Look, people are talking. You aren't hiding it as well as you think, Wild. I mean, look at you. You're huge for a 'fifteen-year-old boy.'"

I took a step, fists clenched, and Ethan took a step back. "Not my fault you can't keep it under your hat."

A strained silence hung in the room for a few beats before Ethan broke it.

"We have half a day." He shrugged. "If there is any chance of finding the goblin or the others, we need more help. Colt will help. I trust him."

He wasn't wrong, but he wasn't right either.

It struck me that Ethan shouldn't care enough to bring in outside help. He didn't even like Gregory. Orin ghosted up behind me, just the slightest change in air pressure tipping me off. Low and quiet, he whispered in my ear, "He thinks Gregory has the cheat sheets."

Bingo. Then we'd use Ethan, just like he planned to use us.

I made myself smile. "Well, let's get going then. Wally, you and Pete find out about the girl, Lisa the snake shifter. Ethan, you go with Colt—"

"No," Orin said, "I will go with Ethan."

Ethan spluttered, obviously not thrilled with that prospect.

I shot a look at Orin. "We need to keep an eye on him," he whispered, his mouth barely moving.

Again, a good point. But for good or for ill, that left me with Colt. "Fine. Check out the House of Shade. Colt and I will see what we can discover about Mason."

When we left the room, Colt quickly fell into step beside me, a few inches taller, broader across the shoulders. Next to a big guy, I didn't look so masculine, even I could see that. Damn it. A few more days, that was all I needed.

"Mason was roomed down this way, with another guy I know," Colt said, pointing to the third floor.

I nodded and let him lead.

"Where are you from?" Colt led the way through the mansion toward where Mason had roomed.

"Texas," I said. Was he flirting with me? How would I know? Me and flirting were *no bueno*. He blew out a big breath, drew another in, but said nothing else.

Apparently, I wasn't the only one not sure what to say.

We reached Mason's room and I knocked on the door. A young guy with shockingly bright red hair opened the door. He wasn't much of a looker, but his eyes were as green as spring grass, and something about him, his stature and the way he held himself, reminded me of Gregory.

"Goblin?" I blurted out. His face fell into a snarl.

Colt snickered. "Jesus, that was badly done."

"I am," the red head snapped, long fingers curling around the door.

I held up both hands, palms out. "Sorry. Gregory is a friend of mine. Do you know him?"

"I thought we were here for Mason?" Colt asked.

"Mason is missing," the goblin snapped, showing sharp teeth. "And Gregory got what was coming to him."

A chill zipped down my spine. "Why would you say that?"

The door slammed in my face. Or would have had I not stuck my foot into the opening. I pushed my way into the room while Colt said something behind me along the lines of "this is not a good idea."

But he followed me in. I booted the door shut and grabbed the red-headed goblin by one arm. "What do you mean Gregory got what was coming to him?"

"He thought he was better than us. Because he looks so human. His mom was half human." He spat the words at me. "He's a damn pretty boy."

I frowned. "You could pass for an ugly human. You know that, right?"

"Don't flatter him," Colt said. "It won't work."

"I wasn't," I growled. "Tell me what you know about Gregory."

The goblin tried to pull away from me, but I tightened my hold on him and locked eyes with him. There was darkness in me, I knew that, and I felt it uncoil like a beast coming awake. It surged up slowly, spreading through my limbs, spilling up into my eyes until everything around me grew still, right down to the pulse of my heart.

The goblin's eyes widened and he gulped. "I overheard one of the vamps say that they needed to speak to Gregory. That he was doing so well, he wouldn't have to finish the trials. That he could just skip the rest. Lucky bastard."

I frowned and the darkness I'd felt leeched out of me like a puff of smoke on the wind. I let go of the goblin and stepped back, shaken by what I'd felt as much as what I'd heard. Like I was a stranger to myself.

Colt gave a low whistle. "I've heard about Shades being able to pull the truth from someone, but I've never seen it. That is seriously badass."

The goblin curled around himself. "Get out of my room, *Shade*."

I made myself ask one more question. "Was it the same way with Mason? He was told that he was able to skip ahead?"

He bobbed his head once. "Yes."

"You just follow people around? Creepy, dude, seriously creepy," Colt said, and the goblin took a swipe at him. Colt was fast, I'd give him that. He danced back and pulled his wand in the space of a heartbeat, pointing the weapon at the goblin.

"I think not. This isn't my first time facing one of your kind."

I headed to the door. "We're done here," I said letting myself out. Colt could follow or not. My mind was whirling.

Someone—no, not just someone, a vampire—had offered Gregory and Mason a way to skip ahead. Because they were doing so well in the trials. Gregory I could believe. Despite the bind he'd been in when I met him, he was smart, wily. "Did you know Mason?"

Colt hurried to catch up to me as I strode through the mansion, heading outside. I needed to breathe the fresh air. I needed to be out of this place so I could think straight.

"I knew him a little. Are you asking me if he was good enough to be called up?"

"Called up, that's what it is?"

Colt shrugged as we pushed the main doors open and walked across the wide lawn. "If you're good enough, you might get asked to skip. Or at least that's the rumor. I've never actually known anyone who was pulled out and given a pass."

"So it's a valid thing. Something the kids might believe?" I drew a breath of the air and let it out slowly.

"Valid, but unlikely. Mason was not the top of his class. Middle or lower would be my guess based on who he hung with. The status of your friends usually indicates where you lie within your group." We'd reached the edge of the trees and I stepped under the cover and kept walking, taking us deeper into the forest.

"He'd go with someone he trusted, someone he thought was actually able to enforce a rule like that. At least in the beginning. Gregory was fighting to get away when I found him," I said, more to myself than to Colt. "He was smart. He figured out pretty quickly that something was wrong."

"What do you mean?" Colt asked.

"I saw him being taken. I tried to stop the people who had him, and he called to me for help." It was only then I realized that was why I'd headed out this way. To look for clues. "They dragged him out here."

I pointed at a small spot at the center of three trees. To the right was a bigger tree and I laid my hand on the wide trunk. This was where Rory had dragged me down and hidden me from the assassin.

A slow turn and the heel of my boot dug into the soil, leaving a distinct mark. There had to be tracks. And tracks never lied.

I crouched by the tree and tried to put my body into the same position it had been in that night. Colt crouched with me, close enough that I could smell the cologne he wore. I couldn't help it, I took a deep breath. Spicy and a little bit sweet.

"What do you smell?" he asked.

I laughed. "Just your perfume."

He laughed right back at me. "Gotta keep the ladies happy."

I rolled my eyes and focused on what was in front of me. This was where I'd seen the tip of the assassin's boot. I had to work to suppress the fear that rose in me. Not a warning, just a true fear of how close I'd come to biting it that night.

I closed my eyes, recalling the direction of Gregory's final shout. Opening them, I pointed in that general direction. "Gregory and his captors, they were out there."

"How do you know?"

"I just do." I wasn't about to tell him all my secrets.

He grabbed my arm as we stood, and then he wobbled and fell against me. I caught him, and he slowly stood, far, far too close. "And here I thought you didn't like me."

Part of me wanted to pull away, the other part thought *oh hell, why not?* For all I knew, I could die tomorrow in the next trial.

The "oh hell" part won. Colt cupped my face, bent his head and brushed his lips against mine. Nice, sweet . . . safe. He tasted like his cologne, a little bit spicy, a little bit sweet, maybe even a little bit magical.

"What the hell is going on here?"

The words cut through the air like a blade as sharp as the one I carried. Worse, Rory was the one who yelled them.

BOOK THREE

CHAPTER 1

Being caught kissing a boy in a forest by Rory shouldn't have bothered me. After all, I'd seen him kissing Missy—a bleach blonde I know for a fact stuffed her bra with her socks—behind the five and dime—twice. The first time, I'd run back the way I'd come, embarrassed and not sure why. The second time, he'd seen me before I could react. Rather than stop, he'd turned so his back was to me, then continued to kiss pretty, girly, hair always perfect, makeup always on straight, stuffed boobs Missy.

I pulled back from Colt, just enough so that I could turn and arch an eyebrow at Rory even though my face was about to combust if the heat rushing to my cheeks was any indication. Before I could form an answer with my tingling, kiss-stung lips, Colt did a very dumb, very male thing.

He stepped between me and Rory.

"Who the hell do you think—"

And that's where the question ended.

I stepped to the side to avoid the sharp right hook I saw coming about three miles off, in time to see Rory's fist connect with the side of Colt's head. Colt's eyes rolled back, and his body went limp like Rory had pulled every pin in every joint of a marionette.

"I told you to stay safe." Rory stepped around the still falling Colt and clamped a hand on my wrist.

My jaw dropped, and heat snapped through me again, although this time it was purely anger. "I *am* safe, you idiot. You said to stay in groups. Two is a group. Or was, until you knocked him out. What's wrong with you?"

I yanked my arm, but his strength topped mine and then some. His fingers didn't budge and the dark glower in his eyes deepened until I wasn't sure if I was looking at the boy I'd grown up with, or a man I didn't know at all.

Excited anticipation fluttered in my stomach and electricity sizzled across my skin, but I didn't have time to wonder at the strange reaction.

He leaned closer and lowered his voice, rough with a warning. "You've never been a stupid girl, Belle, don't start now. He's not the sort that'll keep you safe from what's hunting you. You know that."

A memory of the other night flashed through my head. Uncomfortable heat wormed under my collar.

I shook it off. Sure, it would have been dangerous to be out here alone, or with Colt, in the middle of the night. But it was broad daylight, and Rory was just being an overprotective douche. The man needed to be reminded of boundaries.

I drove my forehead forward, intent on a headbutt. He jerked to the side, missing it. I twisted my arm and yanked at the weak part of his grip, the break between his fingers and thumb. My arm slipped, but he bore down, keeping hold of me. I used his distraction to quickly step to the side and upper cut with my other hand, connecting with his jaw, hard.

He grunted and his head snapped back. His weight followed, forcing him to stagger backward. His hand tightened on my arm for a moment, as if he planned to use me to brace himself. It surely would've worked, dragging me with him, but I was banking on the fact that he didn't want to hurt me. Sure enough, he released his grip, putting him at the mercy of his momentum. First one heel caught on the grass, then the other. He couldn't get his footing and went down hard, his butt slamming into the grass.

I didn't hide my grin, standing over both downed guys. Rory's eyes came up, slowly, and a sparkle of fire lit in their depths. The strange surge and sizzle from a moment ago blasted through me again.

Not surprisingly, given our history, a smile flitted across Rory's full lips. "I see you haven't changed one bit. Same old fire. Same hard head."

I snorted and rolled my eyes. "Like you can talk." I stalked past him, leaving Colt alone in the grass. He could take care of himself and he was already groaning, sitting up, as I took off.

I hit the double door of the mansion hard enough that both sides flung open and banged against the back wall, startling several of the kids, making them leap back, raise their hands and wands lifted in defense. I ignored them, taking the stairs to my dorm.

Wally and Pete startled when I pushed inside, Pete sitting on his bed and Wally leaning against the wall. Her dark brown hair spilled over her shoulder as she tilted her head to the side. "Where are the others? Did you find out anything?"

I pushed past her, out of breath from the stairs, and headed into the bathroom.

"Well, when you've got to go, you've got to go," Wally said. "You know, your chances of damaging your kidneys and colon go up by one-point-five percent every time you hold it in."

"Gross," Pete said.

Their voices droned on, blending together as I leaned over the sink and splashed water over my face. I felt bad about Colt. He'd had no chance against Rory's fist—I didn't know anyone who could stay standing after a full-on punch from Rory. But that strange surge of excitement I'd felt with Rory had my heart pounding. I felt ready to run full speed into trouble. Or sneak into danger and work out a way to get back out again.

Ready to pick up right where we'd left off.

But this wasn't the farm. This game had life-and-death stakes. Which meant I needed to rein in this sensation, no matter how good it felt.

A few splashes of water on my face, and I headed out the door. "I'll be back, you two. I'm going to grab some food," I called over my shoulder, "then you can tell me what you learned."

Wally gave me a salute, and Pete nodded as I strode out of the room. I loaded up two to-go containers of food in the mess hall, barely looking at what I was piling on, only knowing I was starving and needed fuel.

Back in the room, Wally and Pete filled me in on what they'd learned about the missing snake shifter.

"Lisa told her friends that someone higher up suggested she'd get to skip the rest of the trials because she was doing so well." Wally said and shot Pete a look. I stuffed a chunk of potato slathered in cream cheese, bacon, and chives into my mouth.

"Lemme guess," I swallowed my mouthful and jammed in a roast beef chaser. "She wasn't, was she?"

Pete shook his head. "Her friends felt bad talking about her, but they said she was middle of the pack at best. Not even an alpha personality. They weren't surprised that she'd accepted an offer like that. They figured it was the only guarantee she'd get."

A moment later, Ethan and Orin stepped into the room, eyes shooting daggers at one another. Or maybe wands and fangs.

Ethan puffed out his chest. "We got some good info. The ones we talked to thought—"

"That he was going to be moved through the trial?" I offered as I stuck my fork into another potato chunk, this one covered in some sort of gravy and hunks of cheese. If nothing else, the food here was spectacular.

Ethan frowned, and we filled him and Orin in on our findings.

"Where is Colt?" Ethan looked around as if the other boy could be hiding under one of the beds.

"We went our separate ways," I mumbled. I'd cleaned off both plates and a nice food lethargy was stealing over me. "Orin, you want to come with me to get that paper from the director's desk tonight? We can do it at midnight." I yawned and crawled into my bed. It was not quite noon, but I was exhausted and my body was shutting down. "Wake me up when it's time to go."

I'm not even sure that he answered me. My head hit the pillow and I was out like a light. But my sleep was far from restful.

My dreams were disjointed and laced with panic. Shadows chased me, and when I turned to fight them, they engulfed me—my arms and legs went numb, my body slid to the ground. Helpless. I was helpless, and I hated it.

Blink.

I stood at the edge of our old farmhouse, watching it burn. Animals lay dead all around me, their limbs twisted, and the smell of death filled my lungs, tightening them more than the smoke. These animals had been mine to care for, mine to protect. And I'd failed them. Waves of fire rushed straight toward me, faster than I could even turn away from. I threw my hands up—

Blink.

Sam screamed for me on the edge of a cliff, high above me, high above the river of rushing water beyond me. "Wild! Help me!" Her voice cut into me, drove me forward even though there was no way to get to her. I threw myself at the sheer rock face, my fingers digging into it, sliding. "I'm coming!" The rock pulled away in pieces like shale. Her screams filled the air around me, pitching higher and higher, charged with panic and pain, and I couldn't get to her, I couldn't save her—

Blink.

A figure cloaked in darkness stood across from me, less than ten feet away, and yet I couldn't see his face. Everything around him was hidden in shadows. Something about him rang familiar to me. The way he moved, like liquid night, the gesture of one hand as he pointed to me. "I know you, Wild. And I will come for you."

Blink.

I was against that tree in the woods, Rory's arms and legs around me, his finger tapping the pulse point in my throat. Dangerous, he was dangerous. But he was home too. His arms tightened around me, and I relaxed, breathing in his scent. "You shouldn't trust me," he whispered as his arms tightened further, crushing me, snapping the bones in my chest until they pressed into my lungs, my body gasping for air—

"Wake up," the voice growled in my ear. Not Rory, someone else.

I opened my eyes to see Orin's face inches from mine. I slapped him away and rolled out of bed, that last piece of the dream sticking with me. I shook my head once and stood, still in my clothes.

We crept to the door to see Wally and Pete waiting on the other side and, shock of shocks, Ethan.

"Can't let you have all the fun," he said.

I glanced at Orin and Pete. The other two guys shrugged.

Whatever they'd done or said, he'd obviously agreed to join our expedition—or been forced into it, though I rather doubted the forced part. He'd agreed to this for some reason or another, no doubt because he thought it would work for him somehow. I made a motion with one hand for them to follow me, and they fell into a line, spaced out, behind me. We headed down the hall a ways before a warning tingle hit my spine. Orin shot forward and grabbed my arm.

Vampire, he mouthed.

We peeled off, nearly to the stairwell. I motioned for everyone to hide, and we all ducked back, hiding in the shadows as best we could. Orin, of course, blended in completely, and the others . . . well, if you didn't look too closely you could pass by them. Assuming you weren't a vampire sniffing for scents and listening for heartbeats.

Voices drifted up to us from the stairwell, the footsteps silent.

"Watch them closely. It feels like the night is holding its breath." That was . . . Sunshine's voice. Crap!

Pete had tucked in beside me and he shivered, recognizing the Sandman too. I clamped a hand over his mouth. I could almost feel a squeak ready to sneak out past his traitorous lips.

"I was just about to check their room. Wild likes to wander. I'll keep her put."

My belly dropped to the floor. Rory? Rory was checking on me for the Sandman? That last dream with him came crashing back in a sickening flood. My stomach rolled, and I had to fight the nausea that crept up my throat.

"Good. Alert me if anything is amiss," the Sandman growled, his words barely audible.

I held my breath, waiting for Rory to mount the stairs. Waiting for Sunshine to walk with him. They'd notice us for sure. Rory would, at any rate. I'd never been able to hide from him.

Except no one skulked past us. No one crested the stairs. How was Rory planning to check up on me?

Orin stiffened, sharpening my focus.

A familiar vampire materialized *out of thin air* as he worked his way down the stairs to the second floor. If he'd stepped foot on our landing, not far away, I hadn't seen it. It almost seemed like he was following Rory and Sunshine, wherever they'd gone. Who was hunting whom?

I counted another thirty seconds. "Now," I whispered.

Our group hurried to the director's outer office. I reached for the door to her inner sanctum, but Ethan stopped me, putting an arm across the top of my chest.

He lifted his wand, twirled it once, and light blue sparks sprang from it, like the sparklers I'd made with the twins the year before on the Fourth of July.

Ethan waited for the sparks to absorb into the metal knob, then opened it, and the five of us slid through into the dark of the room. The click of the door shutting behind us was loud to my ears, even though I knew it was barely above a whisper.

"All clear," Pete whispered, and he was clearly talking about the assistant. Even the most dedicated employees didn't work around the clock.

"Hurry," Orin said, gesturing toward the door. "If there are any wards, it won't be long before someone shows up to check it out."

Ethan led the way, hurrying to the director's big desk. I raced in after him, knowing *wards* meant an alarm of some kind.

"Where were the papers?" Ethan asked.

"She had it right on top," I said. "A piece of paper on top of a pale green folder. The paper was a list of the missing kids. There had to be more information than that on it too." At least, that was what I was banking on.

Ethan held his wand up, the tip glowing with light. "Well, unless she's a complete fool, it won't still be there."

I did my best not to put my fingers on anything, using the edge of my sleeve to open the drawers and peek inside. Most were strangely empty, as if the desk were just a prop on a stage.

Wally had dived into the books on the shelves, trailing her fingers across the spines. Pete and Orin stood at the door, ears pressed to the wood.

On top of the desk was a single file folder, this one dark red, not the pale green I remembered. I leaned in, grabbing Ethan's hand so as to direct the light from the wand. I read the words on that folder, and then read them again, thinking I'd made a mistake. "That's my name," I said at last. "My real name."

Maribel "Wild" Johnson.

My heart pounded out a wicked drumbeat as I put a single finger to the edge of the folder and flipped it open. Stamped in red across my file was a single word.

Missing.

CHAPTER 2

The next morning came far too fast as far as I was concerned. We'd gotten back to the room without a problem, and everyone had gone to bed, silent. Because what was there to say, really? The file folder said I was missing.

Only I wasn't.

What the hell was going on? Was I the next target of whoever had stolen the other missing kids? The vampires Rory had warned me about, and whatever mages they'd roped into their scheme? Or did this have something to do with the assassin who was after me?

I tossed and turned, my mind unable to shut off until the light in the room began to shift. My eyes drifted shut as the sun rose, and then, seconds later, it seemed, someone shook my shoulder.

"Wild," Wally said. "Wake up, something is happening."

I sat up, blinking, unable to see anything it was so dark. "Open the curtains."

"They are open. It's after nine in the morning," she said. "And the moon is still high."

I rolled out of bed as Pete flicked on a light. Everyone squinted against the glow, and I waved at him. "Turn it off, Pete."

Orin slid to the door. "Someone is here."

The door opened, and Jared stood there holding a flickering torch in one hand, his eyes unreadable in the dancing light. "Are you ready to face the House of Night?"

This was new. I thought this was supposed to be about randomness? "Why aren't we going to choose for ourselves?" I challenged him.

He smiled. "Because the House of Night is about accepting what is, and what you cannot change."

I didn't like the pattern the trials were suddenly taking. And I wasn't sure about Jared. He, himself, didn't bother me, but the fact that he was a vampire did. The same vampire, in fact, we'd seen roaming the halls last night. "Long as none of us go missing, I think we'll be fine."

He jerked as if I'd slapped him, although he caught himself quickly. "Follow me."

Orin fell in behind him first, then Ethan, Pete, and Wally. I paused in the threshold. A warning instantly throbbed through me, tingling across my skin. Something had changed in the mansion overnight, increasing the danger fourfold. I told myself it had nothing to do with our midnight break in. We'd taken nothing from the director's office, and we'd kept our hands off anything that would have left prints.

But I was nobody's fool and wasn't going to lie to myself. We'd tripped something the night before, only we hadn't realized it at the time. I was sure of it.

I jogged to catch up to the others, stepping beside Wally. She glanced at me.

"The House of Night will be interesting," she said.

I made myself grin at her even while my body and mind churned with worry like they were trying to make butter. "You looking forward to it? This will be your house."

"No, I am not," she said softly. "They treat necromancers poorly. The vampires, that is. So, while it is the best fit for me, I am not looking forward to the schooling."

I frowned. "Just like those three girls."

"Yes." She sighed. "If I could slide into one of the other houses, that would be ideal. But you will see soon enough what I am capable of. No other house would have me. My magic can't be anything but what it is. No matter that it is weak."

Before I could respond, Jared led us out through a back door of the mansion and into a courtyard where two buses waited, idling in the darkness.

"You sure that's enough buses?" Pete asked.

"Do not question your betters, boy," Jared said. His eyes landed on each of us in turn, as if daring us to go on. I straightened up and so did Wally. Orin and Pete froze, and Ethan looked away. So be it, the girls would lead the way.

Again. My lips twitched a little at that. It amused me that the guys in our group were so willing to let the girls lead.

We loaded up as two more troops of kids arrived—one of them the trio of girls who'd beaten Wally up two nights previously.

I saw them coming and walked to the front of the bus, waiting for them to take the first step in. "Bus is full. Use the other one."

One of them hissed at me—full on viper hissed—but they did as I said, backing down and moving to the other bus.

The driver shivered. "Thanks, they give me the fecking willies. Shoot! Sorry, fudging. Not supposed to swear in front of you kids and your delicate freaking ears. Likely never heard a word like that before. Am I right or am I right?" He grinned, and the smile stretched from ear to ear, his eyes bugging out a little. Goblin then. His voice had a lilt to it that tugged at me.

I grinned back. "Yeah, never heard a bad word in my life. Surely would never use one. Do you think adults really believe that if they don't swear in front of us, we won't ever use them ourselves?"

He shrugged, grabbed the door handle and pulled the folding doors shut. "Who knows what adults think? I'm just paid to drive the bus."

I crouched down beside him as he pulled out of the mansion's grounds, watching where we were going as he droned on about the different kids he'd seen come through in all his years of driving for the academy.

"The only one that ever done impressed me was a tall kid, Shade, I think he was, but really he ended up being something else." He gave a low whistle and my attention shifted fully to him.

"What do you mean he ended up being something else?"

"Nah, not supposed to talk about it. Like talking about the boogeyman before you put the kiddies to bed." He grinned and winked again. "But if you come back on my bus, I'll tell you all about him." We'd begun to slow, and I could see the gates ahead of us, lit up in unnatural night. Our driver cranked the wheel to the left, taking us to a gate that I would have known was the House of Night even if I'd not been told. Massive wrought iron, solid black, partially covered in the thorny ivy, the gates were right out of a horror movie. Right down to the skulls set up on the spikes at the top. A lovely touch to be sure.

I stuck out my hand. "My name is Wild."

I hadn't thought his grin could get wider, but I'd been wrong. He clasped my hand. "Mighty fine to meet you, Wild. My friends call me Gory." He braked smoothly, rolling the bus to a stop.

Pete pushed up behind me, waiting for me to step down. "Gory Goblin? You related to Gregory? I heard all the clans named their people alphabetically. Like if your dad is a Luke, then all the kids have to start with an L."

Gory laughed. "True, that be true. And often the women who marry in change their names to the same letter. So yup, I am related to Greggy. Where is he anyway? His mam asked me to let her know should I see him. Bit on the pretty side that one, but a right smart head he has on his shoulders."

I shot a look at Pete, whose eyes popped open wide. I grabbed him by the shoulder and all but pushed him down the stairs.

"Thanks for the ride!" I called over my shoulder.

"Say hi to Greggy if you see him! Tell him to keep on keeping on!" Gory called back.

Sweet baby Jesus in a manger of spoiled straw, Gregory's family hadn't been told that he was missing? Just like we hadn't been told anything about Tommy's death. The blood in my veins turned sluggish, not something I needed only moments before stepping into the next trial. One that was bound to be worse than the others we'd faced. How could it not be when it was run by vampires and necromancers and who knew what else?

"We gotta go." I kept moving, forcing my way through the funk. "Come on guys. Let's get this done."

Ethan tried to push to the front of our group, but Orin blocked him.

"This is not your house, Ethan."

Wally bobbed her head. "Exactly."

He cleared his throat and lowered his voice, drawing us all in close. "I remember some of my . . . paperwork."

My eyebrows went up, but I motioned him forward. Fair enough—if he thought he could lead, let him lead. Orin and Wally let him pass, but I could see Orin, especially, was reluctant to do so.

"And?" I asked Ethan, "what exactly do you remember?" Part of me wondered if he'd actually tell us anything. Other than taking note that the cheat papers were exactly that, I hadn't actually looked at them. To be fair, if I'd not slept the previous day away, I would have.

I had never claimed to be a saint. I needed to survive this to keep my siblings alive and well, and for them I'd break all the rules.

Ethan went for his wand holder, pulled out his wand, and lowered his voice further. "Necromancers first. Then ghost walkers. Vampires last. That's the order."

"Then let Wally lead up there with you," I said. "You really want to be the first to get hit by a—Wally, what will the necromancers send after us?"

"Zombies," she said without hesitation. "Lots and lots of zombies. You can take their heads, that will slow them down, but it won't kill them like in the movies. You have to knock out or kill the necromancer to stop them completely. Otherwise, the body parts of the dead things will just keep on coming. I mean, if Ethan wants to try and go first, that's fine by me."

That slowed Ethan and he tipped his head. "Fine. You're right, this is your house, after all."

This morning, no beautiful woman greeted us atop the gates. In fact, no one else was around. Had all the other kids slipped ahead of us? Or had they left? I turned around, realizing that there was no other bus. We were here alone.

A warning shot down my spine. Something was off.

The gate creaked open on its own, and we stepped through, the air around us tensing and cooling rapidly as if we'd stepped not only through the gate but from summer into autumn. I blinked and took in what awaited us.

It looked like a pastoral scene straight out of some fairy tale villain's playbook. A stone wall well over twelve feet high in some places wrapped around what could only be a graveyard, a huge metal gate locked at the front, skulls and crosses welded to it.

"The graves of the five houses," Wally whispered. "It's protected so the dead who served our world can rest."

"That can't be right," Ethan said. "Because we know they're going to raise the dead to challenge us. They would never stick us here."

That warning tingle intensified.

"Could it be an illusion?" Pete asked.

Ethan lifted his wand and did a swooping swirl, whispering a word under his breath. Sparks spat and fizzled. "No," he said, shaking his head, "it's not an illusion."

"These zombies . . . they will be stronger than anything any necromancer could ever raise in the real world," Wally said. "Their strengths when they were alive will be available to them in death. Which is why they are kept here. They are supposed to be kept safe from being raised. They would only send us here if they want to test whether we can rise to an impossible challenge . . . or if they want us to fail."

Slowly, the four members of my crew turned and looked at me. Ethan actually looked upset. Pete horrified. And Wally had tears in her eyes. What the hell?

I shook my head. "What? Why are you all looking at me?"

Orin smiled, slow and sad. "You're supposed to be missing," he said with more than a tinge of sorrow to his voice. "What better way to have it happen than for you to go missing in the middle of the House of Night's trial?"

I shook my head harder. "No, no, no. That makes no sense. The other kids that went missing, they were all asked."

"And what would you say if you were asked?" Orin countered.

"No. She'd say no and we all know it. Anyone who's spoken to her once would know it," Wally answered for me. She wasn't wrong.

Especially now that I knew what had happened to the kids who'd taken up the offer to skip ahead. Or sort of knew what had happened to them.

"Fine, so this is my fault? You want me to go first?" I took a few steps and Wally sighed.

"I want you to walk with me at the front, not Ethan. Your warning system is going to help us get through this. Our odds increase incrementally with you in our group, even if this is a set up." She turned away from me and headed toward the locked gates. They swung open, welcoming us in.

"My warning system?" I stepped up next to her and slowly pulled my knife from my belt. A flicker from that very warning system cut down my spine like tiny little needle jabs. Not enough to hurt but enough to make sure I was aware of what was about to happen.

Wally plucked at a long stalk of grass as her eyes roved the space ahead of us. "I've been reading up on Shades. You have a built-in warning system, better than any of the other houses, as you are meant to survive attacks from many different quarters. You are meant to be aware of the world in a way the rest of us are not. Of course, not all Shades have it. About fifteen percent of Shades have a faulty warning system. Less than five percent have a heightened warning system, one that provides a wider range."

I didn't tell her she was wrong. That warning system, as she called it, had been saving my butt most of my life and since I'd arrived here, it had kicked into high gear.

She stepped to the right, her hand trailing over the tops of the gravestones closest to her, a sigh slipping from her lips. "The dead are so quiet, so simple. So much easier to talk to than the living."

"How big is this magical graveyard?" I asked.

"Acres and acres," she said. "Miles upon miles."

Pete let out a groan. "I'm shifting. If we're going to be running for long distances, I'd prefer to do it as a honey badger."

I didn't disagree with him—he was much more agile in his animal form, and far more aggressive, which wasn't a bad thing in the least. The fact that he said nothing about his clothes told me just how worried he was. He just stripped, tossed his clothes to the side and shifted to his four-legged form.

I reached out and put a hand on Wally, slowing her. "Just take it easy. We don't want to fight or run until we have to."

"Agreed," she whispered. "There is another necromancer here. He is starting to call the dead to life. I've only ever tried to handle two or three at a time. Zombies that is."

"Crap," Ethan whispered, his fear all but tangible. I glanced back at him. He and Orin were side by side, Pete waddling along between them and us, sniffing at the graves. Orin's eyes glittered in the darkness, and for the first time I was worried about him.

Not that he wouldn't make it.

But that he might have been setting us up. According to Rory, vampires were in on this, maybe even behind it. Mason's roommate also thought a vampire was involved with his disappearance. Could Orin have been playing us all along? Vampires hated necromancers, so why had he defended Wally? Thoughts and questions rolled through me like tiny bolts of lightning.

A slow grin spread across Orin's face, and my heart picked up, adrenaline lacing each beat.

What if the vampire Rory had warned me about wasn't Jared, or some nameless blood sucker?

What if it was Orin?

CHAPTER 3

I didn't have time to consider just how deep a game Orin was playing, if he was friend or foe, or whether he would stand by us now that we were here in his house. The graveyard we stood in trembled beneath our feet, the ground rumbling and rocking. A roll of earth rippled toward us like a wave in the ocean, and with it came a warning that was so thick it seemed to smother my lungs, freezing the air in them.

We were in serious trouble.

"Jump!" I said as the wave in the ground got close, and we all leapt into the air. Well, with the exception of Pete, who was tossed up by the rolling earth, flipped like an oversized pancake. His paws scrabbled outward as he twisted, reaching in four separate directions, his teeth bared and his tail jutting straight up before he fell back down. I landed in a crouch, fist to the ground.

The ground gave beneath me, like it had turned into a pile of quicksand. I quickly rolled away, but there wasn't far to go. All around us the ground sunk and dropped around the different markers. "The graves."

"The dead are being wakened!" Wally stood in the center of our group, her head thrown back, her hands outstretched. "The necromancer . . . oh God, he's so strong! How can he do this? This isn't supposed to be possible!"

"You said two or three zombies at best, that's what you can handle?" I spun in a slow circle, counting the graves coming to life. Five, six, seven . . . ten, twelve, fifteen.

I stopped counting when I realized every single grave was stirring.

Every. Single. One.

Hands, elbows, tops of heads, and shoulders pulled themselves free of the now softened ground, clawing their way toward us. Most hands were partially decomposed, others were straight up skeletal with tattered rags hanging off them. Only a few were solid, still holding muscle and bone together with actual flesh—even if that flesh was more than a little decomposed. The smell that wafted up with the emerging bodies sent us all stumbling back, Ethan gagging, and Orin pulling a face. I tried to breathe just through my mouth, but I could taste the rotting flesh which was far worse than just smelling them.

Time to move. "Wally, tell me you can slow them down!" I grabbed her arm and dragged her through the middle of the graveyard, assuming the others would follow, picking up speed as I searched for the best path between the dead, grasping bodies. The three guys stuck close, Orin falling to the back as I tried to find us a way out that didn't involve going over graves.

A hand shot out toward my ankle and I kicked it away, snapping it off at the wrist.

Fore! Pete's voice reverberated through my head as his honey badger form chittered.

"Not playing golf, Pete!" I sidestepped a pair of hands that came at us, closer to knee height. "Keep your wand out, Ethan!" I hollered.

"Really, Sherlock? I thought I'd let them take us." He snapped back then yelped and a burst of light shot up behind us. The darkness and fog faded for the space of two strides, and in that brief moment I could see, we were in far bigger trouble than I'd realized.

Acres of graveyard was an understatement. There was no end to it that I could see, no wall at the far side. And every grave was moving, every occupant climbing out.

We'd been running before. But now . . . "As fast as you can. Orin, take the lead!"

The vampire shot ahead of us, Wally falling way behind him, Pete at her side.

"Ethan. You and me at the back."

We ran, dodging hands and snapping teeth, and my adrenaline ping-ponged inside me. Because I was severely out of my element. I didn't know how to stop the dead.

"Wally, what do we do?" I shouted, and she slowed and looked over her shoulder.

"We have to fight." Her eyes were wide, shell-shocked. "We have to fight our way out. Running will only make this go on and on. In that it *is* an illusion, like a hamster's wheel that keeps going and going. The only way to make it stop is to face them."

A howl went up behind us, gurgling and wet. I dared to look back in time to see shapes bounding across the graves. Clumsy, limping, but bounding.

"Werewolves. Dead werewolves," Ethan snarled.

"Real wolves are afraid of fire," I said. "Can you do anything with that?"

"No problem." He waved his wand with a quick flick of his wrist, and three fireballs popped out of his wand like a roman candle, growing in size as they flew toward their targets.

The first fireball hit the lead wolf square in the chest, knocking it to the ground, lighting it up like a Christmas tree.

"See? This is easy." I could hear the smirk in Ethan's voice.

But I kept my eyes on the burning wolf. It shook itself and slowly got back to its feet, its fur singed in patches and still burning in others. The undead beast bared broken teeth before charging toward us once more. Now we had a werewolf on fire coming at us.

Brilliant.

We backed up until we bumped into Wally, Pete at our feet. "Orin?"

"You told him to run. He ran," Wally said. I turned around to face her.

So much for staying together.

"Best case scenario, what are our odds?"

She closed her eyes for a brief second, squeezing them shut, and then looked at me once more. "The odds are not in our favor. We can fight, but they will keep coming until we are overrun. Thousand to one. Maybe worse."

"You're the necromancer," Ethan snarled. "Shouldn't you be doing something other than giving us cruddy odds?"

For the first time in these trials, he was right. This was Wally's world and we needed her to pull it together. "We'll protect you while you figure this out." I put my back to her. "We'll stand our ground."

"That's suicide!"

I grabbed Ethan by the arm and gave him a shake. "And Wally's right. Running will get us nowhere. Orin is out there by himself figuring that out right now. We stand together, we fall alone."

"Or he's made it to the exit." Ethan turned and squared himself. "Damn vampire. They can't be trusted." We faced the wolves together, the pack of three moving faster than the other undead. As they drew closer, my jaw dropped. I couldn't help it. They looked to be not fully wolf, but not fully human either. Like the wolfman out of the old horror movies we'd watch on Saturday nights. Only they were hunched forward, not running on two legs but four.

"Are they only partially shifted?"

Ethan nodded. "Stuck between shapes in death."

There was no more time for words as the weirdly shaped animals launched at us, snarling and snapping. They were not acting like normal wolves, or even the shifter wolves we'd faced in the previous trial.

These just came straight at us with no effort at stealth or subterfuge. All three of them came for Ethan, ignoring me.

Mistake number one on their part.

He went down under the weight of them with a shout. I grabbed the one closest to me by the scruff of its neck and heaved with everything I had in me. The skin stretched and pulled, tearing as I yanked the dead wolf off Ethan, flinging it to one side and taking down two more zombies with its thick body.

A burst of light cut through the air, sending one of the wolves straight up into the air in pieces that scattered like a burst piñata at the worst kind of party. Ethan rolled from the third, and I went in with my knife, driving it down and into the thing's neck.

The wolf tried to turn his head, and I yanked the handle hard to the side, tearing the blade through the bone and rotting tissue, popping its head off like a daisy.

The dead wolf wobbled, fell to its all-too-human knees, and rolled over as its head tumbled away from its body.

Ethan and I backed up.

"Thanks," he said.

"Don't mention it." I swung my blade to the right, catching a zombie that had risen partially from a grave. "We need to get our backs against something. Stuck in the center like this, we have no chance at all."

"There's a mausoleum in the center of the graveyard," Orin said. "We can climb on top of it."

Ethan and I whipped around at the same time.

"You came back?"

I couldn't help the question. Orin tipped his head, looking like nothing more than an oversized black bird, right down to the flat black eyes.

"We're a team. We've established that. Frankly, I'm surprised at your surprise."

"You're a vampire," Ethan said, "Don't be surprised that we're surprised that you didn't just leave us here."

"That's the pot calling the kettle black," Orin threw back.

"Not the time, boys!" I said as I pushed another zombie back, shoving it with my boot. My foot sunk into its chest, trapped for a second by the partially shattered ribcage. I snarled and shook my foot harder until it was free, although covered in slimy substances I didn't want to identify.

I grabbed Wally by the arm and we bolted for the mausoleum. Part of me still worried Orin would turn on us, that he was potentially leading us into a trap, but I didn't see any other choice.

Orin led the way, cutting through the zombies with his elongated creepy claw fingers. The zombies fell under his hands better than any other weapon we'd used so far. A quick glance down at Pete showed that while his fur was covered in zombie guts, he'd suffered no bites.

"No bites?" I asked the others as we jogged along, Wally in the center of us. She was strangely silent, and I knew why without asking.

This was really *her* test, and so far she'd done nothing but give us crappy odds. She seemed to have frozen.

Orin made getting to the mausoleum seem easy. I should have been happy, but the very fact that it seemed easy felt wrong.

"Slow down." I said. "Something's off."

"If we slow down, we aren't going to make it," Ethan pointed his wand up into the air and shot a burst of light that spread out around us, showing me just what we were facing. Easily a thousand zombies moved in on us. I could see them under the fan of light. Goblins, gargoyles, shifters, and men and women who held splintered wands in their gnarled and rotting hands.

Except . . . I didn't see any vampires.

Or any obvious Shades.

"Once we're up on the building, what then?" I asked. "We'll be surrounded and there will be no way out."

"We have no choice," Ethan yelled. "We can't outrun them!"

A zombie goblin launched itself at Ethan as if to help make his point. Pete shot forward, taking the shambling undead out by the legs, but it wasn't down for good. It rolled over and pushed itself toward us again.

Like a swarm of ants. I'd seen red army ants devour a downed bird. You'd think the bird could escape, but after a thousand tiny bites, it gave up.

And the ants had their prize.

I wanted to vomit. This was not an enemy that could be killed or outrun.

But I also knew that pinning ourselves down without an out could—no, would—get us killed.

Because there was no doubt in my mind that Wally was right. This was no normal trial. It was meant to do one thing and one thing only.

Eliminate me.

CHAPTER 4

We have no choice but to go to the mausoleum. Maybe I can blast them from there," Ethan repeated. The graveyard was full of moving parts, along with the constant groaning and shuffling of the undead as they came for us en masse. I looked to Wally.

"Wally, talk to us. Talk to me."

"We need high ground," she said, her eyes closed. "Then maybe . . . maybe I could do something."

Ethan shook his head and muttered "useless" under his breath.

"Then we go." We started out again, this time without hesitation.

Orin reached the building first, climbed up and then waited, watching with his flat black eyes as we drew close.

The mausoleum was a perfect square building with a few ornate edges, a flat roof, and no visible ladder to the top. I hurried forward, driving Wally and Pete ahead of me.

I bent and grabbed Pete around the middle and threw him up onto the building.

Damn it, I hate it when you do that! his voice echoed in my head.

I grinned. "You just wish you had wings."

"Give me a boost!" Ethan shouted.

"I am right beside you, idiot." I crouched beside him, cupping my hands, and then hoisted him up.

"Come on, Wally, you're next." I turned to see her standing behind me, her eyes despondent, arms wrapped around herself as if she wished she could shrink right where she stood.

"You should just leave me here," she said. "He's right, I'm useless to the group. I know stats, I know numbers, but I've never been trained as a necromancer. I don't know what I'm doing. I don't know how to help our group. I can feel the dead, but I don't know how to stop them. I can't . . . I can't, Wild. I'm not good like the rest of you." Her eyes flooded with tears.

"Look—" I waved a hand at the oncoming horde. "We don't have time for you to doubt yourself. We need you to be the necromancer of this group. We need you to be a badass raiser of the dead." I crouched beside her, and she reluctantly put her foot in the cup of my fingers.

I stood, boosting her high into the air. She scrambled over the edge, and I turned to see the zombies coming for me.

A semi-circle of the undead reached for me as a unit, smiles on their rotting faces. Those smiles sent chills of warning through me, and not the "hey, zombies are coming to eat you" kind of warning. This was more like "hey, whoever is running these zombies is coming for you," which was infinitely worse in my opinion. Like the necromancer controlling them could see through their eyes and knew his prey was right in front of him.

I lashed out, shoving them back, breaking off bits and pieces as fast as I could. Strike, lunge, rinse, repeat. A bite landed on my forearm, and I howled as the zombie's teeth dug into me, tearing flesh. The teeth were jagged, and they clamped on with a ferocity that would give any wolf a run for its money.

I brought my knife down hard on the biter's head, driving the blade all the way into the hilt, but it didn't let go. It shook its head and its broken body began to shift into something else—

House of Claw. Get out of there, Wild! Pete's voice came through loud and clear.

"Yeah, trying!" I yelled as I pulled the knife out and tried a different angle, jamming the blade into the zombie's head sideways, through the jaw bone. The mouth went slack on the one side, and I yanked free, blood running down my arm, my fingers numb on that side.

I backed up and reached up with my good hand. I opened my mouth to ask for help when a zombie shuffling toward me stopped me in my tracks. Instead of trying to get away, I took a step forward.

"No." I struggled to breathe around what I was seeing, the world dipping and curving like I'd held my breath for too long and was about to pass out.

My brother stepped through the crowd, his body not as rotted as the others, as if he'd only just been killed, as if he'd died protecting me as he'd promised to do if it was asked of him. The line of his jaw, the brush of his hair, the hands that had boosted me into the apple trees how many times? It was all so familiar, so unmistakably him.

This could not be happening. This had to be an illusion.

Didn't it?

"Tommy." I could barely say his name as he pushed his way through the crowd, and then he was rushing me, pushing me back against the mausoleum with so much force he knocked the wind out of me. I tried to grab at him, to see his face. I had to see his eyes. I couldn't believe this was where he'd been kept. And now he was fighting me.

"Tommy!" I bellowed his name, pain wrapping around my heart as I fought him.

The necromancer had done this to Tommy, had set my own brother against me. I drove my fist into his side, felt the ribs crack, but it didn't slow him. Not for a damn second.

His hand came up lightning fast, his fingers wrapping around my neck, squeezing.

I kicked as he lifted me, stronger than he'd ever been. Weirdly, I could only wonder if he'd been this strong as a living Shade, or if this was the strength of the undead. My brother was undead.

And he was going to kill me.

"Tommy." I whispered his name, choked on tears. I didn't want to die. But I couldn't stop him. I couldn't bring myself to destroy him.

I tried pulling his fingers off my neck, snapped one of them backward and he didn't so much as blink. Staring into his face, his rheumy eyes, I knew then there was nothing left of my brother in this body. This was not the boy that I'd adored, the one I'd looked up to and wanted to be like. Not the brother who'd shown me how to wrangle cows, ride horses. Not the brother who'd taught me how to track and survive out in the woods.

It was only his body, not his spirit.

"I'm sorry." I mouthed the words rather than spoke them as I lifted a foot and kicked him in the hip, throwing him off balance. We went to the ground and I rolled, driving my elbow into his, snapping the bone. His fingers still clung to me, but I pried them off, one broken finger at a time, gasping for breath.

Orin, Ethan, and Wally were shouting at me to get up, to hurry, but it all seemed so far away. Even the other undead seemed to be waiting to see how this played out between me and Tommy. No, not Tommy. This was not my brother, not anymore.

I spun as another body rushed through the horde. Green eyes, dark hair, and the scent of home. The other half of my childhood, this one alive and desperate. Desperate to watch my back, at all costs.

"Rory—" No words, there were no words, just his name, as Rory thrust himself into peril and rushed over to me. He dragged me back to the mausoleum. He bent and cupped his hands to give me a boost, same as I'd done for Wally and Ethan.

"What about—"

"Go. I'll be fine!" he yelled over the din, fear heavy in his voice.

Like in the trees, I knew it wasn't fear for himself, but fear for me. Fear he'd lose me as he'd lost my brother. Maybe fear that I'd end up like Tommy—

I choked back a sob and took the boost, balancing a hand on his muscular shoulder. I scrambled to hold onto the edge, Ethan helping me up the rest of the way.

I spun on my belly in time to see Rory disappear under a wave of the undead.

"Who was that?" Orin leaned over the edge.

"NO!" My scream echoed through my head. Through my heart. My middle had already been ripped open by seeing Tommy as one of them, by having to fight my own brother. To lose Rory too . . . that was beyond unfair.

A flash of his dark clothes was all I could see as he was rolled under the zombies, like an undercurrent in an ocean of the undead had taken hold of him and swept him away from me. I stood and bolted to the other side of the roof, looking for him, searching the masses with my eyes, frantic to see him one more time.

"RORY!" His name ripped out of me as I frantically searched for him.

Gone, he was gone. This time, I couldn't even see a shred of fabric.

I was no fool. There would be no diving in after him, no saving him from these creatures. He wouldn't want me to throw my own life away when we both knew he was done. That he couldn't be saved.

He'd put his life on the line for me, just like he'd said he would.

I bent at the waist, my entire body shaking. Memories and images cascaded through my head—the first time we'd gone skinny dipping in the river as kids, the two of us grinning at each other as we hid from Tommy, that cheeky ass smile of his, the feeling of his strength pooling around me and protecting me the night he'd hidden me from the assassin.

I couldn't stop the shaking, couldn't stop the tears as they bubbled up. The others were all talking at once—I could hear them in the background discussing what to do, how to get out of here. How to escape.

And all I could think about was Rory.

The way I'd talked to him. My last words to him had been spoken in anger, pushing him away. A wave of nausea rammed its way up my throat, and I threw up over the edge of the roof, right onto a zombie's head. It blinked up at me with a bemused look.

Nice shot, Pete said from beside me. *But what's got you all riled up?*

"Stop it, just stop it!" Wally yelled and I turned to see Ethan pushing her across the roof, toward the edge.

Ethan kept shoving her. "Do something to help. If you can't be useful, then you can be the bait this time. You can draw them away."

Orin just watched.

And the grief in my belly turned to an instant white-hot rage. I would not lose another friend to the army of undead.

I didn't even recall moving across the space between us, I was just there on Ethan, driving him back, my hand wrapped around his throat the way Tommy's had been wrapped around mine. I held him out over the edge of the roof, balancing him on the backs of his heels, his face red from the lack of oxygen. "You don't touch her. You don't hurt her. Got it?"

"Wild, it wasn't that bad," Wally said. "Honestly, this is too far, even for you. Don't drop him. We need him. We need all of us to get through this."

Ethan watched me with wide eyes, his entire body leaning out over the grasping, broken, and rotting hands that reached for him.

I swallowed hard and drew him back onto the roof. He fell to his knees and coughed, shaking his head and looking up at me. "What does it matter? You might as well have dropped me there? We aren't going to make it out of this. None of us are."

We all stared at him.

"What are you talking about?" Orin said. "You want to die now?"

Ethan shook his head. "Don't you get it? This isn't normal." He swept his hand over the dizzying scene. "This isn't a test for the Culling Trials. I was trained in all the variations on the challenges, going back generations. This was never mentioned. *Never.* No, this is meant to kill us. Wally was right about that much. Because even if it was meant for one of us"—he shot a glare at me—"they can't have witnesses. That's how this world works and you all know it. You can't allow witnesses to a death that was an assassination."

While I wanted to tell him he was wrong, that we would make it out of this too, I truly believed our lives hung in the balance.

I would grieve for Rory later, but right now I needed to figure this out. I had to find a way for us to escape this trial.

Wally's hand slid down to my palm and she linked her fingers with my good hand. A burst of awareness flooded over me, and I slowly turned, hanging onto her as I looked down at the sea of dead.

Glowing lights lit up inside each and every one of the bodies, throbbing with a deep green pulse that I knew without understanding belonged to the necromancer controlling them. "Do you see that?" I whispered to her.

She tightened her hold on my hand. "The light? Yes, but I don't know how to stop it."

I nodded and dragged her to the edge of the roof for a better vantage point. The zombies didn't look as rotted. The longer I stared at them, the more they looked . . . alive. "You see them as they were, not as they are."

Wally blew out a slow breath. "You shouldn't be able to see them like I do, Wild. There is only one—"

"If we can pinpoint where the light's coming from, we can stop the necromancer." I looked at her. Really looked. She was as terrified as I'd ever seen her, and I didn't think it was just the fact that we were facing death. "Wally, why does this scare you?"

"The same reason Gregory was afraid during his trial, the same reason Pete was afraid in his," Ethan said. "If she fails her own challenge, her memory will be wiped. She will be cast out of the only world that would have her and her skills."

Her face paled. "He's right. I'm terrified to blow this, not just for me but for all of us. The undead here, they are going to make a push to kill us. I can feel it growing. I don't know why the necromancer is waiting, but he is."

Out in the graveyard the light pulsed and danced, stronger to what I would guess was the north of us. A steady glow of green curled round a bigger clump of stationary zombies.

I watched that group for a beat, and not one of them took a step in our direction. I pointed. "There. That's where the necromancer is."

Wally nodded. "I know, but what good does it do? The odds of me being able to beat a necromancer of this calibre . . . well, they're not good."

"At a loss for stats. Finally," Ethan grumbled.

I stared out at that green glow and the light that radiated from the individual who had done this to us. "We kill that necromancer, and the dead go back to their graves?"

"Yes, in theory. But we only really need to knock the necromancer out," she said.

Orin had been quiet until that moment. "And just who is going to run the gauntlet and knock him out? If someone can get to him, they'll still have to fight the zombies around him, no doubt some of the strongest undead."

Slowly, they all turned to me.

I closed my eyes, taking stock of my body. My arm throbbed, aching deep to the bone where the zombie had chewed on me, and my fingers still tingled as though there had been some nerve damage. Other than that, my body wasn't in bad shape. I wasn't even exhausted. I just felt like my heart had been ripped out of my chest.

Just like when Tommy had died.

It took all my strength to push the grief down, to stuff it to the back of my heart where it wouldn't interfere with what had to happen. My survival wasn't the only thing on the line here. The others were depending on me too.

"Ethan, what kind of range do you have with that wand of yours?" When I opened my eyes, he was looking out over the milling mass. A few of the zombies were climbing on top of each other, trying to get to us. Eventually they would. They'd be just like those red army ants on the bird that should have flown away but couldn't.

There would be no waiting this out. "I'm not sure if I can reach the necromancer," he said.

"Try," I said.

He took a few steps and stood on the edge of the roof, held his wand up and then flicked his hand forward.

Hope he doesn't drop his wand, Pete muttered.

Another time I would have laughed. Another time I would have poked fun at Ethan too. But Wally was right—we needed him, we needed all of us.

A flare of light shot out from Ethan's wand, lighting up the sky with a tail like a comet. It fell about three quarters of the way to the necromancer.

Laughter boomed all around us, the zombies laughing with their master. Pete snarled, and Orin gave a low growl.

I just nodded. "So we know how far you can help us."

"Us?" Ethan raised an eyebrow. "You're going to leave me here by myself?"

I shook my head as I ripped a strip of my shirt off and wrapped it around my arm, pulling the ends with my teeth to tie it off. "No. Pete will stay with you. I'll take Orin and Wally with me, seeing as this is their house and they have the best chance of surviving."

Wally stood a little straighter. Orin rolled his eyes. "Vampires are far superior to any necromancer."

"Right, fine." I was going into battle mode. We had little chance of winning this game, but I intended to give us a chance. "Ethan, can you blast a space clear on this side so we can jump over?"

"Why not ask Wally to do it? Or can't she control even one zombie?"

His words seemed to spark something in her. She stepped forward, and I saw in her a tiny spark, a flare of pink light deep in her center.

"I'll clear the way, Wild." She looked down on the zombies at our feet, and I watched with fascination as she reached a hand out over them. The pink light in her bubbled up and trickled down her arm to drip off her fingers. Like rain drops.

"We need a thunderstorm, not a sprinkler," I said.

Her eyes whipped up to mine. "I can't. I don't know what I'm doing."

You should get Orin to throw you guys down there, see how you like being chucked around, Pete said.

I glanced down at him and he stared up at me with a wide honey badger grin.

He wasn't wrong. There was an opening about twenty feet out from the mausoleum edge.

"I'm going to regret this," I muttered. "Orin, can you throw me and Wally out there?"

Orin grinned. "I thought you'd never ask."

He took hold of me by my forearms and spun. Like he was going to throw a hammer in the Olympics. My bitten arm did not like his grip, but there was nothing for it, I had to go through with this.

Sweet baby Jesus, this was a bad idea.

I swallowed hard with the first rotation, and then he let me go and I was flying through the air, seeing the dead flash below me, their arms raised like I was at a rave and about to crowd surf. It wasn't so bad, not really.

That's the last thought that rolled through me right before I smashed into a grave stone.

Head first.

CHAPTER 5

My first thought as I came to was that I didn't have a dog, so how could a dog be pulling on my leg and my hand at the same time?

My second thought was that the dog would need to have two mouths.

My third was much clearer as I remembered my flight via Orin's throw over the zombies' heads as they reached for me right before I hit the gravestone. "You did that on purpose, Orin!" I managed to open my eyes just as Wally and Orin landed beside me, her cradled in the curve of one of his arms.

I was dragged backward, a low growl reaching my ears. Maybe it was a dog. The pounding in my head told me just how hard I'd hit that rock.

Gravestone. We were in a graveyard with zombies and a necromancer set on killing us.

"Kill our best chance at survival? I think not," Orin said. "You are more solid than I realized. I couldn't throw you as far as I thought. And I carried Wally so as not to break her."

I lifted my head to see a hunched-over zombie with my foot and boot in its mouth, its clawed fingers digging into the leather sole. I jerked my knee toward me, yanking the zombie closer, then got my foot free and booted the undead thing in the head. It fell onto its back and let out a low groan that sounded suspiciously like "Shiiiiiiiiiiit."

Orin slashed at the zombie attached to my right hand. Its head rolled off, but the hands still reached for us.

I pushed to my feet, Wally helping to steady me. The second she touched my skin, the zombies lit up like fireflies. A steady pulse of green was all around us, the source drawing closer.

"Go, go! He's making his move!" I yelled at Orin.

He ran ahead of us, and Wally and I followed, her right hand in my left.

A sharp warning spun me to the left as a zombie launched straight at Wally, teeth first, eyes missing from its skull, long stringy hair in patches, then more solid, the skin healing as I saw the person as they were before they died.

Even though I saw it differently hanging onto Wally, the thick stench of rotting flesh tickled the back of my throat. Keeping Wally behind me, I gritted my teeth and pinched my lips against the stench, then swung my blade. The knife cut directly across the zombie's neck, through the soft flesh and partially decomposed bone with an ease that surprised me. The head rolled from the shoulders and plopped to the ground, teeth and jaws still snapping.

The arms of the zombie reached for me and I shoved it back, knocking it to the ground.

I pushed another zombie back. We couldn't slow down, not if we were going to make it to the necromancer. Not if we were going to take even a portion of the chance Wally's sight gave us.

The air around us tingled, the smell of ozone cutting it just before a flash of lightning touched down to our right, sending the zombies back a good forty feet. I glanced back over my shoulder to see Ethan waving that boom stick of his around, lightning snapping down with each wave.

Another burst of lightning to our left, and one right in front of us, and the path was as clear as we were going to get it. I grabbed Wally and swung her up onto my back. My arm burned where I'd been bitten, and I could feel an infection growing there, spreading up and down in pulses.

Not good. We had to end this as fast as we could.

I tucked in close to Orin and let him clear the remaining zombies in front of us.

"We're here." He slowed. "I—" He swallowed hard. "I think it was a bad idea to bring me."

Wally let out a low groan. "No, oh no!"

"Oh no what?" I yelled. "What are you two not telling me?"

Wally slid from my back as Orin turned to face us. His eyes were still dark, but through my connection to Wally, I could see the green glow blooming in their depths. The other necromancer had him in his grasp. "Oh crap, are you kidding me? Tell me this is a really bad joke!"

Orin lunged at me and then stopped and shook his head. "I'm trying, I'm trying to fight him."

"Wally, you've got to push back!" I said as I shoved Orin back. "You've got to!"

"I know," she said. "But the odds of me being able to beat him—"

"The odds are bull!" I snapped. "You have to beat him, Wally. No more odds, no more statistics. Embrace what you are, or we are all going to die! You are stronger than you know. You have to believe that!"

I danced away from Orin, trying to keep the zombies shambling our way in sight at the same time. It struck me, not for the first time, that none of the zombies had been using the abilities they'd had in life.

Almost on cue, the air echoed with a boom, a rumble of rocks and stone. I whipped around to see the mausoleum going down, magic circling around it that wasn't Ethan's.

"Wally, now!" I put all the command I could into my voice, and she cried out as if I'd hit her.

Orin jumped on me and we went to the ground. I rolled with him until I was on top, pinning him down, my knees on his arms and my hands free.

Wally stood in front of the necromancer, her arms spread wide. "I can't let you hurt my friends."

The necromancer let out a long, low laugh, and I couldn't help but stare. He was wearing a dark gray robe, and his long beard and hair were the same gray. His mouth and eyes had lines that suggested not laughter, but cruelty. There would be no begging or bargaining with this one. He arched both brows at Wally. "You are a child from a blood line that is known for being weak. For letting your heart rule your power. I see it in you, a soft color. Weak. Dilute. You cannot stop me."

Orin tried to buck me off, and I punched him in the side of the head, knocking him out. "Sorry."

His eyes rolled and I leapt off him, heading for Wally. But my back had been to the zombies, and several of them grabbed me from behind. Before I knew it, my limbs had been stretched out like I was on a drying rack.

Wally's head dropped and a soft sob tore out of her that I could just barely hear. This was it, she would either beat him or I'd be torn apart. We'd all die.

"He's wrong, Wally! He's so wrong! I'm here for my family—I've only fought like I have because of love! We're a family now, too, Wally, and you damn well know it! We need you to dig deep like you've never dug before."

Her shoulders shook and she slowly turned her face to me, tears streaking her cheeks. "I'm so afraid. I don't want to be like him."

The zombies pulled, and the muscles and tendons in my limbs shrieked. I tipped my head back and screamed.

There was a clatter and the zombies released me as a snarl rent the air. I'd never been so happy to see a honey badger in my life. Pete ripped through the zombies' legs, sending them flying, and I hit the ground, my joints feeling loose. Wobbly.

Pete slammed into Wally's legs. *Tell her she can do this, I believe in her!*

"Pete believes in you, Wally. You can do this!"

Ethan fell next to me, shooting backward. "Wally, even I believe you can do this. Your family isn't weak, or I wouldn't have let you stay on this team!"

Orin groaned. "Me too."

Wally lifted her hands, her breath coming in huge gulps, her chest heaving, and I watched as the pink glow suffused her body and jumped from Pete, to me, to Orin, and even Ethan.

"I won't let you hurt my friends," she said. The green energy from the other necromancer pulsed as he laughed.

"You are untrained. You can't beat me."

"You don't need training to have heart," I said. "To have the grit to see this through. You just do it."

Nice, now we're a Nike commercial? Pete said.

Wally smiled, as if she'd heard him too. "Yeah. I can beat you. For my friends."

There was a moment of complete and utter silence and then light erupted from her, blasting into the zombies and knocking the other necromancer off his feet.

I wasn't sure what the others saw, but to me, Wally looked like she was on fire, the magic flickering up around her, protecting her as she walked toward the other necromancer. Each zombie she touched sighed and slid down into the ground.

"*Thaaaank youuuuuu.*"

Wally stood over the necromancer. "Nobody hurts my friends. Nobody hurts my family."

"This is impossible." His eyes were wide. "Impossible."

I stood and made my way to Wally's side. "Not a word we know." With a swift move, I bent and slammed the butt of my knife into his skull.

His eyes rolled back, and he slumped to the ground.

The remainder of the zombies sunk back into the earth, one by one.

I took a few steps back. "Well done, Wally, well done."

Her eyes were shining, and a grin trembled on her lips. "I'm not useless."

"Nope." I grinned back, my own eyes stupidly full. "Not for a second did I ever believe that."

Knew what you were made of all along, Pete said.

Wally bent and scooped him into her arms, squeezing him. "Thank you. All of you."

Ethan grunted something and stood, holding a hand out to Orin. The vampire blew out a breath as he rose, his eyes his own. He gave a full-body shudder. "That's not allowed, you know. Necromancers taking over vampires."

Wally nodded. "I know. He was not a good necromancer."

"What do we do with him?" Ethan asked. "I mean, we can't kill him."

I arched an eyebrow, still breathing hard, my body shaking from the beating it had taken. "What do you think he was going to do to us? Take us out shopping for new clothes and lunch at Mickey D's?"

They all looked at me. Of course, they did—I was the killer. And I didn't particularly feel bad about killing someone who'd been set on us. But he *was* knocked out.

"We're going to see vampires at some point, right?" I let the idea tumble out of my mouth. "What if we hand him over, like an offering of sorts? They'd believe you, Orin, right? If you told them what he'd done?"

Orin's face slowly transformed into a wide grin that flashed his fangs. "Oh, they would love that. Yes, let's take him along."

And just like that our five turned into six, although number six was, to be fair, bound and gagged with Ethan's magic. He kept the necromancer in front of him, kind of a human shield as we made our way out of the graveyard. With the necromancer muzzled, we could see the exit clear as day.

"He had a spell with him," Ethan said. "To cloak the exit."

Wally shook her head, a frown creasing her eyebrows. "That means this was more than just a necromancer trying to kill us. Someone from the House of Wonder must have given him that spell."

"They weren't really out to kill us, to be fair," Orin pointed out. "Just Wild. We were collateral damage."

I looked back once we reached the gate. The graves were silent, quiet . . . and a figure stood among them. My heart picked up speed as I watched Tommy staring at us. His arm was twisted where I'd broken it, but his eyes . . . his eyes were his own.

He tipped his head to me, and when he lifted it, he mouthed two words. *Keep fighting.*

My heart beat so hard, I thought it would leap out of my chest. I glanced at Wally, to ask her if she was holding him up, and then back to Tommy, only he was gone. Back into the grave he'd been assigned.

And what about Rory? I knew that he was gone—there was no surviving the way the zombies had taken him down—but there was no sign of a body.

I had to bite the inside of my cheek to keep the sob back. I was not a crier. I usually didn't give myself over to my emotions, but seeing Tommy and losing Rory . . . it wasn't just losing him. It was losing Tommy all over again. Losing my mom.

Three of the most important people in my life were gone, their lives blown out like candles. I drew a slow breath and nodded. "Let's go."

This trial wasn't done, and if the first test was any indication, I needed to keep my crap together. When we were out, when I was in the shower washing away the dirt and blood, then I could let the tears fall, then I would sob my heart out. But not before. Not while we still had dangers to face.

The moment we stepped out of the graveyard, the moon broke through the clouds, illuminating what we faced next.

I held my arm where the bite throbbed. My head felt like it was stuffed with cotton, and a quick glance at the wound told me what I'd already known. Red lines raced across my skin, angry and deep. A serious infection from the zombie bite, one that was growing at a speed that was far from normal.

"We need to hurry," I said, and even to my own ears the words were sloppy, as if I'd gotten into Dad's moonshine.

"Oh, crap, she's got an infection from the bite!" Ethan growled. He grabbed my face with his hands and peered into my eyes, pulling my lids up with his thumbs. "It's moving fast. I can't even believe I'm going to say this. We need to pick her up and carry her."

"I've got her," Orin said.

"Thought I was too big." I mumbled as he flipped me over his shoulder like a sack of potatoes.

"You are too big to throw a hundred feet. Not too big to pack around," he grumbled back.

The world spun as he stepped, my head bobbing, their voices fading in and out.

We walked through a fog that swirled all around us, the whispers of unfamiliar voices crawling inside my ears like bugs, like mosquitoes trapped in my skull. I swatted with my one hand, heat rushing through me even though I was no longer walking.

Distantly, I knew it was fever. Maybe the zombie's mouths had been deliberately infected with something? Possible. No matter how I looked at it, someone had done this on purpose. No one else had been bitten, just me. Did they really want me dead? Or was it still possible they only wanted to kidnap me? The questions rolled through me, and I fought to stay awake. I was so tired. I just wanted to sleep, to rest.

"Her heart is slowing!" Orin said, and then we were bouncing along. Running. They were running. That couldn't be good.

My crew was trying to save me. Something warm and fuzzy flowed through me. They really were family. No matter that none of us seemed to fit.

You've got to hang in there, Wild! Pete's voice burst through the static, and then the other voices were back. The whispering voices.

I could almost make out words through the static. The harder I listened, the more I could pick up.

Orin lowered me to the ground, and I somehow found my legs strong enough to stand. We were in front of a castle, the drawbridge closed, and fog rolled all around us. No, not fog. Ghosts. We were surrounded by ghosts.

"You see them?" I held a hand out and one of the ghosts reached for me. A woman.

"See what? We can't see anything in this fog. Stay close!" Ethan snapped, fear thick in his voice.

The woman in front of me smiled, her features slowly coming into focus.

"Mom?"

"We're losing her!" Orin yelled. "Her heart rate just dropped!"

Only they weren't losing me. I was with my mom and my mom was here and I was . . .

"Oh, my sweet Wild girl, it isn't your time," Mom said, her smile gentle and sad at the same time. *"You know that, don't you?"*

"It's so hard, Mom. This place is so hard. And the people are assholes." I drew a breath and reached for her, and miracle of miracles, she was solid under my hands. She grabbed me and pulled me tight to her chest and the smell of lilacs and baby powder surrounded me. Safe, home, love, family. This was all I needed.

"I know it's hard, and yes, people are always going to be assholes." She laughed, her chest shaking lightly. *"You'll have your days too, my girl, where you'll be the asshole. The one to get the job done. Because you are the only one who can protect them all, Wild. Do you understand? You are the best of me. The best of your father. The best of our family."* She pressed her lips against my forehead and I clung to her, already feeling her pushing away. A burst of energy flowed from her into me, pushing back the infection, pushing back the fatigue. *"Go, my girl. Go and don't forget. You must get up now. Get up."*

"Get up!" Pete screamed in my face, his breath smelling vaguely of death. Was it from biting the zombies? Gross, that's exactly what it was from, I was sure of it. "You have to get up!"

He was back on two legs, his freckles bright from the strain of his yelling in my face. I rolled onto my belly and lifted my head. Across the drawbridge stood Ethan, Orin, and Wally. The captured necromancer sat behind them on his knees.

Pete grabbed me by the shoulders, shaking me hard. Something had happened while I'd been out cold. Apparently. We'd passed through the ghosts like they were actual mist.

Or maybe they'd had to face the ghosts on their own?

"If you don't cross the bridge under your own power, it doesn't count," he said. "You have to get up, Wild. You have to. I won't finish this trial without you, not after everything we've been through together."

I pushed to my hands and knees. My guts rolled, my bad arm shaking and buckling under me, but I sat back on my knees and then slowly got to my feet, Pete hovering like an old lady the whole time. He had sweat pants on, thank God. That was about all I took note of besides the planks under my feet as I took step after step toward the others. Though I did wonder where he'd gotten them from.

This was the worst time to be at my worst. The vampires came last, Ethan had said so, and I was pretty much useless. With my good arm, I went for my knife and pulled it out, fingers trembling. If I was going to have to fight, I needed to be ready.

My footsteps echoed loudly on the wooden planks, and as soon as my boots reached cobblestone, I stopped. The world around me swam, sweat dribbling off my face and onto the stone.

"Is this real?" I asked, my words still thick and slurred. The castle around us was massive, and even in my very addled state I could appreciate the scope of it. My heart skipped a beat.

"How are you even standing?" Wally asked softly. "A few minutes ago, your heart was faltering, even Orin felt it."

"The ghosts," Ethan said. "They can give energy. She must have known one of them. That's why they let us through. Damn it, even when she's out of it she's getting us through this." He shook his head, and I just kind of rolled with it.

"My mom," I said. "She gave me energy."

"Yes," Orin said. "This part, this castle is real. This is where the council of the undead oversee their portion of the magical world." He paused. "They allow us to use it for the purpose of the Culling Trials as they want a chance to view the contestants in person."

Pete grumbled under his breath and hitched at his sweatpants. "Contestants or new play toys?"

Orin didn't so much as miss a beat. "Either. You, though, they'd likely put on a spit and slow roast for their next gathering."

I wasn't sure if he was joking or not and didn't have the energy to tell him not to be a dick.

Apparently, Pete wasn't sure if it was a joke either. He dropped back next to Wally, grumbling, "What a jerk. He's lucky I don't mind him so much now."

"Statistically speaking, he's not wrong," she said. "Four to six percent of the trial entrants fall under the spell of one of the vampires and chose to stay here as servants. They aren't strong enough to live in the magical world anyway if they can be taken that easily, but the statistics don't lie."

"Wish they would once in a while," Pete said.

Orin and Ethan led the way, and warning tingles danced up and down my spine with each step. I let out a low groan as my stomach rolled with nausea. The vampires had better hurry the hell up, or I was going to be flat on my back again before I could be of any help to my crew.

The two guys approached the center of the courtyard, Ethan with his wand raised and Orin with his hands clasped at his back as he float-walked along. One day he'd make a fine Dracula. I grinned at the thought, feeling the crazy that came with a high fever and infection. Then another warning blared through all that crazy, demanding my attention.

I pushed Wally and Pete ahead of me, still trying to guard the rear. "Eyes open."

"As if I'd close them now," Pete muttered.

"It's a saying, Pete," Wally said, "and as she is our resident Shade, we should listen to her. As I mentioned before, she has a highly tuned inner warning system." Wally continued on in that thread, giving stats about how many Shades made it through the trials versus the rest of the blood lines.

That warning system was ringing a thousand bells at once, my adrenaline pulsing so fast, it pushed back the fog of the infection, clearing my mind. I struggled to keep my breathing normal, slow and even. Ethan and Orin stopped in the center of the courtyard.

"Which way?" Ethan did a slow turn, pointing at each of the four doors leading out of the castle. Four doors, none of which we needed to go through.

This was the wrong way.

"Stop!" I whisper-yelled the word.

Ethan and Orin slowed, and I motioned for them to come back to us. Ethan took a step, but Orin didn't.

"I think I would know my own house," he said, turning away from us.

Ethan looked between me and Orin. "Yeah, he should."

Wally and Pete backed up until they were beside me. "Listen to her," Wally said. "If she's picking up on something, then we need to—"

The slightest creak of hinges squeaked through the air, and four figures emerged from the four doors.

I grabbed Wally and Pete and dragged them farther back. Maybe it was because I had *missing* stamped on my file. Maybe it was because of Rory's warning about the vampires. Maybe it was because I was so close to death. But this was bad, beyond bad.

"This will be worse than dealing with the necromancer," I said.

Please, God, let me be wrong for once.

CHAPTER 6

The four vampires rushed out at us from the doorways in the castle, their speed blinding. There was no way I could fight, no way any of us could physically best them. We had to outsmart them instead.

"PARLAY!" I screamed the word and the vampires came to a dead stop.

"We are vampires, not pirates, you stupid girl." The one to the left of us laughed, and the other three joined in, their laughter rolling around us, amplified by the stone walls until it felt like a hundred vampires were laughing at us.

"And if we have a necromancer who can control vampires? How much would that be worth to you?" Ethan asked, taking over.

"Necromancers can't control vampires," one of them said. "That is an old myth to scare the young ones into being obedient."

Orin shrunk where he stood, just a little, but I saw it. "It is true." He shook the necromancer at his feet and the vampires seemed to really see him for the first time. With his heavily lined face and thick beard, he was for sure no kid.

"I can do no such thing," the necromancer purred.

"Then how did I learn it from you?" Wally held out a hand and her necromancer power crawled down her arm and latched onto the vampire closest to us.

"I would never have figured it out if I hadn't seen you control Orin."

Orin nodded. "He made me attack my crew. He was inside my head and I couldn't stop him."

Three of the vampires laughed. The fourth tried to join them, but Wally made a fist. The laugh strangled, and she pointed at the other vampires. "Protect us from them."

Pride suffused me as my crew closed ranks. I only wished Gregory were here, that he could be a part of this moment. Ethan and Orin went shoulder to shoulder, keeping the necromancer on the ground in front of them. Pete stayed near me, and Wally was to our left, directing the vampire she'd taken hold of.

"Damn it, she's in my head!" He stepped forward, claws extended at his fellow blood suckers. He put his back to us and let out a snarl. "This should not be possible!"

A moment of tension, and then the world seemed to explode in a flurry of movement, shouts and emotion.

People burst through the doorways, not all of them vamps. One was Director Frost, and another was Ethan's dad, his wand out as he blasted one of the vampires away from our group, flipping him end over end.

Behind them strolled the Sandman, his eyes on me. He gave me a slow nod, and I knew who'd sounded the alarm that something was wrong with our trial. The only question was, why?

Why had Sunshine helped me? Was it because Rory had died?

I went to my knees, the chaos around me white noise buzzing along my skin. Yelling, flares of magic, vampires hissing . . . it all unrolled around me as I stayed there on my knees.

Pete grabbed one arm, and Wally the other. "We've got to get you to the healer," Pete said.

I closed my eyes and let them carry me.

"She dropped her knife," Ethan called from behind us, slipping the blade back into its sheath. Only he'd said the wrong thing.

She. He'd said she.

A new burst of excitement whipped up behind us, but I couldn't bring myself to care as I was hauled through a doorway, out of the House of Night, and into the bright sunshine of upstate New York, as if everything behind us had been a dream.

"Nightmare more like it," Pete said. "Holy cats. Wild, that was . . . do you really think they were trying to kill us all?"

They laid me on a table and the healer shushed him, the same healer as that first day. What was her name again? Was I mumbling?

"It's the infection," the healer smiled down at me. "It's almost to your brain. They got you out just in time."

"What would happen if it reached her brain?" Pete asked.

"Zombie," Wally said.

The healer—Mara, that was her name—tsked. "Don't go upsetting her. She's here and that's that."

Of course, she knew I was a girl too. She had from the beginning but hadn't said anything. But every other thought scattered as her hands pressed against the bite wound. I arched my back as pain rippled outward from her touch.

"This will not be pleasant," Mara said, her voice grim.

Fire and ice, knives and snapping teeth, tearing flesh and broken limbs, I couldn't think past the pain that erupted through my veins. "Bite down."

Something was shoved between my teeth and I bit down hard, snapping it in half.

"Holy cats, are we sure she isn't a shifter?"

A chunk of leather was shoved in next and I bit into it, my teeth almost touching through the thick material as I screamed.

For a moment, I thought about just letting it go, because the pain was surely not worth the prize. We still had one more trial to go through, one more chance at being killed. Because I was sure that this botched attempt wouldn't be the last. Whoever was doing it would try again, and again, until they had what they wanted—our deaths, a kidnapping, it didn't matter. They would not give up.

Was that why the Sandman had been there? Was he after me? The pain receded and my mind went into overdrive with theories and questions. Had the Sandman killed Rory for looking out for me?

Had my friend died trying to protect me, or had he been just thrown under the bus to throw me off the track?

The shakes took me, starting in my legs and working all the way up through my middle to my chest and arms. A heavy blanket was tossed over me, and then Orin and Ethan swept into the tent, followed by . . . Colt.

His eyes shot to me, one still bruised from his encounter with Rory in the forest. It felt like a lifetime ago even though it had been less than a day.

"She can stay here," Mara said, dusting her hands. "She needs rest and food. And I fixed her nose while I was at it, seeing as . . ." As everyone knew I wasn't a boy. That thought tripped through my brain.

Ethan shook his head. "No, she comes with us. Colt, can you pick her up?"

Orin took a step, but Colt beat him to it. "Yeah, of course." He scooped me up, blanket and all, as if I weighed nothing.

"I can walk." I moved to push him away, but my arms were weighted lead and I couldn't so much as lift them.

Colt held me tightly to his chest as he walked out of the tent, the others falling in around us. All the way to a bus that took us back to the mansion. I dozed, unable to keep my eyes open.

I was warm, safe. I fell asleep in Colt's arms.

When I came to, we were back in the room, and I was tucked into my bed. My crew was there, talking softly.

"What are we going to do?" Wally asked. "We know someone's after her, the whole school knows she's a girl now, but they haven't kicked her out. Why? That makes no sense."

"You want her to be kicked out?" Orin countered.

"No, of course not." Wally huffed. "But they are acting like they don't know. Why? What do they want with her?"

"She's strong," Ethan said. "It's possible they want her for a specific job. That's . . ." he cleared his throat, "that's what my dad said. That maybe someone wants her specifically. That's why she's being tested so hard. Maybe it wasn't a trial meant to kill her after all."

Pete paced beside my bed, identifiable by his footsteps. "But for what?"

They were all quiet at that, and I sat up. Colt was there too, surprising me. He gave me a smile and I tried to smile back.

Except that when I looked at him, all I could see was Rory.

I swallowed hard. "I need to shower. Can . . . I get some privacy?"

"I'll be just outside," Wally said. "Pete and I will guard the door."

Colt grabbed Ethan. "And we'll get some food."

Ethan rolled his eyes. "I should never have told you she was a girl."

They filed out, all of them, except Orin. I looked up at him. "What?"

"We all passed that trial. But we shouldn't have. You tie us together in a way that is not normal." He frowned. "I'm not sure how I feel about that. I do not think these ties will be easily broken. I should be bothered by it. Vampires are by nature loners, but . . . now I don't want that."

I stood, hanging on to the bed to make sure I didn't fall over. I wasn't hurting anymore, but I felt like I'd been sick for weeks. "That your way of saying we're friends?"

He tipped his head to the side. "I suppose it is. I've never had friends before. Is it normal to want to protect them?"

I wanted to laugh at him, but he was serious. "Yeah. Yeah, it is."

"I see." He sighed. "Well, I will guard the door with Wally and Pete then. Because you are my friend."

He did his float-walk to the door and closed it quietly behind him. Call me crazy, but the doubts that had ghosted through me about Orin slid away with the last of our conversation. He might be weird. He might be bloodthirsty, but I didn't think he'd turn on us. I headed to the bathroom, peeling off my clothes as I went. The smell of the undead, of sweat and blood and fear, clung to them and I just needed them off.

The water was scalding hot as I stepped into it, but I didn't care. It rolled off my face and shoulders, mingling with my tears. My body was healed. I could feel every inch of it coming up to full speed even while I stood there, right down to my nose. But I wasn't sure that the rest of me would ever come back from this. From fighting Tommy. From watching Rory disappear under that wave of zombies.

As angry as I'd been with him, I'd never thought I'd truly lose him. Not Rory.

He'd dodged death so many times even when we were kids. How could this have happened? Sobs ripped out of me and I let them. I wouldn't get another chance to grieve, not until we made it through the final trial.

I stood there, crying and smacking my hand against the wall, until the water began to cool. I forced myself to scrub off the dirt at that point and wash my hair.

When I stepped out of the shower, a single pulse of warning cut through me. "Are you freaking kidding me?"

Wrapped in a towel, angrier than a hen tossed in the pond, I snatched my knife from my belt and stormed to the bathroom door. Done. I was so damn done with this crap, with the constant warnings and danger.

But that didn't mean I was going to be stupid. I turned the knob slowly and peeked out.

Colt stood there, his hands under Ethan's mattress. Looking for the cheat sheets? "Really?"

He spun on his heels, but there was no shame on his face. "He left me behind in that first trial. I broke my leg and he left me."

I remembered that. The House of Shade challenge had seemed so hard, so treacherous, but now I would have paid to go back to it instead of facing the last house. "And you want to get back at him?"

He shrugged as he stood, the papers in his hands. Rather than pocket the cheat sheets, he took his wand out and waved it over them. Then he pulled a blank sheet out of his pocket and waved his wand over it. The words reappeared on the previously blank sheet, as perfect as a photocopy. He tucked away the copy, then stuffed the originals back in place. "Maybe. Maybe I just want to take what he thinks is his for once."

His blue eyes were locked on mine and I stared back, forgetting that I was standing there soaking wet in nothing more than a towel.

Colt took two steps, cupped my face and kissed me, gently, as if I would break. "Maybe he doesn't deserve the best, Wild."

I put a hand on his chest, pushing him and the confusion away. One thing at a time.

"Ethan is what he is. But you promised me food, and I'm starving. Also, how did you get in past the others?"

Colt turned and headed to the window. "I have more skills than most." He winked at me over his shoulder and slid out, gone without a sound.

As quiet as any Shade. I had more questions for him, for this place, for this world. My stomach growled angrily, and I nodded. Food first.

Questions later.

CHAPTER 7

"Okay." I clapped my hands as my crew walked down the hall, using the noise to chase away the lingering fatigue from the night before. It felt like I'd woken up every five minutes last night, drowning in a never-ending loop of zombies, assassins, claws, and gleaming knives. To top it off, Rory's face kept drifting up out of the abyss, pulling at my heart. Reminding me of all I'd lost to be here.

I took a big, shuddering breath, willing away tears. A huge, gaping hole that felt like a wind tunnel cut through my middle. Memories of Rory kept shoving their way into my thoughts. I kept remembering how it had felt to be near him—dangerous, edgy, raw, exhilarating, and yet safe. Protected. Those feelings had only amplified over time, becoming a thousand times stronger.

And now he was gone.

My childhood was being ripped from me, piece by piece. I could barely think under the weight of grief. But I had to survive. He hadn't given away his life so I could throw away mine.

"Okay," I said again, hurrying down the steps to the cafeteria for breakfast. "Here's what we have. The missing kids are being offered a leg up, so to speak. Then they disappear. Fine. The director seems to be on the case, but she's obviously too slow to catch up with whomever is doing this. Whatever intel she is getting is old. Not abnormal, since the people in charge are usually clueless. I—*we're* being hunted," I amended, "but that seems like a different situation than the kidnappings. We were meant to be killed last night, not taken. No matter what Ethan's dad thinks."

"Um, ya *think*?" Pete asked with wide eyes.

"I *have* been thinking on it, and I don't think Gregory would've taken an easy out," Orin said thoughtfully. "His family isn't rich—he'd want the gold. It would improve his standing going into the academy."

I nodded, chewing my lip as we pushed through the doors into the cafeteria. The promise of bacon made my mouth salivate, competing with the smell of burnt toast, steaming sausages, scrambled eggs, and fluffy pancakes. I loved eating at this place, especially since I didn't have to cook any of the meals myself.

"I found the sheets you stuffed under my mattress," Ethan said in a low hum.

"Like a princess with a pea," Wally murmured.

"So obviously he wasn't going to sell those," Ethan finished, nodding at a group of guys seated in the back corner. Colt stood from among them, fresh and clean, with stylishly tousled hair. Those entrancing eyes found me and stuck, and a smile quirked up one side of his mouth, sending a rush of heat through me. Ethan went on. "But what was he doing outside?"

"Being hauled away." I grabbed a plate and started heaping it with food from the buffet. "They, whoever they are, got him when he was still inside. For all we know they tried to convince him to go and he initially agreed."

"Right, right," Ethan whispered to himself.

"They weren't taking the fastest route to the parking lot," Orin said, following too closely behind me. I had the distinct feeling he was staring at my neck.

I rolled my shoulders without meaning to. "That's true. They would have had to circle around through the trees." My mind spun. "Do you think they're keeping the missing kids on campus somewhere? That seems risky."

"We have a day to look around and find out," Wally said. "The odds of someone going missing in the woods around here—"

"He didn't go missing; he was taken," Ethan corrected dryly, heaping eggs onto his plate.

"The odds of someone being kidnapped and hauled into the woods—"

I let Wally's statistics drift into the background as I quickly went over the events of the last free day. One thing I hadn't really paid attention to jogged to the front of my mind.

"Where is the director's assistant?" I asked, following Ethan to a middle table, front and center so all his adoring fans could see him. Colt met us there, giving me a small smile as he sat. I hadn't told the others about him copying Ethan's notes. Mostly because I had a feeling my crew would be facing a different trial than the one described in Ethan's papers. "That guy seemed more than competent when we met him, yet he wasn't there when Jared hauled us up to the director's office the other night. Where could he have been, rather than in the office, doing his job?" Adam hadn't been there when we'd broken into the office either, but that had happened late at night, and I didn't think it wise to mention our criminal activities in front of Colt.

"Maybe he was finding out more info for the director?" Pete asked, holding up his fork with a half-eaten sausage skewered on the end.

"More info that didn't reach her in time to actually help?" I frowned and pushed the hash browns around my plate. "When

I first met him, it felt like he could read right through me with a single glance." I shivered. "He doesn't seem like a guy who is satisfied with second-rate intelligence."

"I forgot about that," Pete murmured. "Yeah, Adam is a creepy dude."

"I didn't see anything wrong with him," Orin said.

"Not surprising," Ethan returned.

"If he's not the type to settle for second-rate info, that would explain why he was out, trying to find answers. Maybe that's what he's been doing all along?" Wally said.

Ethan pushed food into his cheek so he could talk around it. "Maybe he was just getting coffee."

"Maybe you shouldn't talk with your mouth full," Pete said.

Ethan rolled his eyes and went back to his plate. "Okay, *Mom*."

"Besides him," I cut in, "there is Jared to think about, who *was* hanging around, despite the fact that he and the director clearly don't like each other."

"He thinks she's soft," Orin said. "That's no secret. He wants the job, so whenever she slips up, he lets everyone know. He wants her out. Gone. She's old."

"I've seen that guy Adam around." Colt leaned forward, looking between Ethan and me, ignoring everyone else. "The assistant? I saw him yesterday after the trials, walking from the portables to the mansion. He looked pissed."

"I'm sure he always looks like he's pissed." I dropped my napkin onto my plate and stood. "I say we check in on him, see what he's up to. If he *is* trying to find out info for the director, great. If not, we might learn something by tailing him."

"What about Jared?" Wally asked, standing with me. The others followed suit, except for Ethan, who clearly wasn't going to leave until he'd eaten every scrap off of his plate. "I say we tail him."

Orin nodded. "Vampires like to have their fingers in everything even though they don't get involved in much of it. He might know something, even if he hasn't acted on it."

"Sounds good. I'll take Adam. Who's going with me?" I asked.

"I will."

"Me."

"I'll go."

"Might as well."

The chorus died down and everyone exchanged looks.

I stared down at Ethan, the only one who hadn't piped up. He surely didn't want to be in my proximity any more than I wanted to be in his, but he also liked to be the center of attention, meaning he could keep eyes off me, and if we got caught, he could also keep me in the school. He'd proven that he would.

"Orin, you take the lead on tailing the vampire," I said, picking up my plate. "Direct the others on how not to get caught. Keep your eyes open for anything that looks suspicious. Ethan and Colt, you come with me."

An hour later, I paced the dorm room, anticipation firing through my limbs and impatience dragging down my features. Colt sat on Ethan's bed, gazing out the window at the grounds below. The others had already taken off to find their mark and hopefully tail him without getting caught. I didn't have high hopes for either expedition, but at least it was daylight. Following someone around wasn't against school policy, just social norms.

"Honestly, Ethan, what is taking you so long?" I barked, turning toward the bathroom door for the umpteenth time.

He emerged in a halo of fragrance, with his sweats clinging to his solid frame, his shoulders swaying with his casual yet calculated saunter, and his hair styled *just so.*

"Are you under the impression we are going to a garden party?" My voice carried a distinct bite to it. "We're trying *not* to stand out."

He flicked his gaze my way, taking in my overall appearance. "You're still trying to look like a boy even though anyone who matters knows you're a girl, your sweats have a stain on them from breakfast, and you're an Amazon woman. We're going to stand out regardless of what I look like."

It was annoying that he was probably right.

"Fine. Whatever. Come on, the day is wasting." I gestured them both toward the door.

Colt stood, just as unhurried as Ethan. I rolled my eyes and pulled the door open. I already regretted bringing them along. But Rory had said not to go alone, and that had been his last piece of advice for me.

"Okay," I started as we trekked down the hall.

"Your strategic vocabulary is limited," Ethan said as he kept pace, his demeanor blasé. It was a real skill to move quickly and look slow, I had to hand it to him. He and Colt both had mastered *cool.*

"I like a good jumping off point. Okay." I exited into the stairwell. "Let's see if Adam is at the director's office where he belongs."

"He isn't," Colt said, slowing my progress. "I saw him walk across the grounds twenty minutes ago."

I stopped and turned to him with an incredulous expression. "What?"

"I saw him—"

"Yes, I know what you said. Why didn't you mention it?"

Colt gestured at Ethan. "He wasn't ready to get going."

"But you could've—" I breathed through my nose, willing patience. "Right. Fine. Okay. Lead the way."

"You'll never get accepted into the House of Shade with that attitude," Ethan said as we turned on the stairs, heading down. "You need to work on being cool and collected."

"I need to work on better decision-making when choosing my partners."

At the bottom of the stairs, we turned toward the back of the mansion, retracing my steps the night I'd seen Gregory taken. Flashes of the scene rolled through my head. I tried to summon up information about the men who'd taken him—their stature, the bulge of their lean muscle as they struggled to contain him, the plain shoes they wore. Images rose of possible body types, what they might've looked like, what their magical talents might've been. Not vampires, surely. They'd been much too coarse in their movements. Yes, I'd seen a wand, but only in the hands of one of them. Not Shades, either, unless they were lower on the scale. They'd looked too human to be goblins or trolls. Shifters would be stronger, well able to handle a half-pint goblin like Gregory. But a necromancer or someone who didn't use strength and speed in their craft might fit the bill.

My eyes cut sideways as we reached the back door, noticing Colt's lean muscle against Ethan's more robust body.

"Do you work out, Ethan?" I asked, following the curve of his bicep with my gaze before eyeing the size of his thighs.

His bored amusement spoke volumes.

"It's just that," I hurried to say, ready to die if he thought I was interested in any way, "spell workers don't physically fight, right? Where'd you get all the muscle?"

His chest puffed up slightly, preening at the notice. "I lift."

"Right." I drew the word out. "But why bother? You do all your defensive fighting with a wand. I haven't seen you throw so much as a single punch."

A smirk graced his lips. "Don't you like your men fit? Or are you more the dominatrix type?"

My face annoyingly flamed red. "So that's why, then? Body image issues?"

His smirk broadened into a knowing smile, his ego of steel deflecting my light jab.

I glanced toward the trees where I'd last seen Gregory. Memories flooded me, of Rory's lips pressed against the shell of my ear, quieting me, of fingers tapping against the pulse in my neck. I remembered the feel of his solid strength as we cried against each other about Tommy.

I blinked away the tears and gritted my teeth. I had surviving to do.

"There," Colt said in a hush, grabbing my elbow and jerking his head to the left. "Near the portables. See him?"

Even with the distance, I could recognize him moving with the grace of a predator, his hair cropped short and his posture straight and strong. No suit adorned his muscular physique. Instead, he wore the sweats we all did, larger to fit his heartier frame.

Adam. And he was far, far away from his desk.

CHAPTER 8

I s he trying to blend in?" I asked, an incredulous giggle escaping me. Adam was huge next to the students, both in stature and in presence. How could he not be noticed near the rundown portables? "He's like a wolf wandering around a pack of poodles and trying to act like he's tame."

"Poodles are actually very intelligent dogs," Ethan said, still sauntering for all he was worth, but a little less gracefully, now. A little more on edge.

Good. He was taking this seriously.

"Intelligent, sure. Trainable, definitely." I let Colt lead me, his instincts right on. If we veered from our path, we'd get noticed, especially since Adam had just looked around to see if anyone was near. He was up to something, clear as day. "But adept at stalking prey and then ripping their throats out? Probably not."

Adam went up the steps and stopped at one of the portable doors. His hands pulled up in front of him and his head was lowered as he worked at the knob. It had to be locked. It wouldn't be for long.

"Whose portable is that?" Colt asked, quickening our pace as we reached the line of portables in front of us. "Ethel Wiseman?"

"No idea," Ethan replied. "We didn't get friendly with the neighbors the night we stayed."

No, we just stole their food.

"Who's Ethel Wiseman?" I asked.

Colt slipped in between the buildings with incredibly light feet. He sped up to a jog, staying close to the buildings so he could duck into the small alleys between at a moment's notice. It's exactly what I would've done had I been leading. Just like the way he'd slipped in and out of my bedroom window without any of my guard dogs noticing. "Are you sure you're not a Shade?"

"His mother is a Shade," Ethan said with condescension ringing through his voice.

"I didn't get any of her magic," Colt said, his step faltering. "But I noticed how she went about certain things. It's common sense, if you think about it. How to sneak up on someone."

"It's lower class," Ethan murmured.

I rolled my eyes, so many arguments springing to mind that my tongue locked. Now wasn't the time, anyway.

"I heard Ethel was approached after the trial yesterday," Colt said, slowing before looking back the way we'd come. His eyebrows lowered, and it occurred to me that he didn't know how many portables separated us from Adam.

I stepped around him, taking over, and resumed the jog, albeit slower. We didn't have far to go.

"I thought you guys must've heard about that," he continued. "The guys in my dorm were talking about it last night. Robby's girlfriend heard it from her friend Sarah, who heard it from Ethel first hand. She got asked to skip the rest of the trials and asked everyone's advice."

"Is she daft?" I frowned as a slight tingle of warning washed through my blood. *Here we go.*

I lowered my voice to a whisper, working on those light steps that Colt had seemed to master. Why was I so far behind on that?

"People who get asked to skip disappear. Surely one of her friends would've told her that."

"That's the thing about being mediocre," Ethan whispered. "You take any hand up you can get. You're happy just to get noticed. At least, that's what I assume, anyway. You'd know best, Wild."

"I wasn't the one using my daddy to cheat, Einstein. But keep throwing rocks in that glass house."

Colt muffled a laugh. "I don't think anyone else has put it together, that the missing kids were all offered a leg up."

I held up my hand for quiet as I peered around the corner of the portable, not feeling the pressure of danger thickening the air. Not yet. Adam had to be inside.

Soft laughter floated by, along with a female voice, gay and light. Another voice joined the first, two people up the way probably headed out to enjoy the soft sunshine in this rare break between trials.

Tightly drawn curtains shielded the back window of the portable, so I led the others down the narrow gap between portables to the front, racking my brain for a plan.

A thought occurred to me. Out of all the portables in this row, of which there were tons, why would Colt assume that Adam was choosing Ethel's? Did he already know, or was it a blind assumption?

Metal jingled, a handle being grabbed. I paused, breath trapped in my lungs. A warning signal prickled down my spine.

Colt clutched my shoulder, but neither of the guys made a sound. I nodded to show I'd heard it. A tiny squeak was the only indication that the door had swung open. Boots tapped against the wood of the porch, soft sounds but not up to par for a Shade.

He wasn't an assassin—at least not a good one. The door clicked into place a moment later.

If he took off across the lawn toward the mansion and glanced back, there was a good chance he'd see us, three people stooped in stalker mode between the portables. His suspicion would likely compel him to take a closer look . . . unless what he saw embarrassed or disgusted him.

Moving quickly, I pushed in between the guys. Colt's hand came out to steady me, low on my hip. Ethan grunted and tried to move away, but I stopped him with a hand on his pec. The muscle popped against my palm and he froze, his eyes widening.

"What are you doing?" he asked in a release of breath, his gaze heating and dipping to my lips. Maybe he hated me, but it was clear his brain had just shut off.

"Pretending, you moron," I ground out, leaning heavily against Colt and feeling his hand slide across my stomach. "Play the part in case he looks. Only a voyeur will stop to gawk, and it won't be out of criminal suspicion."

A shape passed by with a swing of a large arm. I recognized his crew cut and caught something in his opposite hand that I couldn't make out. His face turned, and I caught a glimpse of nose before his figure disappeared. Steamy versus stalky—if he saw three people stuffed in the gap, he would take a second to look if he thought they were making out. It worked, he didn't. That had to be a good sign.

"Come on," I said as Ethan's large hand touched down on my hip and Colt's hand headed south to my butt. Heavy breathing and shifting bodies said I was the only one pretending, and I was suddenly encompassed in a circle of muscle and handsomeness most women would dream of.

I wasn't most women.

"All right, show's over." I flicked Ethan's crotch, jerking a little at the hardness but immediately gratified when he jolted away. He thunked his head against the portable wall and scowled, reality seeping through the burning gaze from a moment before. "Really? You hate me, but you'd do me, anyway?"

He shrugged, wiping the edge of his mouth with the back of his hand. "Why not? Not like I'd call you in the morning."

I shook my head and turned to elbow Colt in the stomach, but he was already moving away.

"Sorry. I was caught off guard. Stopped thinking." Colt gave me a mouth-watering smile. "I'd definitely call."

I couldn't hold a grudge against his disarming wink.

"Whatever," I said, "come on. He's getting away."

At the edge of the portable, I caught the figure again, standing in the middle of the grass, facing the mansion. Sticking out like a sore thumb. Eyes found him, stuck for a moment, then darted away, no one wanting to spend too long gawking at an authority figure.

He stared down into his hands for a moment in what seemed like contemplation, then dropped them again and looked around.

"Can you see what he's holding?" I asked, no idea why I was whispering.

"No," Ethan said, pushing in close so he could see around the corner, and jabbing me with a part of his body that would've been strapped down by the right underwear.

This time I did throw an elbow, forcing him back. "We need to see if it really is Ethel's room, and maybe figure out what he took. Or at least where he took it from." I dragged my teeth over my lip. "But if we do that, we'll lose him."

Even as I said it, Adam pivoted and pushed forward, walking in the opposite direction of where Gregory had been taken. If he was looking for the lost kids, he was either on the wrong track or going the roundabout way.

"I'll look," Colt said, slipping by me. "I know what she looks like, and I've rooted around in other people's things a few times in my life." He smirked, and I knew we were both thinking of Ethan's cheat sheets. "I'll meet you guys back at the dorm."

"Okay, sounds good. Let's go." I plucked at Ethan's sleeve and hurried forward before he could, without shame, poke me with his anatomy again. Too much confidence clearly wasn't always a good thing.

"What are we going to do when we catch him?" Ethan asked. The heat had thankfully cooled from his voice, but it was obvious the blood hadn't yet made it back to his brain.

"We're not going to catch him. He'd bash our heads together. We're going to stalk him. See where he goes, and what he does with whatever he grabbed."

Adam cut another diagonal, this time to the corner of the mansion, clearly intending to go around. Something was still clutched tightly in the hand swinging at his side. A small black object. He wasn't doing anything to hide its presence.

"I didn't hear any names announced this morning, did you?" I asked Ethan, ignoring the pull to follow Gregory's trail off toward the trees. I'd been interrupted twice so far. I needed to follow it through. The answers lay that way. I felt it in my gut.

But Adam looked like a concrete lead at this point. It would be foolish to ignore him.

"No. I was listening for them too," Ethan replied.

"So if Ethel got asked, she didn't get taken."

"Not yet, unless they just didn't announce it."

Intuition churned my gut now, and my feet slowed without my direction.

"Hurry up, what are you doing?" Ethan grabbed my arm and hurried me forward.

"Maybe we can stop her from getting taken."

He yanked me harder, and I couldn't help but go with him, logic telling me this was right. That Adam knew something, had something, and was going somewhere we needed to know. But my intuition . . .

"Maybe she was already taken, and they want some info before they make the announcement."

"If Colt's roommate's girlfriend is such a gossip, wouldn't he know all that and have told us?"

"If Colt didn't have such a jonesing hard on for you, he might have waited around for his roommate to invite his girl over. Then maybe he would, yes."

At the corner of the mansion, Ethan pushed me against the wall, flattened, and peeked around. A hand came out of nowhere. Thick fingers wrapped around Ethan's neck. Muscles pulled, and Ethan went airborne.

CHAPTER 9

H oly sh—" I stepped forward before launching myself without thought, punching out and connecting with a cheek, then wrapping my arms around the assailant's neck and using my momentum to rip him around.

He had no choice but to go, his grip slipping from Ethan's neck. Ethan's feet hit the ground and he dropped, gasping and coughing.

I twisted and ripped again before letting go, forcefully directing the falling body to the grass. The ground came up too fast and my foot hit it wrong, sending me rolling. Ethan was already up, his wand out and pointed.

"What the hell are you kids doing?" Adam rose from the ground like a cage fighter ready to get even, juiced up with power and strength and grisly know-how. Whatever type of magical he was, he'd gotten those muscles from violence and experience.

Tingles of terror blazed out through my bloodstream, giving me the jitters like a triple espresso. I either needed to run or throw another punch—standing there chatting was not in my wheelhouse at the moment. Thankfully, Ethan had a better weapon at his disposal. Entitlement.

"You'd better have a damn good explanation for grabbing me," he berated, his wand hand steady and his shoulders squared, an elite member of the magical society talking down to a lesser one, no matter their relative size. "We were walking around the building on our day off, perfectly within the rules."

Adam's weight shifted, a small movement. Almost imperceptible. It spoke volumes.

"Let's go." I grabbed Ethan's arm urgently and tugged him back the way we'd come. Adam didn't seem like the kind of guy who'd bow down to arrogant pricks, no matter how influential. This pause was the best we'd get.

"No." Ethan dug in his heels, his chin raised and his indignation firing on all cylinders. "I want to hear an explanation."

Adam stared him down, fire glimmering in his eyes.

"Come on." I yanked Ethan again. "We can go to that other spot."

"Your superiors will be hearing about this," Ethan said, finally allowing me to pull him away.

"Best watch yourself," I heard, low and rough and spreading shivers up my spine. Adam's gaze had shifted to me, piercing, locking me in so that I couldn't look away. "Your number is up, and your protection is dead. Best thing you can do is run. Get out of the trials and don't come back. *Run.*"

Pain welled up at his mention of Rory's death. Tears clouded my vision. A laugh bubbled up, out of nowhere.

"Then what?" I asked, rage quickly replacing the sorrow. I shook with it. "Run and hide? Cower in the shadows?" I spat, something I despised, but it really got the point across. "That's not my style."

I turned and shoved Ethan in front of me.

"Heed my warning," Adam said, the words trailing after me like tin cans.

"Make yourself useful, and catch whoever is stealing kids and threatening my life, or do your reflexes only work when teenagers are sneaking after you?"

Silence stretched as we distanced ourselves from Adam. I didn't look back.

Finally, faintly, delivered directly to my ear, I heard, "I'm working on the kidnapping. There's nothing I can do about the other. It's beyond me, now."

I stopped and spun, taken aback. Emptiness greeted me.

"I hate this place. Everyone always disappears," I said, wanting to run back. To chase Adam around the corner and beg for answers.

"Come on." Ethan plucked at my sleeve. "We have to let him go for now and pick him up somewhere else. He probably smelled your arousal earlier. That's how he knew we were around."

"Gross. I don't even have a comeback, I'm too busy trying not to gag."

He huffed out a laugh. "Nice way to step up back there. Perfect. I couldn't have coached you better. You might not be completely useless, for a Shade."

"Way to step up?"

"Pulling me away before I had to threaten something I might not be able to deliver. I can let the director know what he did, easy. Getting him fired, on the other hand . . ."

It dawned on me what he was saying, and surprise flitted through me. "You were playing a part," I said with a grin. "I wondered how one person could be so entitled. I was thinking about getting you a cape."

"I'm always playing a part. How do you think my family maintains status? But I might have overdone it a bit that time. That guy . . ."

Another shiver crawled up my spine. I nodded, unable to form words. That guy was more of a feeling than something to be explained.

"What is he?" I asked, still feeling the intuition tugging at me.

"Shade, obviously."

"No, couldn't be. There's no way he could be an assassin. He's much too loud." I pointed toward the trees, feeling the need to head back there. To follow the trail I should've followed the other day instead of dallying with Colt and getting caught by Rory. To sit down and cry until I couldn't breathe.

"It's not just assassins in the House of Shade." He huffed. "All of them are low-level grunts, as far as magical society goes, but still highly useful in situations the civilized world doesn't like to speak of. Some of them specialize in getting information out of people the hard way, some of them are poison masters, some excellent thieves, and some, like him, are adept bodyguards, able to read people and threats. The good ones can mask their whereabouts, like a shadow. The great ones can mask themselves *and* others. Often, a Shade is brought in to protect someone against a fellow Shade."

I slowed as we neared the trees I'd hidden in the other night. My mind shifted to Rory. To the way he'd covered me with his body, slowed my heart rate, and masked us from danger. Saved us. Me.

"Why would a Shade go against their own people?"

He shrugged. "Why would a magical person go against another magical person? A human against a human? The world is complex, the magical world more complex."

"Still, why do you think Adam's playing detective? Is he actually working for the director or himself?" I walked around the trees and surveyed the direction in which Gregory had been carried off.

"No way to know for sure. But did you see what he had with him?" Ethan asked. "He'd set it next to the fence. A memory ball."

"What's that?"

He scoffed. "Under what crusty rock were you living before you came here?"

And just like that, helpful Ethan vanished, and douche Ethan resurfaced. An act, my butt.

"A memory ball is a magical photo album, but instead of pictures, it records feelings, sounds, smells, images . . . it's the *whole* memory, not just a flat version of it."

"He's probably planning to go through it for clues. If she's gone, maybe she took a . . . memory selfie right before it happened."

"Do you realize how dumb you sound?" He shook his head, waiting while I took in the landscape. "Besides, if she has disappeared, he'll never get it open."

This side of the mansion had more trees with the woods creeping up within fifty yards of the building. A few benches dotted the way, a couple horseshoe pits sat off to the side, and a green wooden shed with the door closed pushed up against the wall down the way.

Ethan's last words filtered in through my head, taking a second to register.

"How do they open?"

"With a matching retina. Memory balls are connected to the user. He'd need her eyeball."

I turned to him slowly, my own eyes widening. "Can you magically bypass it?"

"Only if she died, and only then if you were the registered next of kin. Memory balls are personal. Like phones."

I clutched his arm. "Maybe he has her eyeball."

"I thought about that. We can work back around to him. Finding him again shouldn't be a problem. He's a blunt instrument. No wonder the director is always one or more steps behind."

Once again, I had to ask, "Why? What do you mean?"

"He's a bodyguard, not a detective. It's like giving a garbage man a chemistry set and saying, 'here, make . . . '" His example tapered off.

"Do *you* know how dumb you sound right now?" I asked.

He scowled.

I started forward, not really knowing where I was going, just feeling things out. I wasn't a detective, either, but when the fox got into the henhouse, you found the threat, or you went hungry. I'd spent my whole life rooting out threats, large and small. That wasn't about to change now.

Windows lined this side of the mansion, all four floors of it.

"Screaming would draw people to the windows." I pointed up at them, imagining the darkness pressing in from all sides as the guys jogged the kicking and yelling Gregory through the lane of grass. Sound would bounce off those glass panes, and it hadn't been quite late enough for the attack to go unnoticed.

But then, I'd only heard the two shouts. Was that because Rory had knocked me down and dragged me into the trees? Or maybe they'd knocked Gregory out?

I scanned the tree line across the expanse of small clearing.

Or could it be because they were nearly at their destination?

"Come on," I said, jogging left.

Trees welcomed us into their shade, the air cooling immediately and the sun's potency reducing down to a warm glow.

"Why not have a place near campus?" I said to myself, feeling excitement unfurl in my gut. I was close, I could tell. My intuition was practically vibrating through me. "You can take kids at your leisure. Draw them out to chat, then snatch them when everyone else is headed back to their dorms. If all went to plan, no one would be the wiser."

"Do you need me here for this conversation?" Ethan asked, trailing behind me with his wand out. I was thankful he was still taking this seriously.

"No. You're no detective, either. Not without your cheat sheets, at any rate." I scanned the shaded ground, rocks pounded into the soft earth. I held up a finger and backtracked, hitting the tree line again and hooking my arm into his.

"It's back on, then?" Ethan asked, but I knew he didn't really mean it. His grip was too tight on his wand. His body too tense. He might ignore it, but he had intuition, too, and it was telling him exactly what mine was telling me.

Here. Somewhere here!

"Lovers' stroll," I murmured, scanning the ground as we walked, trying not to make it obvious. Three guys running through, struggling, carrying a load of any kind, would leave prints, and since there was no rain, those prints weren't getting naturally erased. Would they think to erase them themselves? Or were they too cocky for that? "Bingo."

Boot prints, their tread obvious. Deep marks scored the soft dirt on the side of one print, indicating the person who'd left it had held something heavy. Then on the other side, the same thing, the weight shifting. Four times they would have brought someone here. Heath. Gregory. Lisa. Mason.

I let Ethan go and followed, pointing at a disturbance in the leaves, a small drag mark, and then the continuing tracks. "They dropped him, picked him up, and kept running. Slower, though. See how the tracks change?"

"You *sure* you don't change into an animal?"

"Only a she-devil in the throes of passion." I frowned at myself. "Stop putting dirty thoughts in my head."

Broken twigs littered the ground in one place and the tracks lightened before disappearing totally.

So someone *did* care enough to try and conceal where they'd gone.

"They turned through here. Through these . . ." A broken branch led the way. Then another. At a dead end, I looked around, momentarily lost. It was Ethan who spotted it.

"Is that stone?" He pointed through a narrow gap between two huge trunks, each fighting for space in the crowded forest.

A surge of adrenaline flooded me. My breathing sped up.

"Yup." I jogged around the tree, feeling no warning and therefore not being as careful as I should have been.

My breath left me as I fell. Blackness enveloped me. Ethan's fingers curled around my wrist, halting my descent with a jerk, popping my back. His strong hand pinched the skin of my wrist, and my feet dangled in the empty air.

"Help." It was barely more than a whisper. Blackness pulsed all around me.

CHAPTER 10

Thisisaglamour, you idiot," he said through the strain of holding me. A second hand joined the first. All that working out served a purpose after all—he hauled me up out of the black nothingness I'd fallen into.

I clutched at the forest floor as soon as I could reach it, breathing heavily, my toes tingling. I hadn't gotten one flare of warning. Not a twinge of uncertainty. Was it only living things that alerted my internal warning system?

"There are stairs." Ethan, out of breath, grabbed me by the waistband of my sweats and yanked me the rest of the way up.

I slid onto my stomach and face, reaching back to shove his hand away from my half-exposed butt cheeks, but he'd already let go, stood, and flicked his wand. A few words and the ground cover cleared away, revealing a large hole in a solid mass of black stone. On the side, stairs descended into the cavern of unnatural darkness below.

"That's dangerous," I said, out of breath. "Someone could just fall down that."

"Yeah. Maybe one of the missing students did." Ethan jerked his head to get me moving. His tone suggested he didn't believe his own words any more than I did. He descended the stairs, wand out. Clearly, he wasn't going to make me go first, this time.

Halfway down, the darkness clung to his legs, then crawled up his body, so thick it looked like a physical thing. When it reached his waist, he lifted his arms, as though inching into cold water. He shivered, completing the image.

"Can't you dispel that darkness?" I whispered, following him down.

"I don't know how. I've had tutors to give me an edge for the academy, but I'm still freshman level, maybe sophomore at best. This is beyond me. I don't know how they did it."

"You need to talk to your dad about cheating a little more thoroughly," I said as I closed the distance between us and put my hand on his shoulder. If this murky shadow blinded us, I didn't want to get separated.

"Apparently so," he said, and I didn't think he was kidding.

The inky fingers reached his chest, then inched onto his neck. Right behind him, it slid over my breasts, dousing me with a chill that couldn't be explained by a mere change in altitude.

"Here we go," Ethan said softly as the darkness slid over his full lips. "Gregory better be worth—"

The shadow cut off his volume, or maybe stole his words. I dug my fingers into his muscled shoulder and pushed up close, my front glued to his back. Black slid up my nose and then stole my sight.

"Oh God," I said, clutching Ethan with two hands now, both of us stopped dead still, the warmth between us the only thing grounding me. I didn't hear the words I'd just uttered. I was either deaf or mute, and we were both trapped in our fear of the unknown.

I came to first, fighting through the paralysis. Fingers relaxing on one hand, I shoved him with the other, forcing him to move forward. He staggered, clearly missed a step, and fell, yanked from my grip. My heel hit the step I'd been steering him toward, and I careened forward.

His body hard but thankfully not bony, a prone Ethan caught my fall.

"*Oomph*," I grunted, and thankfully heard the noise. He groaned and I rolled off, allowing him to sit up. Blood dripped from his nose. The ground wasn't as forgiving as the backside of his body had been.

We'd reached the bottom.

Darkness pressed in around us, but it was the kind caused by an absence of sunlight, brightened only by a small glow from a distant torch flickering from its bracket on the stone wall. A narrow corridor into the earth led away from us and a funky smell tickled my nose—stagnant water, mildew, and gym socks, if I had to guess. I leaned closer to Ethan to inhale his pleasant-smelling cologne and dispel the stink of the place.

"Whatever this place is, it isn't open to students," Ethan whispered, wiping his nose and standing slowly. "They wouldn't have hidden it so well if it were."

"Thank you, Professor, for your fantastic insight." I moved around him, peering down the long corridor and spying three more flickering torches perched against the wall, two on the left, and one on the right. Green lined the cracks of the old stone, pock-marked and dingy, which looked like it predated the mansion. Who'd built this place, and why? "Shall we?"

"I don't think winning the trials is worth all this," Ethan murmured under his breath, but he started forward anyway, his wand slightly shaking. Entitlement wouldn't do him a damn bit of good down here and we both knew it.

"The director must know this place exists," I said. "It's old—really old—and it wasn't hard to find."

"It wasn't hard to find *for you*," he replied as we inched down the long corridor. The dank surroundings seeped into my bones, sending a chill down my spine. "You've already set a record at the school. You're the first female to win three trials, and the second person to do so in history."

"We all won."

"You're the driving force. I won't admit it in public because—"

"Your reputation, yeah." I rolled my eyes.

"What everyone has said is true—you've brought us together as a unit. Even with my cheat sheets, I wouldn't have been able to get through some of those challenges. And you would've knocked out four, not three, if it wasn't for that ambush yesterday, which was . . ."

His words died away.

"What did your father *really* say about it? Not what you told everyone in public, but what he really thinks?" I finally asked as a gap in the stone came into view on the right, draped in fuzzy lines of deep shadow. A familiar warning vibrated through my body, slowing my forward progress.

"He's looking into it. No one knows who is behind it, which usually points to one person."

"Who?"

He made an exasperated sound. "You really don't know anything about this world, do you? We'll just say, a very bad dude."

"A very. Bad. Dude." I nodded sarcastically, which was probably lost in the dim light, as I pulled my knife from its sheath, not having done so before now because Ethan had been leading and I hadn't wanted to accidentally stab him. Which would've happened when I'd fallen.

"The Shadowkiller." He breathed the name and it ghosted down my spine like cold fingers. Shivers ran through me, and I had to work to force my body to stop.

"Regardless." The word barely made a sound. My shoulder blades itched, like someone was watching from the many shadows. "The director at this school should know of this place."

"The director of the elite graduate academy probably does. But if it is top secret, or a school secret, he wouldn't pass that info on to a bunch of low hanging fruit, like Director Frost or the staff for the trials."

Derision dripped off of every word. Clearly, he thought the trials were run by a bunch of lackeys. That didn't make me feel any safer.

Your number is up, and your protection is dead. Best thing you can do is run. Get out of the trials and don't come back. Run.

I pushed Adam's voice out of my head.

"Well then, wouldn't the *elite* director check it out if he heard about the disappearances?" I asked.

Ethan snorted. "The graduate director is on vacation. He takes one every year during the Culling Trials."

I pressed my lips closed. There was no point in arguing further. It wasn't going to get us anywhere.

At the end of the corridor, more shadows cut across stone, almost making another corridor. Warning blared at me from all around. I clutched Ethan's sleeve. Gregory was down here somewhere, I could feel it, like a direct connection to him.

"Get ready for defensive spells," I murmured, steeling my courage and stepping forward. "Maybe strap on Captain Entitlement's cape too. Couldn't hurt."

A glint made my heart lurch, and I was twisting and then bending to the side before it registered as a throwing star. The metal flashed as it sailed past my face and clinked against stone at my back. A flurry of movement caught my attention from the way we'd just come. A man running at us.

"Move!" Ethan shoved me aside and blasted a stream of red from his wand.

The man, dressed in black and blending with the shadows, turned his shoulders just enough that the flare of magic zipped harmlessly by. His movements, lithe and graceful, barely hitched as he righted himself and kept on coming.

In the gap we'd been facing, light bent and pulled away as a face inched into view. Sweat glistened within overgrown sideburns. My heart lodged in my throat.

"The Sandman," I uttered through numb lips. His hand came up, another throwing star between his fingers.

Adrenaline flooded me as Ethan got off another shot at the guy creeping at us. New Guy dove gracefully to the side, Ethan barely missing him that time.

"Come on!" I yanked Ethan toward me, bent, and snatched up the throwing star that had tinkled to a stop five feet away. I spun and threw it at the Sandman. The weapon flew through the air, smoothly as though I'd been doing it all my life.

The Sandman batted it away lazily, close enough now that I could see the two pricks of blood welling up against his skin. He stepped out of the gap.

Ethan zapped off two more spells, one for each man. Both men moved like they were on liquid joints, making me feel like a rusty tin man in comparison. New Guy pulled a knife out of nowhere and sent it flying from his gloved hand.

The Sandman—crap, when had he reached us, I hadn't even seen him move—shoved at Ethan to further expose me. Thankfully, it also cut me off from the airborne knife. Unfortunately for Ethan, the knife dug into his shoulder.

He cried out, clutching at it. A throwing star zipped by my head, slicing my earlobe.

I gritted my teeth and spun away, pain flaring from the wound. A touch said my ear was still there, so I ignored the throbbing as another knife appeared between New Guy's fingers. The Sandman pivoted, throwing star in hand one moment, launched the next. The man moved like a striking cobra. The star caught the light as it flew at New Guy, who pivoted on a dime to twist away.

New Guy's next knife wasn't aimed at us.

They probably both wanted me dead, but it seemed they weren't on the same side. I'd take it as a win.

"Come on, Ethan." He grunted when I grabbed him, his fist around the knife hilt, ready to pull it out. "No." I stopped him. "Leave it in. It's plugging up the hole—"

The stranger reached the Sandman and warning prickled every inch of my body, raising the small hairs on my arms and back of my neck. I couldn't move, I had to watch the two masters meet. The Sandman threw a punch he didn't seem to think would land, because he was prepared when it didn't—the second the stranger blocked him, the Sandman jabbed forward with a knife in his other hand. The stranger blocked that with two arms before flourishing a knife he seemed to have grabbed from empty air. He struck to the side, but the Sandman was already moving, their dance as beautiful as it was lethal. These guys were unbelievably skilled.

I snapped out of it. "Hurry, hurry, hurry." I dragged Ethan to the end of the corridor, ignoring his pained protests. Flickering light played across the cracked and scarred ground, as though centuries of moving heavy things through here had taken its toll on the stone. Or maybe it had been a lifetime of duels like the one behind us. Warning still bled through my body, but it felt nothing like what was going on behind me, so I pressed on, eyes peeled.

"Did your dad teach you to cheat while injured?" I asked in a hush, turning right with the corridor.

"No," he ground out, his voice soaked with pain.

"And now we know the limits of entitlement, eh?"

"Stop. Saying. That. Word."

I chuckled, giddy in my terror, as I saw a gap in the stone away to the left.

"Light." Ethan struggled to point ahead of us, to a soft glow that chased away most of shadows. It wasn't daylight, though. Logic pointed to a guard's station or office for whoever came down here. We didn't need to run into any more magical people if we could help it. Or get stuck in a dead end.

"Here." I yanked him with me, his forward movement greatly hampered by the pain in his shoulder. "You need to work on your pain tolerance."

Only one torch lit this corridor, and in a dozen or so feet, I saw why. Bars lined the right side, separated by columns of stone blocks. Benches were pushed up against the opposite wall, as though for viewing.

We inched closer and movement caught my eye, someone stirring from behind the bars. A girl, my age, with an oval face, large blue eyes, and scabbed-over bite marks on her neck.

"Hello?" she asked in a small voice.

A foot scraped against stone. Fingers wrapped around the bars, just visible down the way. A longish nose pushed out and my heart leapt.

"Gregory?"

"Wild?"

My heart swelling with excitement, I started down the line of occupied cells, but didn't get far. Gregory was in the first one. A smile took over his face, big and broad and so relieved.

"You came! You found me! How'd you find me?" he asked, words tumbling over each other.

A strangled sound dragged my focus back the way I'd come. There, filling the gap posing as a doorway, short and compact and sporting those hideous sideburns, was the victor of the battle of masters. The Sandman. And now, nothing stood in his way.

Well, nothing except a wounded mage in training.

"Ethan—"

I didn't get to finish the command to move.

The Sandman charged so fast, I lost track of his limbs. Ethan cried out and an axe went flying, revolving end over end until the gleaming edge crashed against the only torch lighting the area. The blade sliced off the flaming top, sending it fluttering to the floor. Once there, it dulled before going out.

Darkness washed through the room—the only light coming from somewhere deeper in the tunnel—and the last thing I saw was Ethan sprawled across the floor, curling around his hurt shoulder. A spear of pain drove through my thigh, a knife blade. Another embedded in my upper arm, shallow but no less painful for it. My knife clattered to the ground, having fallen from suddenly relaxed fingers.

"No, Wild!" Gregory yelled, his voice weak. Shouts and screams echoed off the walls and chased each other around the room. A blur of movement made me flinch, the pain throbbing, dulling my reactions. A fist came around, aiming for my cheek.

I pulled back at the last second. The fist smashed into the wall beside me. The Sandman cursed, but he didn't stop. His leg whipped out, unreal fast, clipping my ankles. My legs went out from under me, my balance already in jeopardy from my wounded leg. I struck out with my good arm as I went down, hitting the second crotch that day. This time, I put a lot more strength behind the punch.

The breath gushed out of the Sandman and he doubled over. I snatched my knife from the ground even as my hip crashed into the stone. Pain rolled through my other side, vibrating through my body now, hard to ignore. I did my best, lashing out with my knife and catching his shin.

The Sandman swore, his voice rough, and pulled his foot back. Adrenaline blasted me one moment before the boot hit my face and darkness stole my consciousness.

CHAPTER 11

S leep peeled away slowly, and soft warmth greeted me, cushioning me on all sides. I blinked my eyes open into an unfamiliar room. The beds were arranged in rows, all of them empty except for the one I lay in. Etched into the wall across from me were the words:

Strength is Life. Honor is Life. Loyalty is Life. Death is Life.

I knew without understanding how that I was for the first time seeing the creed of Shadowspell Academy.

A wave of pain washed through my head that drew a groan out of me. I must be in the medic rooms inside the mansion, or at least that was my best guess based on the ache in my head and the astringent smell that curled up my nose.

Darkness pressed against the windows. What had happened to the day? Had the zombie poisoning somehow returned? I remembered the trial, remembered coming out of it, and then . . . nothing.

I winced, curling my fingers around my forehead, and struggled to remember what had landed me in with the healers.

Adam. Ethan and I had been following Adam, and he'd caught us. He'd grabbed Ethan around the neck and I'd rushed in to help. Had Adam done this to me?

A familiar face approached the bed as a fuzzy recollection took shape of dark eyes staring at me through a mess of long brunette curls.

"Are you okay?" Wally asked, her face somber. "The nurse said she healed what she could of the concussion so you could sleep, but your head will likely be sore for a while. Is it sore?"

I squinted, letting Wally's words drift around me, trying to remember beyond that encounter with Adam. I'd grabbed his neck and whipped him around. I'd . . .

I dug my fingertips into my skin, willing the throbbing pain to cease. My memories frayed at the edges and drifted away. There was still half a day unaccounted for.

"What happened?" I asked, dropping my head back onto the pillow. Some pain relief would sure be great. Where was a bottle of Tylenol when you needed it?

"You got into a fight with Ethan," Wally said, anger lighting up her eyes. "He dragged you in here, unconscious, with a broken nose and two knives sticking out of you."

I frowned up at her and shook my head, the movement sending waves of agony pinging through my skull. "Ethan? No, that can't be right. Knives? He doesn't even carry knives."

"He got the drop on you, didn't he?" she asked, searching my eyes for answers to questions that didn't make any sense. "Why did he slash your ear? Was he actually trying to kill you? I mean, you stabbed him, so all wasn't lost, but Pete said—"

"So." A slick voice filled the room, velvety and decadent. Jared drifted closer, his attractive face hard and eyes glimmering with suspicion. He didn't glance at Wally when he stopped next to my bed. "It seems you provoked another student of reputable standing. It is becoming clear that your goal is to get kicked out of this establishment. Luckily for you, Master Helix has decided not to press charges. I cannot think as to why."

"Probably because I wasn't fighting with him. I was following—"

The words died on my lips. Adam stood behind and a little to the side of Jared, the sound of his approach hidden by the pounding of my cranium. His eyes shot sparks of warning at me. Tingles of it stopped my tongue.

"You were following Ethan, yes, he mentioned that," Jared said, his mouth twisted in distaste. He turned slightly, glancing over his shoulder at Adam, before his expression darkened. "Ah. Lovely. I see the director's minion has arrived. Another reason to leave the office unattended, Adam?"

"Thank you, Jared, you can go," Adam said, his eyes not leaving mine, his voice steel.

Jared made a frustrated sound. "Surely Madam Director sees that this . . . creature should be kicked out. Her presence waters down the prestige of the whole school. Attacking a fellow student? A *Helix*, no less? She amused me in the beginning—thinking to take on three vampires—but that has faded. It is clear she is a danger to everyone here."

"I didn't attack *him*," I said, pounding my stare into Adam as hard as the pain pounded into me.

"How many more will she attack before your office actually *does* something?" Jared said.

"Thank you, Jared," Adam said again, his tone icy and his gaze spitting fire. He chewed off each word. "You. May. Go."

Jared's eyes narrowed as they surveyed me. "I will get to the bottom of this. Something isn't adding up. A full report should be made, regardless of the Helix boy's decision not to press charges. If it were up to me—"

Adam leaned forward, a small movement. Pressure increased in the room. He didn't have to say a word.

Jared's body tensed, and he drew himself up straighter and lifted his chin. "Very well." He glided out, indignation covering him like a cloak. "This is not forgotten. You can rest assured of that."

A hard look from Adam sent Wally scurrying from the room, as well. "I'll just be outside," she said over her shoulder, clearly not wanting to leave.

"What do you remember?" Adam said, his voice deep and low, sending tremors over my limbs.

"Everything," I bluffed, looking at him through narrowed eyes.

"That right?" He studied me. "Ethan did this to you, then?"

"There is no way Ethan could stab me. Twice. He's not fast enough, and you know it."

"Then who did?" His blank face didn't give anything away.

I hesitated in naming him, suddenly unsure of my own hazy memories. Besides, at the moment, I had no proof.

"Where's Ethan?" I asked.

"In your dorm, healed up and preening over his victory against a woman with the potential to be the best Shade the house has seen in years." Adam's face gave nothing away.

I shook my head slowly, the effort costing me. What was the point in arguing when I didn't have the knowledge to do it successfully?

He must've realized that from my silence.

"You can't be the best Shade dead, Wild," he said, his voice low and rough. "I'd really think about your options if I were you. I'd think about leaving." Without another word, Adam took a step back, turned, and stalked from the room.

A memory flitted through my mind: *Your number is up, and your protection is dead. Best thing you can do is run. Get out of the trials and don't come back.* Run.

I'd been walking away from Adam, I remembered that now. We'd fought, but we'd walked away. He hadn't done this to me. But then who had? Not Ethan. I was sure of it.

I took a deep breath and palmed my head again. "Healer! I need aspirin! Or a lobotomy."

I also needed to get to Ethan and compare stories. I needed this gap in my memory filled.

Unfortunately, it quickly became clear I wouldn't get that opportunity. The director's office had reached a compromise with Jared, who wanted me gone now seeing as I was such a *danger*. I wondered though what had turned him suddenly against me, because before he *had* seemed more amused than anything. What had changed? Was it because he'd noticed the others following him? Or was it more than that?

The healer, Mara, mentioned she'd keep me under surveillance, monitoring the concussion to make sure it really had healed. If I was in good enough health by morning, I could continue on in the trials. If she deemed it a health risk, I'd be kicked out with a standing invitation to return next year.

No way in hell was I getting kicked out. I doubted they'd have me back. And what would happen to Billy in that case? Would he be forced to come with me? The idea of going through the trials, trying to protect Billy at the same time, made my skin crawl and my stomach roll.

The next morning came slowly between fits of pain and nightmares I couldn't escape no matter how far I ran in my dreams.

Shaky and determined, I boarded the last bus in the row, the one I'd been told my crew would be riding. There in the back, where Ethan normally claimed space for us, sat a hard-faced crew behind a douche who had either lied or kicked me when I was down. Because there was no way in hell he'd beat me fair and square. If he had, I'd never forgive myself.

Smirks and snickers followed me down the aisle, and if not for my headache and Jared's threat, I would've distributed a dozen knuckle sandwiches.

Ethan glanced up as I made my approach, the seat next to him vacant, and a shadow crossed his deep blue eyes. His gaze hit my arm, then my thigh, before he glanced out the window.

"Well. Hello, master-at-arms," I sat down beside him.

"Wild!" Pete pushed up in the seat behind me, concerned. "Are you okay? What really happened? Because no way could—"

I held up a hand to stop him. "Great question, Pete. Because the last memory I have is jumping to Ethan's aid."

It was a small lie, but I was going to roll with it.

Ethan's face swung around, confusion marring his features.

"Jumping to my aid?" he said. "He wasn't after me, he—" That shadow passed over his eyes again, something unsettled moving in their depths, before he turned away. "You shouldn't try to pick fights with your betters, Wild. Now you know why."

"Them's fightin' words," Wally said in her deep Walter Cronkite voice.

I clenched my fist and leaned into him, so angry I could spit, no matter how disgusting it was. "You just corroborated my story in one sentence, then changed it to a bullcrap story in the next. *Which is it?*"

Ethan's jaw clenched and he waved his hand, annoyed and frustrated. That made two of us.

"Just forget anything happened, Wild," he said softly, for my ears alone. "Forget it, okay? This is bigger than us. Some people you just can't mess with. I believe that. Just forget it, and we'll get through the trials. That's all we need to do right now. Everything else will work itself out."

"Are you kidding me right now?" The bus shimmied to a start and the chatter around us raised in volume to compete with the motor. Our crew leaned in closer to hear Ethan and me arguing. "Those kids are still missing, and we were—*are* clearly on the right track. We can free them, I know it. Or at least find out who's responsible for their disappearance." Free them? Why had I said that? My head throbbed and I pinched the bridge of my nose, breathing through the pain.

Ethan's face closed down again. "What's the last thing you remember?"

I told him slowly, clutching at the foggy memories like a man with arthritis would a small gold coin. When I hit the part where Adam had told me to run, Wally sucked in a breath.

"That's a threat, right?" she asked. "Is he behind all of this? We got nothing by following Jared, literally not a single clue. He just sat in the cafeteria reading a book."

Ethan's lips tightened and he minutely shook his head, looking away again. "Adam had Ethel's memory ball. That's it."

More flutters of memory surfaced, about a conversation I'd had with Ethan. Something about an eyeball to open it . . . Next of kin . . .

"What's the last thing *you* remember?" I asked him, the black hole in my memory scaring me a little, but more than the fear, it frustrated me to the point of tears. I had the key to unlock all of these mysteries, I could feel it, only it was lost in the swamp of blackness that was a time lapse.

. . . *swamp of blackness crawling up his legs* . . .

Ethan spoke over the flutter of memory, crushing it.

"I remember kicking your ass and stabbing you with Shade knives I could never have acquired on my own," he murmured, so softly I wondered if I was half making up the words. The bus came to a stop and he shoved me out of the seat, something he could only do because I'd grabbed my head to stop the dull pounding. It didn't work. "Let it go, Wild. Keep your eyes open and your ass down, or you'll get everyone killed. That's a warning *from a friend*."

"Oh yeah, a friend?" I jabbed him in the ribs, following close behind him. "Since when are we friends?"

"Since never." He hopped off the bus and walked toward the fifth and final gate. The House of Wonder. The magical house. Just like the House of Night, this gate clearly belonged to the House of Wonder. The metal was a brilliant silver accented with gold down long curving spindles that resembled a climbing rose that had been set in with cut red glass or rubies. I was suspecting those of his house wouldn't allow mere glass to be used. But even the beauty and craftsmanship of the gate couldn't detract from the situation at hand. Namely my memory loss.

"What's going on with you two?" Orin said as he drifted to my side. "Things aren't adding up. And Ethan is lying. I can smell it all over him." Pete nodded and added a *me too*.

"I know. But I can't . . ." I gritted my teeth. "There is a hole in my memory."

"But he knows? Ethan knows you can't remember?"

"Yeah. He knows, but he's not talking."

Orin stared at the ornate gate in front of us. He nodded silently as Pete dropped in on my other side, and Wally stepped up beside him. "We'll just have to get the truth out of him."

"Yes," I said, cracking my knuckles. "We will."

"But after the trial. We'll need him for this trial," Pete said. Orin and Wally bobbed their heads in agreement. They weren't wrong.

I took a deep breath, calming the frustration and the anger and the fear of what had happened in that black space in my memory. "Right. After this trial." I palmed my head as we caught up with Ethan. "We need to check with Colt, too. See if there was anything else missing from Ethel's room." I glanced around, looking for his crew.

The others exchanged pointed looks. It was Ethan who broke it to me.

"He's gone. Missing. He never met us in our dorm, and he didn't show up to his." He didn't look at me as he said it. "There's nothing we can do about it. We need to get through this trial and get on with our lives."

CHAPTER 12

I wondered if I'd have a stress fracture in my jaw from clenching my teeth so hard. Something was seriously wrong with Ethan. He seemed . . . defeated, somehow. Like the wind had been stolen from his sails. His pompous arrogance was gone, replaced with hollow indifference. Whatever had him spooked, he didn't plan to fight back. And that dug into me almost more than the missing memories. It wasn't like him.

"What happened?" I asked softly, needing more info so I could fight back for him. I wasn't the type to say die, even when I was obviously being thrown into the deep end with weights around my ankles. "And why would Colt get taken while we ended up in the infirmary with knives sticking out of us? Shade knives, did you say?"

The beautiful woman strode along the top of the gates, just as she'd done with the first three trials. I wondered if her failure to appear the other day had anything to do with how badly our trip through the House of Night had gone. She waved a hand forward as she stood to the side of the gates. "Good luck to you all. Have fun."

Fun.

We walked through the gates, Ethan leading the way, and a shiver cascaded over me as a magical wall slid behind us, closing us off from turning around and running for the exit. The timing was not surprising. A roar boomed through the air as soon as the wall descended, the sound vibrating through my body. I remembered it from that first day, when Wally had spouted off T-rex statistics, and everyone around us shifted and practically danced in fearful anticipation.

Thoughts of the day before fled. I was sure blood left my face in a rapid flood, if the numbing of my lips was any indication.

"Is there a reason the only magical worker among us waited to do this trial last?" My boot crunched against the brittle grass one moment and thudded against the rustic wooden floor of a saloon the next. Wooden walls had sprung up around us. An old-timey piano played in the corner, the keys pressing down and lifting again in a creepy mime without fingers to propel them. A long bar sat in front of us with a bartender behind it, one hand wrapped around the neck of a bottle of whiskey, and the other resting behind five shot glasses.

The man grinned from under his long gray mustache that curled up at the corners in twin perfect swoops. His leather vest hung flat on his stomach and his long, pointed wizard hat indicated he wasn't great at putting together a costume.

"Welcome," the man said, his voice gruff, like I'd expect, but with a lilting sort of accent that spoke of posh England, which I wouldn't expect. "Pick your poison, my young friends."

"Should be pick *yer* poison, if you're going for the Old West vibe." I glanced around at the establishment we'd found ourselves in. Card tables filled the space, each partially occupied. Men hunched over their cards with drinks by their elbows and ladies in fancy dresses and corsets by their sides. The dealers opposite them wore pointed wizard hats, like the bartender, and each had a little chest of gold by his stack of cards.

We were the only crew present.

"This is the most important trial for him," Orin said, at my elbow, looking around as I was doing. "He'll need to impress daddy and all his peers to make it in his world. A failure here could mean his entire future comes crashing down. Society gives guys like him a lot of leeway, except when it comes to living up to expectations. I would go so far as to say that he will have the hardest trial of all of us. For us, there were no expectations, per se. For him . . . all of them."

"Shut up," Ethan said, the truth of what Orin was saying evident in the tightness of his voice.

"That's good." I blew out a breath, trying to ignore the throbbing of my head and the warning shivers coating my body. "I was worried it would be harder, somehow."

"That, too," Orin said.

A shadow zipped by in my peripheral vision and I swung my gaze that way. My vision dizzied for a moment before I saw a group of women in the corner, their breasts heaving out of the tops of their gowns to the point where I struggled to understand how their nipples stayed covered. Poofy skirts flared out from their corseted waists. They stared at me, one and all, some with knowing looks, others with expectant expressions. One laughed suggestively.

"What is the deal with this trial?" I asked as Ethan chose a table to his right and sat in the single empty chair. A distant roar permeated the walls and shook the bottles against the mirror behind the bar. That creature did not belong in the Old West. I knew that much.

"Pick a table, and best the dealer, who'll use magic to try and confuse you," Ethan said, determination in his voice. "They use mind tricks. Persuasion. It's a test of your strength of mind. You need to be able to throw off the magic. Or you can choose the bar. See if you can do the same with the potion you ingest."

Orin drifted to the bar. "It is rare the House of Wonder can concoct a poison that can befuddle a vampire. That ability is usually limited to the House of Shade, poisoners of the highest calibre."

"It really doesn't make sense that two houses would rely on the same craft when the House of Wonder thinks so little of Shades," I said, wandering through the tables.

"Two sides of the same coin," Orin said. "The same result, but different methods. Anyone from the House of Wonder would consider it an insult to create a potion without magic."

"Snobs," I said.

Something else was at work here. I could feel it. Something . . . not right. Much as I wanted to believe this trial wouldn't be rigged after the last disaster, I didn't trust it.

"It is the same craft, but with different intentions," Orin said.

"One has no morals," Ethan added, but without any heat, placing his elbows on the green velvet of the card table.

"So, then . . ." Wally pulled out an empty chair, but the players at the table weren't looking at her. They were all looking at me.

My head pounded. My heart thudded. My sense of warning, slower to develop than usual, flared, so intense it nearly made me scream.

The man in the wizarding hat jumped up from behind the bar, wand out, and blasted me before I could dive to the side. The spell wrapped around my body, holding me in place as Pete shed his clothes and changed shape.

Orin turned from the bar with a sour face, an empty glass held between his fingers, his eyes on the bare bottom. "Shade," he said in a strangled release. The glass fell from his suddenly lifeless fingers. He grabbed at his throat, eyes bulging, and took two staggering steps. "The Shade . . . infiltrated . . ."

"What's he saying?" Wally yelled.

The Shade had infiltrated the House of Wonder. They were coming for me. Sideburns was finally making his move.

Almost as the thought formed, a man in black burst from behind the group of women in the corner. Limbs and skirts went flying.

Anxiety riding me like an unbroken horse, I forced myself to calm down and focus. The throb in my head drifted into the background. My intense desire to break free surged, firing hot through my blood.

The spell holding me cracked like an egg.

I snapped my eyes open and yanked out my knife. A split second later the man was on me, his own knife already slashing for my face.

I dodged to the side and slapped at his hand, using his momentum to knock him off balance. My blade parted black fabric. He turned and thrust, slower than I would expect, clearly not the best of his House. I knocked my forearm against his before ripping it down, following with my blade. It slashed against his wrist and over the top of his gloved hand. Red welled up in the cut and he jerked back.

People jumped up from chairs, wands or weapons raised. Wally grabbed the edge of the table and flung it, overturning everything. Money and cards rained down as she charged forward, a little alley cat of power. I could see the pink of her magic lighting her up. I wasn't sure what good it would do against the living, but she was embracing it.

Honey badger Pete snarled and dove under the heavy green skirt of a woman with a hard expression and a poised throwing knife. Another dagger thudded to the ground from under her skirts, followed by a small hand-gun—her hidden weapons. She gasped and kicked out before staggering to the side in an effort to dislodge the honey badger latched onto her legs.

"We gotta get out of here," I called as a glint of metal flew through the air, end over end. There was too much going on, too fast. I couldn't keep up with it all.

A knife, the blade gleaming in the saloon light, sped toward my chest. I dropped and rolled before popping up again and grabbing a shocked trial worker who clearly hadn't gotten the memo regarding the change in plans, and shoved him in front of me as a human shield.

"Ethan, shrug it off," I yelled, seeing him frozen in his seat, his eyes dodging all around but his body still. "Don't let the panic rule you. *You* rule you. Shrug it off. We need you!"

"Raaaaahhhhh," I heard before a body went flying. Wally straightened, a strange glowing sheen around her, and I took a moment to marvel that a little chick like her had just thrown a grown man across the room. Something in me said that the spells they were trying to use on her were being deflected by her magic.

A spell tore at me from the bar. I swung my human shield around, and he raised his wand to deflect the assault.

"Good choice in shields," I murmured, marching him forward.

Another spell hit his legs from the side. His legs stopped moving, frozen stiff. I continued pushing him forward anyway, his heels skidding along the wooden floor, hoping his brain and muscle memory would override the spell.

SHADOWSPELL ACADEMY: THE CULLING TRIALS

They didn't.

Timber, Pete said.

"Crap." I threw aside my now useless shield and reached Orin as Pete, growling and spitting, chased a wand waver out of the swinging saloon door.

Orin's eyes stared up at the ceiling from his position flat on his back. Tex, the English Wizard with his stupid hat, smirked from behind the bar.

"Didn't expect that, now did he?" Tex said, leaning against the counter.

"Wally, get my back," I yelled as I reached over, grabbed Tex's shirt, and yanked him toward me. His eyes widened then narrowed and his hands flew out to protect himself. I was one step ahead. I rested the blade of my knife against his throat and dug in, drawing blood.

Tex's hands lifted into the air.

"Is he dead?" I asked through gritted teeth. "Is the vampire dead?"

"Not eternally, no. The vamps want him after all this is over. The necromancer too. The wizard and the weird raccoon thing got placements as well already. All this is for you. Don't you feel special? Let them take you, and your friends go free."

A beam of red blasted him in the face, ripping him from my hands and sending him flying. His back hit the shelves of bottles and his eyes rolled back in his head. He sank to the ground, bottles tumbling down after him, breaking against the ground or thunking on him.

Ethan stood behind me, his wand held in a steady hand and his eyes alight. "That was the strongest persuasion spell I've ever pushed off," he said, taking two quick steps to me, his expression triumphant. "I broke it, thanks to you." He grabbed me around the middle and pulled me toward him, his soft lips a contrast to his hard body.

Electricity sizzled through me, but not from him—from the sense of victory. Two combatants sharing a win.

He broke away. "No way in hell are you going to turn yourself over in this trial," he said. "We'll beat this like we beat all the others. I have a reputation to uphold." He winked. "So let's go. Hurry."

I liked this new Ethan better. The confidence was real. Who-ever'd beaten him down had lost their hold on him. I grinned. "Let's."

He spun and cast a spell, slamming a woman dressed in black center mass and dropping her. Clearly, he had been thoroughly tutored on attack spells.

"Leave Orin," Wally said, shoving a frozen woman out of the way and heading toward the door. "He'll understand, and we can't carry him." Her voice dropped. "Always question your drink of choice when there is danger afoot."

"That voice . . . It doesn't get any less weird," Ethan mum-bled, running at my side.

We shoved out of the door, and Pete looked back at us as a woman took off running for a stand of horses. The scene melted into a dusky prairie, not unlike the savannah scene from the shifter trial, before changing yet again with a flicker, like a com-puter screen glitching. The Old West town flickered back to life.

"This trial is being tampered with," Ethan said, slowing and looking at the sky. He brought out his cheat sheet, running his finger down the page.

"How was it?" Wally asked me quietly, standing very close. Her eyes roved my face as she waited for me to answer.

I palmed my head as the pounding returned, feeling a vague sort of danger but nothing imminent. Not yet. That last trial probably hadn't gone the way they'd expected. We were a helluva lot stronger and quicker than most other trial goers. Working together made us shine.

"How was what?" I asked, smelling lilac on the air, a strange fragrance for the Old West town.

"Kissing a Helix. I mean, he's the worst, don't get me wrong, but he's hot. Can't say I'm not curious . . ." She waggled her eyebrows at me.

I ignored her, focusing on Ethan and his notes. "Let's concentrate on getting out of this trial. Not winning it, but just getting out of it with all of us alive."

Ethan looked up at me, and for a wonder, I didn't see disappointment in his eyes. "Are you sure about that?" he asked.

All eyes turned my way, and I hated that Orin wasn't there to lend us another strategic brain. I hated that we'd have to leave him behind. It went against everything in me. Just like Rory, though, I couldn't fix this. He would live. We might not.

"Nothing we encounter is going to go how your cheat sheet tells you, Ethan," I said, feeling the urgency to get moving. "It won't do us any good, and I doubt we'll be able to beat any of the challenges. We didn't even get to do the last one."

"You did." Wally pointed at me. "And he did." Her finger swung to Ethan. "Orin failed at it, but they cheated—"

"The best course of action is getting out of here and getting to safety," I said. "No amount of gold or glory is worth our lives."

Ethan nodded and looked down at his sheet. "We can stick to the easier challenges, then. After what just happened, my father will understand the rationale behind that. He can push for a retesting if necessary. I can all but fast track us through the next one, but we'll all have to do the final one."

"What's the final—"

As if on cue, an enormous roar ripped through the air, sparking fear in my heart.

"T-rex," Wally said, suddenly out of breath. I knew how she felt. "We're going to take on the T-rex."

"How the hell is that magical?" I asked as Ethan started jogging, heading northwest. "And do you know where you're going?"

"The scenery isn't how it should be." He picked up his pace. "I don't know who you pissed off, Wild, but you sure don't have many friends in the magical world. My father won't be impressed that the security is so lax. Going after you is one thing, but dragging me into it isn't a good look. Not when he's on the board."

"Sometimes you're a good guy, Ethan, and sometimes I want to bitch slap you." I increased my speed, knowing it wouldn't be long before the next attack came.

The scenery around us changed again, turning rocky with surprise dips and falls dug into the landscaping. Mountains rose on one side and waves crashed away on the other. It was like the engineers had gotten into a fight about what they wanted the scene to look like, and settled it by drawing a line and each doing their own thing.

"This isn't an easy one, Ethan," Wally said, frustration ringing loud and clear. "You're the only one that can do it."

"What?" I asked as white lines appeared near our feet, rolling to a stop ten yards away. Sand filled in between the lines. Four people, two men and two women in robes of all shades, decorated with stitched moons and stars and a dusting of glitter, stood at the end of the white lines, facing our way. Like a weird bowling alley . . . and we were the pins. "What can't we do?"

"He's planning to leave us behind again," Wally accused, grabbing his arm and getting in his face. "You low-life, cheating—"

"We're a group," Ethan yelled over her comments, shaking her off. "As long as one member can defeat the enemy, the group can continue on."

"Then why do we each get our own lane?" Wally demanded amid Pete's growling.

Ethan gestured everyone toward the lines. "Trust me. Just keep yourself from being taken down until I deal with this guy. You'll see."

"We'll see? *Trust you?* What kind of a stupid idea is that?" Wally screeched, closer to losing it than I'd thought possible. "We trusted you on that tower. We trusted you when we faced that troll. We trusted—"

"Okay, okay." I put out my hands, eyeing the people on the other end of the lines. Their robes hid their bodies, but these were mages—trained to attack with magic, not their bodies.

They expected to face off and trade spells. That was it.

"Whoever is messing with these trials probably expected us to go for gold. They planned for the wrong contingency. So this is just a simple challenge, like Ethan said." I wished I felt as confident as I sounded.

"There's nothing simple about this, Wild. Do you know the type of spells they hit people with in these—"

I put up my hand to quiet Wally. She'd clearly reached the end of her rope. I couldn't blame her, but I also couldn't let her give in to it.

"This is fine," I said, walking along the end of the lines, reading our opponents. I silently noted their stance and balance, judging how they'd react to a charge and, more importantly, their general stance on violence. All the information I needed was right there in front of me—in the way they held themselves, in the way they sized us up or didn't.

"In poker, they say play the player, not the hand. This is the same." I pointed at the line leading to a man in a black robe with more glitter than was really necessary. "Wally, you here. Act like a damsel in distress. He'll take it easier on you. Deflect his spells like you did back at the saloon. Ethan . . ." I pointed at a woman with a bob and a pink robe. "She's the meanest. You'd better take her."

"No." Ethan pointed at the man across from him, with a drab brown robe and impatience written all over his face. "I'll take him. He's the highest magical worker."

"He's bored, look at him. He won't try as hard as—"

Ethan didn't wait for my assessment. He stepped up to the lane, aligning each foot with the lines on either side of it. With a snap, he, the lane, and the man on the end disappeared.

"Damn it," I whispered, shoving Wally to her lane. "I'll take the pink robe then. Pete, you're the last. The woman in purple. Charge her, move fast, lots of snarling."

"Watch yourself, Wild," Wally said, her eyes solemn. "If you fail this challenge, you don't come back to the trial. They'll have you alone. We won't be able to get to you."

Wally's words sunk in slowly, casting a new light on Ethan's sudden interest in being a team player. He was passing up an opportunity for gold. He was taking an easy challenge.

He was not acting like he'd always acted, and I'd fallen for it, hook, line, and sinker.

You'll see. Trust me.

CHAPTER 13

I'll be fine." I put a hand on Wally's shoulder. "You watch you, okay? Use your power. Charge him. Dodge his attacks and throw him around. Knock his wand away—anything you can. Try to beat him, or hold out until Ethan finishes and saves us." Maybe he was playing us, maybe he wasn't. All we could do now was hope for the best. Orin wasn't even there to point out a logical solution.

She gave me a dry look, as though asking, *He kissed you and now you believe in him?*

I was thankful she didn't ask me outright. It seemed shallow to blame my lack of judgement on my continuously pounding headache.

Pete snarled, snorted, and trotted to his lane, kicking at the dirt with his back feet as though prepping for a race. Wally gave me a slow wave before doing the same, minus the dirt kicking.

I faced off against the woman in soft pink before purposely placing my feet on either side of the lane. The scene around me dizzied, but I ignored it.

Play the player.

"You love that color, don't you?" I asked in an easy tone, my feet magically stuck to the ground. I didn't know if it was a preliminary measure, keeping everyone put as the challenge got underway, or I'd have to leave my boots behind when I charged her. "Not because of the actual color, but because that color tells people certain things about the wearer. It makes you seem more feminine, which people read as softer, gentler, more eager to please." The woman's expression didn't change. "But I bet you're an old battle-axe under that godawful robe, aren't you?"

Her lips pressed together and her eyes tightened at the edges.

A farm spread out around us, and with a start, I realized it was *my* farm back home, my house hunkering in the distance and the barn not far away. No cows grazed in the fields, though, and no horses flicked their tails in their pens.

"Ah. Trying to make me homesick?" I guessed. It was working. At least the place wasn't burning like in my dream.

"More comfortable, actually," she responded in a flat, dry voice. "But Shades are always comfortable, are they not?"

"No, but it's interesting that you think so."

"You must make contact with me with three spells," she went on as though reading from a rule book. "The types of spells do not matter. They simply must get past my defenses. In addition, you will need to counteract my attacks. Any questions?"

"Yeah. What happens when your opponent doesn't have a wand and can't hit you with a spell?"

"You lose."

"Right."

"And . . ."

A small chime sounded. My feet came unstuck. She brandished her wand like a quick draw and flicked her wrist at me.

But I was already off and running.

I dove under the beam of magic, rolled, nearly stood, and realized she'd already gotten off another shot. I flung myself to the side, hit an invisible wall, and rolled the other way as a flare of green dug into the ground at my side.

"How many spells have to hit me before I lose?" I grunted out, popping up and ripping out my knife. I sliced at the invisible wall, throwing up sparks. It didn't help. I was stuck in this ten-foot-wide space that was part of the game. .

"As many as you can stand." She flicked her wrist and the stream of yellow turned into a blob of yellow, spreading out to catch me.

"Good call with that spell." I ran and jumped at the wall, hit it high with my toes, pushed off, and attempted a really cool backflip. I landed on my stomach and the air pushed out of me. "Ouch," I wheezed.

"Spirited, this shall be enjoyable," she murmured.

I leapt up and zagged right, drawing her fire, before pivoting. She moved her wand, expecting me to run left. Instead, I dashed right again, scraped against the wall, barely missed by the spell, and sprinted straight at her. Her eyes widened and her wand hand jerked, a muscle memory reaction, no doubt. I rolled under it, but not fast enough. The spell screamed across my shoulder, ripping away my shirt and slashing my skin.

"Ouch," I said again. But at least it took my mind off my headache.

I bounced up, five feet away, as she swept her wand from one side to the other. A spell materialized, and I knew I wouldn't be able to dodge it.

So I didn't try.

Knife held out, teeth gritted, I sprinted at her and launched myself through the spell. It parted around my knife, but the sides clung to my body. It didn't stop my forward progress.

I slammed into the mage as heat flared across my skin. It seeped down into my blood, burning so hot, I had to glance down to make sure they weren't real flames. She landed with an *oomph*, then grunted when I smashed down on top of her, taller and stronger.

Without thinking, body burning, I went for her weapon, knowing that if I could get it from her, we'd be at an impasse. Or, at least, she couldn't magically light me on fire again.

Screaming with the pain, I grabbed her wand hand and jammed my other elbow across her face. Her lips curled and her fingers loosened. I elbowed her again. And again, forcing out a whimper. As expected, she wasn't used to physical violence.

"Let . . . go," I said, banging her wand hand against the ground.

"It'll . . . kill . . . you!"

Too late. Another elbowing made her cry out, and her fingers released their grip. The wand was in my hand before her words had properly sunk in.

The agony of the magical fire cut off, but a sharp blast of pain shot up through my hand, my arm, and into my chest. My middle turned to ice, spreading out before sinking into my limbs. I sucked in a breath, trying to let go of the wand, but I couldn't. Like a wave pulling back to the sea, the cold dimmed before leaving my body all together.

Shaking, confused, I pushed back to standing, holding the small stick that now sent vibrations through my body. It felt . . . wrong, somehow. Off. Not as natural as Ethan's wand had. But it didn't kill me.

Liar, liar, pants on fire.

"Give me that back!" She flopped, trying to turn over and stand, but wasn't able to push through the pain. "That's mine!" Her voice was weak.

I frowned at the vehemence of her reaction. It struck me, again, that this was the second wand I'd handled without any serious injury. Maybe the danger of stealing someone's wand was a myth magic users drummed up to deter theft.

"I need to get out of here. What's a spell I can do on you?" I asked, flicking the wand like she'd done. Red sparkles flew from the end and cracked all around us.

"No! How?" Her eyes widened as she looked at me. "How are you doing that?"

"Presto change-o," I said, flicking the wand again. This time blue sparks curled into the air. "What if I just . . ." I did the same again, but right next to her leg so the sparks would hit her.

"Ah!" Surprise lit her features and she scooted away. Mud spread across her light pink robe.

"I bet you hope that's mud, at any rate," I said, remembering how I'd wrestled with Bluebell the day before I left the farm. Not allowing myself to dwell, I bent and did the swooping move again. Then a third time.

The scene wobbled. She disappeared. My farm melted around me. Ethan, his wand freshly stowed in his stupid holster, pulled out his sheet of paper ten feet away, back on the open plains that we'd started with.

There was no sign of the others.

I walked over and punched him in the face.

"You lying piece of crap!" I yelled, waiting for him to sprawl out before kicking him in the side. "You were setting us up the whole time!" I bent over and blasted some wand sparks at him.

"What in the—" His hand shot out and he gripped my wrist, his eyes pinned to the wand.

I grabbed his wrist with my other hand, twisted so he'd have to turn onto his belly, then pushed up, keeping him in place. "Not wise," I ground out.

"Whose wand is that?" he asked, his voice high pitched in pain.

"Don't ask stupid questions." I dropped the wand since the sparks didn't seem to have an effect, then punched him in the ribs. He grunted and tried to move away. I did it again, but his thick slab of muscle shielded him from my blows.

"Stop," he said, his body tensed. "Stop!"

I picked up the wand again. The annoying vibrating feeling ran up my arm, so I stuffed it into my back pocket.

"Trust me, huh?" I said, my hands on my hips. "We'll see?" It was my turn for high pitched. "Now the other two are lost in limbo!"

"All they had to do was hang on, like I said," Ethan shouted back at me, his face red and dirt smeared across his cheek. "Who do you think got you out?"

"I did." I pulled out the wand for emphasis. "With this."

"With what, a few sparks? That wasn't a spell! It wouldn't trigger your win." He jabbed his chest. "I won. I shut everything down."

Breathing heavily, I stowed my stolen wand. The timing was close enough that he could be right, especially since he hadn't reacted to the sparks I'd made with the wand. They'd surprised the wand owner, but they hadn't really hurt her. Still, it was possible the bit of magic I'd done had been enough. Either way, Wally and Pete hadn't been so lucky.

"This challenge would be impossible for anyone but a wand wielder." I stalled, waiting just a bit longer to make sure Wally or Pete wouldn't materialize near us. "It's not fair."

Ethan painfully rose to his feet and dusted himself off. "Everyone is supposed to be in groups. All a group needs is one wielder."

"Well, clearly that isn't the case, since the one wielder was the only one to make it through. Where are Pete and Wally? They should be here too if you're right."

"What about you?"

"I don't count. I cheated."

He made a disgusted sound and snatched his fallen paper up off the ground. "I don't get you, Wild. You didn't know anything about magic, yet you made it through to the gold on the Shade trial. It's in your nature, so okay, I guess. But you practically led the Claw and Unmentionables trials, and you saved our asses in the Night trial by *speaking* to ghosts. Now here you are, probably the first trial goer in history to steal an instructor's wand, and you're yelling about the fairness of things. No one should be this good at everything. No one. And that's coming from someone who is *expected* to be this good at everything." He shook his head and took off walking. "Something isn't right with you. I mean, you've got people trying to kill you for Christ's sake. You! A girl!"

"Girls aren't good enough to be targeted, is that what you're saying?"

He shot me a narrowed-eyed glare. "You're supposed to be a fifteen-year-old boy, aren't you? Well, that cover has been blown, and yet people are still after you. Doesn't that seem odd to you?"

My step hitched, because I'd never thought of it like that. Yes, as a matter of fact, it kind of did.

He threw up his hands. "This whole thing is messed up. All of it. And I hate that I've been dragged into it. I don't want anything to do with the Sandman. My father can rein in most people, but the Sandman isn't one of them. I've got no protection from him. None of us do. I don't need any part of—"

"Wait, the Sandman? What do you mean?" Memories fluttered my awareness, so close, I could practically grab them. Darkness lining a face. Sweat dripping from sideburns. A twinkle of light on something metallic. The missing day was *right there* on the edge of my mind.

A sudden ground-shaking roar blotted out my thoughts. My feet nearly started dancing, ready to run without my body attached if need be. The scene around us dissolved, replaced with a big open area, a cave to one side, a cropping of rocks to the other, and an enormous beast out of the past directly in front of us. Green and black mottled skin, flesh hanging from its jagged bottom teeth, and too-small eyes zeroing in on us.

A freaking T-Rex, so big that our heads wouldn't even touch the bottom of its belly.

"We're gonna die."

CHAPTER 14

Wally's voice drifted into my mind from the first day of the trials, which felt so damn long ago.

"To date, in this century, there has never been a death by mauling as pertains to the T-Rex."

Regardless of the strongholds in place, and there didn't look to be any, a real T-Rex was liable to kill people.

. . . in this century . . .

. . . never been a death . . .

"It's an illusion," I said, clutching Ethan's sleeve as he stared up at the monster, slack mouthed. "It has to be an illusion. It's magic, like everything else. Wally said no one's died from one of these in this century."

"It is magic, yes. We're in the House of Wonder." Ethan shook himself into movement and straightened the sheet of paper he'd fearfully clutched in his hand moments before. "Of course, it's magic. We might not die, but we'll fail."

"I'm less concerned with failing than dying, though that first challenge might've amounted to the same thing."

"Failing is not an option. We have to make it through. That's the plan, right?" Ethan turned and ran for the cave while stuffing the sheet of paper into his pocket.

"I'm sensing daddy issues." I ran right beside him, holding the uncomfortably vibrating wand in a shaking hand. Another roar rumbled through the space, squashing all other sound and making my heart flutter.

"I've prepared for this." Ethan was muttering, and I got the distinct impression he was trying to bolster his confidence. "I've studied. I've practiced."

"There is no preparing for the size of this beast," I said, my heart stopping dead when the huge head swung our way. The T-Rex regarded us from its small eyes, before bending forward and slamming us with a blood-freezing roar. "Its teeth are the size of a human foot."

"Yeah. I learned that in grade school." He put on a burst of speed.

I ran faster still, passing him, and made a beeline for that cave. "There's a difference . . . between learning it . . . and *living* it."

The ground shook with the imprint of one massive foot carrying a whole lot of tonnage.

"A big . . . difference." Another foot. The beast was coming after us. "Every man . . . for himself!"

I slid into the cave, feet first, as another footfall shook the ground, this one faster than the previous two. The fourth thud was faster still, the beast chasing its prey.

I rolled, finishing the slide on my belly. The T-Rex swung its head down, faster than a creature that size should have been capable of moving, and chomped at Ethan. The enormous teeth just missed him. Screaming, Ethan ducked into the cave so fast, he slammed his head against the rock roof. He staggered and fell into me.

He clutched his head and curled up, but I was already pulling him farther back into the recesses, a space too small for the huge reptile to reach. Frantic breathing filled the hollow silence left by the dinosaur.

"Failing is not an option," I said, replaying the memory of those huge teeth stained with blood and bits of flesh, snapping shut. "We might not die, but it'll hurt like hell. Failing is definitely not an option. How do we bring it down?"

"My head is pounding. You'll have to do it."

"Nice try, gorgeous. My head has been pounding since this morning. How do *we* bring it down?"

He fumbled for his pocket, whatever he'd read before running to the cave clearly forgotten.

"I got it." I dug my hand into his pocket and pulled out the piece of paper. Organized, typed directions filled the sheet, ending with "Notes." In that space, various spells and details had been added in a surprisingly delicate hand. "Did your sister help you with this?"

"I am literate," he said dryly. "The best spells to use are at the bottom."

I was literate, too, but my handwriting looked like it had been scrawled out by a five-year-old with an attention problem.

I muttered a few of the handwritten words—some foreign, like "Olumpah," and some I understood, like "Levitate." The wand spat sparks of blue, and I pointed it toward the wall.

"So spells can just be common words?" A monstrous foot slammed down outside the cave, followed by a roar that filled our small space to bursting.

Both of us grabbed our heads.

"It's not *just* anything. The words, intention, and wand movement work together, driven by your inner strength and power." He pushed up a little and touched the bump forming on the side of his head. He looked at his fingertips, didn't see blood, and glanced out of the cave. "Countless hours are spent learning spell work, and only the best can ever master it. Most people are merely proficient."

"Awesome. Well, I would like to be proficient enough to cause havoc. What do I say?"

He sniffed and shook his head before taking a deep breath. "I've trained for this. I can do it in my sleep."

He lightly touched his head. He hadn't trained for this when at anything other than a hundred percent. Welcome to real life, Wonder Bread.

"Right." I nodded in determination. Clearly, he wasn't going to teach me to use magic without a little prodding. "Then jog on out there and start throwing some spells. I'll be right behind you, with this tiny knife."

His gaze cut my way, and he watched me grab for my knife. He sighed. "Look, we can't really practice in here or the spells will bounce off the walls and hit us." I grimaced and directed the boom part of the wand toward the cave opening, where the T-Rex waited.

I doubted the predators of old would've been so patient. Or tolerant.

"You're better at overall combat," he went on. "I'm obviously better with the actual spells. So we'll have to work together—"

"That's what some of us have been doing all along . . ."

His blue eyes flared. "Do you want to win this, or not?"

"Sorry, sorry."

Outside the cave, the T-rex shifted and lifted a foot. This one landed farther away, back toward its initial position. Its default setting, I guessed.

"What we can do is this . . ." He licked his lips and crawled nearer the opening. "Use your—the wand. React with it how you would normally react with a knife. If you'd go for the eyes, or belly, aim and shoot the sparks. I'll then follow it up with an actual spell."

"The eyes are much too small and far away for a target," I said, my brain whirling, shedding off the panic of fighting a huge predator that had terrorized prehistoric earth. "The belly is covered in that thick skin. Are your spells more potent than foot-long teeth?"

Ethan blinked and looked down at his wand. He hadn't thought of that.

"Who the hell is training you that you don't already have a strategy?" I berated. "And what important branch of the government is he or she making a mockery of?"

"It was my weapons instructor," he replied.

"Ever heard the saying, those who can, do, and those who can't, teach?" I shook my head and crawled toward the mouth of the cave on hands and knees until the roof allowed me to stand, hunched over. I eyed the T-Rex, looking around the empty space, waiting for us to bring the fight to it.

Whiskers, my pissed off bull, had nothing on this situation.

"So, it's either bring down the beast or get eaten?" I asked.

"Or let time run out." He braced a scratched hand against a rock, leaning heavily and squinting. I looked at my watch to see a timer ticking down. We had less than thirty minutes left to deal with the T-Rex. Ethan's head was probably throbbing to the same beat as mine. "But I got the impression that time running out would be worse than losing to the beast. Something about lava . . ."

My jaw dropped, and I spluttered before I managed to actually speak words. "Oh my God, what is wrong with magical people?"

He took a deep breath. "Are you ready?"

"No. You?"

He released a shaky laugh. "Nope."

"But what choice do we have, right? We need to impress your daddy, right? We need to finish this and hope that Orin, Wally, and Pete are okay."

He sobered. "Yes," he said softly. His pink tongue left a wet trail across his bottom lip. "Look," he said, not looking over at me. "Between us, I'm glad it worked out this way. I'm glad we ended up in a crew. You're insane, but you have a way about you. You make all this . . . bearable."

"Same," I said, and it wasn't a complete lie. Sometimes he was actually pretty okay.

His grin said he heard everything I didn't say in my voice. "We can't all be team players, Wild. What fun is there in that? Some of us have been groomed to be separate, whether we like it or not."

And with those words, he pushed out of the cave and ran right. I surged after him a moment later, really wishing he'd given me a heads up.

As expected, the T-Rex's head swung around, tracking our movements. It roared as it stepped forward, on the chase once more. Ethan pivoted and headed back toward it at an angle.

"Go," he said, yelling at me. "Go, go!"

"Go where?" The T-Rex gained speed, each step cutting the distance between us by a quarter.

"I hate this," I muttered, letting intuition kick in and changing my angle. "This is terrible. Why did I decide to come?" Not that I could have let Billy come instead, but I found myself wishing we'd cut and run like my dad had suggested.

The T-Rex either didn't catch my change in direction or wanted Ethan more, because it kept moving straight for him.

"Levitate!" I heard, imagining him using a lovely little wand flick while standing stationary, like that woman in the last challenge.

"It's too heavy," I said, changing my direction again and running back at him. He couldn't get eaten yet. If he did, I'd have no chance. The T-Rex didn't have a wand I could steal, and it wouldn't care about my punches. "Use an attack spell!"

"Surl-ah-age!"

The word was garbled. I couldn't see the accompanying flick. I had no idea what he was going for.

The beast roared, a surprised, pain-filled sound. Its feet stomped and shuffled. Whatever that spell was supposed to do had worked.

"Surlahage," I shouted, aiming for an ankle, the easiest thing to hit, and flicking my wand in a clumsy fist. The movement was more a whip crack than a flick.

A jet of white flew, arcing through the air and pinging into the dinosaur's knee area. It blistered the tough skin. The T-Rex roared, though it didn't sound as pained this time, and bent its opened mouth toward the ground. Toward Ethan.

I swung the wand again, wanting to really explode that knee. "Surlage!"

The second try was wrong, I could feel it. Everything felt wrong, from the movement to the instrument to the word itself.

Gray-black light erupted from the wand this time, in a straight shot, flung with some vigor. It hit the beast's ankle, as hoped, slashing a line of red.

"Yes, yes!" I shouted, giddy from my accomplishment.

The T-Rex roared, almost a howl of pain, before whipping its big head around to me. Its tiny yellow eye took me in. Oops.

"Oh no! Oh no!"

I turned and ran, unable to quell the instinct to flee something that big. The ground shook as the predator changed direction and charged.

"Throw another spell. Throw another spell!" I shouted over my shoulder, probably not heard over all the commotion. "Take out its feet!" I flicked the wand over my shoulder, following my words. "Surblage. No, surfledge. Surlahedge!"

Various streams of color zipped out. An explosion took me off my feet and flung me forward. I twisted in the air and landed on my side in time to see the last spell splat way up onto the dinosaur's chest. The beast rocked back and forth, waving its little arms and roaring at the sky, teeth snapping together over and over.

Another stream of light came at it from the other side. "Gar-gant-rain-*ium*."

"Gar-gant-rainium," I said quickly, trying for the proper word flow and attempting an artful flick. It looked like something was stuck on the end of the wand and I was trying to flick it off. "Garg . . . antum. Dang it, I forgot the rain. Gargant-*rain*-ium!"

I wasn't great at remembering the words, they were too damn weird.

The wand vibrated like a broken washing machine, and I nearly dropped it in discomfort. The beast roared as a spell hit it from behind. It turned, in time for my streams of brown and murky green to hit it broadside.

"Those colors aren't right," I said, hopping up as a splash of red washed across the T-Rex's side.

It roared, worse than before, and shook its great head. Red gushed down its body, and I realized I'd opened that wound with one of those garbled spells.

"Which one?" I murmured through my teeth, not running back to Ethan. Hitting it from both sides was better, as long as each of us could keep it from chomping down on the other. "Gargant-ium!" I slapped the wand at the air and more horrible vibrations ran up my arm. "Rain! Damn it. Gargant*rain*ium!"

Pus-yellow light flew out this time, hitting the creature's hip. Blisters preceded smoke and then flame, curling up the T-Rex's skin. A clear, vibrant green light flew toward it from the opposite side, exploding.

The beast's little arms clawed at the air as it shook its head again, its mighty mouth open and its body sagging a little. I could just barely see Ethan behind the thick leg, advancing with swagger, wand held out confidently, slipping into striking range to deliver his killing shot.

"No, no, no!" I ran at him, all my senses firing. Fear driving my legs faster than they'd normally go. "Not so close—"

Ethan shot out, his wand flicking gracefully, his body broad and powerful. His instructor had obviously been a complete idiot. He was making himself a perfect target.

"Entitlement doesn't work on a beast," I yelled, readying my wand again. "Back away, Ethan! Get out of the striking range! It's not ready to die!"

A beautiful deep crimson stream flew through the air, slicing into the creature as it bent toward its target, its mouth open wide.

"No! Surpledge!"—wand slash—"Geranium!"—wand slap—"Gargant-*rain*-um!" I was basically waving my wand like it was a whip now, something I actually knew how to do. It was helping . . .

but not enough. The scene spilled out in front of me, a horror show I couldn't escape.

The beast moved faster than ever before as it shot toward a wide-eyed Ethan. The T-Rex's teeth snapped closed on his middle with a sickening crunch.

I sucked in a horrified breath as my murky, hideous spells slapped and slashed at the beast, one ripping a hunk of skin off its back, another peeling all the skin from its leg, and the third exploding against it. A tiny arm was flung off.

The beast staggered, opening its mouth to roar. Ethan fell out to the side, stiff from fear-driven paralysis or the first death in this challenge. I was hoping for the former.

I ran toward him, throwing up more spells haphazardly as I moved, dodging the clumsy feet of the agonized T-Rex. My spells hit home without the damage of the previous few.

My wand waving. I was too panicked for Ethan. I hadn't waved it as forcefully the last few times.

"Help," Ethan moaned as I got close. The T-Rex's clawed foot slammed down, forty feet away, the creature howling in pain as it spun and clawed uselessly at itself.

"You're alive," I said as I reached him, my relief short-lived. Four puncture marks in all, two in his front and two in his back, each round as a coffee mug. They almost met in the middle, and he was seeping blood and . . . other parts. He didn't have long.

This death was meant for me. I was sure of it.

And Ethan had taken the blow.

"We need to win," I said, terror fueling me. "We need to win this so we can get you to a healer."

"I can't feel my legs." His eyes widened as he looked down. His arms pushed against the ground, as though he didn't realize what he was seeing was a part of him and he wanted to get away from it.

The tail swung overhead, enough to take me out had I been standing.

"We gotta go." I grabbed him under the arms and dragged him behind me to put distance between us and the creature. I didn't know what else to do. "Give me a nasty spell. Nastiest you know."

"You can't—"

"Give me a spell!"

"Darn-*at*-re. A. Dis-*a*-trium."

"What happened to the spells with actual words?" The T-Rex's tail whipped the other way and it roared, sounding like it was so through with this crap. I knew how it felt. "Here we go. Give me your wand. It felt better than this one . . ."

"Wands . . . intimate."

"Well then, we're about to get intimate." I snatched his wand out of his hand, looked at the stolen one in my other hand, and decided *screw it.*

The creature came at me, its mouth open and hell in its eyes.

"Darn-*a*-trium. Ah. *Dis*-a . . . trum." That wasn't right, but I flicked both wands, anyway.

A stream of poo-colored brown magic came out of the instructor's wand, and baby puke green magic came out of Ethan's. Both hit the T-Rex on its right leg, a little higher than I'd intended, but nearly at the knee. Red holes opened up in its scaly hide before an explosion of fire shot out. Heat and light and propulsive energy slapped me, pushing me off my feet for the second time and flinging me back. My head knocked the ground and black spots swam within my vision.

The T-Rex's roar was soaked through with horrible pain. I pushed to my elbows as its body hit the ground. Half of its leg had been blown off, blood spray coating the dirt.

My stomach pinched and bile rose in my throat. These challenges weren't for the faint of heart.

"Terrible spell work," I heard, a pain-filled, wet, gargled whisper. A smile covered Ethan's face, and he coughed up a wet laugh.

"Oh no." I crawled to him, my head pounding, my body aching, the wands clutched in my hands shooting sparks with each movement. "How do I end this, Ethan? How do I end the challenge?" I dropped the wands and clutched his bloody hand in my own. "Ethan!"

His blue eyes found me lazily, the light within them dimming. "You know . . ." Wet coughs racked his body. "You're pretty . . . hot when you . . . clean yourself up. I . . . like 'em tall." He laughed again, as though that was a merry joke. "Good work, Johnson." His eyes swung the other way, as though he didn't have control over them anymore. "You win."

A breath released from his mouth, and his body went slack in the pool of blood under us. His eyes were sightless.

"No." I grabbed his chin with my fingers and turned his face my way. "Hold on, Ethan. Please. *Please*, don't die on me! The dinosaur is down!" I looked around us, wide-eyed. The T-Rex kicked the foot that was still intact, weakly waving the one tiny arm it had left, and then stilled. "The T-Rex is down! *Why is this not ending?*"

Tears clouded my vision as a boot crunched against the dirt behind me. I pushed up and swung around, grabbing my knife and protecting Ethan's body with my own.

The Sandman stopped ten feet from me, his expression unreadable. "That was meant to be you." He jerked his head, and I knew he meant Ethan. "You were meant to die in here. You're a Shade, or so they thought. You shouldn't be able to use a wand." His eyes flicked to the two wands next to me, lying deserted. "But you chose a different path than they expected. An impossible path. You should've been captured twice over. Or killed. And yet, here you are, with the man who was supposed to win it all . . . lying dead at your side. I was right, and they were wrong."

Anger seethed through me, burning away the grief and fear, the guilt from letting Ethan and my crew down and reaching the end alone. I grabbed Ethan's wand and stood on wobbly legs. "What do you want from me?" I hollered.

His dark, dangerous eyes beheld me. "Everything."

CHAPTER 15

That last word reverberated in the air between the Sandman and I. *Everything*. He wanted everything from me? What the hell did that mean?

"What, you want to marry me?" I blurted out, my brain muddled from the concussion, from the unrelenting terror and the horror of Ethan's lifeless body at my feet. "Aren't you supposed to get on one knee for that?"

There was a split second where I thought the Sandman would laugh in my face. I mean, it was ridiculous, but so was everything else.

"Perhaps not everything," he said.

The Sandman took a step back, his eyes locking on something or someone coming up from behind on my left. I tensed, but no warning tingles raced through my body. Friend, not foe.

"We are not done here." The Sandman turned and strode away, and I thought about shooting him in the back with the wand.

Well, screw it. I'd never second-guessed myself before—why start now? I whipped the wand in a circle, then pointed it at the Sandman's back. The sparks that shot out were a mix of black and red, and for a moment—just a split second—I could see my rage in the magic, my anger and strength propelling it forward to slam into the Sandman's back, spinning him around. He fell back and *through* something, like an invisible fence that was keeping us in. One minute he was there, the next he was gone.

"Wild!" Pete was all but on top of me when he yelled my name, and I startled. "Holy cats, what . . . is Ethan . . . dead?"

I dropped to my knees, tucked the wand down the back of my pants and put my fingers to Ethan's neck. The blood that had pooled out from his puncture wounds seeped through the knees of my jeans. Warm, his blood was still warm. *Please don't be dead. Please don't be dead. Please don't be dead.* I couldn't bear the thought of losing him. I wasn't sure if it was because he was part of my crew, because I'd already lost so much, or because of that tiny spark that had jumped so unexpectedly between us.

A single pulse of his heart thumped under my fingers. That was enough for me. "Help me get him up, Pete!" I got my arms under Ethan's and Pete grabbed his feet. "We need to get him over there." I pointed at the place I'd seen the Sandman fall through.

Wally came running, bursting out of seemingly nowhere. Her face was scratched and her clothes sizzled, but she was intact. "Oh my God!"

That was all she said as she caught up to us, and her silence scared me more than if she'd spewed off all the numbers, all the reasons why Ethan wouldn't make it. She took one of his hands and just held it.

We reached the place where the Sandman had fallen out of the test . . . and nothing happened. We kept on running across the open plain with Ethan bouncing between us.

"We do not have time for this!" I snapped.

"Where are we going?" Pete struggled to speak as we ran. "Why isn't this over?"

I didn't have an answer. What I had was a dying boy and . . . a couple of wands in my back pocket. One of which would work for me, even if I had no idea what the hell I was doing.

"Wally, come grab Ethan."

"I can help." Orin slid in from the right, out of shadows that hadn't been there a moment before, his face beyond pale and green in spots.

"Why can you all get in, but we can't get out?" I raged as Orin took Ethan's arms from me. I grabbed the wand from my back pocket. Ethan's wand. I pointed it in front of us at nothing. But there had to be something there. Something holding us in.

"I need a word, a trigger word, something!" I yelled and the others startled.

"Bascilium-oroco," Wally whispered. "It can break another person's spell."

I didn't hesitate, trusting her. Trusting my crew. Hell, I didn't even stumble over the word for once. "Bascilium-oroco!" The word tasted like copper pennies on my tongue as I pointed Ethan's wand at the landscape.

The tip glowed like a lighter, heating brighter and brighter until it was like a mini sun in both light and heat. I couldn't look at it, but felt it drawing strength from me to make this spell, whatever it was, work.

"Say it again!" Wally yelled. "Three times, you have to say it three times with a pause in between!"

"Bascilium-oroco!" I shouted the word and the light grew impossibly brighter until I was on my knees and the others were yelling. The wand began to heat in my hand, burning into my flesh. It smelled of charred meat, and still I hung on.

My friends were depending on me.

Billy and Sam were depending on me.

Ethan's life depended on me.

If there was a chance this would work, that it would break the spell of this place, then I had to hang on.

"Bascilium-oroco!" I put everything I had into that final scream, every ounce of energy and then some. The world around us shattered into a thousand colors, the light from the wand bursting through everything around us, splintering images and throwing them back in broken reflections. When I opened my eyes, the plains and the T-Rex were gone, and we were sitting on a chunk of land that looked very normal.

Other groups of kids huddled at various points around us.

I hadn't just shattered our test, but everyone's test. Someone was going to be pissed.

But that was the least of my worries. "We need a medic! A healer!" I yelled, stumbling to my feet. I would have dropped the wand, but it was seared to my palm. Orin was running, carrying Ethan in his arms easily despite whatever poison he'd ingested in the first challenge.

The teachers and testers were like an ant nest that had been kicked repeatedly. I wanted to believe it was because Ethan was a Helix and Helixes were important. But the number of eyes that went to my hand, still glued to the wand, told me otherwise.

I didn't care. I ran after Orin, Wally and Pete right with me. We hit the medic station at full speed, and the woman who'd cared for us each time was there. Inside the tent was hushed, for all the world like we were alone.

Mara had her hands on Ethan in a flash, her eyes closed and eyes moving rapidly under her eyelids. "Bad, this is bad."

Someone poked their head in. Jared. The vampire's eyes widened and then narrowed into a glare.

"Jared, get his father!" Mara said.

I went to my knees beside the cot and found Ethan's hand with the one not seared to his wand. Wally went to her knees beside me. Pete and Orin were behind us, and we waited like that—a united crew—as Mara worked her magic on Ethan. The punctures in his side closed, the wounds on his face closed, and the pallor of his skin improved. But his chest didn't lift and lower.

Mara stumbled back, breathing hard after maybe thirty seconds, sweat rolling from her face. "There is nothing more I can do. He was too deep into death for me to pull him back." Her eyes opened wide with unshed tears, but she tipped her head at Ethan and then looked hard at me. What was she trying to tell me? "I'm sorry about your friend."

Too deep into death. What did she mean by that? Now that we were out of the trial, my head was pounding once more, all the adrenaline that had kept the worst of it at bay had burned off.

I was shaking my head before she even finished. "No, that can't be. He can't die."

But she was already walking away, pausing only to look back at me. The tent was empty except for the five of us. Five. I refused for it to be four.

I looked at Wally. "Tell me you can do something, Wally. She said *too deep into death*, that means he's in your realm now. There has to be—"

Orin sucked in a breath. "Once death has taken—"

I waved my wand hand at him. "Too far into death is not dead. Am I right?"

Wally's eyes were as wide as Mara's had been. "I'm not sure I'm strong enough to do what you're asking."

"Try," I whispered. "Please try." I kept my hand on Ethan's. Still warm, he was *still warm*. I had to believe that we could save him yet.

Wally put her hands on Ethan's chest and bowed her head. The magic I'd seen around her in the graveyard spilled out of her body, pink and soft and gentle, and for a moment, I thought I saw a darkness around Ethan. Like his body was engulfed in shadows even though I knew for a fact that it wasn't.

Noise erupted outside the tent—angry shouts, the wail of a woman, the bellow of a voice that likely belonged to the elder Helix. I understood that cry of grief and could easily guess who'd made it. Ethan's mother.

"Hurry, Wally, hurry," I said.

Pete slipped up beside Wally and put a hand on her shoulder. "We can do this."

Orin put his hand on my shoulder, too, and the circle was complete, our crew linked together in a way I hadn't thought possible. Wally blew out a breath and the magic she carried pushed the darkness clinging to Ethan back, lighting it up.

"It is not his time," she said, and her voice radiated power that rippled outward, flapping the edges of the tent. Everyone outside went silent for a moment, then a hand pushed on the flap but didn't make it in. They were trying to get in, but something held them back. I didn't know if it was Wally's power, or the presence of death.

A voice that was anything but human chimed back, answering Wally. *"He is in my grasp. You cannot take him from me."*

Pete and Orin gave identical gasps. But Wally just shook her head, her hands clenching against Ethan's chest, digging into his shirt. "But he is not fully with you, and so I command you to release your hold on him. You obey me. I rule you, *Bani*." Wally's Cronkite voice was in full effect and the power it radiated was anything but funny.

The darkness around Ethan surged, wisps wrapping around him, but Wally pushed it back again, her shoulders tightening, the pale pink light glowing hotter, brighter. "I will not be ignored. No longer!" There was a snap of power to her words, like a whip being cracked, and the shadows slid back from Ethan, slowly, and then faster until there was nothing left but Wally's glowing pink power.

"Death is held at bay, for a minute or two at best," Wally whispered, slumping, Pete catching her.

I leaned forward. "Ethan?"

His chest still didn't rise.

Orin slapped Ethan's chest. "CPR, we need to restart his heart."

He started compressions, and I just stared at him in shock for a moment. Who the hell would think a vampire would know CPR? It hit me in a flash. A vampire who didn't want to kill his human victims would need to have at least basic CPR and medical knowledge.

"You need to breathe for him." Orin said. "Now, two breaths."

I leaned over Ethan, pinching his nose, and breathed into his mouth, forcing his chest to rise and fall. Two puffs. Orin did another round of compressions. "Again, two more."

I held my mouth to Ethan's and closed my eyes, putting more than my own air into him—trying to give him my energy too, if that were even possible.

Orin pressed long pale fingers to Ethan's neck. "There's a pulse. Very weak. Breathe for him again. We keep breathing for him until he takes one on his own."

I didn't question Orin, just put my lips over Ethan's and breathed into him.

One. *Open your eyes, don't give up!*

Two. *Come back, Wonder Bread. We aren't done, you and I.*

I pulled back a little, enough that I could look straight into Ethan's face, watching for any sign that he was alive. Any sign at all.

His left eyelid flickered and then the right, and those blue eyes opened and stared right into mine. Had he heard me calling him back?

"Wild." His voice was hoarse, a mere croak of my name.

"Yeah?"

"Personal space, it's a real thing."

CHAPTER 16

I stared into Ethan's eyes a beat longer as his words sunk in, the air in the tent lightening up as I realized we'd done it, we'd saved him. "Personal space might be a thing when you aren't dying," I said as I pulled back. "You get no say when your heart isn't beating, Wonder Bread."

His eyes widened, and he took a slow breath. "Was I dead?"

I nodded, not able to say we'd brought him back. Because even in my head the truth sounded like a lie. If we could bring Ethan back, why hadn't someone tried to bring Tommy back? Why hadn't I found Rory and brought him back?

The entrance to the tent flapped again, and this time it opened. An older man with an air of power and prestige strode into the room. Ethan's father. A woman of similar age hurried in behind him, worry etching her eyes. His mother.

"No, not my boy," she said, makeup making tracks down her face. It was probably the only time she'd ever present herself like that. She was beautiful, like Ethan, and put together.

Grief, thicker than over-floured gravy filled the room, sucking the air out of it.

Wally put a hand on my shoulder and the four of us stepped back, giving Ethan's parents space.

"Time to leave," Pete said. I nodded my agreement and we slipped out of the tent as Ethan's mother fell on him, sobbing and kissing his face.

Outside the tent, I took a deep breath. Crazy, this whole place was crazy, but it was sinking in that we'd done it. We'd finished all the trials.

And we were still alive. All of us.

A flash of Gregory's face, his hands grabbing at mine through bars that held him back, cut through the haze of the concussion. Had I seen him? I lifted a hand to my head, but it was still stuck to the wand as if glued.

"You've got to get that looked at." Orin grabbed my hand. No, not glued, scorched.

"I can't even feel it," I said, turning my hand to get a good look it, the crackled skin, the black char in places. Part of me knew it was shock, the other part was morbidly fascinated that this burned up hand was mine. Orin and Wally shook their heads in unison.

"That's because your hand is nearly dead," Wally said. "We've got to get you to a healer right away."

I followed her toward another medic tent, empty except for a healer I didn't know. A guy with messy brown hair, glasses, and a pair of light green scrubs. He took one look at my hand and sat me down on the edge of a bed, his hands cradling mine. "How did you do this?"

"The trial?" I offered.

He shook his head and pushed his glasses up with a finger. "No, what spell?"

"Bascilium—"

He cut me off, slapping his hand over my mouth, his eyes wide. "You used *that* spell?"

I shot a look to Wally and she nodded for me. "It was the only chance we had."

The healer blew out a shaky breath. "The director is going to want me to report this."

"Will it get me kicked out?" I asked.

"No. Not if you can handle a spell like that." He readjusted his hands on mine and began to mumble words under his breath. His magic was immediate, the glow of it lighting up the small space between us with a faint green light.

I sucked in a breath as the healing started, the pain sharp as the burn wounds were reversed, the skin reforming with each second. I closed my eyes and lay back on the bed.

To block the pain, I focused on what was going on around us, outside the tent.

"You said he was dead," Mr. Helix roared.

"Then you should be happy he isn't!" Mara yelled back. "When I left him in the tent, there was no heartbeat. *He was dead!* You felt that magic holding us back, we all know—"

"That is impossible. Bringing people back from the shadow of death . . ."

"Not impossible. Forbidden." The director's voice cut through all the yelling. "And if I am correct, his teammates were the ones who did it."

My eyes flew open and I stared at Wally, Orin, and Pete. "Go, get out of here!" I growled at them, a sharp stab in my hand making me grimace.

Wally shook her head, fatigue heavy in her words. "They will know it wasn't you alone. There is no point in running. The odds of us escaping . . . very low. I don't know what they would be exactly but very low indeed."

The two guys stood up a little straighter as the tent flapped open and Mr. Helix strode in, followed by the director. She looked damn good for late seventies—closer to her early fifties at best, maybe even a rough forty something.

Mr. Helix was a big guy, though not as muscular as his son. "You four . . . saved him?"

The healer let go of my hand and I flexed my fingers, opening and closing them on the wand. I held it out to his father. "We did what we had to do. He is part of our crew."

He stared at the wand in my hand. "I do not like being in others' debts."

I stood slowly. "Would you rather we had let him die?"

The fact that he paused before answering said it all. His son's life was of value to him. But that value only went so far—he seemed more interested in his family legacy than in Ethan's life. Damn it, I really didn't want to feel bad for Ethan.

There was no stopping my mouth from curling into a sneer. I turned my back on him, but the director had moved to stand in front of me. "To my office with the four of you. Now."

And just like that we went from the frying pan into the fire.

The director sat across from us in her office, her fingers laced together in front of her full lips. Seriously, she looked like she'd knocked off another fifteen years at least. I wanted to ask her how she'd done it. Likely just an illusion, like so much of this place was. Vanity at its best.

"What am I to do with you four? You've broken one of the most sacred laws of our world. We do not bring the dead back to life!"

"We didn't know." I crossed my arms and frowned at her. How the hell did they expect us to know their rules? We were just students—no, future students.

The other three shifted beside me, their furtive movement saying it all. Crap, they *had* known. I straightened up a little more and deepened my frown. "*I* didn't know, and I pushed them to it."

"I see." Director Frost's eyes stayed locked on me, the edges of them definitely smoother than the last time I'd seen her. Those icy blues were weighing my worth, and I had a niggling feeling that perhaps she saw me the way Mr. Helix saw Ethan. A tool, and if that tool was broken, she'd find another. Or maybe she'd finally realized my troublesome ways weren't worth the possible gain.

"If the heads of your soon-to-be houses were not so damn ecstatic to welcome you four in, I'd have all of you removed from the trials and sent home with wiped memories. As it is . . ." She tapped her fingers on a thin stack of papers. "You have made too much of an impression to just *disappear.*"

She was silent as she stared down at the papers. "All of you have passed the trials and will be welcomed into your respective houses," she said softly. "But let me make this crystal clear. You will speak of this event to no one. As far as anyone is concerned, you came through the trial of Wonder because of Ethan Helix and his final spells. He was injured gravely, but a healer fixed him up." Her eyes locked on each of us, one at a time, as if she could force us to agree. The other three lowered their eyes, cowed by her.

"Why?" The single-word question popped out of me. "I get that we broke a rule, but why the rest? Because you don't want people to know that someone's infiltrating the trials? Someone who's stealing kids? Trying to kill us?" With each of my questions, my friends tensed further until I thought they would spring forward and slap their hands over my mouth. But I couldn't stop. Not now, not after everything we'd been through. "We did better than survive those damn trials. We survived when we should have died, and you damn well know it!"

Director Frost smiled at me, the gesture as cold as her name. "Again, let me be clear, since you seem to be thick as most Shades when it comes to understanding the why of things. Those who did indeed infiltrate the trials were not trying to kill all of you. Just one of you. And they nearly succeeded."

My head spun. "Ethan? They were trying to kill Ethan?"

"His father has many enemies. Powerful enemies that wanted to destroy his family legacy. He is the last of his blood-line," Director Frost said. "You didn't seriously think they would be here to kill you, a Shade impersonating her brother? As much as you thought you were hiding, everyone knew by the second day who you were. The shifters were the first to sniff you out, then the vampires, and those vampires are nothing if not gossips. We let you stay because it was too much bother to send you back and take your brother instead. You are a tool, Wild. Nothing more than a blunt instrument."

Orin stiffened at the gossip comment.

Anger flashed through me like a bolt of lightning, there and gone, leaving behind the residue. They'd all known. And they'd let me keep trying to hide it? I opened my mouth to give her my thoughts on that matter, but she cut me off. But what about Sideburns? And Rory? They'd said nothing about Ethan being in danger.

Her eyes never flicked to the others, not once. "You are all dismissed for the remainder of the day. The advancement ball will begin at 10 p.m. While I'd rather you four weren't there, again, your heads of houses will expect your presence."

Just like that, we were done, out of the room and headed to the dorm. We walked in silence all the way to our room, but as soon as the door was shut, Pete let out a whoop that set my heart racing.

Talk about PTSD—I reached for my blade without even feeling a warning tingle. Pete grabbed Wally and spun her around, then grabbed Orin and attempted to spin him about too. Orin was stiff as a board, and the spin was beyond awkward, falling into comical.

"We did it! We all did it!" Pete shouted.

His excitement was contagious, and laughter bubbled out of me. We *had* done it. Despite the odds that Wally had insisted on spewing, despite the fact that we were the underdogs, the outcasts, we'd done it.

I grabbed Pete and hugged him, then Orin and Wally.

The door opened and we all turned to see Ethan standing there, pale but upright. His father behind him, gripping his shoulder just this side of too hard.

There was an uncomfortable silence. For about two seconds.

"Wonder Bread. We weren't sure you had it in you to make it up the stairs." I grinned at him.

Ethan's lips twitched. "Well, I couldn't let you have all the glory considering I did save you all back there."

Wally, Pete, and Orin tensed, but I could see the truth in Ethan's eyes—he'd been fed the same cover story we had. "Sure, sure. But let's be honest. You screamed like a girl when that T-Rex was coming at us, and I'm pretty sure you peed your pants. Even if you did save us in the end."

The hand on Ethan's shoulder relaxed and Mr. Helix nodded. "I see that you all understand then. Even so, I'd like to speak to Ms. Johnson alone."

The others didn't hesitate. They just filed out of the room quickly, and even Ethan turned to leave.

Mr. Helix shut the door behind them. "I know what really happened, Ms. Johnson. You saved my son, and for that you have my gratitude."

That was not what I'd expected. "He's part of my crew, like I said. I couldn't leave him there."

He tipped his chin up. "As grateful as I am to you for saving him, I want to be sure that we understand one another. He is not of your kind, Ms. Johnson—an untrained, unkempt, wild thing that has no concept of decorum or her place in this world."

My jaw dropped. "I'm sorry, do you think I saved him because I *like* him?"

He frowned, and I could see that was exactly what he thought. I started to laugh, and then I was laughing so hard I could barely breathe. He waited me out.

"Helix, let me be clear. Your son is an ass. I wouldn't be interested in him for all the money in the world." I held up both hands as if surrendering.

"I see. Perhaps I misread him then." He turned and walked out the door, shutting it with a soft click.

He'd misread Ethan? What could he have possibly misread?

CHAPTER 17

Wally and I were no longer allowed to room with the guys now that "everyone knew" I was a girl.

I was disappointed to leave the guys, especially after the experience we'd just been through together, but the new digs we'd been given were totally worth it. Two queen-sized beds and two full bathrooms all to ourselves, complete with oversized clawfoot bathtubs. Manna from heaven couldn't have been more welcome. The healer had worked on my hand, but he hadn't done anything for the rest of my aching body.

A booming announcement rippled through the mansion as we stood in our bedroom.

"The advancement ball will begin at 10 p.m. sharp. Bring your pieces of five, along with your watch for your final sorting."

Wally, seeing my face, picked up a tiny black jewelry bag out of her pile of clothes. "We got them at the beginning, remember?"

The five tokens. I pulled my own out from the original envelope the Sandman had brought me, and took them with me into the bathroom.

I soaked in the bathtub a long time, letting the Epsom salts and hot water pull the last of the tension from me. My head throbbed, but a double dose of pain killers had numbed the worst of it. It struck me that while Mara had healed Ethan's puncture wounds when he was near death, the healers hadn't been able to cure my concussion. Why? I let that question sit for a moment, swirling it around as I swirled the water in the tub with one finger.

"They were after Ethan," I said to myself and sunk lower into the water, sticking a foot out on the edge. "Not you. You were just in the wrong place at the wrong time."

"Statistically speaking," Wally called out from the bedroom. "People who talk to themselves are 58 percent more likely to find themselves in a mental institute."

"You made that one up!" I yelled back, smiling.

She laughed. "Maybe, but you can't be sure."

The banter with Wally and the heat of the water helped release some of the tension in my muscles.

I told myself that as soon as I got out, I'd start looking for Gregory and the other missing kids again. Only *that* thought kept slipping away from me like a bar of wet soap in the tub.

This wasn't like me. I wanted to find them. Didn't I?

On the edge of the tub, I placed the five trinkets I'd been given in the first envelope from the Sandman. Like the tokens for a game of monopoly, I understood them now. The knife represented the House of Shade. The wand the House of Wonder. The gravestone the House of Night. The paw the House of Claw. The plain blank silver coin the House of Unmentionables. Five houses, five trinkets. As I touched each, a flare of recognition rolled through me, and I wondered just where I would be placed. I would have assumed in the House of Shade, but after handling wands . . . I wasn't so sure.

Wally knocked on the door then stuck her head in, hair wrapped up in a big white towel that made her skin look even paler than usual. She flapped an envelope at me. "This just came for you. Someone slid it under the door."

She flipped the thick envelope to me and I caught it easily with the hand that had been fused to the wand, still amazed at how the magic here could heal so many injuries. Now that the trials were over, what harm could come from an envelope?

The material was thick, not unlike that first envelope that had shown up with the Sandman what felt like months ago. A week, it had barely been a week since he'd come to the ranch.

"Thanks," I said, and Wally backed out.

I held the envelope up to the light to see if there was any indication of what was in it, but the material was too thick. I ran my hands over it, squeezing it. Not much in it, a couple sheets of paper at most, and no warning tingle to indicate it might be something like poison or a spell. I grabbed my knife from the counter closest to me, put the tip of the blade into the top of the envelope and cut it open.

I peered inside, seeing a single piece of paper folded in half. What the hell was this?

Putting my knife on the side counter again, I reached into the envelope and pulled the note out, flipping it open with my thumb.

It's not over. Watch yourself.

R.

R. Rory had always signed his name with the same swirly R.

My heart kicked up a notch and a tear slid down my cheek. He must have arranged for this note to be delivered before the House of Night trial.

I folded the note and slid it into the envelope and set it next to my blade. Then I dunked under the water and blew out a stream of bubbles, letting the water hide my tears.

I forced myself into autopilot, once more shoving my grief away to be dealt with—or not—at a later date. We had a freaking advancement ball to go to, and apparently, we were not to miss it. Wrapped in a towel, I stepped out of the bathroom and into the bedroom in time to see Wally accept two boxes from someone at the door.

"What is this?"

"Something from Mrs. Helix," she said, handing me one of the long boxes and pushing the door shut with her hip. I was surprised by the weight of it, lighter than I'd expected given the size.

Wally squealed from her side of the room as she pulled out a stunning burgundy gown with more taffeta and crinoline than I had thought possible on a single dress. "Look, Mrs. Helix sent us gowns!"

Holding my towel with one hand, I opened my box with the other—slowly, as if I were half expecting a snake to leap out and bite me. Inside was a bundle of dark material covered in tissue paper, with a note pinned to the front.

With all my thanks.

M. Helix.

"What is it with notes today?" I mumbled under my breath. I pulled the dress out, gasping as the jet black material slithered from the box. Black, but covered in iridescent flecks that once more made me think of a snake. With a twist of my wrist, the material caught the light and those flecks danced.

"Wow."

There was no taffeta or crinoline on my dress. I saw lace, but other than that it was hard to really make out the shape.

Mrs. Helix had sent shoes along with the dresses, heels that fit perfectly. Wally's heels were higher than mine, though the style was almost dainty. Mine were a solid three inches with a thicker heel, a scale design that complemented the dress, and straps that wrapped up and over my ankle.

"What is she trying to say?" I asked. Wally looked at me from across from the room, where she sat doing her hair.

"Each house has at least one sigil attached to it. The serpent is one of them for the House of Shade. She's saying you're a Shade and everyone had better believe it."

I didn't want Mr. or Mrs. Helix to be nice to me and the thought that had been put into the clothes and shoes was no small thing. I held up the black dress, still not quite ready to put it on. "How did she find something so perfect for us?"

"She had these made with magic, obviously. She has a team of fashion designers at her beck and call. Everyone jumps to dress a Helix." Wally ran a comb through a thin strand of hair before attempting to curl it with an old school curling iron. "She is *very* fashion forward. We're going to be the best dressed, just you watch. Oh my God, I'm freaking out a little."

I sighed and pulled the dress on over my head, the material cool and smooth against my skin. I slid on the heels and turned to look in the mirror.

The bodice top was off the shoulder and made of lace. A subtle design of blades and various other weapons was woven through the curling vines. If you weren't looking for it, you wouldn't have seen the details. You'd just think it was pretty lace.

The lower half of the dress was a slippery material that I wanted to call satin, only it was heavier and definitely not any material I'd come into contact with before.

"So . . . magic." I plucked at the iridescent black skirt that clung to my legs, noting the slit up one side, and Wally grinned.

"Yes. Very expensive magic."

Wally slipped in behind me and pulled the zipper up, and I realized there were corset bones hidden in the dress. Once pulled tight, my waistline and minimal chest were accentuated. I touched the boyish cut of my hair. Wally frowned.

I laughed and brushed it, but left it hanging. Sam had cut it for me, and I'd be damned if I was going to change it now. Besides, my sister had been right—the longer front gave me an edgy look as a girl.

I dusted on some makeup I'd borrowed from Wally with serious difficulty, managing to finally pull off mascara and a bit of lip gloss. That would have to do. I grimaced.

Someone knocked at the door and Wally flounced over to open it. Pete stood there in a full suit and tie, his mouth dropping open as he stared at the burgundy fluff that was Wally. "You want to go to the dance with me?" he blurted out.

She laughed. "Well, yeah, we're all going with you, silly."

I rolled my eyes and gave her a push from behind. "Go on with Pete. I'll catch up."

With them both gone, the room felt too quiet and a soft warning trickled up my spine. Not an immediate danger, more like there was something coming. Like maybe the note from Rory had arrived right when I needed it. I grabbed my five trinkets off the edge of the tub and tossed them lightly in my hand. These had to come with me. I held them loosely in one hand, then went to the bedside table and opened the drawer. My knife was resting there in its sheath. "Supposed to be a night off for you." I pulled my skirt up, baring one thigh. With a few adjustments, I got the strap to hold to my upper thigh. I'd have to flash people to get to it, but at least I'd have it with me.

"Too bad I don't have pockets," I said. A tingle spread through me wherever the dress touched. I slid my hands down the skirt of the dress, finding a pocket on either side that opened to my bare skin underneath. "No way."

Sure enough, I could easily grasp my knife handle through the opening on the right. I hurried to the bathroom and pulled out one of the long ribbons we'd found from the previous occupants of the room. I lifted the skirt and bared my left leg, tying the ribbon around as tightly as I dared, making a loop in it that would be perfect for another weapon.

A wand.

Where could I find a wand that no one would notice missing? What had the director said? That when someone was booted out or chose to leave, they had to give up their gifts to the school.

Shades gave up their weapons.

Shifters their ability to change form.

Vampires their speed and need for blood.

Necromancers their power over the dead.

Mages their magic and their wands.

Wands. Plural.

I was moving before I thought better of it. Maybe it was stupid, but I didn't think so. My instincts were saying I would need a wand of my own, so that's what I was going to get. A grin slid over my lips. One more rule to break, and I'd be done.

Honest.

CHAPTER 18

My plan consisted of very few details. Go right into the director's office, ask her a few questions about what I could do to keep my brother and sister out of this place, see if I could distract her enough to lift a wand. She'd been so proud of how many of them she'd collected in that mahogany box. There was no way she'd miss one.

I should have been nervous. But all I could feel was excitement. I was getting me a wand, dang it, one way or another. Maybe Ethan could help me learn how to use it? Train me on the side?

That conjured up an image I hadn't been expecting. Ethan smiling at me as he faded. *I like 'em tall.*

A hot flush spread through me, but I pushed past it. Nope, a whole lot of nope on that one. Ethan was a very bad, if very hot, idea. I hadn't been lying when I'd told his father it would never happen between us.

There was no sign of Adam, so I walked right up to the director's door, knocked once, and then turned the handle as if I belonged there. "Director, I need to speak to you."

Because let's be honest, with my track record so far, anyone who saw me walk into the director's office would assume I'd been summoned.

Shockingly, the door was unlocked and the room was empty.

"Well, hot damn," I whispered, shutting the door behind me.

I went right to the box on the desk, flipping it open, and looked down at a dozen or so wands. Which one did I take?

The door clicked behind me and I spun, my hand going for my right pocket.

Ethan stood in the doorway. His suit jacket, pants, and vest were a deep midnight blue, and his collared shirt was white as fresh-fallen snow. Hair slicked back, he was . . . damn it, he was gorgeous. He raised an eyebrow. "What are you doing?"

I wasn't sure I trusted him, even now, and that hesitation seemed to bother him. "What are you doing?" I countered.

"I figured you might be in trouble again. Thought you could use a hand." He walked toward me, and I thought about closing the box. But if I wanted him to teach me to use a wand, I'd have to tell him about said wand.

"No. I'm here for a wand." I swept my hand over the box and stepped back. His eyebrows shot all the way up to his hairline, his eyes darting from the box to me.

"It's not a bad idea. It would be smart to have a wand of your own, to train yourself with it. Even if there's no real reason you should have such an ability with magic." He leaned over the box and I caught a whiff of his cologne. Expensive was my first thought. My second was that I wanted a closer sniff.

No. Bad, bad, Wild.

"How do I choose one? Yours felt . . . better in my hands than the tester's. Her wand was clunky and uncomfortable," I said, forcing myself to focus on the task at hand.

"You pick them up. See what feels good." He didn't touch any of them.

I stared into the box, dipped one finger into it, and soaked in the energy of the different wands. When I reached the bottom, it felt like a tiny spark of electricity shot through me.

Voices came from the other side of the door.

"Hurry!" Ethan whispered.

I grabbed the wand that was calling to me, yanked it out and shoved my hand into my left pocket. The wand slid into the loop I'd created, fitting against my leg more securely than it should have, as though it wanted to ensure it stayed put. For just a moment, I thought I'd end up with another burn mark on my leg, but there was nothing like that. Just the reassuring warmth of the wand's presence.

I flipped the box top down and sat in one of the visitors' chairs. Ethan sat next to me and we both turned as the door opened and the director stepped in, annoyance written across her very young face.

Her eyes flew to us. "What are you two doing here?" And then she caught herself. "You broke into my office?"

We both shook our heads. "No, I came to speak to you about my siblings," I said. "I knocked and thought I heard you say come in. The door was open."

Her eyes narrowed and her full lips pinched. "And you, Mr. Helix?"

Ethan smiled. "Just keeping my graduation date company."

Well, hell, there was no way I'd get out of dancing with him now. The smug look on his lips said it all. He'd planned that last little bit. Because if I denied him, it would be obvious he'd just followed me in.

He was good, I'd give him that.

Ethan stood and offered me his arm. "We're going to be late. We waited too long for the director."

Just like that, he swept us out of the room, past the frowning director, and into the hall. I hung onto his arm with my right hand. "I can't believe that worked."

"Confidence usually works, especially when you're bluffing."

"Ah, so you have a date already." I let go of his arm, but he caught my hand and returned it to the crook of his elbow.

"No, I'd planned to ask you. The least I could do since you broke the rules to bring me back from the dead." His calm tone caught me off guard.

"No, Wally brought you back."

Ethan glanced at me. "No, she wouldn't have even tried if you hadn't made it happen. Everyone knows that. She's strong enough, we know that now, but it's forbidden. The only reason we aren't all being kicked out is your obvious lack of education when it comes to our world."

The usual condescension that dripped from his voice was gone. This was fact to him, pure and simple. Maybe almost dying had changed him. Maybe he realized he wasn't invulnerable after all.

"Besides, you wouldn't have survived that challenge without me coaching you through the spells."

And *there* he was, teaching "How to Look Down Your Nose at Someone 101."

I rolled my eyes. In my heels, I was a good three inches taller than him at least and could give him a solid downward glare I'd been wanting to blast him with all week. "Please. You were too busy getting eaten by a T-Rex to coach me. I guessed at the words."

We walked by a girl in a bright red dress as I said that. She gasped, tears gathering in her eyes. "How can you talk to him like that? He almost died!"

I scrunched up my nose at her and Ethan laughed. "That's what I like about you, Wild. You don't pull punches, not ever. Not even when society dictates that you probably shouldn't talk about someone's near death experience mere hours after it happened."

"I do what I can to keep it real," I said as we turned the corner at the end of the hall. A wide set of double doors loomed ahead of us. They were closed, and from behind them came the steady thump of bass, music playing loud enough that it rumbled through my head, setting off the ache of the concussion.

"Shall we?" He gave me a mocking half bow. I would have curtseyed if I'd known how.

"Attitude before skill." I waved him forward. And again he laughed.

Damn it, I'd taken a pot shot at him and he'd just laughed it off. Ethan went to the door first, pushing both sides wide open. Music spilled out around us as the kids who'd survived the culling trials danced, grateful to have survived, to have made it this far.

The mass of bodies sent an instant wave of paranoia through me. I hesitated and Ethan came back for me and leaned in close.

"Are you getting any warnings?"

I wasn't sure I liked this new Ethan. Laughing with me. Listening to me. I certainly didn't know what to make of him. "No, nothing."

"Come on then." He tugged me forward, taking me by the hand like we were really on a date. Maybe I should have pulled away, but he was my lifeline in this crowd of people I didn't know. People I didn't trust. At least I knew where I stood with him.

Standing on my tiptoes, I searched the crowd for Wally, Pete, and Orin. They were all the way across the floor, near the food. Even at that distance, I could see Wally's mouth moving, Pete's head bobbing, and Orin's trademark bored expression.

I lifted a hand to them. Orin put two fingers to his head and saluted me. "I'm going over there," I said.

Ethan held my hand fast. "Stay here, with me and my friends."

I turned to see his friends were all magic users, of course. Within seconds, they were patting him on the shoulder, congratulating him on winning so many of the trials. Telling him how strong and amazing he was because he'd survived when everyone had thought he was dead. The girls batted their eyelashes, and the guys weren't much better. Colt was missing though.

Colt was missing.

My brain tried to get me to care, and I struggled around the throbbing in my head to want to go find him.

Ethan lapped all the love and attention up. I shook my head. Yeah, he was an ass, although of the good-looking, smelled so good I wanted to stick my nose against his neck and breathe him in variety.

I turned away and started through the crowd toward Wally and the two guys. There were far more people here than those of us who'd finished trials. Distantly, I recalled someone saying that the academy students had been invited so they could meet the new kids.

I let the music pull my feet forward, let it call to me, and though I was no dancer, it moved through me.

It felt no different than fighting. I sidestepped the other bodies with ease, my magic skirt trailing around me. The shadows seemed to cling to me and the dress, and it was like people weren't even seeing me. I spun around an entangled couple and found myself face to face with a ghost. My feet slammed to a stop, and I'm not entirely sure my heart didn't follow suit.

"I warned you to be careful, and you're on the goddamn dance floor in a dress at a party full of people who could kill you at the drop of a hat?" Rory snarled the words at me. Like he wasn't supposed to be dead. Like I hadn't seen him go under a mass of zombies. Like he hadn't broken my heart into a thousand pieces.

He'd survived, and he hadn't told me. He'd let me suffer.

Just like he hadn't told me he'd come to this school.

"Son of a bitch!"

I snapped a fist out so hard and fast there wasn't even time for his face to register shock. In my haste, I landed the blow on his cheek, rather than his nose.

He stumbled back and a few people laughed and made way for us. The music didn't slow. I turned away from him and pushed through the crowd, knowing without a shadow of a doubt he'd follow. I wanted to hug him tight, to cry and kiss his face and tell him I was glad he was alive.

But I was damned pissed that he'd let me believe—again—that he was gone forever.

I passed Ethan, who arched a brow, but I shook my head. I didn't need help for this. A side hall opened up and I turned down it, heading deep into the shadows. There was the softest of footsteps behind me, and I spun. "You should have told me!"

Only it wasn't Rory behind me. Jared stared at me and I stared back, shocked by how disheveled he looked. His normally immaculate clothes were torn in places and there was a smudge of dirt across his one cheek.

"You need to come with me, now. I was wrong about you." He grabbed me by the arm and propelled me forward.

"Why, what happened?" I tried to put on the brakes, but between his strength and my heels, it wasn't happening.

"Your sister is here. They have her."

All the wind in me left in a whoosh that made me light-headed. Sam is here?

"The ones who took the other kids, they snagged her too." Jared loosened his hold on me but didn't let go.

I wasn't fighting him, mostly because my mind had gone into a tailspin. I slowed my feet as the sound of a loudspeaker squealing came through the sound system.

"Everyone, please line up, we will now commence the cauldron ceremony where you will have your final House chosen."

The announcers words distantly registered, barely, through the shock. "How did they get Sam? She's back in Texas!"

Jared paused. "Look, I know that you and I have not seen eye to eye. I've done what I've done to protect those whose job it is of mine to protect. You, a Shade, would understand that, I think."

Damn it. I didn't want to trust him, but the sincerity rolling off him was just that—completely sincere. And I did understand that need to protect your own, maybe better than he realized.

"Barry Darkson . . . House of Shade. Killian Irish . . . House of Shade . . . Farley Whitehall House of Wonder . . ." The names rattled off, one after another.

Jared ran a hand through his hair and started forward again. "Your sister came looking for you. Apparently, your father needs to be reminded of how to keep secrets," he pushed open a door and led me outside. The distant music thumped along until the door shut behind us.

Jared let my arm go. "Are you able to run?"

I kicked off the heels. "Yes."

He led the way across the lawn and to the east side of the mansion. Adrenaline snapped and zinged through me. If the kidnappers thought they were going to take Sam, I was about to show them how very wrong they were. Nobody messed with my family.

Nobody.

CHAPTER 19

The grass was cool and damp against the soles of my bare feet as Jared led me away from the mansion. Away from my friends. Away from Rory.

I slowed a split second before the warning tingle whipped through me. Jared turned. "You are picking up on the danger?"

I nodded, feeling the memories start to surge inside me. I'd been here before. With Ethan. I tried to piece the broken memories together. There was something dangerous here, of that I had no doubt.

But where . . . and what?

Jared kept moving, forcing me to either keep up with him or fall too far behind. A cry cut the air, a girl's cry.

Sam.

I bolted forward. Screw the danger.

The ground ahead of us glowed, as if lit from within.

My breathing kicked up several notches. Even if my memories were sketchy, my body knew this place.

And it didn't like it.

Another cry cut off as though forcefully smashed . . . Jared was already down the stairs and I followed, ignoring the screaming of my instincts. I needed to get to Sam, danger be damned.

Jared lifted his hand and I took it. There was darkness ahead, creeping and pooling, and it swallowed us whole. A spell.

One I'd been through before, only last time I'd been with Ethan. We stepped out of the other side of the darkness. Moved down a hall, past torchlight and a room that looked to be a guard's room. Jared shifted to the side and I kept moving forward. Hands reached out of the cells on my right, and I found myself reaching back.

"Gregory?"

"Wild, you shouldn't have come back." His voice was weak.

Come back. "I was here before?"

"You were," said a voice I knew and shouldn't have been surprised to find at the bottom of a dungeon. Adam stepped out of the shadows. "And you should not have come back."

Jared snarled. "I'll take care of him. You get the other kids. There's a way out if you keep following the tunnels." He tossed me a ring of keys.

Adam shook his head. "Jared, you should know better by now. You can't beat me."

Jared grinned. "Maybe not, but you can't beat us both. We have you now, Adam."

Both? If I was getting the kids out, who was he referring to? Footsteps approached us from behind, and I couldn't help but turn and look. Director Frost stepped out of the same darkness from which Jared and I had emerged. It was unmistakably her, but her skin was unlined. An illusion?

She smiled at Adam. "Indeed. He cannot beat us both."

Jared launched at Adam and the director looked at me as the two men tumbled down a tunnel to our right, the sounds of their blows and grunts fading quickly. "Get the others out. We will deal with Adam."

All along. Adam had been orchestrating this all along.

I nodded and hurried to the first cell. Gregory was so eager to leave, he fell out when I opened the door. I caught him with one hand and dragged him with me to the other cells. All the missing kids were there, including Colt.

"Thought you could avoid dancing with me at the graduation, did you?" I asked.

His eyes were haggard, but he smiled at me. "Never. I'd never run away from you."

"Sweet, really, but can we get out of here before they take us all?" Gregory snapped his long fingers up in my face. Same old Gregory.

"There should be one more kid. They brought my sister in." I spun around, counting the cells, but there was no one left.

"Maybe they already got her out? They kept everything dark, we couldn't see who took us, or who was in here if they were quiet," Colt winced as he spoke, the bruises on his jaw a testament to Adam's violence.

A bellow followed by a wall-shaking boom stopped us in our tracks.

"You all go." I paused and then shook my head. "Look, go out the way I came in. Through the darkness and up the stairs. It'll be faster. Get to the mansion, tell Ethan and the rest of the crew that I'm here." I pushed the missing kids back through the darkness. Not the way the director wanted them to go. But I knew for sure it was a way out. I didn't want them to get stuck.

And I wasn't leaving until I found Sam.

I waited until the kids—more of them than I'd expected—disappeared into the darkness, led by the one vampire in the crew.

A burst of warning cut through me and I spun, pulling my blade out through the pocket of my skirt as I turned. I stopped the blade only a breath away from Jared's heart.

"Good stop. You sent the others out?" He tipped his head toward the tunnel Director Frost had pointed out, away from the stairs. I nodded, lying, though I didn't know why.

"What about Adam?" I looked past the vampire in time to see Director Frost drag Adam out by the scruff of his neck.

Her face wasn't the only thing that had changed—her body was lithe, young and fit. She smiled at me. "I see the confusion. Put your blade away, and let me explain just what has happened here."

Rory's note flashed in front of my eyes.

I didn't put my knife away. Adam rolled his head toward me, blood dripping from his face in a continuous flow. Frost dropped him on the ground. "He's no good without his wand, like most from the House of Wonder." House of Wonder? I'd thought he was a Shade. And then it hit me.

He was like Colt, one of the rare people who straddled two houses.

Adam lifted his head. "Run. Get out."

He was telling *me* to go.

Oh crap.

Jared's hand shot out and clamped on my wrist. "Don't even think about fighting me, Wild. You'll lose. And my love over there needs you intact."

Frost laughed. "Oh, the look on your face, Wild. You are trying to put the pieces together, but you can't, can you?"

I jerked my hand, trying to free it from the vampire's iron-clad grip. He grinned at me. "You aren't going anywhere. You and the other kids are going to go permanently missing. But the cause is good, great even."

The urge to fight, to slash at him with everything I had, was overwhelming and it took a great deal of effort to hold it down. I needed answers before I cut his lying tongue out of his face. "You don't have my sister here, do you?"

He shook his head. "No, but it was an easy way to make you ignore your natural instincts, wasn't it? You are a child yet, untrained if strong."

Normally I wasn't at a loss for words, but I didn't want to admit that Sam and Billy and my dad were weak spots for me. That I would always come for them if they called. So instead I clamped my mouth shut and smoothed my face.

"So is there no fight left in you, Wild? To be sure, let me show you just how serious I am about this situation." Frost bent over Adam and, with a quick slicing motion, opened his throat up from ear to ear.

He gurgled and grabbed at his throat, blood spurting out through his fingers as he tried to keep it in. I watched the fear and shock in his eyes as his life bled out of him, as he bent slowly to the ground and then went still.

"Are we clear?" Frost said quietly.

I nodded once. "What are you?"

Frost smiled, and again I was struck by the difference in her appearance. She had to be a shifter of some sort to appear as an old lady when we'd first met, and now as a woman not much older than me. "You've noticed, have you? You see through the glamor I had on me, seeing my true age, while others saw me as you see me now—as young and beautiful. Most people don't, but that is because they are not like you and me. Of course, this is no longer a glamor. But I'll explain that later."

"I am *nothing* like you." I wanted to spit at her, disgusting though it was, but wasn't sure she wouldn't slit my throat. "You kidnapped all those kids? Locked them up?"

"Yes, and I drank them up." She licked her lips.

Vampire was my first thought. But if Adam and Colt both possessed two gifts, it couldn't be as rare as Wally had indicated. "You're a shifter and a vampire, aren't you? Like Adam was a magic user and a Shade."

"Oh, she's getting closer, Jared. I knew she was smart." She walked up and linked our arms together. "Should I tell her?"

He laughed. "It's rather fun watching her guess."

"True. We have a few minutes before we reach the other end." His hand tightened on my wrist. I was pinned between them as they began to march me down the tunnel Director Frost had pointed out earlier. But despite the blaring warning going off in my body, I knew it wasn't time to act.

My moment would come—I just had to wait.

Director Frost sighed. "You understand that there are some people who carry more than one line of magical ability? Like your friend Colt. Mage and Shade blended together deliciously, equally strong in both. He's an oops, you know? His father strayed." She smiled and winked at me as if we were at a slumber party playing truth or dare. "That's rather uncommon though. Perhaps five out of every hundred gain multiple abilities and most often they are pushed toward one or another in their training, allowing the secondary ability to wither on the vine."

My jaw ticked, and I struggled not to pull away from them. "So?"

"Well, rarer yet is someone who carries three abilities. Perhaps one in a hundred. Your friend Drexia would know the exact stats." She made a motion with her hand and the tunnel brightened ahead of us, lit up along the edges with flickering torches. Drexia? Oh right, she meant Wally.

"Let me guess. You have a trio of abilities?"

"Not quite. You see, you and I are very special, Maribel Johnson. One for every generation. According to the records, our abilities are never bestowed on a woman. I had a hand in that, to help hide myself. To help hide others like me."

Chills swept through me, and they had nothing to do with the cold stone beneath my bare feet.

"What do you mean?"

"You are a Chameleon, Wild. A child who carries the ability to tap into all five gifts that the gods of the north bestowed upon supernaturals. All five. As you've seen in the trials, you are proficient in them all."

Her words might as well have been a blow to my head I was so stunned.

And yet it made sense. This explained my raw ability with magic, my connection to the others in my crew.

"Yes, that is why you excelled in the trials. And why it was so difficult to capture you." She leaned into me. "But better that I should be the one to catch you. He hunts for you too, Wild, and he will not be so gentle."

The tunnel was narrowing, and I could see my chance coming up. I slowed my feet, forcing them to slow too. "Wait, who do you mean, *him*?"

"The one that everyone fears. The one whose blood you share. The Shadowkiller." Director Frost looked at me. "You mean your mother never told you about him? She never warned you that he tried to kill her too? He was the reason she ran, the reason she hid you and your siblings away."

Her words hammered into my skull. Bits and pieces of partially overheard conversations between my parents trembled at the edge of my mind.

Whispered fears heard through the floorboard.

The click of a gun being chambered.

Shouts in the yard.

Jared's voice was silken. "Her mother sheltered them far more than I'd have thought. Stupid of Lexi."

Director Frost snorted delicately, and the corner of her right eye drooped, wrinkles appearing even as I watched. "She was a fool who thought she could outrun death, and look where it got her. Dead. Just like her oldest son."

My jaw ticked, the urge to defend my mother rising sharp and fast. "Your Botox is wearing off."

She gasped and lifted a hand to her face as the skin began to loosen, wrinkling in front of my eyes. "What did you do?"

We were at the end of the tunnel exit. The moon was bright overhead, and I'd barely noticed that Frost had released my arm so that she could step out ahead of us.

"Where are the others?"

I smiled at her, not fully understanding but knowing I'd ruined her plans. "I sent them back."

Director Frost turned on me, her eyes glittering. "Just like your mother. Weak. And alone."

As if her words sparked the memory, my mother's voice whispered to me: *"No matter what, you fight to the end. You never give up. You never give in. You give them hellfire and brimstone, my wild girl."*

I glared at the director. "She was not weak. And neither am I."

Hellfire and brimstone, here we come.

CHAPTER 20

Director Frost lifted a shaking hand to me and dug her nails into my chin. A light pulsed through her fingers and into me, quick as a rattlesnake's strike, and her venom was as sure. My knees went weak as I slumped under her hands. She threw her head back and laughed, her face smoothing and her hair growing longer, thicker right in front of me. Blonde, loose curls wove over her shoulders.

"Rich, I won't need the others anyway. Wild will fill me for years." When Director Frost tipped her head back, the lines in her face were gone. "What do you think, Jared?"

"As beautiful as ever," he murmured, lifting her one hand to his mouth, pressing his lips hard against her skin.

I wobbled in place, on my knees in my prom dress, my heart racing and my muscles weak.

"You—"

"Sucked the life right out of you." She smiled and snapped her fingers at Jared. "Get her in the van."

Jared bent to lift me, and I swung up with my left hand with everything I had left, landing a punch perfectly under his jaw. His head snapped back, teeth clicking, and I stumbled forward. We were surrounded by forest, but that didn't bother me.

"Get her!" Frost yelled, and I knew I had only seconds before he was on me.

I fumbled for the wand on my left side, pulled it out and pointed it behind me. I needed light. Blinding light.

"Stroblightus!" I yelled, hoping a made-up word, powered by all the intent in the world, would work for me. Please God, let it work for me.

The wand shook, warmed, and then brilliant light blasted out of it, illuminating the forest in a blinding flash.

Jared yelled and the sound of him skidding to a stop was music to my ears. I bolted forward, diving deep into the trees. The light behind me faded, but not before I saw people I recognized. People I hadn't thought would be there to save me this time.

Two dark figures shot through the shadows ahead of me, one catching me around the arms.

"Rory." He'd come for me.

He gave me a light shake. "Where is she? Where is Frost?"

"Back there," I said.

"I'll end this. Use your crew. You've got this." He dropped me, and he and the other dark figure ran back the way I'd come. The Sandman. So much for coming to rescue me.

I stumbled back a few more steps, so tired it was as if I'd run the whole set of trials without a single visit to a healer's tent.

Jared gave a low laugh and I spun, trying to see him. But he wasn't the only one whose vision had been damaged by the flash of light.

That is when I saw them. My crew, their dark shadows creeping forward from between the trees. "Guys, I could use some help!"

Jared laughed, but the sound slid away as my friends emerged from the trees, stepping up beside me, all still wearing their high-end grad clothes. All except for Pete, who was already in his honey badger suit.

I faced Jared. "I'm not alone. And we are not weak."

He snarled and shot forward, and Orin met him with his claws extended, shocking the older vampire.

"You cannot fight me!" Jared yelled.

"I'm not yours to command anymore!" Orin yelled back and I knew that it was because he was with us. He'd switched allegiances. The two vampires collided, hissing and snarling like wild animals. Pete shot into the fray, grabbing at Jared's ankles, tearing the flesh and then finally clamping on like some living version of a parking boot. Jared swung and stepped, trying to shake him off, but Pete was on good and tight.

"Coming, Pete!" Wally yelled. She lifted her hands and the ground softened around us, turning into quicksand. But it wasn't the ground she was controlling. "The dead are everywhere. Statistically speaking, there is not one place on the planet's surface that doesn't contain dead material of some sort or another."

The ground beneath Jared's feet began to give way and Pete jumped back. Orin landed several blows, one right after the other.

Ethan pointed his wand. "Orin!"

Orin stepped back and turned his face as Ethan shot Jared in the face with a blast of light that was stronger than the one I'd produced, and far more direct. Jared went down howling. The smell of burning flesh wafted over to me. I tucked the wand back into my pocket and pulled my knife. As much as the wand was good, the knife was real.

The knife was my home.

Jared shook, his knees embedded in the softened ground. "Fools, you are all fools!"

"Stay where you are," I said. "Ethan, is someone else coming?"

"I don't think so." He shook his head. "That guy Rory told me to get your crew and head to the dungeon without telling anyone else. I assumed he'd handle the rest."

He'd gotten the Sandman. He'd more than handled it.

Ethan had known where to come.

The memory banks that had been locked for the last two days finally opened, and I saw it all over again. The first time Ethan and I had found the hidden dungeon.

The Sandman sneaking up on us.

The other assassin attempting to kill us—only to be stopped by the Sandman.

Gregory reaching for me.

The Sandman had saved my life, only to boot me in the head and somehow take my memory. To effectively make me butt out of his operation while the kids stayed locked in the cells. To use them all as bait. To use me as bait.

And Ethan had helped him do it.

I stared hard at Ethan, feeling the distinct urge to strangle him. "You and I are going to have a chat about lying to each other after this is done. And it will involve me kicking you in the balls to make sure you get my point."

Ethan's face was flat, emotionless. "No one goes against the Sandman."

"Except me."

We spun as Director Frost stepped from the shadows, wand in hand. With a flick of it, she threw the five of us up and back, pummeling us against the various trees.

I slid down the tree I'd been tossed into, tumbling through the branches, the rough bark tearing at my dress. I wished I were wearing jeans and a shirt instead, but I might as well have wished the ground wasn't going to hurt when I landed.

The ground came up fast and was as hard as I'd thought it was going to be. But that didn't stop me from picking myself up and charging the director. Her eyes widened and she smiled as she pointed her wand at me, the tip glowing deep red. I dove to the right, rolled, and came up as she sent another shot my way. One after another, she kept on firing away.

I was doing what I could to pull her eyes to me, to give the others a chance. But they weren't getting up.

"Waiting for your friends? You're drawing from them, taking their energy and abilities." She laughed. "So much natural talent, so raw."

Part of me knew she was trying to distract me, but I still tried to shut down whatever it was that I was drawing off my crew. Only she was right, I had no idea what I was doing and there was no way I could stop It.

Jared was on his knees still, holding his hands over his face, moaning. "My eyes, my eyes are gone."

An idea formed, and before I could question it, I acted. I bolted for Jared, spinning him around to use him as a shield as I put my knife to his throat. "You want him back?"

The shadows behind her moved. She'd notice them if I didn't do something. The fact that she'd bested both the Sandman and Rory spoke volumes.

She was better than them, which meant they would need my help to take her down.

Her eyes hardened and then she laughed, tinkling and light. "You don't have it in you."

Only I did. I wouldn't hesitate to kill to protect those I loved.

I tightened my hold on Jared. "I'll kill any wolf that comes for my family. No matter what clothing they wear." I slid my blade across his throat, cutting through to the spine. Just like they'd done with Adam. The blood flowed down over my hands, impossibly cold for fresh blood, as if it had been dead for a long time.

He gurgled and slumped in my arms as the director screamed. "NO!"

With her focus broken, she didn't see them coming for her.

The Sandman burst out from the shadows on her right side and took her down, wrenched her arms behind her and wrapped them in a gold ribbon of all things, faster than a cowboy hogtying a calf. Then he pulled a golden clamp from under his jacket and snapped it around her neck.

"That will keep you, Frost. You're done."

Rory limped out of the shadows, holding his side. Injured, but alive.

I thought for sure she'd keep on screaming, but her silence was almost worse. Cold, deadly silence that spoke volumes. Her eyes locked on mine, and I knew a promise of death when I saw one.

She would not forget what I'd done. That I'd killed her love, Jared, that I'd helped them take her down.

Moments later, the forest was alive with lights as more teachers and students ventured into the trees. I wiped my blade on the back of Jared's shirt and tucked it away.

For the first time since I'd arrived, I knew for certain I wouldn't need it.

At least for a minute or two.

After the arrival of the other teachers, testers, and students, everything went to hell. Frost was hauled off to some magical jail that Wally whispered to me was the place where all the baddies went.

We were sent back to our dorms. Wally let me shower first. I couldn't get the water hot enough to wash off the feeling of Jared's blood. I couldn't get warm even though it wasn't by any means cold outside this late in the summer.

I pulled on cotton pj's and climbed into bed. Wally kept talking, but I just wanted to sleep. I didn't want to think about what I'd done. Despite everything we'd faced in the trials, Jared was the first person I'd ever killed. He was a vampire, sure, but I was the reason he'd died.

And Frost's words clung to me. I wasn't just a freak of nature for being a Shade, but a Chameleon who could drink down the power of others. Fear jangled my nerves and kept me awake far longer than I wanted.

"Wally?" I spoke to her after the lights were out.

"Yeah?" Apparently, I wasn't the only one wide awake.

"Why did my blade kill him? I thought . . . that it would hurt him, but I honestly didn't think it would kill him."

Her bed squeaked as she shifted her weight. "Magical blades can do a lot of things, Wild. And that blade might seem like an ordinary hunting knife to you, but whoever made it had magical skill. And they gave you an extraordinary weapon. But I thought you knew that already?"

Magical skill? But my dad had said he was a null, and that he and mom had made the knife together. Or had he just said that so my mom would bring him with her when she ran away from . . . well, from the Shadowkiller.

The director had said I shared blood with him . . . how?

Sleep came eventually in fits and starts, and I tossed and turned. I realized only a couple hours in that I had a solution for my lack of sleep. We were just in the wrong room. "Wally, get up," I grumbled, grabbing my pillow and leading the way.

She mumbled something under her breath but wasn't far behind me.

The door on the second floor wasn't even locked. What a bunch of ding dongs.

At least the four of them woke up when I opened the door. "What are you doing here, Wild?" Orin asked.

"Can't sleep." I went straight to the bed Pete was on. "Shift."

"You could say please," Pete muttered, but he shifted to his honey badger form. I crawled into the bed, and Wally tucked in behind me. Pete lay on our legs. Orin grumbled and moved to the side of the bed, laid down on the floor and flung an arm up. Wally took his hand. Gregory muttered something about crazy girls, but he slid his mattress onto the floor and scooted it close enough that he could reach us. I took his hand.

"And where do I fit in?" Ethan asked.

"Wherever you like," I mumbled, already feeling sleep pull itself over me. Ethan grunted and then arranged some pillows at the foot of the bed. He leaned back and reached an arm up and over one of my legs. His hand rested on Pete's back.

I didn't see him do it, but I felt it. Now that we were together, I could feel all of them, weirdly enough, kind of in the back of my head. They had been my crew, the misfits no one thought would make it through the culling trials, but we were more than that now. No matter what I was, if Frost was even right about me being a Chameleon.

We were family.

CHAPTER 21

The next day announcements came on loud and clear, snapping us all out of a deep sleep.

"Director Frost has been removed from the grounds due to unprofessional conduct. Director Rufus will oversee the final advancement ceremony. Please be advised that the ceremony will take place in one hour for those who missed it last night."

I would have rolled out of bed, but the others had me pinned down. I smiled to myself. "Up and at 'em, boys." I wiggled my legs, disturbing both Pete and Ethan as I let go of Gregory's hand and saw Wally let go of Orin. You'd think we would have been uncomfortable sleeping like that all night, but no one had complained.

Not even Ethan.

Wally and I headed back to our room and quickly dressed. So the Sandman was taking the director's spot? Did that mean he would stay on with the academy?

Rory's words came back to me.

The Sandman. He's not what he seems. I can feel it. His position in the school is a cover.

Whatever the Sandman's game was, it wasn't over. Whatever plans he had, he was in a prime position to execute them now. Cold washed over me. Did he know I was a Chameleon? Was that why he was on my case? I kept my thoughts to myself, unable to spill the beans, even to my crew. Maybe later.

Maybe never.

Dressed in clean jeans, a dark green T-shirt and my ball cap, I headed out. Or tried to. Wally stopped me. "You don't have to wear that hat anymore, you know. Everyone knows you're a girl."

I touched the brim of the hat. "Yeah, I know." The thing was, they might know I was a girl, but they'd given me wide berth as a boy. And maybe I wanted that respect. I didn't want to have to go through earning it all over again because suddenly people realized I had boobs instead of balls.

We hurried down to the front hall and into the ballroom I'd rushed out of the night before. In the center of the room a cauldron rose out of a trap door, flames curling up around the black bulbous pot. Steam swirled up from the surface, flickers of light dancing through it.

Wally nodded. "You weren't the only student who didn't get to toss their tokens into the cauldron."

"Crap, I lost my tokens!" I put my hands to my pockets as if I'd find them there.

She smiled and held up a little bag. "My mom sent me with an extra set, in case I lost mine."

A sigh of relief slid out of me. Ethan was ahead of us, along with Gregory, Colt, Mason, Ethel, and Lisa. Pete and Orin hurried to our side. Okay, Pete hurried, Orin glided.

"I'm kinda glad I missed it," Pete said. "It's better this way, just us."

"Not quite." I tipped my chin at the kids who'd been missing. They lined up first and I watched, excited to see how this played out. That is until the Sandman strode across the ballroom floor. His eyes were hidden behind his aviators, but I saw the bruise on the side of his face. He'd not escaped the fight unscathed.

"Line up, throw your tokens in, and when you're called to your house, get your ass in gear. The buses are waiting."

"Such pretty words," I said, just loud enough for my crew to hear. Pete snickered and even Orin's mouth tipped up.

Lisa was the first, and when she threw her tokens in they bubbled and hissed and one was thrown back out of the cauldron, spinning in the air, catching the light. She reached up and snagged it. "House of Claw." She clutched it to her chest and hurried away.

Mason went next. Then Heath. Then the other kids who'd been taken and not noticed. Two of them threw their tokens in and got nothing back.

"Nulls." Sideburns said. "Wait outside my office."

Those two, a boy and a girl, left with their eyes low and their shoulders hunched. Just watching them, I wasn't surprised they were nulls. This place had eaten them up and spit them out.

Colt was next. He threw his tokens in and the cauldron shook and hissed harder than before, the steam turning from a clear mist to a red burst of magic and sparkles.

I grabbed Wally's arm. "He won't be a null, will he?"

She shook her head I think, but I only caught it from my peripheral as I stared hard at Colt.

Sideburns gave a slow smile. That could not be good.

The cauldron spit out not one, but *two* tokens. Colt caught them both. "House of Wonder and House of Shade."

Sideburns tipped his head at him. "Your choice where you train. But you can only train one."

Colt stared at them and slowly left the ballroom, but not before he shot a look at me. I couldn't decipher what was in his eyes. He couldn't be confused about what to choose, he was obviously a mage.

Ethan was up next and got—surprise!—House of Wonder.

Gregory, House of Unmentionables.

Orin, House of Night.

Pete, House of Claw.

Wally, House of Night.

My friends waited to the side of the cauldron for me. I stepped up to the black pot and stared into it.

"Wait." Sideburns put his hand out, stopping me. "Everyone else, leave."

"What? Why? Are you going to try and kill me again?" I took a few steps back, my hands going for my weapons.

Even underneath those aviator glasses, I could feel him glaring at me. "Not yet, I'm not."

"That's a threat!" Pete yelled.

It was, but something passed between Sideburns and me that I couldn't quite explain. He was trying to protect me.

Because what if I had more than one token come out? What if Director Frost had been right about me and I was a chameleon? What kind of danger would that put me and my friends in. I swallowed hard and gave him a small nod. "It's fine, I'll be out in a minute."

The others were reluctant but did as I asked. Ethan was the one who stopped at the doorway. "Just shout, we'll be right here."

"Don't start being a nice guy now," I said. "I just got used to you being a douche."

He grinned and closed the door, and I turned back to the cauldron. "You think I'm going to be like her. Like Frost."

"I do. And the fewer people who know that the better." Sideburns made a motion to the cauldron. I lifted my hand over it, tokens in my palm.

"Why even make me do it then?"

"Because we could all be wrong about you. You could just be a talented human, a null like your father. Which would be worse?" he asked.

"Null," I answered without hesitation and dropped my tokens into the cauldron.

They hit the tumbling, boiling water with tiny little plops. The water hissed and bubbled, turning a distinct shade of gray that slid into silver, then to red, not unlike Colt's.

I held my breath as the cauldron shook, rattling on its bed so hard I thought it would tip over.

I didn't dare take a step back. The steam rose, smelling of apples and lilac bushes, and then five tokens shot back out and into the air. I caught them as they fell, snagging them like a juggler.

Or like a Shade.

"House of Shade," Sideburns said. "That is where you will train."

"Under you?"

"God no." He grunted. "I am no trainer. But I will be watching you. If you look even for an instant that you are going down the path of the other Chameleons, you'll be dead faster than you can blink."

I clutched the tokens in my hands. "Eloquent as always." I turned my back on him, something I wouldn't have done even a week ago and headed out to where the others waited. I tucked the tokens into my pockets, all except one. I held it up. "House of Shade!"

They grinned along with me and I let them think I was happy, excited, and not a little bit freaked out.

A host of buses were lined up at five intervals, ready to take us to the academy. Each of the houses had a retinue, and most had two flag bearers holding up a banner. They were decked out in colors and designs matching the house they represented. The House of Wonder was a trio of triangles, the lines interlocked, made out of silver and gold of course.

House of Night's banner was a deep blue, a pair of back to back ravens holding a bone between them.

The House of Claw was a giant multi-branched tree and each branch was covered with animals in a forest scene, from wolves to squirrels to the alicorns, and even . . . "Pete, there's a honey badger on that banner!"

He grinned and high fived me. "Hot damn, cats on fire, there is!"

The House of Unmentionables had a simple sign, the unfinished figure eight, the ends of it curling in on itself. Two gargoyles waited at the front of that bus.

And then there was the House of Shade. Black on black, the banner seemed to be one color, but within it was the Web of Wyrd, just like the patch on the Sandman's jacket. The more you looked at the banner, the more things you saw in the darkness. Figures. Weapons. A man on his knees. I gasped and started shaking. It was Jared in the banner. I was sure of it.

We started forward and then suddenly we were walking apart from one another. I wanted to tell them to stop, that we couldn't separate. But that wasn't how this worked.

Wally waved at me, but she was sad. Pete wasn't much better. Orin stared straight ahead, and Gregory kept shooting glances my way.

Ethan didn't look at any of us. Of course not, he was done with us now that we'd finished the trials.

That hurt more than I'd thought it would.

I stopped walking and spoke without looking at them. "We're still a crew. No matter how far we go."

I felt more than saw each of them straighten.

"Damn right," Pete said. "To the end."

"Well, let's hope it doesn't come to that. Again," Ethan said, and I laughed.

"Yeah, let's not do that again."

We all stepped out at the same time to our individual houses.

At the banner of the House of Shade, I waited. There was a good cluster around us, and damned if everyone wasn't shooting me fervent glances. No one spoke, though. I noticed some of the girls from the Shade challenge, those who'd baited the group of dumb boys to follow them. I nodded at one of them. She nodded back, an eyebrow arched.

"I will be your chaperone to get you to your new home, the campus of the House of Shade." Rory's voice cut through all the other noise as he stepped out of the passenger side of the nearest bus. "If you have any questions, I will be the one to answer them."

My mouth got ahead of my filter. "How do you punish someone when they've wronged you in the House of Shade?"

Rory didn't miss a beat. "You challenge them to a sparring match."

I nodded. "I challenge you to a sparring match, Rory. You need an ass kicking."

The other kids pulled away from me. But I wasn't afraid, not of Rory.

He grinned at me, and a piece of the hurt I'd been carrying slid away from my heart. History was a strange thing. It made you forgive when you otherwise might not.

I sure hoped it would help him forgive the ass whooping I would be giving him.

I sure hoped I could fit into this new world. Maybe I would find out what it meant to be a Chameleon.

I crossed my arms. "And you need to tell me how you survived zombies."

"Only if you win." His grin widened, and I found myself grinning back.

He stepped back from the bus and waved a hand toward the many behind it.

"Welcome to the House of Shade."

Let the games begin.

ALSO BY THE AUTHORS

Also by K.F. Breene

DEMON DAYS VAMPIRE NIGHTS WORLD
Born in Fire
Raised in Fire
Fused in Fire
Natural Witch
Natural Mage
Natural Dual-Mage

Also by Shannon Mayer

DESERT CURSED SERIES
Witch's Reign
Dragon's Ground
Jinn's Dominion
Oracle's Haunt

Shannon Mayer is the *USA Today*, *Wall Street Journal*, and *Washington Post* bestselling author of urban fantasy, epic fantasy, and paranormal romance novels and series. She has sold more copies of her books than she can count on one hand—close to three million. She lives in the southwestern tip of Canada with her husband, son, and a menagerie of animals, many of which show up in her books as sassy side characters.

www.shannonmayer.com
shannonmayerauthor@gmail.com

K.F. Breene is a *Wall Street Journal*, *USA Today*, *Washington Post*, and *Amazon Charts* bestselling author of paranormal romance, urban fantasy, and fantasy novels. With nearly three million books sold, when she's not penning stories about magic and what goes bump in the night, she's sipping wine and planning shenanigans. She lives in Northern California with her husband, two children, and out of work treadmill.

Sign up for her newsletter to hear about the latest news and receive free bonus content.

www.kfbreene.com
books@kfbreene.com